Planning perfect weddings...
finding happy endings!

The *Wedding*
PLANNERS
BRIDES-TO-BE

It's the biggest and most important day of a
woman's life – and it has to be perfect.

At least, that's what The Wedding Belles believe,
and that's why they're Boston's top wedding
planner agency. But amidst the beautiful bouquets, divine dresses and rose-petal confetti,
these six wedding planners long to be
planning their own big day!
But first they have to find Mr Right...

**And don't miss the exciting wedding-
planner tips and author reminiscences
that accompany each book!**

The *Wedding* PLANNERS

MILLIONAIRE GROOMS

The three last Wedding Belles
will meet their perfect matches!

Winning the Single Mum's Heart
by Linda Goodnight

Chef: Who will Natalie cut her
own wedding cake with?

Millionaire Dad, Nanny Needed!
by Susan Meier

Accountant: Will Audra's budget for the
big day include a millionaire groom?

The Bridegroom's Secret
by Melissa James

Planner: Julie's always been the wedding planner –
will she ever be the bride?

The *Wedding* PLANNERS

BRIDES-TO-BE

Sweetheart Lost
and Found
SHIRLEY JUMP

The Heir's Convenient Wife
MYRNA MACKENZIE

SOS Marry Me!
MELISSA McCLONE

*M&B™ and M&B™ with the Rose Device
are trademarks of the publisher.
Harlequin Mills & Boon Limited, Eton House,
18-24 Paradise Road, Richmond, Surrey TW9 1SR*

WEDDING PLANNERS: BRIDES-TO-BE
© by Harlequin Books S.A. 2009

Sweetheart Lost and Found © Shirley Kawa-Jump LLC 2008
The Heir's Convenient Wife © Myrna Topol 2008
SOS Marry Me! © Melissa Martinez McClone

ISBN: 978 0 263 86893 7

012-0209

Harlequin Mills & Boon policy is to use papers that are natural, renewable and recyclable products and made from wood grown in sustainable forests. The logging and manufacturing processes conform to the legal environmental regulations of the country of origin.

*Printed and bound in Spain
by Litografia Rosés S.A., Barcelona*

Sweetheart Lost and Found

SHIRLEY JUMP

To Kathy,
who has brought music and laughter into our
lives, and who graciously forgave me for tripping
on the altar in the middle of her wedding.

Shirley tells all about her own big day:

"You seriously can't take me anywhere without a calamity happening. I'm a walking *America's Funniest Home Video*. Even my own wedding had a near disaster. My husband got laryngitis the day of the wedding (hmm...was that a convenient way of not having to say any vows?), so his vows came out as a squeak. I forgot our toasting glasses and we had to borrow other guests' champagne glasses when the best man made his speech.

But all of that was nothing compared to my veil catching on fire.

Let's just say tulle and candles aren't a good mix. When my husband and I went to blow out the unity candle, it was before he kissed me, so my veil was still down. I tried to blow through the tulle. The netting swooped forward into the flame and, *whoosh*, caught on fire. Not a big flame, thank goodness, but a nice little spark. So here I am, madly blowing out my veil, then trying to lift the veil and get the unity candle blown out at the same time. I have a nice round hole in my veil as a memento.

Don't even get me started on the time I tripped and fell on the church altar in front of two hundred people at someone else's wedding. And just don't ask me to do a reading at your wedding – not unless you're planning on splitting the prize money from *AFHV* with me.

At least in my fictional world of *Sweetheart Lost and Found* I can create weddings where almost nothing goes wrong!"

**Catch up with Shirley's latest news at
www.shirleyjump.com**

Callie Stevens is the florist at The Wedding Belles. Here are her tips for your big day:

♥ A little visual can go a long way towards making sure you and the florist are on the same page. So bring along pictures of floral arrangements you like, or flowers you find special, to give your florist an image of the perfect bouquet.

♥ If you get married around a holiday, remember that the church will probably already be fully decked out with great flowers. Save some money by utilising the beautiful arrangements already in place.

♥ To save money, don't go for cheap flowers – choose one striking bloom in a less expensive vase arrangement for a centre-piece, or a simple bouquet with a few colourful flowers. Sometimes less is more.

♥ On the big day be sure someone has been designated to be in charge of distributing and pinning on the boutonnieres and corsages so you don't have to worry about that detail.

♥ If you want your guests to be able to see each other across the table, be sure to keep centre-pieces under fourteen inches high. Also, keep highly fragrant flowers to a minimum at table settings, as some guests may have scent allergies.

CHAPTER ONE

CALLIE Phillips slipped the final flower into the cheery wedding bouquet, stepped back to admire her handiwork and marveled at the irony of her career choice.

A woman who didn't believe in happily ever after, crafting floral dreams for starry-eyed, Cinderella-was-no-fairy-tale brides.

Callie fingered the greenery surrounding the flowers symbolizing hope. True love. A happy ending. Her clients at Wedding Belles were paying her to act like she believed fairy tales came true. But all the while Callie created those dreams with vibrant blooming white roses and delicate pastel freesia, she hid the fact that the petals had long ago dropped from her own jaded heart.

"My goodness, will you look at that. Another beautiful creation, darlin'." Belle Mackenzie, the owner of the Wedding Belles and Callie's employer, breezed into the basement floral design area. She was impeccable as always in a skirt and bright red sweater set that offset her gray hair and shaved years off her fifty-plus age. "You are incredible. Whatever made you think of this combination?" Belle bent to inhale the fragrance of the burnt-orange tulips, paired with deep purple calla and crimson gloriosa lilies.

"The bride, actually," Callie said. "Becky was just so outgoing, and this design seemed to suit her personality, not to mention the unique colors of her wedding party dresses."

"I don't know how you do it. You read people like novels." Belle smiled. "Best thing I ever did was hire you."

Callie smiled. "No, I think it's the opposite. Best thing I ever did was walk in here and apply for a job." Belle had taken Callie under her wing years ago, seeing a budding creative talent and someone who needed a stable, maternal figure. She'd taught Callie the art of flower arranging, even paid for her to go to classes, then when she'd expanded her wedding planning company into the much bigger Wedding Belles, had given Callie the job of florist. And through that job, a group of close friends who had since become Callie's rock.

Giving Callie's unstable life a firm basis for the first time in her life.

Now Callie spent her days discussing calla lilies and Candia roses with starry-eyed brides, but never for one moment believing she would hold another bouquet, opening her heart a second time, believing once again that one man would be by her side forever.

Just the idea of forever made her consider heading for the hills. She'd tried it once, on a whim, and it hadn't worked at all. Callie wasn't slipping on that gold band of permanence again under any circumstances.

Belle gave her a grin. "We all make a good team, don't we? The Wedding Belles."

"Even if one of us has never been swayed to the dark side?"

Belle's laughter was hearty. "You mean the white side of the aisle? It's not as bad as you think over there. And one day, darlin', I'll convince you that falling in love and getting married isn't the prison sentence you think."

Ever since Belle had hired her three years ago, she'd been

working on convincing Callie that marriage was an institution for everyone, sort of like a One Size Fits All suit. Callie wasn't surprised—the gregarious owner of the wedding planner company had been married several times and had gone into the business because she loved happy endings. The other women on the Belles team echoed that sentiment—and most had already found their happily ever after.

But Callie knew better. For some people, love was an emotion best left for greeting cards.

"Belle, I already tried marriage once and it didn't work." Callie cut the end of the crimson satin ribbon that she'd tied in a ballet slipper style around the stems of the bouquet, then tucked a few strands of reflective wires and delicate crystal sprays into the flowers, adding a touch of bling.

"That's called practice," Belle said, laughing. "Second time's always better. And if not, third time's a charm. Or in my case, maybe the fourth."

Callie rolled her eyes. "I'm certainly not going to get married that many times." If at all, ever again. Her divorce was only eighteen months in the past, and if there was one thing her marriage to Tony had taught Callie—

It was that she, of all people, should never get married again.

"You know what you should do?" Belle said. "Celebrate."

"Celebrate what?"

"Being single again. You've been back on the market for over a year, Callie, and you have yet to take a step out of the barn."

"A step out of the barn?"

"And pick another stallion in the corral." Belle winked. "There are plenty of 'em out there, honey. All you need to do is pick the one that gets your hooves beatin' the fastest."

"Oh, no, not me." Callie waved off the idea, even as she laughed at Belle's advice. "I'll keep on working with the flowers. They don't let me down."

"They also don't keep your bed toasty at night."

"So I'll buy an electric blanket." Callie put the bouquet, along with the rest of the wedding party flowers, inside the large walk-in refrigerator, then turned to walk upstairs with Belle. In a couple of hours, she and the other Belles would deliver everything to the wedding party, and see one more bride down the aisle.

"Well, before you go choosing a blanket over a beau, will you run on down to O'Malley's tonight and drop off the new invitations for his daughter's wedding? Apparently the first time the printer changed the groom's name from Clarence to Clarice. Thankfully we caught the mistake just before they got mailed."

Callie eyed Belle. "Is this some way of forcing me out?"

Belle gave a suspicious up and down of her shoulders, a teasing smile playing at her lips. "Maybe."

Audra Green, the company's accountant, greeted the two of them as they entered the reception area of the Belles' office. The entire room spoke of Belle's sunny personality, with its bright yellow walls, gleaming oak floors and bright white woodwork. It welcomed and warmed everyone who entered, just as Belle herself did. "What's Belle cooking up now?" Audra asked. "I read something mischievous in her eyes."

"Proving to Callie that Mr. Right could be right down the street."

"Along with the Easter Bunny and Santa Claus," Callie deadpanned, retrieving the box of invitations from the desk.

"So I thought she should go down to O'Malley's tonight and maybe deliver these invitations, scope out the dating scene," Belle went on, optimistically ignoring Callie. "Get back on the horse before she forgets where the stirrups are."

Callie and Audra laughed, then the straitlaced accountant sobered and gave Callie a sympathetic smile. "Do you want some company?" Audra asked.

"Thanks, but I won't need it. Contrary to Belle's match-making plans, I'm going to drop off these wedding invitations and nothing more," Callie said.

"And if Mr. Right happens to be sitting at the end of the bar?" Belle asked.

"If he is," Callie laughed at Belle's indomitable belief in Disney endings and picked up one of the thick silver envelopes in the box and wagged it in Belle's direction for emphasis, "then I'm sure you'll be the first to announce it to the world."

Jared Townsend believed in the power of proof. If something could be proved beyond a shadow of a doubt, then he accepted it as fact.

His quest for proof was why he had excelled in geometry but not abstract thought. Why he'd nearly failed poetic analysis and instead discovered a home in the concrete world of statistics.

But now he found himself in the most unlikely of places, to prove the most unprovable of statistics. A bar on a Thursday night.

To prove that true love could be measured and analyzed, weighed and researched. For that reason, he had a clipboard and a pen and intended to interview at least a dozen couples before the bar closed, assuming he stayed awake that long.

A party animal, he was not. He wasn't even a party puppy.

"Welcome to O'Malley's. What can I get you?" A rotund bartender with a gray goatee came over to Jared, a ready smile on his face, his hand already on a pint glass. At the other end of the bar sat an older man, his shoulders hunched, head hung, staring into a beer.

"Beer sounds good." Jared slid his clipboard onto the bar, along with a few already sharpened pencils. Raring to go.

If anything spelled geek, that was it. No wonder Jared hadn't had a date in three months. Carry a clipboard—an instant death knell for attracting women.

The bartender arched a brow at the pencils and clipboard, apparently agreeing with that mental assessment, but kept his counsel and poured the draft. He slid the frosty mug over to Jared without a word.

A couple walked in. Jared grabbed a pencil, readying himself. At first glance, they looked perfect for his survey. Early twenties, blond girl, brunette guy, walking close, talking fast, as if they were—

Arguing.

"You're a moron," the girl said. "I don't know what I ever saw in you. Seriously, Joey, my toaster has more brains than you and that's *after* I burned my bagel."

"Dude, that's mean."

"And quit calling me dude. I'm your *girl*friend, or at least I was. Not your dude." She flung off his hand and stalked away, ordering a tequila shot, which she knocked back in one swift, easy movement that said she'd done this before. More than once.

Jared put down his pencil. He let out a sigh, settled back on his stool and took a long, deep gulp of beer. No one else was in the bar, even though it was nearly nine and the sign outside promised karaoke night would start in a little while. Maybe he should have picked a place further downtown, rather than one so close to his apartment.

"Hey, O'Malley, how 'bout another for the road?" the man sitting at the opposite end of the bar said. He raised his glass, but it trembled and he nearly dropped it.

"I think you've had enough," the bartender, apparently the O'Malley namesake of the bar, said.

The man swayed in his seat. "No, no. Not enough, not yet."

Jared heard the words—so familiar—and turned away,

fiddling with his clipboard. His memory raced back all the same to someone else, to another slurred voice, determined to have one more round.

O'Malley let out a grunt of disgust. "You're cut off. Why don't you go home?"

"Don't wanna go home." The man heaved a sigh, stumbled off the stool and careened down the bar. "No one there. No one t'all." He crashed into a couple more stools, then gripped the edge of the polished oak surface and teetered.

The memories slammed into Jared until he couldn't ignore them any longer. He shook his head, then got to his feet and caught the man's elbow, righting the stranger just before he lost his balance.

"Get him some coffee," Jared said, signaling to the bartender. "And call him a cab."

"I ain't paying for that." O'Malley scowled. "If I took care of every drunk—"

"I'll pay." The man may be a stranger, but his story hit a familiar note in Jared's chest, one he had to heed. He turned to the man, and helped him onto one of the seats, ignoring the nearly overpowering stench of alcohol. "Sir, why don't you sit here a bit? Have some coffee, wait for the cab."

It took a second, then understanding filtered into the older man's bleary gaze. "You're a good man." He patted Jared on the back. "My new best friend. And I don't even know your name."

"Jared Townsend." Jared doubted the man would remember his name in the morning, but it didn't matter. Jared had been down this road often enough to know where it led.

"I'm Sam." His inebriated tongue slurred the "s," and his handshake had a decided wave to it, but the sentiment was there. Jared slid the coffee in front of Sam, and encouraged him to drink up.

The door opened again and Jared swiveled toward the sound, once again grabbing his clipboard and pencil. This time a single woman walked in, but no man followed behind her. Jared's spirits plummeted. Clearly he'd picked the wrong bar. Not a big surprise, given how little experience he had with this kind of scene.

Maybe he should leave, try another place, one with more atmosphere—*some* atmosphere at least—or try a restaurant, a diner, a—

Holy cow. Callie Phillips.

Jared's breath caught, held. The pencil in his hands dropped to the floor, and rolled across the hardwood surface. A woman sang about a broken heart on the jukebox, Sam said something about the quality of the coffee and the tequila toting couple went on fighting, but Jared didn't pay attention. He pushed his glasses up his nose, refocused and made two hundred percent sure.

Yes, it was Callie.

She'd just walked into the bar and upset his perfectly ordered, perfectly balanced life.

Again.

He had the advantage of watching her while her eyes adjusted to the dim interior. He studied her, noting the difference nine years had made. It could have been nine days for all his heart noticed.

She'd cut her hair, and now the dark blond locks curled around her ears, framed her face, teased at her cheeks. But she still had the same delicate, fine boned face, wide green eyes, and those lips—

Bright crimson lipstick danced across her lips, lips that had always seemed to beg him to kiss them, mesmerized him whenever she talked. He watched her approach, his gaze sweeping over her still lithe curves, outlined in jeans and a bright turquoise top, then returning to her face, to her mouth, and something tightened in his gut.

And Jared Townsend, who never did anything without a reason, a plan, completely forgot why he was here.

CHAPTER TWO

"JARED? Jared Townsend? Is that you? Oh... Wow." She inhaled, her breasts rising with the action, along with Jared's internal temperature. "My goodness. What a...a shock." Callie stopped in front of him, clutching a large box to her chest, her mouth shaped in an O of surprise. "What are you doing here?"

"Uh..." His brain fired, sputtered, fired again. "Research."

She smiled. "Let me guess. You're trying to determine the best beer for forgetting a broken heart?"

"Coors," Sam put in. "Best in sh-sh-show." Then he sent the two of them a wave and headed off to the rest rooms.

Jared glanced down at his icy mug. Beer hadn't helped him get over the broken heart he'd suffered after her, but he kept that ancient history buried, didn't talk about it or drag it out.

Only a masochist dug up a skeleton like that. But damned if his body didn't start playing archaeologist all the same, resurrecting old feelings...and a lot more. There was nothing analytical, statistical or sensible about it. There never had been, not when it came to Callie.

Still, he reminded himself, she had hurt him—and hurt him badly. If he was smart, he'd simply greet her as an old acquaintance and leave it at that.

"I'm here for work," he told her. "Really. Even if it doesn't look it."

Her smile widened. "It doesn't, except for the clipboard, which is so…you." She shrugged, laughed a little, then started to move away. "Well, it was nice to see you again, Jared."

Clipboard was so *him?* Well, damn it, maybe it was, but once upon a time she'd thought of him in a very different way.

Yeah, and how well had that ended up?

He shut off his inner voice. No matter what had happened in the past, a part of Jared wanted Callie to see he had grown and changed. Become a different man. One who wasn't the nerdy professor she had so cavalierly left behind.

A man who could—contrary to his plan five seconds ago— have a conversation with her and be completely unaffected.

Cool with it, even.

"Callie." She pivoted back. "Are you meeting someone here tonight?"

In the space of time it took her to answer, Jared's heartbeat doubled. He caught his breath, waiting. And not because it would make a damned bit of difference to the sheets on his clipboard.

Tonight, he'd stepped into unfamiliar liquor-infused territory to analyze couples, to take that data, feed it into a computer then hand the information over to Wiley Games so they could use it to develop the next generation of couple-oriented games and products. Not exactly the high end research Jared had set out to be doing after he'd received his doctoral degree, but the work at Wiley Games paid the bills and kept him in spreadsheets.

Either way, if there was one particular half of a couple he didn't want to add to his sheaf of papers, it was Callie Phillips.

"No, I'm not meeting anyone, not tonight," she said.

Not an answer that gave him any indication of her status. Single? Attached? No ring adorned her left hand ring finger, so she wasn't married or engaged. What happened? Where was Tony?

"Hey, Callie, what brings you by?" The bartender crossed to them, a friendly smile on his face.

Callie raised the box in her hands. "Your daughter is now marrying Clarence instead of Clarice."

O'Malley chuckled and took the box from her. "Thank you. Glad you guys caught the mistake before we sent them out. That would have been quite the mess."

"You're more than welcome. The wedding's going to be beautiful."

O'Malley's face softened. "My Jenny, she's an angel. I can't believe she's going to be a bride. Or that I'm old enough to be the father of the bride." He laughed, then thanked her again and moved down to the far end of the bar to refill the other couple's shot glasses.

Callie called a goodbye to O'Malley and turned to go. Before Jared could think about what he was doing—and whether it was a mistake—Jared gestured toward the empty seat beside him. "Would you like to join me?"

What was he doing? Inviting her to stay?

Simple curiosity, that's all it was. Getting caught up on where she'd been all these years.

"I thought you were working," she said.

"It's not busy here, so I'm taking a break." He waved the bartender over to them. "A margarita, on the rocks, with salt."

Callie smiled. "You remembered?"

"I did." He remembered a lot more than just her favorite drink, but he kept that to himself. Jared reminded himself that he and Callie had broken up for a reason—and staying broken up had been in their best interests.

She took the seat, brushing by him as she did. He inhaled, and with the breath came the light, sweet floral scent of her perfume. "Thanks," she said, when the bartender laid the drink before her.

"No problem, Callie." O'Malley gave Jared another arched brow, this time one of appreciation that the "geek" had a beautiful woman sitting beside him.

Jared tapped the clipboard and grinned. "Nothing's sexier than statistics."

"If you say so, buddy," the bartender said, then headed down to the fighting couple at the other end, who were working on their second set of tequila shots before gearing up for Round Two.

"What kind of research are you doing?" Callie asked.

"Counting the number of beautiful women who come into a bar alone. I'm up to one. I think I should quit while I'm ahead." He grinned. "Actually it's a questionnaire of sorts for couples. A research project for the company I'm working for."

"Sounds exciting."

"It's actually a lot more exciting once you feed all the information into a computer and start manipulating the data, using it to run statistical probabilities and forecasts. And if I get lucky, hopefully I'll come up with enough data to create some real, hard evidence to bring to a peer-reviewed journal. Something more respectable than the basis of the next 'Twenty Tantalizing Bedroom Teasers.'"

"'Bedroom Teasers'?" Callie chuckled, then raised a dubious brow. "This from the man who dressed up as a biker on Halloween in college? What happened to the leather jacket? The boots? The chaps?"

"Probably shoved in a closet somewhere. I'm strictly a suit and tie guy now. No more of that crazy open road, living by the seat of my pants talk."

His brief, one-night foray into that different persona had been a bad idea. He'd thought that by slipping on a black jacket, climbing on a Harley, he could get Callie to notice him in a way she never had in high school. She had—for a heart-beat—until Tony had stolen her back again, leaving Jared with an extra helmet and a lot of regrets.

No more. He wouldn't journey that road again.

"Pity." Callie took a sip of her drink.

"What's that supposed to mean?"

She shrugged. "You were a lot of fun when you were a...well, not exactly a *bad* boy, but a bad-*ish* boy."

"You make me sound like a five-year-old who wouldn't obey his bedtime."

"If I remember correctly, there wasn't much trouble getting you to bed." Then Callie's face colored and she directed her attention to her drink again.

Jared remembered, too. Remembered too well. One night—a night he'd never forgotten, but she had begged him to never mention again, so that she could marry Tony, with a clear conscience.

Tony—Jared's former best friend. Tony—the man who had stood between them both and been everything Jared wasn't.

And everything Callie wanted.

The memory sucker-punched Jared in the gut and he had to swallow hard before he could breathe again. He'd let Callie go, left college, leaving them behind without a second glance, because he'd thought she was better off—

Had she been? Had he made the right choice?

Hell yes, he had. She would have never been happy with Jared—she'd made that clear. Jared thought that after nine years that last night with Callie wouldn't still sting, would have become some distant memory, fog on his past's horizon.

But nothing about Callie Phillips was foggy in his mind. And he'd be fooling himself if he thought otherwise.

He cleared his throat and took a swig of beer. "So what are you doing now? I take it you're not the bohemian I remember."

She chuckled. "No. I'm now a responsible tax-paying florist."

"A florist?" He assessed her. "That, I can believe. You transformed that hovel I called an apartment into a respectable home, something that didn't scream bachelor dive. You always did have an eye for color and design." Jared straightened his glasses again, then asked the one question that had lingered on the tip of his tongue ever since she'd walked into the bar. Was she still with *him?* "So, how are things with Tony?" he said, nonchalant, taking a sip of beer. "Did you guys have any kids?"

"We're divorced. No kids."

Pain flickered in her gaze, and he wanted to ask more, but they'd only been sitting together for five minutes. It wouldn't be right to probe. No matter how curious he was, how the need to know nearly overwhelmed him. What had happened? When had the tarnish appeared on the golden couple? And did Callie ever regret what had happened? Did she ever think about how her leaving Jared had affected him?

Jared took a sip of beer and navigated toward safer subjects. "Do you live here, in the city?"

She nodded. "I settled back in Boston three years ago when Tony got a job in the city. That's when I was hired to be a florist for the Wedding Belles."

"The Wedding Belles?"

"It's a wedding planning company over on Newbury Street. There are six of us, all working for a woman named Belle, hence the name."

"Wow. We're practically neighbors," Jared said. "I live right around the corner from here and the research division of the company I work for is five blocks from Newbury Street."

"All those times we could have run into each other and never did."

"Until now." Jared's gaze met hers. Heat brewed between

them, a connection never really lost, even though many years had passed since they'd last seen each other. "Serendipity brings us together again."

"Either that or bad taste in bars." She raised her drink toward his.

"Always the optimist." He smiled, teasing her, then tapped her glass with his own. "You haven't changed, Callie." He paused, and searched her face, looking for the woman he used to know. The one who had made his pulse race, encouraged him to take chances, to think bigger, wilder, to dream of possibilities he'd never dared to have—not until she'd come along. And never dared to have again after she'd gone. "Have you?"

"I should probably go," Callie said suddenly, pushing her margarita to the side. "You have work to do and this…" She looked around the empty bar. "This was not a good idea."

"What do you mean?" She'd just arrived and already she was leaving?

"I just stopped by to drop off the invitations. Thanks for the drink, Jared, and the trip down Memory Lane."

He wasn't going to let her get away that easily. He couldn't, not again. When Callie had been in his life, she'd brought something special, something he'd never found again. Losing her had hurt, hurt like hell. And for just a moment, even though he knew it was crazy and knew she was all wrong for him, he wanted her. "Don't go. Not yet."

"I have a busy day ahead of me tomorrow." She started to slip off the stool, grabbing her clutch purse from the bar.

He reached for her arm, intending only to stop her, to keep her from leaving too soon. But the fire that rocketed through Jared's veins told him that nothing had died between them, at least not on his end. Every bit of the attraction that had been left undone in high school, barely explored in college, lurked under the surface, like tinder simply waiting for that spark.

"Callie—" He cut off the sentence. What ending did he have? He hadn't had a "Cool" transplant in the last nine years, which meant he was still the man he'd always been, the kind of man she hadn't wanted.

Only a fool went for a third strike. Yet, Jared found himself drawn again, wondering if the distance of years would give each of them another shot.

"I should get home," Callie said, stepping out of his grasp. "Nice seeing you again, Jared."

And then she was gone. The door shut behind her, whisking in a cool burst of air as a goodbye.

In an instant, regrets blasted Jared. What the hell was he thinking, letting her get away again? At the very least, he should have asked her out, just to see…

What?

He didn't know, really. They'd been over for a long time—if they'd ever really been anything at all—yet something inside him still wanted to know. Still felt that sense of something undone, that insistent need to complete the storyline.

Why didn't he just leave the past alone—leave her alone?

When he met her gaze, he knew why. Because a part of him still wanted answers to his questions. Wanted to know how Callie felt about those days. Jared didn't want a relationship. He wanted closure.

"Hey, where'd sh-she go? The pretty lady?"

Sam. Jared had forgotten all about him. He turned to find the man, looking a little better with his face washed, and a cup of coffee in him. "She had to leave."

Sam sighed. "The pretty ones always have to go, don't they?"

"Seems that way."

Several people trickled into the bar. None of them Callie. Jared didn't look for couples, no longer cared about his research.

Sam sank onto one of the stools. Jared signaled for a refill of the coffee cup. "My Angie, sh-she's gone now. Lost her, lost my res-sh-tauraunt, lost everything," Sam said. "That's why I'm a…a drunk." He ran a hand through his hair, then shook his head. "My Angie, she'd yell at me, tell me to straighten up. Get it together for the grandkids."

"Why don't you?" Jared asked, his voice almost bitter and angry. As the words left him, he knew the question wasn't just for Sam, but for someone else, someone who wasn't here, and who couldn't answer.

Sam shrugged, then paused for a long moment, staring into the coffee. "Would they really care?" he asked, his voice low, full of regret. "After all I've done?"

"Yeah," Jared said. "They would."

Sam looked up, the bleariness in his eyes cleared and for a second, he seemed as sober as a minister. "You think we all get second chances, Jared?"

Jared's chest tightened. He hoped so. If his father had lived longer, Jared knew now, with the wisdom of age and experience, that he would have given him a second chance, too. "I'd like to think so."

O'Malley cleared his throat. "Cab's here."

"That's my cue," Sam said, rising. He put out a hand to stop Jared from paying the tab. "I've got it from here. You've done enough. Go after her. Don't wait too long, like me."

Jared watched Sam leave. The words "we all get second chances" rang in his ears. Maybe it was possible.

Jared scrambled off the stool, tossed a few more bills onto the pile for the tip and moved to grab his clipboard. As he picked it up, a germ of an idea sprang to his mind.

What if…he combined a little research with the answers he wanted? What if he found a way to not only peek inside Callie's mind but also use their time together to analyze her reactions? He could do his research—

And find his answers to the past, all at once.

It would solve his problem perfectly. Give him exactly the kind of intimate knowledge his game research needed.

What harm could come of a few days with Callie Phillips? Not a real relationship, just a few dates. After all, Callie hadn't been divorced for very long. Surely she wasn't interested in anything permanent. And neither was he. Once his research was done, he'd be hip deep in work anyway, which meant no time for a life—

Again. Which was what he had done in his last two relationships. Yet, even as he told himself this was the perfect solution for both of them, a tiny bell of doubt rang, telling him things with Callie always had been more complicated than that.

Jared ignored the warning signals and strode out of the bar. Had to be the buzz of beer. Or the part of himself that wasn't interested in signing up for Broken Heart Duty a second time in a decade.

But seeing her, for just a little while—

He couldn't resist that, no matter how much he tried.

He caught up to her a little ways down the sidewalk, her arms wrapped around herself, to ward off the evening chill. He slipped off his jacket and slid it over her shoulders before she could protest.

"Thanks," Callie said. "You were always Sir Galahad."

"That's me. The nerd in waiting." He tipped at his glasses.

"You're not so nerdy, Jared. Just…nice." She smiled. "And that's not so bad, or so easy to find."

Damn, he was tired of her thinking he was nice. Tired of being seen as "just Jared."

Nice guys finished last. And Jared had been left in Tony and Callie's dust.

For one brief moment, she had seen him as something— someone else. Maybe he could give her that peek again. His mind scrambled for a way to connect, to find a path back to who she used to be, to the people they had been nine years ago. And in the process find out what had gone wrong. Why she had found him so lacking and Tony, the heartbreaker, such a better choice.

Then maybe that continual ache would stop hurting.

Music drifted out of O'Malley's bar as the door opened and closed, releasing the fighting couple, who had apparently made up and were now holding hands and snuggling as they left. Other people headed in, the place finally beginning to fill as the night deepened. The music's volume swelled, bass nearly drumming the sidewalk.

Jared took a step forward, and leaned close, his pulse ratcheting up with the nearness of her. "Do you still do that one thing you used to do?"

Her eyebrows arched. "What one thing?"

Jared took another step closer, invading her space now, inhaling her perfume, his research forgotten, his reason for being here long since left by the wayside. "You know what I'm talking about, Mariah Callie."

Callie took in a breath, her chest rising with the movement, and it was all Jared could do not to bend forward and kiss her, just to see if she would still taste as she did. Feel like she used to, her mouth beneath his, her sweet lips against his.

Damn. What kind of game was he playing?

"Yes," she said.

He grinned. "Good. Then let's go do it now."

"You're crazy."

"Maybe," Jared said. "But since when did that ever stop you?"

Callie returned the smile, hers now curving up into one filled with a bit of a dare, a challenge. "Are you sure you can keep up with me?"

Jared leaned forward. His lips brushed against the edge of

her hair, nearly kissed the delicate curve of her ear. "Absolutely. I've been practicing."

Callie laughed, the deep, throaty sound Jared remembered, sending his mind roaring down a heady path he thought he'd forgotten. Clearly he hadn't forgotten it. Not at all.

Telling him his plan had one hell of a serious flaw.

CHAPTER THREE

CALLIE hadn't laughed this hard in years. She sat back down at the table in O'Malley's, the bar much more crowded now, clutching her stomach. "Do you really think you had to go that far?"

Jared grinned. His blue eyes captured hers and Callie's pulse quickened. "Absolutely. What's a good Madonna performance without adding in the high-pitched 'oops' at the end?"

"For one, I don't think that's what she says and for another, the whole gyrating thing was more than enough." Callie shook her head, chuckling. "You have to be the worst karaoke singer in the universe. And contrary to what you told me, you have *not* improved since the high school talent show."

"Which is why I have you." He waved a hand in her direction, then at himself. "Baby, you make me look good. You are the Cher to my Sonny."

Callie groaned. "Jared, even your karaoke jokes are bad."

He laughed, then flipped open the menu and slid it her way. "Time for some appetizers. We need fortification if we're going to do the Ike and Tina Turner catalog later."

Callie looked away. Twice, Jared had gone and made references to them as a couple. She hadn't seen the man in nine years and now, wham, it seemed as if they were picking up like a knitter who'd started again on a forgotten afghan.

But wasn't that what her body wanted to do? Heck, every part of her was reacting as if not a moment had passed between the last time she'd seen him and now. Every time he looked at her, every time he smiled, the room seemed to disappear.

And when they'd been on stage, singing together—even though he'd had all the talent of a second-grader in Carnegie Hall—a connection had extended between them, the thread tightening whenever Jared's smile winged Callie's way.

Callie's gaze roamed O'Malley's. The now-busy bartender sent her a friendly thumbs-up, apparently approving of her stage performance, too. Callie waved back, trying to look anywhere but at the man across from her. Maybe if she directed her attention away from Jared, she wouldn't feel so attracted to him.

Behind them, a young man with a blond Mohawk and a goatee had taken the stage, holding the mike in both hands with a white-knuckled death grip. He stuttered through the first few lines of a Police song, then gave up, to the razzing of a group of drinking buddies in the back corner.

"Poor guy. Probably gearing up for the *American Idol* tryouts, too." Jared shook his head. "Everyone thinks they're a singer."

Callie returned her gaze to Jared. *"Et tú Brute?"*

He laughed. "At least I admit I stink. I'm really only here for moral support for you and for the nachos." He signaled to one of two waiters who were busy juggling the room's tables. "Do you want to order some?" he asked her.

"Nachos are always good, of course." Had he read her mind again? She sat back against her chair, watching as Jared ordered the cheesy chips and some colas for them, impressed for a second time at how much he remembered about her. Nearly a decade had passed since they'd been together and yet, he'd recalled a lot of details. Her favorite drink. Her favorite snack. Her favorite hobby.

When the waiter left, Callie leaned forward. "Okay, what gives? I know you're not some kind of savant, so tell me why you're all over my favorite things. What do you want from me?"

Jared's gaze didn't divert from hers. "Nothing. Just an evening getting to know you again. Catching up on old times."

"Then how come you remembered everything I love?"

"Is it that hard to think you might have been a memorable person in my life, Callie?"

Silence extended between them, taut, filled with heat, with expectation. He hadn't forgotten her? He'd remembered all those details?

She grabbed the menu again, pretending to study it, which was a lot easier than trying to figure out this odd tension between her and Jared. "I wonder what they have for desserts here."

He tipped the laminated edge downward. "Are you changing the subject?"

"Of course not."

"Then tell me. Have you ever thought about us? About that night? About what might have happened if we—"

"Jared, that's in the past—"

"I meant if we'd gone on tour, of course," he said, his voice shifting into a tease, and Callie wondered if she'd read him wrong, and he didn't mean a relationship "them" at all. Jared reached out and took one of her hands and pulled her out of her chair.

"What are you doing?"

"Do you remember that night, Callie?"

Of course she did. She'd never forgotten that Halloween, that one night in college when she and Jared had stepped over the line from friends and become lovers. One night.

One completely unforgettable night.

Sometimes she wondered what might have happened, had they ended up together, but then her better sense got a hold of her and reminded Callie that happy endings, tied up with a nice neat true love bow, weren't always realistic.

"We sang 'Baby, It's Cold Outside,' and we were terrible," she said, focusing instead on the funny memory of their mangled duet, but then feeling her cheeks heating when she remembered the innuendo in the song, the heat singing it had brewed between them that night. "We were drinking margaritas and probably not thinking entirely straight. I don't know why we even got up on the stage at that college contest."

"We were having fun. A lot of fun."

They had laughed. Laughed so hard, she'd tumbled into his arms outside the bar, seeing Jared in an entirely different light. It had been as if he'd put on that leather jacket, picked up that microphone and become someone else. For the first time, she'd seen him as not a friend, but a man, a very desirable man. When they'd touched, an electricity had erupted between them, bursting into a kiss, a kiss that became more, became everything.

Became an absolutely wonderful, incredible night. Never in her life had Callie ever felt as loved as she had with Jared. He'd made love to her with incredible care, taking his time to treasure her, cherish her.

Love her.

It had been as if he'd memorized her body, knew the sentences of her soul and could finish them with every touch. She'd found herself wondering how she could have missed seeing this side of him, missed this man, and for a moment, considered a future between her and Jared.

But then, in the morning, he'd pulled her into his arms and started talking about where he wanted to go after college. About his plans to buy a house, get married, settle down. Create a forever future.

It had all sounded so fast, nearly chokehold fast, and Callie had panicked and run straight to Tony—the one man who turned out not to be so good at forever.

"Callie?" Jared said, drawing her back to the present. "Are you ready to reprise our greatest hits?"

"Of course." Keep it to music only. Even if the rest of her remembered the details of that night and conveniently kept forgetting the morning after.

"If we're going to do this, then this time," he said, weaving their way past the tables and back toward the small stage at the back of the bar, "I think we need to choose a couple that ended happily. Think Faith Hill and Tim McGraw."

"If *you're* planning on singing, I think we'd be better off with a couple where one of them is a mime," she said, pressing a finger to Jared's lips, knowing this was a crazy idea even as she stepped back onto the stage with him.

Ten songs later, Jared accepted that he would never have a career in music. "There goes my dream of being on the radio. Even O'Malley threatened to buy earplugs on that last one."

Callie laughed and slipped into place beside him as they left the bar. "You clearly have a masochistic urge to embarrass yourself in public."

"It's not so bad as long as I'm in front of total strangers I'll never see again, and as long as you're beside me."

She laughed. "Still playing it safe, huh, Jared?"

"That's me. Safe to a T." He grinned.

"Well, I think you accomplished the total humiliation goal tonight. But you really should have drawn the line at that last pop song."

"That one was purely for your amusement." He caught her eye. "And were you? Amused?"

"Very." The lights above twinkled in her eyes, like stars dancing.

Jared moved closer, unable to maintain his distance another second. All night, she'd enticed him, drawing him closer with every breath, every note. He kept telling himself it was all because he'd missed her, but even Jared knew it was about much, much more. He knew better…and yet, he kept doing the exact opposite of what was smart. "You, on the other hand, were incredible. You can really sing. Why didn't you ever pursue that professionally?"

Callie shrugged, noncommittally. "I don't know. Not my thing, I guess."

"Not your thing? Callie, you are amazing. Seriously. Maybe you should add singing to the wedding business that you're doing."

"Oh, no. The other women don't know I sing at all." She blushed and turned away. "No one knows."

For some reason, it thrilled Jared that he knew. That she'd shared this with him, and no one else. "So you're a closet karaoke-er?"

She laughed. "Yeah, I guess you could say that."

He reached up and cupped her jaw, finally touching the face he'd been dying to feel all night. Her skin was satin against his palm, her delicate features cast by the soft evening light. He moved closer, closing the gap between them, the night providing its soft, quiet blanket of intimacy. "Seems a shame," Jared said. "To have a gift and keep it wrapped up so tight."

"Jared, it's complicated."

"If I remember right, everything with you was complicated."

She lifted her chin, so close he could kiss her with nothing more than a whisper of effort. He shouldn't. He needed to maintain his distance. His professionalism, the research. That's what he told himself he'd come here for, not a relationship with the woman who had always been the complete opposite of him, who'd broken his heart, left the shards in her wake when she'd run off with his best friend.

But she was smiling and he kept having trouble remembering any of that.

"If I remember right," Callie said, "that was part of what you liked about me…and part of what drove you crazy."

"That wasn't all that drove me crazy," he murmured.

A heartbeat passed between them. Another, and all Jared could see, hear, think about, was the movement of her crimson lips, the sound of her breath. Her mouth opened again, lips parted ever so slightly, like an invitation.

And Jared dipped down, so close his lips could almost brush against hers. Desire drummed hard in his veins.

Then common sense sent an icy shower of reality across his senses and Jared drew back, his gaze lingering on hers for one long moment before he released her. "Now that we're all grown up, it seems you're not the only one who can make things complicated."

CHAPTER FOUR

IF THERE had ever been a time when Callie wished she had better bluffing skills, it was the next night at the monthly poker game for the Wedding Belles. "So, Callie, how'd it go at O'Malley's?" Audra asked. "Did you stick to your resolution and not meet a man?"

Callie dipped her head, avoiding Audra's inquisitive gaze. "Of course not."

She'd run into an old friend. That didn't technically make it meeting a man.

The heat on Callie's neck told her the entire assemblage of women was staring at her. So much for bluffing. "So, shall we get back to the card game?" Callie asked, picking up her pile of five cards and fanning them out in her hand.

"Are you going to tell us his name?" Audra asked. She shifted her slender body in the kitchen chair, her blue eyes wide with suspicion.

"Whose name?"

"This man who has you blushing like a teenager with her first crush."

Regina O'Ryan, the company photographer, chuckled, then dipped her head to look at her poker hand. Her brown hair swung forward, the locks curving around her heart-shaped face. "Audra, maybe Callie wants to keep him a secret."

"No secrets. I just want to play cards."

"Uh-huh," Audra said, not believing her for a second.

Callie rolled her eyes at Audra's persistence, then glanced down at her cards. Two jacks, an ace, a three and a four. She slipped the three and the four out, laid them facedown on the table and slid them over to Audra, who, as the hostess, was also the dealer for the monthly ladies' poker game.

The Wedding Belles played for pocket change because they looked forward to the camaraderie and the margaritas more than anything else.

Only four of the six Belles sat in Audra's sunflower-yellow kitchen today, two-thirds of the hardworking, dynamic team. Natalie Thompson was busy teaching a cake decorating class to high school students in downtown Boston; Julie Montgomery was running some last-minute errands. Belle was closing up the shop.

"Audra, I think you might be onto something. Callie does seem awfully evasive." Regina picked up her cards, but didn't glance at her hand.

"That's because she doesn't believe Mr. Right exists," Audra said, rising to refill the chip bowl.

"Are you serious?" Serena asked. Serena, the wedding dress designer, was the biggest Prince Charming proponent in the group. "You have to believe in Mr. Right. It's like a job requirement to be a wedding planner."

"Exactly," Regina agreed. "How many weddings have you helped put together in the three years you've been working here, Callie? Dozens and dozens, right?" Regina finally decided on her poker hand, and slipped Audra a card for exchange. "Our clients sure seem to find good guys and plenty of great picks."

Callie scoffed. "So do the bargain shoppers who shove you out of the way at the annual Filene's Basement wedding gown sale."

"I still have a bruise from the last one," Serena added. "Those women are vicious."

Regina chuckled. "Seriously. We're in the business of creating dream weddings. We're *supposed* to believe in true love and happy endings."

"She has a point, Callie." Audra handed Regina a card from the deck. Regina smiled. Audra eyed her friend, weighing her expression. As the Wedding Belles financial guru, if anyone could spot someone bluffing about their money, it was Audra. "What do you have there, Regina? Anything good?"

"Of course not." Regina's voice raised a couple octaves. The company's photographer might be great at taking pictures, but most of them could call her on her bluffs. "And I'd never tell you if I did. How about you, Callie? You planning on trying out for the Texas Hold 'Em competitions?"

"You all know how bad I am at bluffing." Callie took a sip of her frosty margarita, the cold drink a perfect accompaniment to the chips and dip Audra had set out for an appetizer. "Plus, I usually attract low cards like dogs attract fleas."

Regina laughed. "Maybe that's what we all need. A Labrador. All you have to do is feed him and he's not only loyal for life, he never asks for the remote."

"Seriously, I don't think you should give up on love or men," Audra added. "I mean, we all need to have hope, don't you agree? I don't care what the statistics say, I believe in happy endings. It's just not logical to assume Mr. Right doesn't exist. Especially when we watch all these clients walk down the aisle and know we helped create that perfect moment. Mr. Right is out there, I'm sure of it, especially since I'm planning my own wedding to him right now." Audra took a sip from her drink. "Besides, we've all met more than our share of Mr. Wrongs—"

"Absolutely. Look at me. I've got a Mr. Pretty-Sure-He's-Right," Serena James piped in. The bubbly blond dress designer was currently in a long-term relationship, and a huge champion for the opinion that there was a Mr. Right out there for everyone.

"I used to think that, too," Callie said. "But then I met Tony."

"One bad apple doesn't spoil the whole harvest," Serena said. "What was wrong with the man you met last night?"

"Nothing." Callie sighed. "Everything. He used to be Tony's best friend."

"Oh," Regina said, then realization dawned further. "*Oh.*"

"It means there's history between us," Callie said, plucking a chip from the bowl.

"No, it means you're not starting from scratch," Serena said.

"I'm not starting anything," Callie insisted. Though a part of her wondered where things might have gone if Jared had kissed her. Would they have started something—

Something they had begun, but left undone all those years ago?

"Would finding true love be so bad?" Audra asked.

"No, not at all," Callie replied. "I just think it's not realistic to think all of us end up happy."

"Why not?" Serena asked. "Look at the odds. I have a great guy. Audra's engaged. Regina's married."

"And don't forget Julie," Regina said. "She's found a great guy in Matt."

Serena sighed. "They are *so* cute together. I think it's kinda sad, though, that they're just planning to go down to city hall. Julie's been working for us since day one. She deserves the kind of weddings she plans."

"I agree," Callie said, glad for the change of subject away from her own life, and for the focus on someone who truly needed a happy ending.

Julie, the Belles assistant, had been hit financially from left and right, both from her own personal life and from her fiancé Matt's business struggles. After Matt's custom plane building business lost a huge account, Julie and Matt had decided to pour their entire wedding savings into the company, in order to save everyone's jobs. Things were still rocky at his business, but they were on the upswing.

Julie and Matt were good people, who'd simply hit a financial road bump.

Callie might not believe in true love for herself, but she was happy to see Julie had found a wonderful man. If anyone deserved a happy ending, Julie did.

"Those hospital bills from her mom and that flood in her house last spring..." Callie's voice trailed off in sympathy. Hard times had slammed her before, too, and she'd been battered by the twin winds of financial and personal pressures. She'd gone through both during her marriage to Tony, who hadn't been much for holding down a job—or remembering a word of what he'd promised during the wedding ceremony. "Julie said it was too much and she and Matt need to save every penny they have, until his business is finally on its feet."

"And then, they can have kids," Serena said with a dreamy sigh. Serena, always the one who had dreams for the future, the one with the vision. "Julie's been eager to start a family and would make such a great mom."

"She definitely would." Regina beamed, the photographer's generous smile taking over her face.

Callie and Tony had never had children. A blessing, her mother had said, when the judge finalized the divorce decree. But to Callie, it had been the final ironic twist in her life story. The woman who had never put down roots, who'd married a man who couldn't sit still, had been left with nothing more to show for all those years than a piece of paper and a few sticks of furniture. Not exactly a monument to achievement.

"Every woman deserves a wonderful wedding," Serena said, glancing down at her hand, then her pile of coins, clearly agonizing over whether to bet on the cards she'd been dealt. "I wish we could do something for Julie to help her out."

"Of course there is something." Audra brightened and laid her cards facedown on the table. "We're the Wedding Belles. Why don't we throw Julie and Matt a wedding? I'm sure Belle would be all over it. She's such a romantic. Natalie would make a killer cake. If all of us worked on it and contributed our amazing skills—" she grinned at her friends "—we'd be able to pull this off."

"That's a great idea," Callie said, warmth spreading through her heart for these women, her friends, who had been with her through the trauma of her divorce. Always ready with a hug, a sympathetic ear, or a simple chocolate bar left on her worktable. What would she have done without them?

They were the best friends Callie could have imagined. Better that than some fairy tale concocted by a couple of brothers. What kind of happy endings could two guys with a last name of Grimm create anyway?

Serena put her cards down, her eyes bright with excitement, the wheels of dress designs clearly turning in her head. "I can already imagine the dress I'd like to create for Julie. She'll look like an angel."

"And I'll take black and white photos of the wedding," Regina added, the sense of energy soaring through the group. Callie felt it, as surely as a breeze. This was the energy that comprised the Belles, that gave every one of their weddings its unique flavor. "Julie saw some in my portfolio and loved them."

"I can just see it," Audra said. "What about you, Callie?"

Callie nodded, already picturing the kind of bouquets and

arrangements she'd design. "I can imagine it, too. If there's one thing I can always see, it's someone else's wedding." She smiled. "Julie loves gardenias. I'll make sure she has flowers that would make the Dutch drool."

"Good. It's settled. We'll give Julie and Matt a wedding they won't forget. And we'll make it a huge surprise." Audra smiled, then picked up her cards again. "She's going to be so thrilled."

"She already is. Matt's a dream. I think Julie got the last Mr. Right on earth," Callie said, truly happy for her friend. She didn't envy Julie's happiness a bit. But there were days, especially after she'd watched one more couple ride off into a sunset full of happiness and promises, when she wondered if maybe there would ever be a little of that for her, too.

Callie shook her head, dismissing the blue funk. Dwelling on the disaster that had been her marriage did nothing but stir a pot best left alone.

She picked up her new cards and slipped them into her hand. A jack and an ace. Full house. Maybe her luck was looking up—at least pokerwise. She tossed two dimes into the center pile.

"Ooh, Callie's betting high," Regina said, matching the bet. "Must be a good hand."

"I'm out," Serena said, folding her cards and laying them on the table. "I've got nothing."

Audra's deep blue gaze met Callie's. For a second, she measured what she saw in her friend's eyes, then threw in two dimes. "I'll meet your twenty cents. And raise you a quarter." She tossed in the silver coin.

"Too rich for my blood," Regina said, laughing and setting her pile of cards aside. "Especially when all I have is a pair of twos."

"I'll match your quarter and call." Callie moved to add another coin to the pile.

Audra reached out and put a hand over Callie's. "Wait. Let's up the ante a bit."

"Up the ante? But we always bet pocket change."

"I mean something more interesting. We are, after all, the Wedding Belles. We're supposed to believe in happily ever after, but you don't, Callie, and I happen to think you're wrong. If we're going to pull off this wedding for Julie and Matt, then I think you should test your theory about there not being enough Mr. Rights in the world to go around. If you win, then we'll put on Julie's wedding, congratulate her for getting the last great guy and resign ourselves to the fact that there aren't any other Mr. Rights left, but if I win…"

Callie narrowed her gaze. "If you win…what?"

"Then you have to go along with an experiment. A challenge." Audra smiled. "Because I happen to think you're wrong. I mean, I work on weddings all day and I'm engaged myself. If I don't believe in Mr. Right, then I should go into a different field."

"Yeah, funeral planning," Regina interjected. The four of them burst out laughing.

"It would be nice if you were right, Audra." Callie thought of Jared. He'd awakened something in her last night, something that had lain dormant in her for years. Could Audra be right or was Callie merely wishing on an impossible star? "It's been a long, dry spell, girls, and I could use a guy who doesn't shred my heart like a Ginsu knife."

"Or one who doesn't look like a guilty puppy every time he looks my way," Regina muttered.

"Everything okay with Dell, Regina?" Audra asked.

"Oh, yeah, just fine." Regina let out a laugh. "I'm kidding, that's all."

For a second Callie wondered if everything wasn't as perfect as Regina was leading them to believe. She scanned her friend's face, but the shadow had passed and Regina's regular sunny countenance had returned. Perhaps Callie had imagined it.

"So, Callie, are you game?" Audra asked. "For an experiment if you lose?"

At first, Callie opened her mouth to protest, but then the whisper of a challenge tickled at her. It raced through her blood, sending a shiver of excitement, of possibilities, down her spine. When had she last felt like that? Excited about her future?

Last night with Jared had reawakened the Callie she used to be. When they'd sung together, he'd reminded her of the woman she'd been in college.

And when he'd leaned down, his breath warm on hers, a kiss only a whisper away, he'd made her heart race in a way it hadn't raced in…forever.

Like it had when she'd been the girl who had dropped everything at a moment's notice to jet off for an adventure. The woman who had taken the detours, tried a new city, a different town. She'd done almost anything once, playing a game of spontaneity with every single day.

She'd lost that Callie somewhere in her marriage, buried her under a lot of disappointments and hurts. Did she still exist?

And if she found that woman, would returning to who she used to be ruin Callie's carefully built life?

A crazy thought, she told herself. Surely she could take on this simple little bet from Audra. Maybe this was exactly what Callie needed to get out of this emotional funk she'd been in since the divorce and start moving forward.

She folded her cards together and leaned forward, excitement increasing her pulse. "What kind of challenge are you talking about? Exactly?"

"One where we see if your theory holds up in the real

world. Meaning, you get back in the dating game and see if Mr. Right doesn't just pop up."

"Yeah, from underneath a rock," Regina put in with a chuckle.

"Girls, this is just penny poker," Serena said, putting a hand of caution over the pot of change in the center of the table. "We never bet anything real. It's just for fun."

Audra's eyes glittered and a smile crossed her face. "This could be fun, too. And besides, Callie, it's about time you jumped into the deep end." Her grin widened and a tease edged her words. "Come on in the dating pool. The water's warm, and with some guys, really hot. And who knows? You might find true love in the process."

"What exactly are we betting here, Audra?" Callie asked.

"You take a chance with this Jared—" Audra put up a finger "—and don't try to pretend he didn't affect you because it's all over your face."

"Take a chance?"

"Go out with him again, if you lose this hand, on a *real* date. And see where it goes."

See where things went with Jared? Callie had already done that years ago. And yet…

Hadn't that almost-kiss between them been on her mind nonstop since last night? Didn't a part of her wonder what might have happened if he had kissed her? Or if she had closed the gap?

It had been eighteen months since Callie's divorce. Eighteen months spent rehashing her marriage, trying to figure out where things had gone wrong. Fourteen months of going over every conversation, every argument. But not of dating seriously.

What was that theory about hitting your thumb? Something about quit doing it if it hurts. Well, Callie had quit men. Because they hurt her heart.

Audra waited across from her, a friendly challenge on her

face. Callie thought of the full house she held in her five cards. One of the best hands she'd had in months. Surely Audra didn't hold anything better. And then, they could all drop this crazy idea. She and Jared weren't right for each other. He was the practical, suburbs kind of guy and she was the wild one who'd never been able to stay in one place for long.

Either way, there was almost no chance Audra's cards could beat Callie's. The whole issue was probably moot.

"Yeah, I'm game," Callie said. "I call. Let's see what you've got."

Callie fanned out her cards, splaying them proudly across the laminate surface of Audra's kitchen table. Three jacks, two red, one black, paired with two red aces.

She watched Audra do the same. One red card—a six. Another—a seven. A third—an eight. A fourth—a nine.

When the fifth red card—a ten—appeared, Callie knew she'd just been roped into dating Jared again by a straight flush. In hearts, no less.

CHAPTER FIVE

BELLE's eagle eye didn't miss a thing, either.

"Did you meet a man at O'Malley's the other night, darlin'?" Belle asked the second Callie walked into work the next morning.

Callie avoided her boss's inquisitive gaze by flipping through a stack of mail. "Are you all in on some big conspiracy?" Callie laughed. "He was an old friend, nothing more."

"Uh-huh," Belle said, the lilt in her Southern accent making it clear she didn't believe Callie one bit and already heard i all from the other women. "Well, when this man you *didn'* meet calls again looking for you, what should I tell him?"

"He called here?"

Belle laughed and settled her ample frame onto the settee ir the reception area. On a small table beside her sat a bouquet of white roses, a daily arrangement Callie made for Belle, a tribute to Belle's late and much loved first husband Matthew. "He called twice. Wanted to know what time you came in and if you had time for lunch. That boy sounded positively smitten to me.'

Callie bit back the smile that threatened to take over her face. Already she was smiling about Jared's call? Oh, this was so not a good sign. "What did you tell him?"

"I said I'm not your social secretary, honey, but he's

welcome to call back after ten and find out for himself. Make him do a little work and he'll appreciate the chase all that much more." Belle laughed.

"After ten?" Callie glanced at the clock. "Why so late?"

"My, my, that man does have you off your game today. Did you forget that Marsha Schumacher is coming in at nine to discuss the flowers for her wedding?"

Callie groaned. "Oh, no. I did. Is she bringing her mother?"

"Doesn't she always? I can stay, darlin'. Run some interference, block any unwanted matriarchal meddlin'. I've been married a few times. I know how to handle meddlin'."

Callie laughed. "I'll be fine, Belle. But thank you."

"Hey, I'm here for you, honey, anytime you need me." Belle rose and came around the coffee table to Callie's side. "And I mean that about more than just Marsha."

"I know."

Belle drew Callie into a hug. "Oh, darlin', your sunshine brightened my days after my last husband died. And I'm just so proud of the Callie you've become since I met you."

The world Callie had lived in before existed light years away from the cheery, tulle-filled world of Wedding Belles. A hundred times over, Callie had been grateful for Belle, who'd brought her under her ample wing, and given her not just a regular, stable job, but a voice of wisdom and love. When she met Belle, Callie felt as if she'd finally be able to escape the weeds and settle in among the daisies, become one herself. Though there were days when Callie wondered if she really fit in here. Maybe…

She shook off the thought. She was happy. A little desire to travel was nothing more than that.

"I'm a lot different from that wild woman," she said.

"You are, indeed." Belle laughed. "You've circled around like a cat who's found a new end to her tail."

Callie echoed Belle's laughter. "You are one of a kind, Belle. You and your sayings."

"That's what I told all my husbands." She winked, then headed out the door, just as Marsha and Barbara Schumacher whisked inside, early for their appointment.

Marsha had clad herself head to toe in her favorite color— pink. From her pink sweater to her pink skirt, a pink faux fur coat and even, Lord help her, pink boots. Barbara had opted for real fur, a dark brown mink, which made her daughter look all the more like a piece of cotton candy.

The Schumachers weren't bossy, just…needy. They reminded Callie of her own mother, who made marrying often a sport. Her mother, however, hadn't accompanied marrying often with marrying well, and was usually divorced as quickly as she was remarried. This morning, her mother had called—again—to announce another impending breakup, one where she was expecting her daughter to offer emotional support.

Callie hadn't had time to do much more than listen before her mother had said she had to go, off to play golf at a singles' event. "On the hunt again," her mother said, laughing, the conversation over before it really began. Par for the mother-daughter relationship course.

Barbara Schumacher clutched a sleeping Pomeranian in her arms like a prize from Ed McMahon. Maybe Callie should stop at a pet store on the way home, get her mother a portable dog. It would at least give Vanessa something else to focus on besides finding her next fiancé.

"Oh, Callie, I can't wait to see my flowers!" Marsha rushed forward. "Do you have my designs ready?"

"Absolutely," Callie said, greeting both bride and mother and leading them toward the French doors connecting to a dining room adjacent to the main reception room. The Belles used the area as a way to showcase tablescapes, linens and flowers, giving brides a visual preview of their wedding designs.

"The florist *should* have the designs ready," Barbara said to her daughter, giving the little dog a pat on the head. The Pomeranian roused, then went back to sleep. "That's what you expected, baby, and you should always get what you expect. And then some."

"Last week, we talked about something tall to really wow your guests, yet make the most of your spring theme," Callie said, ignoring the mother of the bride's barb. "Tell me what you think of this." With a flourish, she opened the doors, revealing the grand display she'd set up at the end of the day yesterday.

"Oh, those are *beautiful!*" Marsha exclaimed, dashing forward, one hand over her mouth. She reached out and fingered a lily petal, gently, as if it were crystal, then stepped back to admire the towering topiary arrangement of stargazer lilies, Gerbera daisies, godetia and calla lilies springing out of a thin, twenty-inch-high silver fluted vase. Ming fern and bear grass provided a touch of greenery and soft accent to the bright color, while delicate English ivy trailed like fingers to the table. "But…do you think it's pink enough?"

"It's very pink," Callie replied, thinking that if she'd used any more colored flowers, the whole thing would look like a bottle of indigestion medicine.

Marsha tapped her lip, thinking. "Maybe we should sprinkle the whole thing with, like, pinkish gold dust. I saw that once on one of those craft shows and oh—" she pressed a hand to her chest "—it was like it had been kissed by pink angels. I loved it."

"Oh, baby," Barbara said. "If that's what you want, we'll do just that. Angel kisses for my angel."

Callie forced herself not to cringe. "I really don't think that would add to the arrangement. It might…ah, overpower and detract from the surrounding beauty. I'd hate to see anything steal attention away from the bride." Callie smiled at Marsha.

"That's true. I wouldn't want that. Well, maybe we could throw in some pink carnations or other pink flowers. Or—" Marsha got so excited by her idea she nearly jumped up and down "—we could glue little pink bows all over the flowers and then on the vase and then we could scatter them all over the table and—"

Callie groaned inwardly. Her mind flitted to Jared, imagining how he'd react to such an illogical, over the top feminine proposition. "How about we keep it simple, elegant, like your dress?"

"How would you do that?"

"We could drape a pink tablecloth over the white tablecloth that you were going to have. That would add an extra layer of your favorite color." Again, Callie thought of Jared, picturing his reaction to the entire hilarious scene of arguing over pink fairy dust and pink bows, while a sleepy Pomeranian looked on, letting out little yawns from time to time. She shook off the thoughts.

Focus on work. Not him. Especially not him. Jeez, get her on the stage for a few songs with the guy and suddenly she became as infatuated as a teenager at a pop concert. Maybe she needed more sleep. Or maybe she was just in serious pink overload.

"Could it be the exact same pink as my bridesmaids' dresses and the ties and cummerbunds?" Marsha asked.

"Oh, Marsha," her mother said, "you always have the most creative ideas. Why, if you had the time, you could have designed this whole wedding yourself."

"I could have, couldn't I? It's too bad we couldn't have found a way to make the cotton candy favors I wanted." Marsha pouted and sent a look Callie's way as if it were all her fault she couldn't produce a way to make miniature print-able cotton candy figurines.

"I think that pink color will certainly be doable," Callie said, hoping that concession would soothe her bride, and also get her own mind back on the Schumacher wedding. Thank goodness ninety percent of the Belles brides were a whole lot easier to work with. She picked up her pen. "Now, back to the flowers. For the boutonnieres and the corsages…"

She began to work down the list of floral arrangements with Marsha, trying to talk the bride out of one pink addition after another, her mother chiming in about price and her baby's desires. Marsha was a likable client, but one with an incredible fixation on that single color. Her mother and Serena had thank-fully talked her out of the hot-pink wedding dress, and Marsha's fiancé had firmly put his foot down about wearing a pink tuxedo. He'd pulled the Belles aside during the first meeting and begged them to keep his bride-to-be's pink passion to a minimum, if only to make the wedding palatable to the male guests.

But all the while Callie was dealing with Marsha, her gaze kept straying away from the flowers and toward the clock. Nine-fifteen, nine-thirty, nine-forty-five. The phone rang from time to time, and Callie would excuse herself from Marsha's incessant debate over fuchsia versus pale cherry to answer the calls, but every time it was someone other than Jared.

After Callie hung up, she'd berate herself for even being disappointed that she'd been waiting for Jared to call in the first place.

He was part of her past—a past she'd worked hard to put behind her—and that's where he should stay.

Uh-huh. If that were so, then why did she keep mentally replaying the other night? The way a much more adult Jared had sent her hormones raging in ways she hadn't even imag-ined all those years ago?

She reminded herself that she and Jared had had one brief ill-timed night together. Then Tony had come back, begging her for one more chance, and any thoughts of any kind of relationship with Jared Townsend had been washed away as easily as sand on a beach.

Yeah, and look where that choice got you, her mind whispered. Still, she'd do her best to forget Jared. To forget the past.

But when the phone rang again at nine-fifty-five, Callie nearly lunged for the receiver, thankful that Marsha had just left and she didn't have the added distraction of the client. "Wedding Belles, this is Callie speaking."

"Is this the woman who can make magic with magnolias and bring a man to his knees with a song?"

Jared's voice. Everything inside of Callie roared to life, awakened again, as if it had lain dormant all these years. She laughed. "It is. And is this the man who can turn spreadsheets into works of art?"

"Data DaVinci, that's me." He chuckled. "What are you doing for lunch today?"

"I, ah, have an appointment." Bet or no bet, he was a friend, always had been. She should keep it that way, if she were smart. Keep her past where it was, because if she got caught up in that old Callie—

"That's not what I heard. Your boss said your schedule is free from twelve to two."

Belle. Matchmaking again. That woman would manufacture a happy ending if she couldn't find one. Probably working in concert with the other Belles. Callie immediately swore off the monthly poker games. "Jared, the other night was fun, but—"

"Stop. What's so wrong with a little fun? Because I know that's one thing I could use more of. What's happened to you, Callie?"

"Nothing."

"Really? Because the Callie I remember would have found any excuse to live it up a little."

She closed her eyes and pinched the bridge of her nose. "I'm not like that anymore. I don't take risks." Yet even as she said the words, the old urge to do just that tugged at her.

Hadn't her friends encouraged her to do just that? Told her to get out of her rut, providing a little impetus with that bet? Maybe they'd seen something she'd missed.

Maybe they were right.

"Jared—"

"I'll see you at twelve." Then he hung up, cutting off her objections.

Callie held the phone in her hand for a long time, staring at it and wondering what she had just gotten herself into. Jared seemed determined to bring back the very past she'd done so much work to escape.

A past that still whispered at the fringes of her mind, with a familiar tune of wanderlust. She was happy here, she reminded herself. Happy with her job. Her friends. Her life.

But still…some days, it seemed as if a piece of the puzzle had been dropped on the floor, left behind in a closet. She'd get this overwhelming urge to leave, go find the piece, fill in that one personal gap that had always seemed open.

And that, Callie knew, was what scared her because it led her to make impetuous decisions, the kind she'd made with Tony.

She shrugged off the worries. It was all hormones or something. Nothing more.

"The telephone won't bite, you know."

Callie turned to find Natalie standing in the doorway, a bemused smile on the cake decorator's face, her blond hair in its perpetually mussed bun on top of her head. Callie laughed and replaced the receiver in the cradle. "Sorry. Just thinking."

"What about?" Natalie started walking toward the kitchen,

a load of bags from the local decorating supply store in her arms. Callie took two of them and followed along, helping Natalie unload the cake decorations she'd bought. Miniature brides and grooms, little Grecian pillars, edible pearls, luster dust, cake boards and decorating foil all went into the various cabinet drawers and shelves that organized Natalie's small kitchen area.

"I'll give you three guesses."

Natalie turned to Callie and grinned, her fist on her hip. "Given the look on your face, I only need one. A guy."

"I must have man trouble written all over my forehead today. Either that or you and Belle have suddenly become psychic."

Natalie poured each of them a cup of coffee, then handed one of the mugs to Callie. "Nope. Audra, Regina and the others have just been talking. You didn't think they'd keep that bet to themselves, did you?"

Callie groaned. "Is everyone in this business invested in my romantic future?"

Natalie's hand covered Callie's, the touch of a longtime friend, one who had weathered a difficult path of her own, but one with a far more tragic ending after her husband had died in a motorcycle accident, leaving her with eight-year-old twins. Still, the petite woman maintained her sunny perspective and kept the mood light and the sweets abundant at the Wedding Belles. "Yeah, we are. It comes with the deluxe friend package."

Callie chuckled. "You guys are the best."

"That's why we're the Belles." Natalie turned to the refrigerator and withdrew a sliver of cake. "Here, you need to taste this one. Tell me what you think."

"Nat, I really think this whole part of your job is a shame. What kind of cake maker is a diabetic?" Callie bit into the cake and nearly moaned at the white chocolate cake with raspberry filling that hit her palate with a burst of flavor. "Oh, this is your best."

Natalie grinned. "I thought you said my devil's food cake was my best."

Callie laughed, then scooped up another bite. "So you have two bests. You're an incredible baker, what can I say?"

"Speaking of which, I have an appointment with a client in a couple hours, so I better get some more samples prepared. And don't forget, we have a group meeting for the Cross wedding at two."

Callie nodded. The day would be a long one, as all the spring days were. From April to June spelled wedding season, which meant they'd be working late hours for months. "I'll be here. I have some preliminary designs already worked up that I think Alicia will like and I'll pull together a sample cascading bouquet with those Dendrobium orchids she said she wanted, too."

"Great. See you then." Natalie grabbed her purse off the counter, then paused before she left. "Oh, and enjoy your lunch date."

"Does everyone around here know everything about my love life?"

Natalie laughed. "Of course. That's our job. And your job is to go out on that date, like you agreed."

Callie threw up her hands. "I'm beaten at—"

"—your own game," Natalie finished with a laugh. "And when it comes time to plan *your* wedding, we'll be even more on top of every little detail."

Callie put up her hands, warding off the possibility. "Trust me, we're a long, long, *long* way from that day."

"Uh-huh. That's what they all say." Natalie gave her a grin. "Okay, now I really have to get out of here. And remind me not to bring my kids around here for the next couple of weeks."

"Why not?"

"I saw a sign for free puppies across the street. If my twins see that, they'll be begging me for a puppy. And worse, one *each*." Natalie shuddered. "That's all I need is twins *and* twin puppies." She laughed, then headed out the door.

Callie chuckled, then got to work busying herself with paperwork—completing orders, sketching out some designs and following up with clients—for the next two hours. The hall clock gonged twelve, at the same time that the bell over the front door pealed, announcing a visitor.

But Callie knew—she knew, without even looking up—that this wasn't a client, a delivery, or anyone else but Jared.

She felt his presence as surely as she could a spring breeze, a shift in temperature, a whisper in her ear. Callie paused in the words she was writing and looked up, her gaze meeting his in an instant.

"So," he said, that familiar grin on his face, "what are you in the mood for?"

You.

When he smiled at her like that, she forgot exactly why she objected to dating him. What reason she had against seeing him. And thought about nothing that had to do with food and everything to do with being with him the night before.

"Italian," Callie said, deciding she better darn well get decisive and get there quick. She'd go with him to lunch, tell him that seeing each other on any kind of romantic basis was crazy, despite the bet.

They were polar opposites, with completely different goals in life, and better off, as always, as just friends. Weren't they?

"Good thing I made reservations at Café Donatello." He grinned.

"Pretty confident in my food choice?"

He gave her a cocky smile. "I'm confident about a lot of things."

"That's one thing we have in common."

"Back in high school and college, you used to think we were as different as pencils and fireworks."

"Well, personality wise, sure. But we have things in common."

"Like what?"

"Well, you…" Her voice trailed off. Why was he putting her on the spot like that? And why had he taken a step closer? Every time he did that, she stopped thinking. "You like… singing, and well, so do I."

Oh, smooth answer, Callie. Way to go.

A grin quirked up one side of his face. "All these years and you still don't know me that well, do you? But I know you, Callie. Better than you think." Then Jared moved back, his smile lightening, and he gestured toward the door. "Right now, though, all we're talking about is lunch, right? Ready to go?"

"Uh, yeah." Callie grabbed her purse and followed him out the door. But as she and Jared walked down the street and around the corner to the exclusive Café Donatello, she had to wonder again why he had kept track of a friend from high school, a momentary relationship in college.

Had he cared more than she'd realized? If that had been so, then why hadn't he ever said anything?

A warm spring breeze played at the ends of Callie's hair, tickling up her neck, whispering along her skin. She caught the scent of blooming daffodils, tulips, the dawn of the new season. Spring ushered in that sense of hope, of a renewed beginning, and Callie caught herself glancing at Jared and wondering…

What if.

What if she hadn't run off on that crazy whim and eloped with Tony? What if she'd woken up that morning and gotten swept up in Jared's talk of forever and white picket fences? What if he'd taken her along that road?

Where would she be today? How would her life be different?

But Jared hadn't done that. He'd talked about those dreams, then turned to Callie and read her like a book. *"But that's not the kind of life you want, is it, Callie?"*

In those words, she'd known his four-bedroom dreams weren't meant to include her. And why should they have? Hadn't she made it clear a hundred times over that she wasn't the settling down kind?

But for a moment there, she had thought of settling down with him. And when he'd said that, it had hurt.

"You're awfully deep in thought," Jared said. "Pondering rose and carnation issues?"

She laughed. "No. Something…deeper."

Jared slipped her hand into his. "Like what?"

"To be honest, why you never married." She felt the tension in his touch, telling her she'd touched on a nerve. "Why are you still single all these years later, Jared?"

"To be honest, I don't have time, or room, for anything serious." A couple brushed by them, linked arm in arm, as if bucking that notion. "As soon as this research project is done, I'll be buried in the development phase and I won't have time to do much more than grab some crackers for dinner and wave at my pillow at night."

"You? But I remember you as being Mr. Serious. The man who was going to settle down. Have the house and the minivan and the kids."

He glanced away. "It didn't work out that way."

"Why?" She knew she shouldn't push, should let it be. It was none of her business, after all, but still she cared. This was Jared, after all.

"My life got in the way. Other…aspects of it."

Callie nearly laughed. If anything summed up Jared, that sentence did. All words and less emotion, less getting to the heart of things. That had always been the biggest problem with him—she never knew how he felt, because he kept putting his intellect in the way. He kept so much of him to himself.

"I'm surprised you of all people did get married," he said. "Callie Phillips, the woman who lived on a wing and a prayer."

"It was a whim. One of those, 'Why not?' kind of things," she said. "And after we did it—" she rolled her eyes "—we should have said, 'Why did we?'"

"Marriage wasn't what you expected?"

"Let's just say marriage and I were not a good mix. Tony and I never had the traditional married life anyway. We never stayed in one place, never really settled down. We moved more times than most people go to the grocery store."

"And you liked that kind of life?"

She shrugged. "Sure. Life is an adventure, right?"

They circumvented two mothers chatting on the sidewalk while their babies slept in strollers. "But you're here now and you've lived in Boston for three years. That's called settling down in my book," Jared said.

"I like it here. I like my job, my friends."

"So is this something permanent?"

Permanent. That word did not exist in Callie's vocabulary. "I don't like to think about anything in permanent terms."

"You mean you're just looking for temporary relationships? Nothing deep? Meaningful? Lasting?"

Put like that, it sounded so…crass. So cold.

Yet this was exactly the kind of relationship Callie had sought in the months since her divorce. But suddenly, hearing Jared lay out that kind of temporary affair in black-and-white terms—

Made the opposite sound, well, nice, even as the thought of anything more permanent than a piece of tape scared the heck out of her. But when she looked at Jared—nice, safe, sweet Jared—she wondered if maybe it were possible that she'd been overlooking a good guy all along.

"I wonder if we're both lying to ourselves, Jared. In a way."

His eyes widened in surprise. "Lying?"

"My friends have this crazy idea that I should be looking for Mr. Right." She let out a little laugh. "They even made a bet with me that I'd find him."

Jared didn't say anything for a long moment. Then he coughed and shook his head. "Did you just say Mr. Right? As in the guy you're going to marry, buy a house with, then have kids and get a Labrador with, Mr. Right?"

She nodded. "It's sort of, ah, a dare. I told you, the whole thing was insane."

"A dare?"

"The other women who work at the Wedding Belles, all believe Mr. Right exists. After all, it's practically part of the job description. And they challenged me to find him. Because…" Her voice trailed off. Why tell him all this? What woman poured out her whole sad can't find the right man story?

"Go ahead, tell me more."

Jared, though, seemed genuinely interested. And he hadn't gone running down the nearest highway or faked his own death, both good signs of a noncommitment phobic man. Maybe he was indulging her or maybe he truly wanted to hear what she had to say.

"Because I'm a little jaded, to say the least, and because I'm the least settled out of all of us. I've met my fair share of Mr. Wrongs. One in particular."

"I know." Sympathy flooded his words, another beacon of their shared history. Callie wondered how wise it was to connect with a man who knew her past, who knew about all her mistakes.

They'd reached the restaurant and the conversation paused

while Jared opened the door for her. There was a brief wait, then the maître d' led them to a table.

"And if you find this Mr. Right," Jared said after they were seated and had their drinks, "are you going to marry him?"

Callie nearly choked on the sip of soda in her mouth. "I, ah, hadn't thought that far. And no, that really wasn't in my plans, not again. I already took that road and it led nowhere. You know me, Jared. I'm not a mortgage-signing, minivan-buying kind of person."

Jared grinned. "Don't tell me you'd let your Mr. Perfect get away, and send that one ideal fish back into the dating waters?"

The thought of marrying again, of making that commitment—and possibly being wrong and ending up heartbroken all over again—still terrified her. Add that into the thought of staying in one place, committed to another man—

Callie shook her head. "I'll, ah, cross that bridge when I get to it."

"So your goal is to test the waters, more or less. See if there is such a thing as a right person for everyone?"

"Yes."

He laced his fingers together, then laid his hands on the table. "What if I could prove to you that true love existed?"

"Prove it to me? How?"

"I'm a man of science. You're a woman who takes very little on faith, at least where relationships are concerned. I'd like to show you, beyond a reasonable doubt, that true love does, in fact, exist."

"Like Santa Claus, UFOs and Big Foot?"

"Well, those might be a bit beyond even my capabilities." He took a sip of his soda, then continued. "But I do think it is possible to quantify love. Don't you?"

"As in measure it, weigh it, show it in a tangible manner?" Callie shook her head. "No, sorry, I don't."

Jared leaned closer, and though they were separated by a table in a public restaurant, the intimacy between them increased a dozen degrees. "Then let me prove it to you."

"Prove it to me?" She shook her head. "I've heard those words before, Jared. And I got proof of the exact opposite."

He reached out and touched her hand. Nothing in that connection spoke of charts and data, as far as Callie was concerned. What did Jared want? And for that matter, what did she want? "I'm not Tony, Callie."

She glanced away, thinking of the terrible way her marriage had ended, the bright hopes that had been dashed so quickly, the illusions that had been shattered nearly as quickly as the ring had been slipped on her finger. "No, you're not."

"And we had a wonderful time the other night, didn't we?" She nodded.

"That one night in college, we had chemistry between us, right?"

Chemistry, biology, physics and the entire range of earth sciences. Oh, yeah. Callie nodded again.

"And since then we've both gotten older," Jared said, his voice deepening. "And more experienced."

Heat infused Callie's body. She knew exactly what he meant…and exactly where he could apply that experience, given half the chance. "Where are you going with this?"

"Then why are you so scared to be with me? Haven't I always been a good friend?"

"Yeah," she said, disappointment once again hitting her square in the chest. A friend, he was only a friend. That should, indeed, be all that she wanted. It kept her on the safe relationship ground she liked, kept her heart from being risked, kept her from getting emotionally involved. "You've always been a good friend."

He nodded, as if that were the answer he'd expected. Jared

paused for a moment, then returned his attention to her. "I'm glad you're doing this. Looking for Mr. Right. You deserve a good man. Tony was…" He shook his head. "Let's just say I didn't foresee a happy ending whenever he dated someone."

"What do you mean?"

"Tony had a problem with monogamy. Always did."

The words stung, even though Callie should have been used to them by now. Her divorce had happened over a year in the past, the marriage over long before the piece of paper made it legally so. Her ex-husband's betrayals were common knowledge to her by now, but somehow, coming from Jared, someone who knew her from before, it seemed to hurt all over again. "Why didn't you ever say anything?"

"Would you have believed me?"

She thought of how infatuated she had been with Tony. How he'd seemed to represent everything she wanted. The very symbol of escape from the life she hated. She'd seen him as a savior, a hero—when he'd been anything but. She sighed. "No."

"I tried, a hundred times, to say something, but…" He drew in a breath. "I couldn't break your heart."

Somehow, that touched her in a way she hadn't expected. She thought of the Jared she'd known then, a shyer, quieter man, less sure of himself, someone who kept to himself yet was true to those he made his friends. "Maybe it would have been better if you had."

"It probably would have. And I was wrong. I'm sorry, Callie."

"It's okay." She smiled. "My mother always said I was the kind of hardheaded kid who had to learn the stove was hot by burning my own hand."

He chuckled. "And I was the kind who nearly blew it up trying to test the boiling points of different liquids."

She cocked her head, studying him. "We're very different people, aren't we, Jared?"

His gaze met hers, deep blue eyes so vibrant, for a moment she felt as if she could swim in the ocean of his gaze. "Not so different, not always. I used to wish, though, that you noticed me more. Back in those days. Realized I was more than just your lab partner in high school. Once we turned off the Bunsen burner, you pretty much forgot I existed." He shrugged, as if it didn't matter, but Callie could tell it had. "That's okay. I was...not exactly stud of the year back then."

Had she done that? She remembered being, as he'd said, lab partners with Jared, working on science projects, conducting experiments, filling out worksheets. Other than that, they'd gone their separate ways in high school, she with her friends, then with Tony. Then, later, in college, he'd been in different classes altogether, except for the one class they'd been stuck in together—Humanities and Modern Thinking, where they'd both struggled under a difficult professor and sought each other's help once again, resurrecting the old friendship—

And a new, stronger connection.

Until Tony had come back and Callie had fallen into her old patterns, leaving Jared behind.

She reached for him across the table, knowing nine years had passed and a few words couldn't make up for what had happened back then. "I'm sorry, too, Jared."

"It was nothing. I grew up to be a reasonably well-adjusted adult." He grinned, but once again she got the feeling that she had hurt him in those years and remorse settled heavy on her shoulders. "What you said earlier, about wondering whether there was such a thing as one right person for everyone, is sort of the theory I'm working on."

"Your theory?"

He nodded. "That's what I was doing in the bar. I'm a researcher for Wiley Games, and this time, I was researching love—in a way."

Callie nearly spit onto Jared. "You? Researching love?"

"Hey, it's not that unbelievable." He cleared his throat and something unreadable washed over his gaze. "Not love *exactly,* more love games. The way couples get to know each other. Wiley is using my data to create a bedroom game. I see that face. Don't laugh."

But she did anyway.

"I'm hoping to use some of the research for serious purposes, too. Down the road I hope to extrapolate enough information from the data to write a research paper." He shrugged. "Give some credentials to the whole thing. Something that goes beyond 'Twenty Tantalizing Bedroom Teasers.'"

"That's what you were doing when I ran into you?"

He nodded. "I've already interviewed several dozen couples. The trouble is finding people who are happy together."

"I know plenty of those," Callie said. "We have a database of past clients at Wedding Belles and if there's one thing they love to talk about, it's how they met and got to know each other. If you want, I can put you in touch with some of them."

"I'd appreciate that. It'll expedite my research. It'll be just like the old days," Jared said. "You and me, study partners again. In a way."

"If I remember right, I wasn't much help when it came to studying for those Humanities tests. It was like the blind leading the blind. Don't you think that might not be the best idea?"

"It won't be anything but friends working together, just like the old days."

"Friends who go on dates."

He pushed his glasses up on his nose, as if the mention of that disconcerted him.

"And doesn't that take us out of the realm of friends?"

Jared's cool returned and he met her gaze head-on. "Does it?"

Callie wasn't quite sure herself where she and Jared were

right now. All she knew was that a confusing jumble of feelings rushed through her every time he touched her, looked at her. Those were just as quickly chased by the reminder that Jared had been a good friend for years, and this could be a temporary rush of hormones and nothing more. They were very different people, who wanted very different things, which meant they could never be a couple.

Right?

"Have you decided what you'd like to order?" The waiter's voice cut through the tension between Callie and Jared, drawing them back to mundane items.

"Uh…" Callie glanced down at the menu, realizing she hadn't even opened it yet.

Jared gave her a smile. "Lasagna, extra sauce on the side?"

Once again, he'd read her mind. If the man sent out any more confusing signals, he'd be a blindfolded air traffic controller. "Yes."

After the waiter was gone, Callie turned back to Jared. "So, will you help me?"

She considered him. What could it hurt, really? Spending time with Jared would get her friends off her back about that silly bet and if it didn't work out, would give her the ammunition she needed to once again prove that there was no such thing as true love for everyone. And if it did…well, she'd cross that bridge when she got to it, as she'd said earlier. "Okay. I'll help you, but only for a week. This is the busy season for weddings."

"It's okay. Any help is great."

"Is that enough time, though?"

He grinned. "I don't see why not. Most all the couples I interviewed said that's how it always happened for them. They met, and within the first few minutes of conversation, they just…knew."

Like with a kiss?

If Jared had kissed her the other night, would she have known something then, just as she had felt a connection all those years ago on that one night they'd spent together?

Had it been that special link he was talking about or simply a hormonal overload?

Jared put out his hand. "Let's shake on it."

She took his and did as he asked. It should have been just a simple touch, a sealing of a deal, but when his palm touched hers, Callie's pulse ratcheted up again. "This has to be the weirdest start to a relationship I've ever seen."

"Although, this is more of a partnership, isn't it?" Jared's gaze met hers. "That way, we're clear from the start, and no one gets hurt."

Something flickered in his eyes, and Callie knew—knew for sure now—that she *had* hurt him all those years ago.

Had she read leftover feelings in his touch? Had he never really forgotten her? Never gotten over her?

And if so, where did that leave them?

The waiter brought their lasagna. Steam rose in curls off the pasta, bringing with it the tangy scent of tomato sauce and the sharp notes of parmesan cheese. Callie's stomach rumbled in anticipation.

After they'd each had a few bites, Jared returned his attention to Callie. Every time he did that, it was as if a giant spotlight had shone on her. "So what did you do before you became a florist?"

"Everything. I flopped at burger flipping. Had a problem with authority figures telling me how to apply ketchup."

Jared laughed. "Seriously?"

"I wasn't cut out for fast food. Or grocery packing. Or a number of other jobs. In fact, my personal résumé is pretty cluttered with holes and temporary employment. Thank goodness I found a field I love and a boss I love working for."

Callie buttered a piece of bread, then gestured toward Jared. "What about you? I take it you never veered from the Mr. Straight-and-Narrow path?"

"And why would you guess that?"

"Because I know you, Jared. And because everything about you has always screamed Straight-and-Narrow. The suit, the glasses, the clipboard in a bar, for Pete's sake."

"What's wrong with a suit?"

"Nothing. Nothing at all." In fact, he made a suit look good. Really, really good.

"I admit, I followed the regular route. College, then straight into suit-and-tie world."

"How far did you go in college?"

His gaze met hers. "After I left UMass, I went to CalState, then on to Stanford, and got my master's, then my PhD. On scholarships, thankfully, because I never could have paid my own way. There's an advantage to having good grades."

"I wish I'd finished."

"You dropped out?"

"I've never been one for staying in one place for long and once Tony and I eloped, we were off and running all over the world." She took a bite of food. "This job here is the longest I've been anywhere."

"Why?"

"You know me, Jared. Five minutes in a room and I go stir-crazy." It had been part of what had attracted her to Tony. His constant wanderlust, quest for something new every day. But when she'd divorced him, Callie had made the decision to settle down, plant some roots, at least for a while. So far, she hadn't done anything more permanent than sign a month-to-month lease on her apartment.

"You should have gotten your degree," Jared said. "You were really smart. You did great in Science."

"Thanks to you."

"No, it wasn't me. You had all the brains you needed, Callie."

She looked away, fiddled with her bread. "You were the only reason I ever passed the Periodic Table of Elements test."

"You were the one who made studying for it fun. Who else could turn that into a game?"

"It was pretty boring stuff, you have to admit."

"Okay, it was. But you made it fun." His gaze connected with hers again. "And that's what I want more of."

"More Science? You didn't get enough of E equals mc squared?"

"No. More of the fun you. The wild and crazy Callie I remembered from high school. When we were together…" He paused, drew in a breath, and in the space of that moment, Callie knew something was coming, something she didn't want to hear. "You brought out a side of me that, well, that I wasn't even aware existed."

"What do you mean?"

"I was your resident geek. You were the wild child. All these years, I've stayed the same. So while we're working together, maybe a little of that wildness could rub off like it did the other night—"

"That night was a once in a lifetime thing," Callie said, putting up her hand. "I'm not planning on repeating that."

"Why not?"

"I've changed, Jared. I'm not who I used to be." How could she tell him that doing that had awakened a part of her she'd worked very hard to keep quiet? That she was afraid of becoming the woman who ran out on people at a moment's notice, the one who couldn't stay put? She had friends here, a job—but that itch to leave, to move on, had never really left her.

"No one changes that much."

That scared her, and tempted her, and exactly why Callie

didn't want to go poking around in her past, even with Mr. Straight-and-Narrow Jared.

"I did. So if you're looking for that Callie," she said, her gaze connecting with his, leaving no room for misinterpretation, "she doesn't exist anymore."

"Maybe she should," Jared said. "Because I miss her. Very much."

And in those words, he issued Callie a challenge that half of her very much wanted to take.

CHAPTER SIX

JARED rubbed at his eyes, then leaned back in his chair so far, the office seat tipped precariously on its wheels and let out a creak of warning. The numbers before him swam in a jumble, the words on the screen a blur, but the workload had yet to reduce.

"Dude, you have zero life. You're like one of those Byzantine bald guys."

Jared turned. "Byzantine bald guys?"

Pope, Jared's college intern, spun around a second chair and draped his lean stonewashed jean-clad legs over either side. "Yeah, you know those guys who wear those funny robes and go around chanting all the time."

"You mean monks?" Jared shook his head. "I don't think my love life is that bad."

"Last time you had a date, man had taken his first steps on the moon."

Jared made a face at the spiky-haired blonde. "I'm not even that old."

Pope looked surprised. "Really? 'Cuz, dude, I thought you were at least, like, fifty."

"Thirty-three, Pope. The moon walk was in sixty-nine."

Pope flipped out his fingers, did a little counting. Jared bit back a groan at hiring the intern. The kid had zero common sense, almost no personal skills, but was a whiz with computer programs. If only his technological prowess extended into other areas of his brain. "My bad. Guess you weren't around then. Still, you are like total hermit guy. You need a chick."

"Women aren't chicks, Pope."

Pope shrugged. "Whatever. They aren't PCs either and that's about the only thing you've been intimate with since I started working here." Pope put up his hands. "Now if that's your thing, dude, I'm all for free expression—"

"No!"

"It's cool, it's cool. Totally. You struck me as the straight and narrow type anyway."

"Straight and narrow," Jared repeated. The same thing Callie had said at lunch today. He sighed. "Yeah, that's me."

Except for those few songs on the stage the other night, he was as straight as a fence post. The only time he'd done anything wild had been in college, and all he'd done then was put on a leather jacket, sit astride a Harley and pretend to be a biker for Halloween. He'd ended up on a stage with her, then spending one incredible, amazing night with Callie, only to have her leave for another man in the morning.

And look where that one night of daredevil living had gotten him.

He glanced at the computer beside him. In an intimate relationship with a nineteen-inch monitor.

"Yo, dude, you ever need help with the ladies, call me. I'm a regular Lethargio."

Jared spun back toward Pope. "Don't you mean Lothario?"

"Hell, no. Lethargio. I lay back, and the ladies just come to me." Pope spread his arms wide. "I got the goods, dude. The look, the car, the personality. You on the other hand, could use a little help in those areas."

"What's wrong with the way I look? My car?" Jared wasn't about to compare personalities. He was quite happy with his.

Pope pitched forward and flicked at the tie around Jared's neck. "For one, the strangled chicken look does not scream sexy. For another, pleated pants are advertisements for balloons."

Jared glanced down at his striped tie, his pleated khakis. When he'd gotten dressed this morning, the choices had seemed...normal. The kind of thing he wore every day.

Maybe that was the problem. The clothes he pulled out of his closet were the ones he pulled out every day, had chosen for years on end. He shopped in the same department of the same store, year after year. No deviation from the regular pattern.

He glanced over at Pope. The intern's button-down shirt was open at the neck, untucked, but managed to have a wilder, more approachable look. His jeans were not too tight, but snug enough that a woman looking at Pope would know the guy worked out. No balloon advertisements there.

"Where do you shop?" Jared asked.

"Abercrombie. Hollister. Some Hot Topic, though I'm more a Banana Republic kind of guy when I'm in the flush with the dough."

Jared stared at Pope. Those were names of stores? They had to be on a whole other level of the mall. Maybe in an entirely different mall than the one Jared went to. "Uh, where would I find Abercrumb?"

Pope laughed and popped out of his chair. "Dude, you may be the professor in here, but when it comes to scoring with chicks, you are a total Gilligan."

On Sunday afternoon Callie and Julie rode back from the spacious Markson home in Newton, the Wedding Belles van empty of flowers, but still carrying the scent of the dozens of arrangements and bouquets. "I can't believe we pulled that one off," Callie said. "Another amazing Belles wedding."

Julie shifted in her seat to face Callie and grinned. "Every one of them is amazing, aren't they?"

Callie nodded, then flipped on her directional to turn right onto Boylston Street and head back toward the shop. "When I first started working for Belle, I was astounded at how she could pull something out of nothing. A bride and groom come into the Wedding Belles shop with a simple idea—"

"Sometimes not even that."

"And then Belle and the rest of us took that idea and made it into something like what we just saw."

Julie sighed. "Something magical." She leaned back against the seat, then removed the clip atop her head, releasing her long, curly chestnut hair from its prison. It tumbled past her shoulders. Julie always complained about her locks, but Callie thought her hair was beautiful. "It makes you believe, doesn't it?"

Callie stopped for a red light. "Believe in what?"

"Happy endings. Riding off into the sunset."

"Julie, you get like this after every one of our weddings. All misty-eyed."

Julie turned to her. "And you don't?"

Callie shrugged. "I'm more of a realist." The light changed and Callie moved forward—inched forward, really, with the rest of the slow-moving traffic, turning onto Fairfield. No matter the time of day, downtown Boston always seemed to move at a snail's pace.

"You must have believed at some point. You got married, too."

"I eloped. There's a difference."

"What difference?"

"A stupid mistake difference. A one-night, thinking-he-was-the-one, difference." Rain started to fall, so Callie flipped on the wipers and rolled up her window. She thought of the wedding the Belles were all planning on throwing for Julie, the secret so good, she nearly burst with wanting to tell it, but knew that keeping it would make it all so much more fun when Julie's wedding day came and she saw the fabulous day planned by her friends.

"And then what happened?" Julie said, drawing Callie's attention back to Callie's love life.

"Can we just drop it? My ex is not exactly my favorite topic of conversation." Callie let out a sigh, then turned to Julie. "Sorry. I'm just not in the best of moods. I've got a lot on my mind."

"Your mom again?"

Callie's shoulders sagged, and tears rushed to the back of her eyes. Leave it to her friend to guess, to get right to the heart of the matter. "Yeah. How'd you know?"

"I know you, Cal. That's all it takes."

"She's divorcing husband number four and flying into town to see me in a few days. She needs a shoulder to cry on. Again."

"Number four?"

"My mother really likes weddings, too." Callie tried to work up a smile, but it fell flat. She made the turn onto Newbury Street, and started looking for street-side parking in front of the shop, not an easy thing to find on a rainy day. "She just picks a lot of Mr. Wrongs."

"Well, no wonder." Julie's voice had softened.

"No wonder what?"

"No wonder you're so afraid of doing the same thing again."

"I'm not afraid." Callie drew in a breath, let it out. "Okay, I am. The other night I went over to O'Malley's to deliver the invitations for his daughter's wedding and ran into a guy I used to know. Then, at the poker game the other night, Audra and the other girls made me agree to date him, after I had the losing hand."

Julie laughed. "Never bet against Audra. But how did you know this guy?"

"We were friends, and we went out on one date, years and years ago."

"And how is Mr. Past now?"

"Nice. He was always…nice."

"And that, I take it, was the problem? He was nice, but not…exciting?"

"He has his exciting…moments," Callie said, thinking of that night in college. A totally exciting moment, with a Jared so unlike the one she'd thought she'd known.

"So what are you going to do?"

"Well, I wasn't going to do anything, but then…" She parked the van in front of the Wedding Belles office and shut off the engine. "He came to me with a proposition."

"A proposition? As in 'hey baby, come up and see my etchings' kind of proposition?"

Callie laughed. "No. He's a research scientist and he wants me to help him find couples that he can interview. He's asking them questions about how they met, and what made them stay together."

"Ooh, how romantic." Julie made a face. "Not."

"Well, after Jared left, I got to thinking." She smiled, and the wheels in Callie's head began to turn. For the first time in a long time, she was intrigued. Jared's question had made her wonder about what she had put aside over the past three years. Had she simply been sitting still?

Could it be possible to light that fire in herself—a fire that seemed to have been extinguished by her divorce—without it erupting into the full-force flames of running for the hills? Could she maybe dip into who she used to be, find a bit of that magic she had lost when Tony broke her heart, without losing her newfound life? And in the meantime, maybe make things up to Jared a little?

"What if I took the professor's proposition and messed with his research?"

"How are you intending to do that?"

"What if I turn the tables on him? Maybe take him beyond a little data on hand holding and kissing?"

Julie nodded, putting the pieces together. "And make *his* blood pressure ratchet up?"

"Exactly. In other words, this lab rat puts the *professor* into the maze, at least a little. Jared says he misses the wild side of me and that he wants a little more fun in his life." Callie grinned. "If that's the case, then I have a few experiments of my own I want to conduct. And they'll be fun, but *my* kind of fun."

"You're sure about this?" Jared said. He sent the contraption a dubious glance.

"Absolutely." Callie handed the attendant six tickets, then grasped Jared's hand and got in line behind the dozen children. "Are you *brave* enough for this?"

He tossed her a grin. "Are *you?*"

"Baby, I was born brave."

When she looked at him like that, Jared's gut tightened and he thought of kissing her again. Not just once, but a hundred times. And taking her everywhere but to an amusement park.

Totally not part of the plan. He was supposed to be here to work on his research, to use that to keep his distance, so he could keep his heart out of the fray again. He was a smart man—and a smart man knew enough not to make the same mistake twice.

Just then, the gate opened, the children surged forward and Callie led him onto the platform. They slipped inside a giant curved seat, the sign above it reading Tilt-A-Whirl in a rainbow of letters.

"Grab the center wheel," she told him, "and hold on to your lunch."

He glanced around at their metal surroundings. "Do you know the last time they did a maintenance check? Tightened the bolts? Lubricated the fittings?"

"Quit worrying and just enjoy the ride. Besides, they have him to worry about that." Callie gestured toward the ride attendant, who loped across the platform, checking each of the seats.

Jared cast a doubtful look at the grease-stained, tattered-shirt youth shuffling through his job. "When was the last time he had a drug test?"

Callie laughed. "Has anyone told you that you worry too much?"

"Statistically—"

Callie pressed a finger to Jared's lips. "Focus on having fun, Jared. Not on statistics."

"I'm focused," he said. "But not on the ride." He reached up one hand—the ride, the noisy park, the warm spring evening—all of it forgotten in the space of the second her touch had met his lips, when the car they were in jerked to a start, thrusting Callie against his chest.

"Hold on tight," she whispered.

His arm came down and wrapped around her. "Exactly what I was thinking."

Jared quickly found it harder to do that than he'd expected. The Tilt-A-Whirl began to pick up tempo, matching the rock music pounding out of the sound system. Centrifugal force whipped them around the circle, then Callie reached forward and grabbed the wheel, one hand reaching over the other, spinning it faster and faster, in turn spinning their seat, increasing their circles.

The force flattened her to his chest, but the thrill made her laugh. Jared stopped worrying about bolts and safety inspections and found himself caught in Callie's infectious spirit, his hands walking over hers, increasing the spin factor.

"Having fun?" she called over the music.

"Absolutely."

"Let's go faster then." And she grabbed faster, the dare in her green eyes encouraging him to do the same.

He matched her speed, joining her in laughter, their car whipping in a wild spiral that matched the growing desire in Jared's veins. He glanced over at her, wanting Callie in a way he couldn't remember ever wanting her before.

This wasn't the heated intensity of a college crush. It wasn't the what-if thoughts of a man who had lost a woman to someone else. It wasn't the instant connection of meeting up with a long-lost love. This was full-on, holy-cow, get-off-this-ride and go-somewhere-alone lust.

And then, the music began to ebb, the ride began to slow, the car's spin going from high-speed wash cycle to low-gear and then finally stop. The attendant climbed back onto the platform, but the children had already gotten out of their seats and clambered past him, dashing back to their parents, exclaiming about how much fun they'd had. One little boy stumbled down the steps, clutching his stomach and moaning about too much cotton candy.

Callie turned to Jared, laughter dancing in her eyes. "That was fun."

"It was." A heartbeat passed between them. He knew they should get out of there. Make room for the next flock of kids. But he wasn't ready to leave, not yet.

"Do you want to tackle the Ferris wheel or the—" She stared at him, their little world cocooned in the semiprivate wall of ride. "What? Do I have some mustard on my lips or something?"

"Or something." Jared leaned forward and before he could think about what he was doing, kissed Callie.

When Jared kissed Callie, the world shuddered to a stop. All the thoughts and emotions that had been swirling in her mind, the war of should-she or shouldn't-she screeching to a halt, with one big neon, oh-yes-she-should.

Jared's mouth drifted over hers, at first light and easy, as soft as a cloud, then, when she opened more against him, he gathered her into his arms, pressing her to his chest.

His kiss deepened and she inhaled his warm, male scent, memory spiraling her back all those years, to every one of their touches, as if they'd never been apart, as if she'd never chosen another. She reached up, her hands tangling in his hair, fire rushing through her veins, igniting parts of her that had felt dead for so long, so very, very long.

He cupped her jaw, a tender, sweet gesture that nearly made Callie cry, and then drifted his lips over hers, before coming back to kiss her again, thoroughly, tenderly.

Like a woman should be kissed. Like a man who took his time. Who cared that the woman enjoyed the kiss.

And everything within Callie sang better than her voice had sounded on that stage.

For Jared, kissing Callie rocked him to the core. The analytical part of his mind told himself to measure this kiss. Her response. His own increased heartbeat, rapid pulse. Make it part of his research, stay uninvolved.

The other half of him told the analytical part to shut the hell up for at least five seconds.

And he did, enjoying the feel of her in his arms, the way she curved into his body, the way everything about Callie had always fit exactly right. Fire raced through his veins, ignited every part of his brain, his heart. And told him he was no longer looking at her with the eyes of a researcher.

Jared drew back, his heart thudding hard.

Callie smiled at him. "So, was that part of the grand experiment? Or part of the ride?"

"Oh, you're not part of the experiment at all."

He lied.

He had made Callie part of the research. And he needed to keep it that way. Only by putting his research between them, the familiar world of numbers, could he erect a wall strong enough to protect his heart. Then maybe he wouldn't fall as hard for her as he had before.

Nothing killed a libido faster than a spreadsheet, after all. So, a little note-taking, some analysis of some figures—and hopefully he'd forget all about how sexy her figure was.

It was the only option. After all, Jared knew he hadn't turned into the kind of man Callie wanted. He was, as always, Mr. Straight-and-Narrow.

Unfortunately Mr. Straight-and-Narrow still had a major thing for Ms. Wild-and-Crazy.

He couldn't seem to stop wanting to see her, to keep asking her out. The only solution was to make her part of the numbers, to keep his focus on work. Not an impossible situation, but one where he already knew the probable relationship outcome if he didn't stick to his research guns.

Failure.

"Oh, look, Jared. There's a bunch of couples over there. Maybe you should go talk to them?"

"Oh, yeah," Jared said, trying to draw himself back to work, and away from how amazing Callie looked in jeans and a V-necked T-shirt. He fumbled for his notepad, his pen. Where had his pen gone? It must have slipped out when the ride was flinging them against each other. "I seem to have lost my pen."

"Right here," Callie said, leaning past him, her breasts brushing against his chest, and sending his thoughts way past research territory and down a whole other path that had nothing to do with science and a whole lot to do with anatomy. "You were, ah, sitting on it." Her voice had gone husky, throaty. If he didn't know better, he'd swear she was flirting with him.

"Oh, yeah. Uh, thanks."

She placed it in his palm, her eyes a tease. "No problem. Just doing my job as a research assistant."

"Mister, are you going to get out of there or what?"

They turned and saw a chubby ten-year-old boy standing outside their car, his arms crossed over his chest.

Jared shoved his glasses up on his nose. "We should probably go."

"Unless you want to ride again?" Callie offered.

Everything within him did. But he'd already run this test once. There was no scientific reason to do it again. "No, I'm good."

"As long as you're sure." Then she slipped out of the car and—

Jared was sure, she sauntered off the platform and away from him.

Callie *was* flirting with him?

Was she truly interested in him? He was the one who had started this game, opened this particular can of worms. And now, he didn't know which way it was going. Every time he tried to read her, he seemed to get a different story. He'd gone into this with one hypothesis. That love could be manufactured, measured. That he could stay detached, out of the fray of the experiment.

But with every sway of Callie's hips, Jared knew he was wrong. He was feeling about as detached as a fly caught in a spider's web.

"Let's get something to eat," Callie said, taking Jared's hand and leading him toward a stand-alone hut labeled Snack Shack. The scent of deep fried foods wafted off the small building, with people crowded around it, shouting out orders for things called "elephant ears."

Lord help him. Fried elephant parts?

"I am not getting an elephant ear," Jared said, his stomach rolling at the thought.

Callie laughed. "You haven't lived until you've had one."

"Are you crazy?"

"Trust me." Her green eyes met his, and his objections melted away. She turned back toward the Snack Shack, put up two fingers, had her money out and had paid for two of the treats before Jared could stop her. When the lady behind the trailer window handed them over, Callie spooned on some canned cinnamon apples, then sprinkled the tops with confectionary sugar and gave one to Jared. "Your elephant ear."

He looked down at the bubbled fried disc on the plate. Not gray, but tan, thank God, like bread. "I take it this isn't real fried ear?"

Callie laughed. "No. It's a glob of fried dough. Really bad for your arteries and your heart."

As Jared watched Callie's generous crimson mouth close around a bite of the treat and felt desire stir anew, he knew the fried dough wasn't the only thing bad for his heart.

He kept losing track of his reason for being with her. He'd gone into this project with every intention of keeping his emotions separate. He'd thought, because he'd been down this road with Callie before, that he could compartmentalize his heart from the data. Remind himself not to fall in love again.

Uh-huh. And how well was that plan working?

"Doesn't it tempt you?"

Callie's voice drew Jared back to the present. "Tempt me?" Oh, he was tempted all right. That was the problem.

"Yeah, the elephant ear. They're best when they're hot."

"Oh, yes. Well, you know me. Knife and fork guy all the way." He gave her a grin.

"I thought you wanted to loosen up." Callie leaned forward and flipped his tie. "That means in all aspects. You did it once, remember?"

Jared stepped away, reaching for a set of plastic silverware and a napkin. He gestured toward a picnic table and they each took a seat. "That was a long time ago and it was only for one night."

"Then what was that back in the karaoke bar?"

He grinned. "An aberration."

"The professor loosening his tie after a couple of beers?"

"Something like that." If he was smart, he'd remember to keep his tie tight, and his glasses on. That one foray into the leather jacket had been a mistake. He'd tried to become the kind of guy he'd thought Callie would want—

And she'd left him for a real heartbreaker instead.

He knew better. Knew where walking on the wild side got a man. Why had he ever told her he wanted to add a little wildness to his life? The minute he'd done that—

He'd kissed her.

Jared led a cautious, predictable life for a reason.

Get back to the research. The reason for being here, he reminded himself. Which meant getting close to her, touching her. But not kissing her. Keeping it impersonal.

All in the name of data, of course.

They'd finished their snacks and tossed away the paper plates. Jared stood and slipped his hand into Callie's, the warm feeling of her palm against his sending his mind off track again. "What next?"

A devilish gleam lit her eyes. "Whatever scares you most."

"That's easy." He caught her gaze. "You."

"Me?"

The crowd parted around them, like waves breaking past rocks, the neon lights of the amusement park flashed their rainbow dance across Callie's features, while the rock music of the rides played a rhythmic undertow in the background.

"Why do I scare you?"

"For one," he said, taking a step closer, picking up her other hand, pulling her to the side, out of the fray, "you can sing my pants off. For another, you can tilt that Tilt-A-Whirl like nobody's business."

Beneath his grasp, her pulse ratcheted up, her breathing quickened. Jared made mental notes, but they kept getting jumbled, and he wondered how clear his data would be later. And whether he even cared.

"I had a good partner in crime," Callie said. "Shall we try another ride?"

Jared should say no. He had mountains of work ahead of him tonight. The normal Jared begged off early from a date, went back to his apartment, holed up at his little desk with his laptop and a cold sandwich and worked until the wee hours of the morning. For years, he'd found his job relatively satisfying and rewarding. Loved the challenge of numbers and data.

But for some reason, being with Callie again had awakened an old itch for something crazy, a dangerous feeling, the one that had once made him consider ditching his ambitions and forgetting every shred of responsibility.

Surely, though, he could do that for a few hours. What would it hurt? He could make up the hours tomorrow. The next day.

But what he couldn't make up was this moment, the way Callie looked right this second.

"The Ferris wheel," he said. "I've never been on one."

"Never? Really? Who goes through life missing out on the Ferris wheel?"

"Me, I guess." He didn't elaborate. A guy didn't need to

open the book of his childhood to know it wasn't the kind of story other people wanted to read.

"Well then," Callie said. "Let me show you what you've been missing out on." She led him through the crowds and down the popcorn-strewn path toward the flashing Ferris wheel. It reached three stories up into the air, spinning in a slow, lazy circle, the carts swinging back and forth, filled with necking teenagers, families and elderly couples. "Think you're man enough for this one?"

"Oh, I think I can handle it. If you can."

"Absolutely." She handed their tickets to the ticket taker, who looked like he could have been an older, more tired carbon copy of the one who'd worked the Tilt-A-Whirl. The man reached out, stopped one of the metal seats, then waited while Callie and Jared climbed inside. The bar lowered over their laps, then the ride began its slow backward journey. In a few seconds, the amusement park had disappeared, the people, rides, games of chance shrinking with each upward movement of the wheel.

Soon they were at the top. The car stopped, swaying slightly as the cool spring breeze whistled through the car. "It's chilly up this high," Callie said.

"Here." Jared drew her against him. She fit perfectly, as he'd known she would. Just like she used to. "Is that better?"

"Yes." Callie tipped her chin to face him. "Thank you."

"My pleasure." The stars above reflected in her eyes, the moon danced on her features. Jared's research seemed a thousand miles away.

"Have those couples worked out? The names I gave you?" Callie asked.

It took Jared a second to make the connection with what she was talking about. "Couples?"

"For the game. Your research, remember?"

Oh, he was researching, all right. Every single thing *Callie* was doing. Then he remembered. Callie had given him several names earlier that day. Jared had already completed two interviews. "They were great contacts. Thank you."

"Good." She beamed. "I'm glad to help. If you're looking for any other specific couple types, I can—"

"I don't want to talk about research right now." He pulled her closer.

"Oh." She let out a slight gasp, her mouth opening in surprise, then a smile. "Oh, okay."

The temptation between them ratcheted up a thousand times. To hell with the plan. With staying out of the experiment. With staying neutral, uninvolved. Jared lowered his head, brushed his lips against hers, intending only to kiss her sweetly, softly, but just as quickly realizing he was definitely unable to stop there.

Because he knew how good it would be. Knew what it was like to kiss Callie. To taste her.

And before his better judgment could take the lead, he opened his mouth against hers, his other hand coming up to cup her jaw, his thumb sliding along the delicate edge.

She arched slightly against him, and fire exploded in Jared's brain. For a man who lived his life on strictly analytical terms, it was a heady rush, a journey into a new land, one he'd forgotten existed.

But the very one that had led to him making some very foolish mistakes.

Jared pulled back, just as the ride began to move again with a shudder. He pushed his glasses up on his nose, and straightened his tie, the actions making him feel like himself again.

At least the outside was orderly.

"Sorry," he said. "I didn't mean to lose control, to take things further than—"

"You and your control." Callie shook her head, clearly frustrated with him. "You keep telling me you want to be a little wilder, to loosen up, and yet every time you're with me, you're all research and Mr. Professor again. What's it going to take to get you to let up, Jared? To go back to the guy you were that one night in college?"

"Maybe that was a mistake. An early midlife crisis or something." He thought of how it had ended, of how she'd woken up the next morning and told him what a mistake they had made.

How foolish he had felt, looking at that leather jacket lying over the chair in the bedroom, a silly, empty shell. In the light of day, revealed for what it was—just a costume. Realizing he'd tried to be someone he wasn't. Only to lose Callie in the end anyway.

"What if that was the *real* you? And this—" she tugged on his tie "—isn't?"

"Are we talking about getting real? Because I seem to remember a different Callie from those days myself. You used to be completely spontaneous. Run off to a party at the drop of a hat. Would take a weekend in Vegas, a trip to the beach, just about anything, just because someone asked you to. What happened to that Callie?"

She looked away, avoiding his gaze, the subject at hand. He'd hit a nerve, clearly. "I went to the bar and sang Madonna with you. That's spontaneous."

"So is buying name brand detergent without a coupon." Their seat swung toward the front of the Ferris wheel, then stopped to let off some people at the bottom. Jared wondered why he was pushing Callie on this topic so much.

Why did he care if she had changed? Why was he pushing so hard to have back the old Callie?

The very woman who had walked out on him and married his best friend?

Because he was one serious glutton for punishment, that was clear. So he cleared his throat and returned again to the world he knew, the safe territory of statistics and numbers. "On the other hand, my studies have shown a little spontaneity can be good for a relation—"

"Stop," Callie said, as their ride started and stopped, bringing them closer and closer to the debarking point. "Tell me one thing, Jared. What does spontaneity have to do with your research project?"

"It has everything to do with it. Falling in love is a spontaneous act."

"Oh, yeah?" She arched a brow. Their car had swung into place and the attendant stepped forward to raise the bar, releasing them from the seat. "And tell me exactly how you know this. Because you read it in some scholarly journal or because you have actually done it yourself? Because I *have* fallen in love at first sight. And it was the biggest mistake of my life. One I won't be making again."

Then she slipped away and disappeared into the crowd before Jared could tell her that he, too, had fallen in love.

And maybe never really fallen out.

CHAPTER SEVEN

WHAT had Callie been thinking? That she could turn the tables on Jared and not get involved?

That was like diving into the deep end of the pool and expecting to stay dry. Because every time Jared Townsend touched her, every part of her got involved. Very involved.

And she found herself wanting to do a lot more than just make up for breaking his heart all those years ago. She began thinking beyond the next few days. Actually looking down the road. At a future.

And that was the one thing Callie had learned long ago not to do. Because planning a future only meant that all her plans would go awry.

What's more, it scared her. Caught her in the clutches of a fear worse than anything every horror filmmaker in the world could put on the big screen.

She needed to get out of this whole crazy relationship now, while she still could. Jared was a nice guy and it would only be doing him a disservice to let this thing go any further.

"Callie, are you hearing me?"

Callie sighed and returned her attention to the phone call. "Yes, Mom, I am."

"I'll be there in a couple days. I don't have a definite plan.

Did I tell you? I ran into an old friend the other day and he invited me down to his beach house in Bermuda. So, anyway, I don't really want to book a hotel or anything in Boston. Surely you can put me up for a day or two when I get there."

"Of course." Callie glanced at the sofa bed, already knowing that would be her bedroom, because she'd give her mother the queen mattress. "Have you talked to Dad lately?"

Silence. "I don't even know that man's phone number anymore."

"He's left town again?"

"I presume so." Her mother paused, and on the other end, Callie could hear her take a sip of something with ice—soda or water. Whatever it was, Callie knew it wouldn't have alcohol. Not anymore. "Why do you care?"

"I don't know," Callie said. "I really don't. I guess I keep wondering why."

Her mother snorted. "I stopped wondering that the third time he walked out on us. And then I filed for divorce instead of looking for him. You're better off forgetting him, Callie. Even if he is your father."

"Don't you ever wonder, though? Where he is? Why he keeps running off?"

"No, I don't. I moved on, as should you. Anyway, they're calling my flight. See you later." Her mother hung up.

Callie replaced the receiver in the phone and fingered the list of phone numbers beside it. All of them for her father, who moved as often as some people changed the television station. He'd moved again, last month, and not bothered to leave a forwarding address.

Eventually her father would call. Tell her where he was. Until then, she'd wonder. Look for him on the street. Just as she had in every city she'd visited, every town she'd been to during the years she'd traveled with Tony. Once, she'd run into

him, in Mexico, but before she'd had a chance to talk to him—
really talk—he'd been gone. Again.

The clock in the hall chimed the hour and Callie jerked
to attention, realizing she'd be late for work. There was
something to be said for schedules, for the way one kept
her on track.

Most of all, sticking to a schedule gave her something to
do and think about, something besides her screwed-up family
and Jared Townsend, who had only added fuel to a fire that
was in danger of raging out of control.

"Dude, that's totally you."

Jared cast an unconvinced glance in the mirror outside the
dressing room. Teenage boys milled around them, shopping
and giving Jared cynical looks. Rock music pounded on the
stereo system, its insistent beat seeming to drum home the
message that this store was light years away from Jared's
usual venue. "I look ridiculous."

"You look like a guy who's actually kind of cool." Pope
pointed at the untucked bowling shirt and stonewashed jeans that
he'd talked Jared into buying at one of those stores with the odd
name that Pope frequented. "Any girl will think you're hot now."

Jared scanned the store's high-school-aged demographic.
"Any girl under the age of eighteen."

"Dude, that's like a felony. Don't joke about that." Pope
put up his hands, backed up a couple of steps. "It brings up
bad memories for me."

"Okay, okay." Jared took one last glance in the mirror. "I
still think I look too young. But if you think it's okay—"

Pope pushed him toward the door. "Quit worrying so much
and go see your lady."

"She's not my lady, Pope. I'm actually just using her as part
of the research. Sort of."

"*Dude*. Why? Wait. Is this some new dating method I haven't thought of?"

"No, no, nothing like that. I'm simply trying to maintain my distance."

Pope stared at him. "You seriously need to get away from that computer. I think it's eating your brain."

"It's not like that, Pope." Jared ducked back into the dressing room, changed into his own clothes and hung the new shirt back on the hanger. Then the two of them walked over to the register. "I simply don't have time in my life for a relationship right now."

"Uh-huh. That's like saying you don't have time to run a virus scan, dude."

Jared arched a brow as he handed over his credit card and the shirt to a tattooed and pierced salesclerk. "Virus scan?"

"Yeah. Dating's a necessity for living. You have to do it on a regular basis or you forget how. Start throwing in that research business and you just confuse everything." Pope waved his hands in a wide, peaceful circle. "Keep it simple, and for Pete's sake, don't put your personal test tube into the company data pool."

A few minutes later, Jared left the store wearing his new shirt. He pulled his notebook out of his pants pocket and started flipping through the pages. He passed by his To Do list, each item neatly ordered and prioritized. Then he came to his copious pages of couples research.

And then, a series of pages labeled simply Callie.

His observations about her, with him trying to be so objective. But as he read the words he'd written down, he realized not a single sentence had the detached sound of a scientist. Pope was right. Jared was kidding himself if he thought he could keep up the wall of research between them.

Because any wall built with pencils and paper was too damned thin.

Keep it simple, Pope had said. But when had anything ever been simple with Callie?

If he had any brains at all—and those people at the SAT scoring centers had sure thought he did years ago—he'd concentrate on work, not his love life.

Even if that love life kept intruding on his every thought, kept him up at night, had him spending ungodly sums of money in stores he'd never frequented before, all because Callie had commented on his tie and clipboard. For the first time in a long time, Jared was considering stepping outside of the carefully constructed box he'd lived his life by.

Take that risk a second time, with the same woman. That was about as far from simple as a man could get. And yet, it fired him up in ways he hadn't been in such a long time.

Fine, then. To hell with work. To hell with the research.

A few minutes later, he found himself not at work, but at Callie's doorstep. She opened the door, clearly surprised to see him. "Oh, Jared. I didn't expect to see you."

"I'm sorry for showing up out of the blue, but I wanted to—" He stopped talking, realizing he had no plan. No plan? Jared Townsend never went anywhere or did anything without a plan. It was an odd, but almost liberating feeling. "I just wanted to see you."

She leaned against the doorjamb, about to say something, then her gaze swept over him, and she caught her first sentence and began another. "What are you wearing?"

"Uh…something new."

A smile curved slowly up her face. "Well, it looks nice."

Pope was getting a raise. And a case of beer.

"Thanks." Then he glanced again at her face. A shade dropped over her eyes, her smile gone, spelling something he didn't want to hear, Jared was sure. "If this isn't a good time…" Damn. He should have had a plan. What was he thinking?

"I did want to talk to you—"

"Later," he said, stepping forward, cutting her off. "Let's go down to the beach, Callie. Take a walk, enjoy the day."

She shook her head. "I can't. I have to go to work."

"It's nearly three. Aren't you almost done for the day?"

"There's an emergency with one of our brides. A floral crisis of all things."

Jared laughed. "A floral *crisis?*"

Callie nodded. "She opted to hire an outside florist and he didn't deliver. Literally. Her wedding is in a few hours and she's in a panic, so I need to run to the flower market, get a load of flowers, head over to the Belles office, make up a bunch of arrangements, and get them delivered. All before five."

"Sounds like a lot of work for one woman."

She laughed. "It is. But I've done it before."

"Wouldn't it be more fun with two?" He had a pile of work on his desk. Work he should be getting to, and on any other day, the facts and figures would be interesting, a challenge he'd enjoy.

Except the lithe figure standing before him was ten times more enticing.

She considered him. "You'd help me?"

"Don't I owe you a favor?"

"What favor do you owe me?"

Jared took another step closer, one that allowed him to inhale the floral notes of her perfume, see the golden flecks in her green eyes, catch the hints of sunlight in her hair. "Home ec. Apron making. I sewed my thumb into the seam and you took pity on me." She'd sat at the machine next to him, and that had been the real reason Jared hadn't been able to sew a straight line. Because he'd spent most of the class period watching Callie. Sneaking glances at her hourglass shape, at the way her skirt rose up and exposed a flash of thigh, a curve of calf. He'd asked her dozens of questions about everything from threading needles to working the treadle, just to find an excuse to talk to her.

"I believe you evened the score in Chemistry," Callie said.

"I don't think helping you remember a few elements even comes close to sewing every one of my home ec projects for me."

"I didn't…" Callie thought a second. "Okay, maybe I did."

"And don't forget all the cooking you did in Mrs. Lolly's class, too. I never did master eggs Benedict."

She grinned. "Hollandaise Sauce can be a little tricky."

He stood closer to her now, closer than he'd been five seconds ago. He watched her inhale, exhale, her every breath even more interesting now as it had been before. When had she ever not been fascinating to him? What was it about Callie Phillips? The edge of recklessness to her? Or the way she seemed to call him on all his bluffs?

"And then there was that term paper in college," he continued. "The one on Lady Macbeth." The one he'd called her about, lying when he'd said he'd never read the play, because he'd spotted her across the campus and realized sometimes God threw second chances at a man.

"I'm sure you could have mastered that, Jared," Callie said, her eyes meeting his. "You were always really smart."

"I couldn't have written that paper, not without you. Not that one or the one on Plato at UMass." She was right. He hadn't needed her help on those papers, but for something deeper. For a connection to normalcy.

He wouldn't have survived a single moment of that freshman year in college if he hadn't had her there, but he didn't say that. Didn't tell her how just knowing she was in the same buildings, a few classrooms away, had kept him sane while the rest of his life at home fell apart.

Nor did he tell her that when his life had truly fallen apart and he'd watched her run off to elope with Tony, he'd had to ditch that college and fly clear across the country, thinking that if he could look at the Pacific Ocean and a whole other beach, an entirely different view of the sun, maybe he'd forget about her.

But he never had. Not for a second.

She moved toward him, her green eyes on his, her hand reaching up, fingers grasping his arm, delicate touch curling around his bicep, making him damned glad he'd listened to Pope and opted for a short-sleeved shirt. He was doubling Pope's raise. Promoting him, first thing in the morning. "You didn't need me to help you."

"Oh, but I did."

She watched his mouth form the words, and her lips parted, then closed. "What are we talking about, Jared?"

"Aprons. Term papers." He touched her chin, turned it up. Memorized the feel of her skin beneath his fingers. "Nothing."

She closed her eyes and a heartbeat passed between them.

"Kiss me," Callie whispered, and that was all he needed, all he'd ever needed.

Jared bent down, and covered Callie's mouth with his own. He tangled his fingers in her hair, the curls soft against his hands, her neck warm to his touch. Her body melted into his, fitting perfectly—

Always fitting perfectly, as if Callie had been made for him, no one else.

How he wanted to believe that. For now, Jared would. For now, Jared would kiss her, would taste Callie and would forget all that had happened before. What would happen tomorrow.

She reached up, her hands flat against his back, pulling him closer, her breasts crushing against his chest, inflaming a desire that had never needed anything more than a whisper to spark. Jared deepened his kiss, his tongue darting in to dance with hers, and she returned the gesture, sweet at first, then sparking into a flame, all Callie.

She was fire in his arms, and he shifted to have more of her, his mind catapulting back nearly a decade, remembering what it had been like to be in her bed, to have her with him for one amazing, incredible night.

His touch roved over her body, hands sliding down her back, over her luscious curves, then back up, traveling a path he knew so well. Had memorized, dreamed of so often over the years. Damn, he'd missed her.

She drew back, then laid her head against his chest. "Oh, Jared, what are we doing?"

"I don't know," he said. Because he really didn't. He'd figure it out later. Or maybe, just figure it out as they went along. Even as he knew he shouldn't put this off, should sound the retreat and fall back on the data—

He didn't.

A flicker of the past ran through him, a dangerous, tempting tightrope.

She sighed. "I have to get to work."

His heart thudded in his chest, and he willed it to slow, to remember that they were standing in her doorway and that hauling her off to her bedroom like a caveman probably wouldn't be a good idea. "Flowers first, then fun later?"

She chuckled. "Something like that."

"Well then, I'll definitely have to help you," he said, pressing one quick kiss to her lips again, unable to resist, "so you have plenty of time for fun."

She tipped her chin to look at him, the tease he loved back in her eyes. "If that's the kind of fun you're talking about, then come with me, Flower Boy."

He took her hand, willing to follow her to Holland and

back, if necessary. Especially with that kind of promise waiting at the end of the rose-colored rainbow.

"If that career in research ever falls through, I think you have a second calling in tulips," Callie said, stepping back to admire Jared's handiwork. The two of them had put together a dozen vase centerpieces featuring bright red tulips, white lilies, grape hyacinths, snow drops and ranunculus. Callie had also put together a long table arrangement to run down the bridal banquet table, and created matching corsages and bouton-nieres for the wedding party. She put the finishing touches on the bride's crescent bouquet, then gave Jared a high-five. "You're pretty good at this."

He grinned. "I had a good teacher. But don't let this get back to the guys in the lab or I'll never live it down."

"What, flower designing is less manly than doing research for 'A Hundred Questions To Ask Your Honey In The Bed-room?' or whatever the game is that you're designing?"

"Definitely. Sex research is way more cool." He flexed a bicep beneath his new shirt. "See how cool I look now?"

She laughed. "Last I checked, you weren't getting very far in your sex research."

"Take me home and we'll see how far I get."

She slugged him, sending a couple of tulips tumbling to the floor. "You are turning into quite the incorrigible man."

"All your fault. I was a respectable, tie-wearing, clipboard-carrying research scientist before you came back into my life." He picked up the flowers, then came around behind Callie to place them back on the workbench. Her heart raced, every fiber of her painfully aware of Jared behind her, of the heat of his body, so close. "You have ruined me," he whispered in her ear.

"Well, good," she said back, intending to sound flip, to keep treating this like a game.

Only it had stopped being a game somewhere during that kiss back at her apartment. Something had shifted between them and turned what she'd thought had been a moment of levity into something far more serious.

Something Callie hadn't been prepared to handle. Before he'd arrived, she'd been planning to end their relationship, to go back to being just friends. After all, she'd accomplished her goal. She'd wanted to make up for the way she'd broken up with Jared in college, maybe up-end his research plans a little, but now, there was a decided edge between them—

An edge that had taken their relationship to a whole new level. One she couldn't ignore or dismiss.

The kind of level that spelled permanence. Settling down.

Because she knew Jared. He was a white picket fence, golden retriever, hang your name on the door knocker kind of guy all the way.

Callie lived as far from that as possible. She'd grown up in a family that had disintegrated into chaos, and like a couch potato who'd found his sweet spot on the sofa, she knew that topsy-turvy world better than the one Jared came from. Callie had seen too often how wrong "happily ever after" could go, and even though she made her living at tying all those kinds of happy endings up with a pretty bow and a daisy, she didn't believe for a second that the same could work for her.

Even if, for a moment, a tiny part of her had wanted that very same thing, like a child hoping for a pony on Christmas.

"What's wrong?" Jared said. "You got tense all of a sudden."

"I, ah, just need to get these arrangements over to the Henry wedding. If I don't hurry, I'll be late." She grabbed two of the filled vases and turned toward the door.

"Here, let me help you."

"No, I'm fine—"

"Callie—" He moved at the same time as her, and they

collided, flowers knocking heads, arrangements tumbling to the floor in a gush of water, Oasis floral foam, floral stems and asparagus fern fronds.

"Oh, no!" Callie dropped to her knees and began grabbing the stems, scooping up everything that she could, trying to salvage the ruined flowers, but the delicate petals had already bruised.

Jared bent down beside her, laying one hand over hers. "Callie. Callie, it's okay."

"No, it's not, you don't understand. It's not okay. It's ruined. Everything's ruined."

"It's only two arrangements. We had plenty of flowers and vases left over. We can make two more in a few minutes. Don't worry. It'll be fine."

But she kept grabbing at the ruined pieces on the floor, her vision blurred, no longer seeing the mess before her, but still trying to pick it up all the same. "No, it won't be. You don't understand. It'll all be ruined."

"Callie." Jared stopped her, his hand on top of hers, his voice louder now, more authoritative. "Look at me."

Finally she did. She swiped at her eyes, then looked up. He hauled her to her feet, then grabbed a tissue and wiped away the rest of her tears.

"What's really wrong?" he asked. "This is about way more than some flowers."

She shook her head. "I have to get to work. The Henry wedding—"

"We have time, so stop avoiding me and tell me what's the matter."

"I can't do this, Jared," she said, her heart hammering in her chest. He was so close, too close, and everything he wanted seemed to overwhelm her as much as the work on her desk, the deadline ticking away. "I can't—"

"We can make another arrangement. Heck, we already made more than a dozen, what's two more?"

"It's not that, it's—" But she couldn't finish. She shot to her feet and went to work, assembling the pieces for another set of centerpieces, grabbing two water-soaked squares of Oasis and shoving them into a second pair of squat silver bowls, then quickly shearing the floral stems into points, reinforcing them by wire-wrapping them to wooden sticks, jabbing them into the foam, arranging them in the same pattern as before.

Jared watched her work, silent for a moment, simply handing her whatever would come next. "Are you going to talk to me about this?"

No. No way. "Stress, that's all."

"Uh-huh. You're about as good a liar as I am a singer."

"I need some of that crimson ribbon."

Jared sliced off the right length, handed it to her, but wouldn't let her change the subject. "Did I do something wrong?"

"No." She sighed. "Yes."

"What?"

She laid down the bow in her hands and turned to face him. "You want too much out of me."

"I haven't said I want anything."

"I can read it in your eyes, in the way you kiss me. In everything between us. It's always been there, Jared. That…expectation. You're not the kind of man who enters into anything lightly."

"And you're suddenly the kind of woman who only has flings? One-night stands?"

"I don't want anything serious. I probably should have told you this from the beginning. I don't want to get married again. I never really did."

"This from the woman who makes her living working on weddings?"

She walked away from the bench, pacing the room, trying to find the words that would explain the push-pull running through her, the fear that overcame her every time she thought about getting close to someone again. "I don't want to take that risk, not a second time."

Jared caught her arm, then her gaze. "Not all men are like Tony."

Her green eyes sought his; the connection filled not with heat this time, but with a need for trust, for reassurance. He wondered if he should have pushed this, should have even said all that he had.

What if they took this to the next level and once again, some man came along and stole Callie's heart right out from under Jared? Some man who was more exciting, more her speed? More the kind of dashing, exciting, rock-and-roll sort of man she went for?

Who was he fooling? A change of clothes, a few minutes on a stage, even a pair of contact lenses, didn't change who he was, didn't put him into the same league as some guy with a swagger and a motorcycle. It never had and it never would.

That, he realized, was probably what she'd been trying to tell him all day. Wasn't that what his research had shown him? Sparks flew—as they had years before between Callie and Tony—and people stopped thinking logically.

Why hadn't he been smart and stuck to his facts and figures instead of delving into a story where he already knew the ending?

"I know not all guys are like Tony," Callie said. "But—"

"But if that's the kind of guy you want," Jared said, the words having a bitter tint to them, as he bit them off, spitting them out before she could. He backed up and released her, turning his attention back to the floral arrangements. He didn't have any idea what the hell to do with the tulips, not without

Callie's help, but he made a stab at it anyway. It was far better than hearing her say "Yeah, Tony's the sort of man I want."

"These are done," Callie said, attaching the bows and picking up the arrangements. "I better get them delivered."

"Wait," Jared said, before she could turn away again. "I want to see one more thing."

"What?"

He put down the ribbon in his hands, turned Callie toward him and kissed her, firm and strong, and with everything he had. She responded in an instant, just as heated as she had earlier.

No, he hadn't imagined a second of it. She *did* want him, regardless of anything she had said. But were there enough sparks?

Jared ended the kiss as quickly as it began, a fierce, fast, summer storm. "That's all." He tipped her chin, studying the eyes that he had known most of his life and decided that she may prefer the kind of man that he wasn't, but he was damned if he was going to let her get away this time before he could show her that the professor had a lot to offer, too. He'd made the mistake of giving her up without a fight once before—

And he wasn't going to do it again.

"I've decided," Jared said, "that I need a lot more of that in my life."

"A lot more kissing?" Confusion reigned in her eyes.

"Yeah. And for your information, I'm not looking to get married right now, either. Maybe down the road, yes. But I'm strictly a living by the seat of my pants guy right now."

She arched a brow. "You? *Really.*"

"Yeah. I started with the shirt, the Tilt-A-Whirl and the elephant ears. Now I want to move on to bigger things." He nodded, cementing the resolution and the idea that maybe there was a way to win Callie again—and prove that nice guys could finish first in her heart. It would mean disproving one of his own theories, but perhaps even the research could be wrong. "And since you seem to be the expert in that area, how about tonight we do something else fun? A little wild even?"

"Jared, I—"

He put a finger over her lips, his pulse quickening with the desire to kiss her again. "No objections. And no expectations beyond tonight, contrary to whatever you *think* you might be reading in my lips and my eyes."

"That's all you want?"

"Yes." He might not be able to sing, but Jared could pull off the occasional white lie. He knew Callie and knew if he pushed her too far in the direction of something serious, she'd run from him faster than an Olympic athlete. "So why don't you stop arguing with me and just have a good time, Callie?"

Finally she smiled, too, and he knew he had won her over again. "I don't know about wild, but if you want a good time tonight, then find yourself a suit and meet me at the Lantana in an hour. And wear your dancing shoes."

CHAPTER EIGHT

CRAZY.

She had to be crazy. Callie rarely attended client weddings, not for lack of invitation, but because for one, showing up at a clearly couple oriented event as a single woman wasn't exactly fun and for another, there were only so many dewy-eyed brides and goofy-grinned grooms she wanted to see in a week. She loved working with them, creating their floral arrangements and bouquets, but there was something about being at the actual wedding and reception that reminded her of how she had failed in her own marriage.

So, she did her best to avoid the events, begging off whenever Belle or Serena or any of the other women asked her to go.

Which explained Belle's nearly measurable shock when Callie walked into the Henry reception, with Jared on her arm. "Has hell frozen over, darlin', or are pigs fallin' from the sky out there?"

"Neither." Callie smoothed a hand over her dress, and gave Belle a grin. "I was in the mood for a little dancing. That's all."

Belle gave her a knowing smile, then another, bigger smile when she glimpsed Jared beside her. "Uh-huh. And I see you brought along quite the dancin' partner, too. Who is this nice young man?"

Callie made the introductions. She could see that Belle took to Jared immediately, impressed with his easy charm and quick smile. Soon, they were chatting like old friends, with Belle learning most of Jared's history in ten minutes.

"I approve," Belle whispered in Callie's ear. "He's a catch and a half."

"Oh, he's not—"

"Well, he should be. Now, you two get out there and dance," Belle said, then gave Callie's hand a quick squeeze and headed off to attend to the wedding party.

The band started playing a Frank Sinatra song, sending several couples swinging onto the dance floor. Above them, lights twinkled from the ballroom ceiling, which had been hung with cream-colored shantung silk. The bride's family had spared no expense, and Callie was glad she had opted for one of the fancier dresses in her closet.

"Shall we?" Jared asked, putting out his hand. She inhaled, taking a second look at him. Belle had been right. Jared did indeed make for an attractive dancing partner. He wore a tailored navy suit that seemed custom made for him, the white shirt and red tie ordinary on any other man, but with Jared's dark hair and even with his glasses, he looked almost dashing. He had a way of carrying a suit, perhaps because he was accustomed to being in business clothes, that gave him an air of handsomeness and authority. And made Callie's pulse skitter.

"Are you a better dancer than you are a singer?" she asked, teasing.

"Try me and see."

The deep baritone of his voice sent a thrill running through her. A challenge, a dare, almost. She knew she should say no, should resist him, because every time she got close to him, her plan to simply make up for that one moment in college— and to end it now, before anyone got in too deep, and worse, got hurt—seemed to go off track and spiral into something far, far more profound.

But Jared's hand in hers was warm, the music tempting, the look in his eyes so…

Irresistible.

Jared kept surprising her. Especially today, when he'd kissed her—twice—with fire in his veins. That kiss still had her reeling. But he'd also surprised her when he'd told her he wasn't looking for anything serious.

Could it be that she had read him wrong? That he wasn't the homebody and Mr. Traditional that she'd always thought? A flicker of disappointment ran through her, which was insane. This was, after all, what she wanted, wasn't it?

A man who wouldn't expect anything out of her. Who wouldn't pressure her to make any commitments, to put down any roots.

"If we're going to dance," she said to Jared now, stepping into his arms, forgetting the internal war, "then we're really going to dance."

He grinned. "That sounds like a challenge."

"If you're up to it."

"Hey, don't let the tie fool you. I'm a real Twinkle Toes underneath the pinstripe."

She laughed so hard she nearly tripped. "Is that your secret? Keep telling me jokes so I won't notice that you're out of step?"

Jared's palm went to her back, his other hand slipped under hers and he spun her into a space between an older couple and another, younger couple who were engaged in a hug clench.

Oh, he was most definitely in step. With every beat of her pulse, too.

Callie hardly noticed the blur of pastels, suits and tuxedos, the bride standing on the sidelines, greeting her guests, or the other Belles watching her and chatting with Belle. The only thing she felt or noticed was the feel of Jared's touch, like an iron against her back, hot against her skin, even through the satin of her dress, that she leaned into it slightly, craving more.

"My plan," he said, "is to completely sweep you off your feet and dazzle you so much, you won't want to let go."

He'd already done that. She didn't want to let go. Didn't want *him* to let go.

She was treading on more than his toes right now—she was hitting dangerous, scary territory. The kind that led to a broken heart. Hadn't she already been down that path once before?

And learned that her instincts where men were concerned were about as reliable as a broken lightbulb?

"Relax," Jared said, his breath warm against her ear.

She did, nearly going liquid in his arms, unable to resist the sound of his voice, the romantic melody of the song, and the hum of romance carrying all around them.

"How did you get to be such a good dancer?" she asked.

"My mother insisted on Arthur Murray when I was a kid."

"Really?" Callie arched a brow. "Why?"

A muscle twitched in Jared's jaw. "To keep me busy and out of the house every Tuesday and Thursday afternoon from three to five."

"Were you one of those troublemaker kids?" As soon as the joke left Callie's mouth, she regretted it, because she sensed a tightening in Jared's arms, a tension that hadn't been there before.

"She was having an affair with the next door neighbor's husband. If I was home, I'd tell my father."

Her heart broke for him in that instant, and she wanted to go back in time, make it up to him somehow. "I had no idea, Jared. I'm sorry."

He shrugged. "That's okay. I'm over it."

But Callie knew, because she'd gone through a childhood

marked by trouble and constant upheaval, that you never really get over it, just wore it like a scar. How much had he locked inside himself, the secrets he'd held to his chest, just like she had, always maintaining the facade of a happy family?

"But that had to be terrible." She thought of how quiet he'd been in high school, how he'd kept to himself, never letting on about anything going wrong at home. No wonder they'd become friends. They were each survivors, of a sort, only children in families that redefined dysfunction. She slipped closer to him, laid her head on his shoulder. "I understand that kind of family."

He didn't say anything for a long time, just danced with her, and she could feel the tension ebb a bit at a time, one note after another. "It was never easy," Jared said softly. "Makes trust a little hard."

"I know what you mean. My father was the one who had trouble sticking around."

Jared kept her close, as if soothing her. "Then I'm sorry, too."

She smiled. "I grew up to be reasonably well-adjusted and normal. Just like you."

He chuckled a little. "I vowed when I finally fell in love that I would never cheat, never be untrue. And that's the real reason why I'm still not married."

She drew back to look at him, to connect with those clear blue eyes of the man she'd known most of her life. "I don't understand."

"Because if I'm going to give my heart to someone and settle down, I want to be sure I can do it right. No ifs, ands or buts." His gaze met hers, intense and deep, the lightness of the afternoon's conversation gone. "When I commit to something, Callie, I give it a hundred percent, and I expect the same in return."

Callie swallowed hard and pressed her cheek back to his

shoulder. She shouldn't have been surprised. The Jared she knew was exactly that kind of man. He wasn't the wild man he'd pretended he wanted to be. Heck, he didn't even cross onto wild man streets.

He hadn't changed at all. Somehow, that satisfied her, gave her comfort, like knowing the same store would always be on the same corner, and carry the same inventory. But now, she'd seen that store had something extra, a little something special behind its doors.

True, full-force commitment.

Where she, on the other hand, had never stayed around long enough to give anyone or anything a hundred percent. Except for Tony, and he'd gone and thrown her commitment away as easily as a used tissue.

"Well, you got the Belle seal of approval," Callie said, changing the subject to one that was less serious and as far from commitments and permanence as she could take it. "That's about as good as it gets around here."

"And what about the Callie seal of approval?" Jared asked. "How am I doing in that department?"

"Fine," she said, trying to keep her tone as light as her steps.

Jared tipped her chin to meet his gaze. "Really?"

The song ended and Callie stepped out of his touch. "I should get something to drink. It's hot in here."

Hot between them, hot in the room. A lot of things suddenly bubbling to the surface, and Callie needed space. She spun away before Jared could catch up to her, blending into the crowd. Her heart thundered in her chest, her mind a whirlwind of emotion and racing thoughts. Jared had become more than what she'd expected, and she needed a moment to process it all.

At the bar, she ran into Serena, who had taken a seat at the far end. The usually cheerful blonde's face had a downturned cast to it. Immediately Callie's focus turned to her friend. "Hey, Serena, you okay?"

"Oh, yeah, sure."

But everything in Serena's voice said otherwise. Callie still held some doubts. "If you need me, I'm here, you know."

"I'm fine. Tired." Serena toyed with her wineglass, then gestured at the busy reception. "This turned out to be a really nice wedding. The flowers are gorgeous, Callie. You always do an amazing job, even last minute."

"Look who's talking. I love the dress you designed." Callie glanced over her shoulder at the bride, who wore an elegant sheath dress with an empire bodice beaded in a filigree pattern. Silvery ribbon trimmed the flounced train, a perfect offset to the satin sheen of the fabric. "And thank you again for helping to talk Marsha Schumacher out of a fuchsia wedding dress."

Serena laughed. "That would have been a disaster. I convinced her to limit her pink to some beading and a little ribbon along the hemline. She's going all out with a sweetheart gown, a full skirt and a train that's going to take ten minutes to make its journey down the aisle. That, I told her, would make enough of a statement."

Callie chuckled. "That's Marsha for you. It'll be one of our more interesting weddings."

"Speaking of interesting," Serena said. "Who's that man you're with? Is he the one you told us about at the poker game?"

Callie swallowed and faced the truth that she had been ignoring for days. Five seconds ago, it had just slapped her in the face, in Jared's last few words. All these years, karma had thrown them together again and again, and she'd missed the freeway sign—until now. "He is. And I think…Audra was right. I might have just found one of the last few Mr. Rights on the planet."

"Mr. Right?" Serena's jaw dropped. "You? The big cynic?"

"Don't tell the others. They'll never let me live it down. But…" Callie turned and glanced over her shoulder at Jared, who had stopped to talk to Belle. The two of them were engaged in some kind of conversation that had them both laughing and when Callie looked at him, she recognized the feeling in her gut.

She'd only felt it twice before. Once with Tony.

And once with Jared.

On Halloween night. In college.

Only this time, with Jared, the feeling was ten times stronger than she'd ever felt before. She wanted to burst out of her skin, shout to the world, sing along with the band. Smile, dance…

"Serena, I think I'm falling in love with him."

"You're kidding me, right? You, the one who is so commitment-shy, you'd have to be duct-taped to a chair to even talk about marrying again?"

Callie nodded and laughed, feeling lighter than she had in weeks. Months. Maybe even years. What had happened in the last few hours? She'd gone from thinking she needed to end it with Jared to realizing—

He was a man who was committed to commitment.

And wasn't that, in the end, really, what any woman wanted? A man who would love her and be true. Maybe that was what Callie had needed to keep her from running scared. "It seems that Mr. Nice is actually very, very right for me," she said.

Serena raised her glass of wine in Callie's direction. "Cheers to you."

Still, something in Serena's voice fell flat and Callie returned her attention to her friend. "Everything okay with Rupert?" she asked again.

Serena bit her lip and glanced away. "Yes." She drew in a

breath. "No." Then she spun back to face Callie. "But don't say anything to anyone. I'm sure this is just a momentary thing we're going through and we'll work it out. I don't want to spoil Julie's excitement over getting engaged and Audra's wedding this weekend. Everyone's all excited about those things and if they find out Rupert and I are having a little—" she paused "—fight…they'll feel like they have to pause in their happiness to comfort me and I don't want that. So will you keep it quiet? Not say anything?"

"Sure." Callie had the feeling that there was more than a small fight going on between Serena and Rupert. That made her pause for a moment. If Serena—the one who'd always had the most unshakable faith in Mr. Right—was having problems with her perfect man, then what did that mean about Callie's future with Jared? Could Callie's instincts be wrong again?

Serena laid a hand on Callie's arm. "I think your guy is great. And you seemed really happy on the dance floor. You *deserve* to be happy, Callie. Please don't let me dampen your mood. Go prove us all wrong and find Mr. Right." Serena grinned, the moment of melancholy erased.

"Is that a challenge?" Callie asked, echoing Audra's dare from earlier in the week.

"I'll stake my next poker hand on it."

"You're on." She gave Serena a smile, then headed back in Jared's direction. Willing to take that chance—

Even as it took her breath away.

"Can I steal him away from you?" Callie said when she reached Jared.

Belle laughed. "Certainly, darlin'." She gave Callie a smile, then shared the smile with Jared. "Take care of her, now."

"I will, ma'am."

"I'm sure you will. You seem the type." Belle paused, listening for a second as one of the other members of the Wedding

Belles spoke to her through the wireless headphones the women used to communicate during a wedding. "They're about to cut the cake, so I better head over there. You enjoy yourself, Callie. The rest of us have it under control. And if I'm lucky, there'll be a piece of Natalie's cake left over for me."

After Belle headed toward the cake table, Callie caught Jared's hand. "Do you want to watch them cut the cake?"

"Actually I'd like to catch some air. It's really warm in here."

"Sounds like a good idea." Being alone with him sounded like the best idea of the night, in fact. With Jared leading the way, they slipped outside. A few guests milled outside, the couples huddled together, sharing a quiet moment by the elegant outdoor water fountain. Two of the ushers were laughing and tying cans on the bride and groom's car.

Jared and Callie circled around the building, strolling along the brick pathway. The sun had set, bathing the landscaped grounds in moonlight, giving the venue an intimate air. The music from the band drifted through the open windows, providing a soft undertow of harmony. "It's a gorgeous evening."

"It is," Jared agreed, drawing her to him.

She grinned. "You're not talking about the weather, are you?"

He shook his head. "Nope." He leaned down, brushed his lips against hers and everything within Callie hummed like the music drifting on the evening breeze.

Why had she never really seen how good Jared was before? Why hadn't she been smart years ago and thrown Tony aside, choosing Jared instead? Why had she opted for the one man who had done nothing but break her heart?

Maybe she was, as her mother had often told her, a slow learner when it came to things like this. Either way, Jared was here now, and so was she, and that was enough. And perfect.

Perfect…except for the dropping temperature.

"It's chilly," Callie said, wishing she'd worn a dress with

sleeves. She turned into Jared and slid her arms under his jacket, seeking the warmth of Jared's body. Leaning into him, feeling happy for the first time in so long. So very long. And thinking maybe all those fairy tales she'd helped make come true weren't really fictionalized stories but actual realities—

A reality she, too, could have.

"You know, we're at a wedding, a perfect place to do the rest of those interviews you need to do. It seems you keep forgetting about your research." She snuggled closer, Jared drawing her in, laying a soft kiss on the top of her head.

"That's because you distract me."

"Mmm. And I'm not about to apologize, not while I'm getting warm." As she moved, her arm jostled something on the inside pocket of his jacket, and before she could catch it, the item had slipped past the silky fabric of his jacket and the satin of her dress, then fallen with a soft kerplat onto the ground.

"Whoops. I'm sorry," Callie said, spinning and bending to grab it.

"No, let me—"

They reached for the flash of white on the ground at the same time, but Callie was quicker, her hand grasping the small object before she realized what it was. The handwriting, the sentences processing through her mind, the numbers jumbling together with the words, all of it twisting from a puzzle—

Into one clear conclusion.

No. It couldn't be. Not Jared. He wouldn't.

But he had.

Callie held the notebook, staring at it for a long moment, then looked up at Jared, her mouth opened in a question.

"Callie, let me explain."

"This has my name on it. Notes about me."

"It's for my research. Part of the notes I was taking for Wiley."

"*I* was a part of your research? Part of your hypothesis?

You were taking notes on *me?*" Hurt rocketed through her body, searing her heart, racing across her veins, tearing her apart as surely as a shredder. Still, she stared at the words, disbelieving. "You were using me?"

"No, it wasn't like that, I swear. I mean, it started out like that, in a way, but—"

She flipped through the pages, reading Jared's familiar tight scrawl. His notations about her reactions to him. Her words. Her every step, every breath, every kiss. Every inflection. "I was nothing more than a rat in your maze."

She'd been wrong. So wrong.

The disappointment hurtled to the pit of her stomach like a boulder. She stumbled back, the notebook falling from her hands, tumbling to the ground in a flutter of white, like dove's wings.

"Callie, I had no intention of hurting you. I only wanted to try to figure out what made you tick so I could—"

"So you could use it against me." She shook her head, putting up her hands, not wanting to hear any more. "Don't even try to sugarcoat this, Jared. You and your logic, your hypotheses, your plans. I'm not an experiment. I'm a flesh and blood woman. You keep talking to me about taking risks." She gestured toward the pile of papers on the floor. "Well that's not about taking risks. That's about planning a love life. For a man who supposedly knows everything there is to know about relationships, you are as dumb as they come."

Then she spun on her heel and walked away.

CHAPTER NINE

CALLIE stood by the altar, glancing from the groomsmen to the priest, then to the bridesmaids, knowing something was horribly wrong. The church was full of friends and family, the pews beautifully decorated with twin pink roses tied with pale blue satin bows. Simple, tasteful, elegant. The white runner had been scattered with rose petals, the organist had played the entire round of wedding music in her repertoire, and at the other end of the church, behind closed doors, the bride waited.

But the groom had yet to show.

An empty place marked where he was to stand. The priest looked from one side of the church to the other, as if the bridal party would explain the missing man. "Where is he?" Regina whispered to Callie.

"I have no idea. Do you think he's with Audra?" Callie glanced at the other women, who all shrugged, and sent worried glances down the bridesmaid line that said they had no idea, either.

"He better be," Regina said. "Either that or kidnapped by aliens, because there's no excuse to do this to her."

The people in the church shifted in their seats, then began to talk, the nervous hum of speculation carrying like a virus from pew to pew. Dread curled around Callie. Something had gone wrong. She knew it.

"I'll be back. Try not to look panicked," she whispered to Regina, then she headed down the aisle, knowing the quick disappearance of a bridesmaid toward the vestibule would only hasten the wagging of tongues. But Audra was in trouble—Callie was sure of it—and she didn't care what the guests thought.

She slipped through the double doors of the church. "Audra?"

"O-o-over here."

Callie followed the sound of Audra's voice and found her friend sitting on the stairs that led to the church balcony. Her dress had puddled around her, the simple crepe and chiffon design now wrinkled. Her handheld bouquet of cream and pale pink roses sat on the stairs beside her, seeming to droop, as if commiserating with her. "What's wrong?"

Audra looked up, her face marred by tears. "He's not coming."

"Oh, hon. He's just late. He'll be here."

Audra shook her head. "Callie, I'm a logical person. I should have seen this coming. David's been...distant lately. It was as if he didn't care about the wedding. I had this bad feeling when I woke up this morning and then—" She waved a hand toward the church doors. "I should have looked at the probabilities of this happening and known."

"Audra, who can predict this kind of thing? And really, he could still—"

"Callie, he's not coming." Audra's voice broke on the last word, and Callie surged forward, drawing her friend into a hug. As she did, she felt five other pairs of arms joining in, firm and secure, as comforting as a blanket. Serena, Natalie, Julie, Regina and Belle.

The Wedding Belles, there for each other. As they always

had been. The women pulled together, a sea of bridesmaids in soft blue satin halter dresses, hugging and crying as if it were their wedding, their missing groom. After a while, Audra pulled back, swiped at her face. "You all are the best. I don't know what I'd do without you. Thank you."

"Darlin', if I see that boy, I'll shoot him for you," Belle said.

Audra laughed. "You don't need to do that. Just send him all the bills for the wedding."

"Done." Belle grinned. "Anything else you want us to do?"

"Could you guys go in and tell everyone? I can't face…" Audra's voice trailed off.

The rest of the Belles nodded. "We'll do it. Then I say we go to the reception and have one hell of a party on David's dime. After all, the coq au vin is already cooked, Natalie made a great cake and we're all dressed up." Callie drew her friends together. "What do you say, Audra?"

Audra bit her lip, then rose, her face determined. "Okay. But let me change first. If I'm going to party," she said, a grin curving up her lips, "I'm going to put on some jeans."

"That's the Audra we know." One more hug, and then the Belles were ready to face anything again.

After the last song had been played, all of Natalie's white chocolate raspberry cake had been eaten and Belle had plopped into a chair, exhausted, Callie finally had a moment to breathe.

And deal with what happened last night with Jared. How could she have been so stupid? Trusted him so completely? She glanced over at Audra, the one who thought everything through, added everything up in her columns, made all the numbers balance, and realized that if someone like Audra could be wrong, then what made Callie think she could get it right?

Clearly the thought that there was a Mr. Right for everyone was crazy.

Callie glanced back at her friends, who had settled down around one of the tables. They were laughing, Audra's face finally cheery again.

Callie should join them. Return to that inner circle. But a part of her held back, the part that operated on a long-held protective instinct. Staying too long, wrapping herself up too tight with anyone led to hurt. She'd already been here for three years, the longest she'd ever lived anywhere since her childhood.

If she stayed, she'd always have Jared in her backyard. A few blocks away. A heartbreak right around the corner. Callie closed her eyes and leaned against the wall. In her mind, she pictured a beach. A solitary hut, far from people, from Jared.

An escape.

Surely that would be better than staying here and waiting— waiting to be hurt all over again.

"Dude, you are seriously one clue short of *Jeopardy*," Pope said when he entered the office and took one look at Jared's attire for the day. He shook his head. "Did you learn nothing from me?"

Jared refused to enter into an argument about his reversion to a button-down shirt and tie. The whole foray into a youthful look had gone awry and he wasn't going back there. "I'm not trying to impress anyone. I'm just trying to do my job."

"Yeah, and how's that going? You hate this place."

"So?" Jared scowled, turned away from Pope and went back to entering the data into the computer. He intended to bury himself in work until the project was done. That was a lot easier than thinking about how everything with Callie had gone so wrong the other night. She hadn't returned any of his calls, hadn't been home any of the times he'd been on her doorstep, and if she'd been at the Wedding Belles office either of the times he'd stopped by, she'd been hiding. So far, Callie had disappeared off the face of the earth.

He'd sent flowers. Two cards. Left voice mails. Done everything he could think of to apologize. But since romance wasn't exactly his strong suit—maybe he should open up a few of the games that lay around the Wiley Games building—he had yet to achieve a response from her.

So instead he'd buried himself in his work, interviewing couple after couple, working his way down the list he'd gotten from Callie earlier in the week. He'd sat in restaurants and bars listed as "hot spots" in the local newspapers, clipboard in hand, seeking interview subjects. Basically, not having any love life but plenty of statistical time.

Jared sighed. "You're right. I'm working hard, but I'm not happy about it."

"So, quit working here, dude. Find some big think tank or brain pool where they throw all the brainiacs into a room and solve world hunger or something."

"I tried that. There's no money in it."

"Blah-blah-blah," Pope said. "I think you're just scared."

Jared wheeled around. "Did you just call me scared?"

"Well, yeah. Buddy, you are working here, developing *bedroom* games, for Pete's sake. I'm embarrassed to tell my *dog* I work here. You're the one with all the letters after your name. How do you wake up in the morning and come into this place?"

"It's a paycheck," Jared muttered.

"You could do better."

"Yeah, I could, but—" Jared cut off the sentence.

"But what?" Pope leaned forward, his arms over the back of the chair, his legs, as always, draped over the sides. "But the sky is gonna fall in if you quit, Chicken Little?"

"Hey, that's not even a nice thing to say."

"And that's your biggest problem," Pope said, pointing at Jared, as if he'd just hit the lottery. "You are too *nice*. I heard you talking to the boss yesterday, being all nice when he asked you to work late. He asked me to work late and I told him, 'Later, dude, I got a date.' You know what he told me?"

Jared sighed. "I have no idea. He docked your pay?"

"He said, 'Okay. Make up the time another day then.'"

"I'm doing my job, Pope. There's nothing wrong with that."

"Yeah, there is. When you should be working at a better job. One that actually uses more than three of your brain cells."

Jared scowled. "You're not my mother, or my boss, so let it go."

Pope leaned forward and dropped the classified ads onto Jared's desk. An ad for a position with a Boston think tank had been circled in red. "Go forth and apply, my friend. That's the kind of place where you belong. Not in this rat maze."

Jared shoved the paper to the side. "Pope, I have a deadline to meet."

"You *are* scared. What, did you get burned by the research gods or something?"

"Something like that." Jared wasn't about to talk about it. Not now, not ever.

"It's your funeral," Pope said, getting to his feet. "Your boring, dead-end funeral. I'm going down the hall for a caffeine fix. Want anything?"

Jared shook his head. Pope left the room, leaving Jared to enter the research he'd compiled for the game into the computer. Research that, really, meant nothing, not if Jared didn't turn it into something meaningful. Actually do something more than create a little couples' fun with the statistics he'd compiled.

Meaning take a chance, step outside his comfort zone. Pope was right. Jared did hate the job. He'd give anything to work at a place like what Pope had circled in the newspaper.

Jared stopped typing, read the ad and considered the position. Years ago, that would have been the kind of job he'd have taken in a heartbeat. It had, in fact, been the kind of job he'd had. The kind of career he'd been fast-tracking along, until his life had crossed over and put a stop to a career that came with anything without regular hours, a paycheck that didn't depend on research grants.

"Catch," Pope said.

Jared spun and put out his hands, catching the cola just as it sailed across the room, narrowly missing his monitor. "You could have wiped out my computer, or I could have missed. You live on the edge, Pope."

Pope grinned. "Only way to go."

Jared popped the top, took a long sip, then leaned back in his chair and put his feet up on the desk. "Why?"

"Why what?"

"Why are you the way you are? Why do you skate on the edge of life? Take risks with your job, your relationships, your choice in clothing?"

Pope looked down at his concert T-shirt, the opened button shirt he wore over it and his multipocketed khakis. "*This* is a fashion statement."

"Yeah, that's what I'd call it, too, if I was being polite." Jared snorted, then took another drink from the can. He'd leaned back in the chair, stretching the kinks out of his neck. He had spent too many hours here.

"Dude, you only live once," Pope said. "I don't see any point in doing anything other than living as large and loud as possible. What have I got to lose? My reputation?" Pope snorted. "Hell, I lost that years ago. My job? There's always another one. My girlfriend? Well, isn't fighting for the woman you love half the fun?"

"I thought you didn't believe in committed relationships."

Pope shrugged and Jared could swear he saw a blush rise in Pope's cheeks. "Ah, that's part of the act. You can't be cool if you're running around spouting love sonnets and talking about wanting babies and a Labrador. I have an image to protect."

"You're a softie."

"I prefer the term well-rounded modern man," Pope said, puffing out his chest, "but…yeah. What about you? How are things going with your lady?"

Jared let out a breath. "Let's just say my career is on a faster track than my relationship."

"Whoa, dude, that's not good. You try jewelry? Flowers? Dropping to your knees and begging like a dog?"

"I don't think any of that's going to work." Jared tapped on his computer screen, indicating the facts and figures he'd been working on all morning. "She found out I'd been tabulating some of her responses for the research project."

Pope wagged a finger at him and sat back against his chair. "That is so not you, Doc. Involving people you know in a research project, tampering with the results by getting personally involved. Not a good idea. What were you thinking?"

"That was the problem. I was thinking too much." Jared rose, pacing the room, realizing that the very thing he had prized the most about himself turned out to be his biggest issue. "I didn't want to fall for Callie again and so I decided to keep this wall up between us. I used the only wall I knew, and it was stupid, because she found out and ended things with us."

Pope shook his head. "Man, you've definitely spent too much time cooped up with the lab rats. You became one yourself."

Jared laughed. "Yeah, I did."

Pope crossed to him and laid a hand on his shoulder, his face somber, looking as sage as Solomon's. "There's only one thing to do."

"What's that?"

Pope pointed to the newspaper. "First, get out of the maze

while you still can. And when you do, head straight for Downtown Crossing."

"Downtown Crossing? Why?"

Pope grinned. "That's the diamond district, my friend. You want to start living on the edge? Blow your last paycheck down there, then head right on over to your lady's house and give her an apology she'll never forget. Preferably one made up of two carats or more." Pope nodded, then walked to the exit, pausing in the doorway. "Take it from one who knows. There's not a woman in the world who can say no to an offer like that."

CHAPTER TEN

RIGHT now, Callie hoped she'd never see another engagement or wedding again.

After the debacle at Audra's wedding, and the horrible ending to the Henry wedding, not to mention her own bad experience with the whole process—

Callie was done. Done with anything remotely reminding her of "I do".

Mr. Right did not exist, not in her world. Apparently that message hadn't made it over to Marsha Schumacher, however, who was still happily planning her all-pink, all-the-time wedding.

Callie caught Regina's eye over the table set up in the ballroom and exchanged twin restrained looks of impatience. They'd already been there for a half an hour, waiting while Marsha underwent the most important debate of the century.

Over her champagne glasses.

"I don't know," Marsha said. She tipped her head left, then right. "I still can't decide."

They'd been standing in the ballroom for a half an hour, while Marsha considered swan-pattered crystal champagne flutes over heart-patterned flutes, neither decision which Callie or Regina needed to be a part of, but Marsha and her mother had insisted the wedding planners stay because they needed additional "professional stemware input," regardless of the extra cost for the opinions.

"Whatever makes my baby happy," Marsha's mother said, patting her daughter's hand. "When you look at these, which one makes you feel like a smile?"

Callie saw Regina bite her lip, and had to do the same. Some clients were difficult. Some were annoying. Some were easy as pie. And some…

Were Marshas.

Marsha stepped forward, picked up one glass, then the other. Studied it, put it down, sighed, then tried again. She glanced over at the Polaroids she'd had Regina take, so that she could get an idea of the way the table would look during the wedding, then glanced again at the glasses. "They both do. They both say pink to me."

"Well, which one would Samuel like?"

"Oh, the tall one, for sure. Because he likes things that are tall."

The logic swept right past Callie, but that might have been because her mind wasn't on the bride and her mother, but on Jared. On his research—

And his betrayal. How could he have done that to her?

She'd thought that he'd been a different man, the nice guy she'd known back in high school and college. And for a while there, she'd even thought maybe she was falling for him. Silly plan she'd had to make up for hurting him all those years ago.

Because all she'd done was go and hurt herself in the process.

"Callie? Are you listening?"

Marsha's voice drew her back to the ballroom. "Sorry, what'd you ask?"

"Weren't you listening?" Marsha pouted. "This is a critical decision."

"Oh, yes, it is," Callie said. "I, ah, was thinking about your floral design and how it would look with these glasses."

Regina sent her a thumbs-up and a mouthed, "Good save."

"Which one?" Marsha asked, her face full of panic. "Which one will be better with the flowers?"

Callie picked up the lean, tall glasses with the hearts. "These. They're closer in design to the types of flowers we're using, especially the lilies and the daisies. And, your dress has these same elegant, clean lines." Thanks to Serena and her deft hand at design.

Marsha beamed. "Oh, it does, doesn't it? Oh, yes, these. Definitely these." She let out a sigh. "I feel so much better now. Like the hardest decisions are made."

Marsha's mother patted her daughter's hand, her Pomeranian looking on with a decidedly jealous pout. "Yes, dear, they are. Except for the caterer. We still have that stressful choice between the tuna steaks and the salmon with puff pastry. Perhaps we should just go back to chicken."

Callie wanted to remind Marsha that the most important decisions about her future had nothing to do with puff pastry or stemware or vases, but all to do with the man she was choosing. Whether he would remember the way she took her eggs in the morning or forgot her birthday, or break her heart almost immediately after he put the ring on her finger because he found someone else, and then she'd end up spending the next nine years of her life trying to figure out how to put it back together, thinking it was something that she could fix—

And then realizing it hadn't been fixable after all.

Marsha and her mother finished up their decisions about the rest of the table settings, with Callie making a note for the hall about adding pink bows to the silverware, then the mother-daughter duo finally headed off to their appointment with the caterer. As they walked out the door, they started arguing about the merits of tuna versus salmon, which was more pink, thereby making the meal match the wedding better. Callie shook her head.

"So," Regina said, after the client was gone and Regina began gathering up her photography equipment, "what has you so distracted? Is it Jared?"

Callie let out a sigh. "Yes." She told Regina about what had happened after the Henry wedding, feeling better after she got the story off her chest. It helped, Callie realized, to share the heartache with someone who cared.

"Aw, Callie. Why didn't you tell anyone about this sooner?" Regina asked.

"There was Audra's wedding and all that she was going through. She needed the sympathy more than I did." Audra, though still upset by her fiancé's public betrayal, had rebounded pretty well and was back at work, happily up to her elbows in financial statements. For Audra, keeping busy kept her mind off of what had happened at her botched wedding.

"Callie, we're a team. We're here for each other, no matter what." Regina drew her into a quick hug. "Are you sure you're doing okay?"

Callie nodded. "Besides, he's not really my type."

"Is that something you're telling yourself or is it really true?" The two of them grabbed their coats, shrugged into them and started walking out of the ballroom, sending a wave toward the manager of the venue as they did. He gave them a weary goodbye, clearly glad the Schumacher ordeal was over, too.

"Both, I guess," Callie admitted. "Years ago, I didn't see Jared as the kind of guy I'd go for. Back then, he always had his head in a book. We were lab partners and study partners, but he never seemed like a guy you'd date, more the one you'd ask about your Bunsen burner."

Regina laughed. "I take it from the look on your face that

despite everything that man has been making your Bunsen burner simmer."

Callie shrugged, then grinned. "Okay, yes, he does. And I hate that he does."

"Well, if you're smiling, he can't be all bad, can he?"

"I don't know." Callie sighed. They'd reached the sidewalk, and Callie paused to draw in a burst of cool spring air. "He hurt me, Regina. He really did. I wanted to trust him, to believe he was different from all the other guys and to think maybe…"

"He was the one?" Regina finished.

Callie nodded. "I thought that about him once before. Back in college, but then—"

"What?" Regina asked when Callie didn't finish.

"Tony came roaring back into my life. Tony always seemed so exciting. So daring. Ready to take on the world and ride off into the sunset, with me on the back of his motorcycle." Callie drew in a breath, then let it go. "That's what I was looking for. Someone who would take me away from everything I hated. That was Tony, at least to me. Mr. Excitement."

"What happened?"

"Mr. Excitement got bored with me and went looking for other women." Callie shook her head, then unlocked her Toyota and waited while Regina climbed inside the passenger's side. After Callie had the car started and had pulled away from the curb, she started talking again. "I wasn't enough. And with Jared, it turns out I'm just a research project."

The betrayal stung again, and Callie blinked rapidly, clearing her vision. How could Jared, of all people, have done that?

"Callie, I saw the way that man looked at you at the Henry wedding, and there is no way he's thinking facts and figures when you're with him. Trust me, if Dell looked at me the way Jared looks at you, we'd have the entire Boston Fire Department hosing down the house every single night." Regina laid a hand over Callie's. "Jared may have started out thinking only of his Bunsen burners, but believe me, he's not anymore."

"Maybe. But that isn't what's been worrying me." Callie slowed for a red light, then drummed her fingers on the steering wheel and turned to face Regina. "What if I fall in love?"

"What's so bad about that?"

"I've been down that road before, Regina, and it didn't work out so well."

"That doesn't mean the second time can't go much better."

"That doesn't mean the second time is guaranteed to work out better, though."

"True." Regina glanced away from Callie, watching out the window as a light rain began to fall, misting on the windows, then drizzling down the glass in a zigzag of skinny droplets. "There aren't always guarantees when it comes to love or marriages."

The way Regina said it, Callie got the feeling her friend was talking about more than just Callie's life. "How are things going with Dell?"

"We're okay. We didn't get off to the best of starts, given how fast we got married. But we'll be all right. We just need time together." Regina turned back to Callie. "Anyway, back to you. What's your plan from here?"

Callie gave Regina a lopsided grin. "Run away."

"That's no way to deal with a problem."

"That's the only way I know." Callie had said the words as a joke, but she hadn't meant them that way. Still, she couldn't bring herself to tell any of the Belles her true thoughts about leaving. She knew it would hurt them, and the last thing she wanted to do was that. These women were her friends, and finding a way to explain her need to escape had become an almost insurmountable task. In a few days, she would, Callie decided. She'd have to.

This staying in one place thing clearly wasn't what Callie was meant for. She couldn't go on with her job, helping to put on weddings, designing the flowers, throwing the rice, wishing people well, when she didn't even believe in the concept of happily ever after.

It was time to move on. Trouble was, she couldn't seem to put one foot in front of the other.

Jared took Pope's advice. At least, part of it.

He went to Downtown Crossing, but stopped in at three different places before he found what he was looking for. The salesperson gave him a dubious look, but Jared plunked down his credit card and insisted on the purchase.

Then he went to find the only person he knew who could talk Callie into something as insane as this.

Belle.

There'd be no escape, at least not today.

After Callie dropped Regina off at the Wedding Belles office, she headed home, wanting only to curl up on her couch with a good book, a glass of wine and a little solitude.

But when she pulled in front of her apartment building, she noticed a rental car parked in the space for her unit. Callie groaned, then headed inside.

"Callie!" Her mother exploded forward when Callie rounded the corner. "You're home!"

Callie was immediately enveloped in an Elizabeth Arden-scented hug. "Mom. I thought you were staying on the beach in Bermuda with your friend."

Her mother waved a hand, jeweled rings on her fingers and bracelets dangling from her wrists, all gifts from past husbands and boyfriends. "It didn't work out. He was only interested in me for my tan lines, if you know what I mean. So I hopped on a plane and here I am. Anyway, I couldn't wait to see you and catch up. I want to hear all about what's going on in your life. How work is, who you're dating." Her mother grinned. "If he has any friends."

"Mom, you just got divorced, what last week?"

"Exactly. Which means there's an opening in my heart." She pressed a hand to her chest and grinned, then tipped her head to the side, causing her light brown pageboy to swing. "So, do you want to go out? Go get some dinner?"

"I'm wiped out from the day. Let's order takeout."

Her mother pouted, disappointment shining in her green eyes. "I'd really rather go out. You know how I hate to stay home."

Callie did. Her mother never had been one for being a homebody. She liked to be out, be seen, to meet people, especially the next man to fill the vacancy, as she liked to put it.

And all Callie had ever wanted was a mother who would sit around the kitchen table, share a cup of tea and talk with her about her day—and listen, really listen. But she didn't say any of that. There wouldn't be any point.

Instead she told her mother to give her a minute to change, and agreed to go back into the city again for dinner.

They ended up in a crowded, noisy seafood place that Callie's mother had seen reviewed as *the* hotspot to visit in Boston. "It was at the top of the list in the airline magazine," Vanessa said. "I'm sure we'll meet lots of interesting people there."

"Mom, I don't need to meet interesting people. I'd really rather just visit with you."

"We can do that anytime." She glanced around the crowded bar. "Do you think we'll see any celebrities? Are they filming any movies in Boston right now?"

Callie sighed. "I don't know." They sat down for dinner, ordered two seafood meals that sounded delicious, then sat across from each other and had a people-watching conversation.

"Oh, look over there," Vanessa said, scanning the room. "Isn't that…? No. It couldn't be."

Callie turned and followed the direction her mother indicated and saw—

Jared Townsend, and his ubiquitous clipboard. Of all the restaurants in a city this large, he had to be here? Doing his research?

Was he following her? Callie felt a rush of regret for agreeing to her mother's idea about going out, wishing for the thirtieth time that she had opted to stay home.

But then she looked again and her heart constricted, the part of her that still cared about him, still reacted when she saw him in a suit and tie. Damned hormones. When would she stop reacting to that man? Stop caring about him?

All the more reason to leave town, to get away.

"Is that him?" her mother asked.

"Yes," Callie said, turning back around.

Her mother arched a brow. "You don't sound very surprised. I take it you knew he was in town?"

Callie shrugged, trying to act noncommittal, unconcerned. "I've seen him around."

"Well then, let's call him over. Have a little reunion of sorts. Go ahead, Callie. Invite him to join us." But before Callie could even refuse, her mother rose. "Jared! Jared!"

"Mom," Callie whispered, acutely aware that people were staring. "He's working. Leave him alone."

"How can he be working in a restaurant?" Her mother sucked in a breath, then gaped at Callie. "Oh Lord. He's not a busboy, is he? Oh, and I thought he would go so far. He seemed so smart."

"He's a research scientist. He's working on a survey."

"In a *restaurant?* Is he working for those fast food people?" Her mother finally caught Jared's attention and sat back down. "Oh, good. He's coming over."

Oh, no. Callie did not want to see him. She and Jared were over, let it stay that way. She'd managed to avoid his phone calls, his cards, his flowers, every attempt he'd made to contact her. The last thing she needed was her mother forcing some kind of matchmaking attempt. "Mom, really, let him do his job."

"Why, Calandra January Phillips, if I didn't know better, I'd think you didn't want him to sit with us."

Callie cringed at the use of her full name, which her mother had chosen because it meant "lark," her favorite bird, and the middle name, to remind her of the month of her birth. As soon as Callie could talk, she'd started insisting on her nickname. "Mom, *please*. Can't you and I just visit? For once?"

Her mother gave her a blank look. "What do we have to talk about? I've known you all your life. You'd think we'd have said everything by now."

"Yeah, of course we have." Callie shook her head and muttered a quick prayer that her mother wouldn't launch into another one of her Top Ten Reasons Why This Man Should Marry My Daughter speeches.

As long as Vanessa didn't whip out any visual aids, Callie figured she'd be safe.

"Mrs. Phillips," Jared said, arriving at their table. "It's nice to see you again."

"Actually, I'm not Mrs. Phillips anymore, or Mrs. Linden, or Mrs. Spires, or any of the other names. I'm officially on the market again, if you know any older men." She laughed, then waved at the empty chair beside her. "Sit down, Jared. There's no reason for a man like you to eat alone, especially on a Friday night."

Jared looked to Callie. She tried to send him a mental no, but all he did was grin and pull out the chair. What was he thinking? Hadn't she made it clear she wanted nothing to do with him?

"Why thank you," Jared said. "I don't mind if I do."

"Now tell me, what's with that clipboard?" Vanessa asked. "Callie says it's some kind of research. What exactly are you doing?"

Jared's gaze met Callie's, a burst of heat exchanged in that look—hers in anger, his with something else—before he returned his attention to her mother. "I'm studying relationships and love. Whether real people fall in love at first sight, how true love develops and what makes people who love each other stay together."

Her mother leaned forward, her attention rapt on Jared. "And what'd you find out so far?"

"That sometimes people aren't as honest as they think, at least when it comes to love."

Callie resisted the urge to blurt out a sarcastic retort.

"Isn't that the truth," Vanessa said. "I've been down that aisle four times and not one of my husbands has been honest. I must have liar radar or something, because I just can't pick them very well."

"Maybe you need to quit picking them," Jared said. "If you don't mind me saying so."

Her mother cocked her head and studied him. "What do you mean, stop picking them?"

"Well, my research has shown that the relationships that last work much better when the man has pursued the woman, proving that old axiom about boy chases girl. When the woman makes the choice and makes it a little too…easy on the man, he seems to lose interest and move on, maybe something to do with the hunter instinct, I think. If you make a man work for what he wants, he tends to, ah, toe the line a little better." Jared gestured toward Callie's mother. "Not that I'm implying that you have done anything of the sort, of course."

"Oh, but I have, I have. I'm a total chaser. Like a dog after a Honda, that's me. Except when it came to my first husband, who took off over and over again and I just gave up going after him. Clearly some dogs don't want to stay leashed." Her mother took a sip of wine, then shook her head. "Wow. That's an entirely new way of looking at dating. Sort of *Field of Dreams* for dating."

"*Field of Dreams?*" Jared asked.

Vanessa grinned and then waved a hand over her voluptuous figure. "If you build it, they will come calling." She patted Jared's hand, then rose. "Thank you for that bit of advice, Jared. Now, I'm going to go powder my nose and leave you two alone for a bit. Maybe someone at this table has a little unfinished business to pursue, too. Hmm?"

Callie watched her mother leave, then turned back to Jared. What was all that he'd been talking about with his research? She'd seen nothing of the sort in his notebook. She shrugged it off, and decided to try to convince him to leave while she still had a chance—and before she got distracted by the way he filled out his suit, or the memory of his kiss. Both of which were still imprinted on her mind, seeming to override her better sense, like congressmen vetoing a budget bill. "You don't have to stay, Jared. I can make up an excuse when my mother comes back. I'll tell her that you had to go back to work or something."

Jared grinned. "Oh, but I do want to stay, Callie."

"Even if you're not welcome?"

"I was invited over. Remember?"

"By my mother, not me."

He leaned forward, and when he did, Callie inhaled the scent of his cologne, a mix of woods and man, and everything within her fought against being mad at him. The vetoes were going up fast and furious.

"What's it going to take for you to forgive me?" he said.

"I can't, Jared. I—" She shook her head, refusing to be dissuaded by the grin on his lips, the way she could fall into his eyes. "Let me put it in terms you'd understand. I fed in the numbers for you and me, added the numbers and our two and two came out to five."

"Callie—"

"No, Jared. We don't belong together. We're not even close to the same kind of people. You're a traditionalist and I'm not. In fact, I'm not even staying here."

His eyes widened. "What do you mean?"

"I mean, I'm leaving again," she said, the decision made now. As long as Jared would be nearby, and the possibility of running into him—and falling for him—still existed, she couldn't stay. "I'm going to give my notice to Belle and move on. I can't keep putting on a happy face at all these weddings when I don't even believe in getting married."

He shook his head and sat back. "I never thought I'd see the day."

"What are you talking about?"

Then he pitched toward her again and leaned in close, very close, so close he could have kissed her with nothing more than a breeze to bring them together. "I never thought I'd see the day when Callie Phillips chickened out."

Jared got to his feet, grabbed his clipboard and left her there. Openmouthed, and at a total loss for words.

CHAPTER ELEVEN

CALLIE clicked on screen after screen on her computer. Dozens of options, taking her everywhere from Maine to Monte Carlo.

And not a single one appealed to her.

Instead of the usual rush of anticipation she had always felt before, another emotion clutched at her throat, twisted in her gut.

Loss.

But she saw no other way out. How could she possibly stay here, working all day on weddings? How could she put her heart into creating other women's wedding dreams when that heart no longer believed in those dreams?

"That doesn't look like a floral research trip to me, darlin'." Belle's voice, soft and concerned, came from over Callie's shoulder.

She froze, a lump thick in her throat. Callie minimized the screens, then turned in her chair. "Belle. I didn't know you were there."

"Whatcha doin', honey?"

Callie drew in a breath, then got honest. "Panicking."

Belle's laughter was full of understanding. "I've been there, just before I walked down the aisle the first time, the second time. The third time, too, come to think of it. But your case is a little worse than a touch of cold feet, isn't it?"

Callie nodded. "I've never been one for staying put."

"You've been here for three years."

"I know. That's the longest time I've spent anywhere," Callie said. "Maybe it's time I moved on. Did something else with my life."

Belle pulled up another chair and settled into it. "This doesn't have anything to do with that man you've been dating, does it? Has the professor got your dander all fluffed?"

Callie chuckled. "Dander all fluffed?"

"He's the one who's got you runnin' scared, isn't he?"

"I'm just so scared about all those what-ifs."

"What if what?" Belle said. "What if the earth starts turnin' in the other direction? What if dogs start dancing in the streets?" Belle threw up her hands. "Callie, you can't live your life waitin' on what might happen. You just grab hold and enjoy the ride."

Callie thought of the Tilt-A-Whirl, of how she'd told Jared nearly the exact same thing. But falling for him was a much bigger step than getting on some carnival ride and spinning in a circle for three minutes.

"But there's more, isn't there?" Belle said softly.

There wasn't any sense in hiding the truth from Belle. Heck, from hiding it from herself. Jared, had indeed, been the one who had triggered the old instincts to flee. And if Callie planned to leave, she needed to tell Belle first. It was only fair. "Yes. It's more than Jared, it's something I've done all my life. Why do I do that? Why do I want to run every time a man gets close to me?"

"Well, darlin', if I knew the answer to that, I'd be marryin' again myself." Belle laughed. "I'm trying to stay clear of the aisle, too, but it seems like every man I meet wants either a wife or a maid. Maybe we should book double passage to wherever you're going." She gave Callie a wink.

"Oh, you'd never leave this place. The business. It's your heart and soul."

"No, I wouldn't." Belle's clear blue gaze met Callie's. "And neither should you. You fit here, Callie."

Callie looked around the room, at the elegant setting that somehow managed to feel comfortable, too. Maybe it was the yellow walls or the delicate pattern of the carpet. Maybe it was the spring flowers blooming outside the windows or the portraits of beaming brides and grooms on the walls.

No. Callie suspected what had really made her fit here over the past three years wasn't any of the furnishings or the details. It was Belle, and the women who made up the Belles. They had given her a home, not in a physical sense, but in her heart.

Belle laid a hand over Callie's. "Every time a squirrel runs from what scares him, he gets hit by a truck."

Callie laughed. "That's supposed to make me feel better?"

"No, it's supposed to make you laugh, and it did." Belle rose. "But it's also supposed to make you think. What's out there—" at that, Belle waved toward the windows, to the world beyond the shop "—isn't necessarily better than what is in here. You need to face what's scarin' you, darlin', before you can move on."

"But what if I don't know what I'm so scared of? What if I'm not sure why I want to run?"

"All the more reason to stay where you are, I say. Can't find the answers if you're always running from the questions." Belle gave her a smile that was filled with the wisdom of a woman who had traveled many of life's paths already, then left Callie to figure out the rest.

At the end of the day, Callie was the only one left in the shop. She'd worked extra late, burying herself in sketches, then the tedious task of sorting the mountain of silk flowers, a collection that often got jumbled during the busy season. Somehow, color-coding and cataloging the faux florals kept Callie's mind off Jared and his ridiculous notion that she was chickening out by leaving town.

The bell over the door rang and Callie dropped the bunch of flowers in her arms to the table and headed out to the reception area. A tall, older man with salt-and-pepper hair stood in the middle of the room, looking as lost as a Great Dane at a cat show. "Can I help you?" Callie asked.

"Uh…" The man glanced around, taking in the feminine surroundings, the bridal portraits, the pile of lacy blue garters lying on the table that had arrived by delivery a little while ago and Callie had forgotten to put away. He shuffled from foot to foot, then glanced up at her, as if he expected her to teleport him anywhere but there. "This isn't the kind of place I frequent."

"Most men don't, at least not until a woman drags them in here." Callie laughed.

The man echoed her laughter, then put out his hand. "Name's Charlie Wiley." He had a firm grip, and a friendly smile. "I'm, ah, looking for a woman named Belle."

"She's not here. Everyone's gone home for the day. But Belle lives upstairs and should be back in a half hour or so. She just left for some dinner." Callie gestured toward the settee. "You're welcome to wait."

Just then Marsha Schumacher came running through the door, in a flurry of pink, her polka-dotted dress topped by a pink trench coat to keep her dry from the drizzle outside. "Callie! You have to help me! I'm having a total marital meltdown. I need someone to talk to and Mother's at the spa having her eyes BOTOXed and her lips re-plumped. She won't be able to talk for at least an hour, and even then, I don't think she'll be able to properly emote." Marsha grabbed Callie's arm, as if she were about to hold her hostage. "I need you. This is an *emergency*."

Callie worked a smile to her face. She didn't know what advice she could give Marsha, but comforting the brides was, after all, part of her job for as long as she worked at Wedding Belles. "Sure, Marsha."

"Oh, and there's a man here, too!" Marsha squealed, spying Charlie. "I could get your advice, too. On the whole guy perspective."

Charlie backed up, his discomfort clearly multiplying by the second. "That's, ah, not my area. I'll come back to talk to Belle. Later." He glanced again at Marsha. "Much later."

"Do you want me to give Belle a message?" Callie asked.

But Charlie had already headed out the door, hightailing it as fast as a man could. Callie would be willing to bet dollars to doughnuts that the man was one seriously confirmed bachelor.

"Oh, Callie," Marsha cried, grabbing Callie's hand and dragging her onto the settee, "he's backing out of the wedding!"

"Samuel? Why?"

"He thinks we need more time. That this is too big of a step to take so fast. Like being engaged for three months isn't long enough." Marsha raised tear-filled eyes to Callie's. "Don't you think he should know, in three months, if he loves me or not?"

"Well, Marsha, I don't know if I'm the best one to give you advice—"

"But you're a wedding planner. This is your job. You...you *have* to know." Marsha stared at her, expecting some wisdom to come tumbling from Callie's mouth, some answer to all the engagement questions in the cosmos.

"Well..." Callie paused, stalling, searching for something to say to Marsha. What was she supposed to say?

And then, the answer came to her, or at least, *an* answer.

"Maybe you've been concentrating on the wrong things, Marsha, and Samuel, well, he's been feeling left out."

"Concentrating on the wrong things?" Marsha cocked her head, her dark brown up-do falling a bit as she did. "Like the wedding? But that's the most important thing."

"Actually the marriage is. The relationship. The details, they don't really matter. The wedding is only a single day out of your life. The marriage is for the *rest* of your life."

"Well, that's a weird thing for you to say." Marsha frowned. "Isn't it your job to watch the details?"

"Exactly. That's *my* job, mine and the rest of the Belles," Callie said. "So that you can worry about the rest. You and Samuel."

Marsha sat back against the settee, her mouth opening, then closing. For the first time since Callie had met the outspoken bride, Marsha was at a loss for words. A good five seconds passed before the girl in pink said a thing. "No one really cares about the salmon with puff pastry, do they?"

"Well, maybe only the people who like tuna steaks." Callie grinned. "In the long run, Marsha, none of it matters. You could get married in your backyard and serve peanut butter and jelly sandwiches, or get married in a million dollar ceremony and hand out diamonds for favors, and it won't make a difference in how happy you are ten years down the road, if you're getting married for all the wrong reasons."

Marsha smoothed a hand over her dress, then glanced up at Callie, tears again shimmering in her eyes. "How do I know what the right reasons are?"

"That's easy." Callie smiled. "Your heart will tell you. What's your heart telling you?"

Marsha thought for a minute. "That I love Samuel. And that I don't care about salmon with puff pastry or tuna. Just marrying him."

"I think you answered your own question."

"Thank you," Marsha said. She swiped the tears off her

face. "You made me feel a lot better. I'm going to call Samuel and straighten this all out. And from here on out, I'll let the wedding planners plan the wedding and Samuel and I, we'll plan the marriage." Marsha surged forward and gave Callie a tight, nearly suffocating hug, then drew back. "You've been so great, Callie. You must have a lot of experience with this kind of thing, huh?"

"Not exactly. I was one of those people who didn't listen to my heart until it was too late."

"You mean you let a good man get away?"

"Well, I—" Callie cut off the sentence. Had she done that? She'd been about to tell Marsha about her divorce, but realized that when she thought about her heart, and what it was telling her about who'd gotten away, the first man who came to mind wasn't her ex-husband.

It was Jared.

The only trouble was reading the message.

Jared closed his high school yearbook, the mixed emotions churning in his gut. That period of his life had been immeasurably difficult as he'd tried to hold his family together even as it fractured beneath him.

Then he left his apartment and drove to the cemetery in Brookline. There, he found the graves of his parents. Two people who'd barely been able to live together in life, but who now lay side by side in death.

He bent down beneath his mother's stone, inserting fresh flowers into the vase. "I'm sorry," he whispered.

No one answered him back, of course. She'd been gone a year, his father more than fifteen years. Jared stayed there a long time, wondering if there was anything he could have done differently, knowing as always there really hadn't been, but wishing all the same.

Then he rose. It was well past time to stop living under that shadow.

And there was only one woman he wanted to take with him on his journey forward. Callie Phillips.

"I didn't know you could make puff pastry pink," Audra whispered to Callie when they arrived at the Schumacher wedding the next afternoon.

"Apparently anything can be made pink if you pay for it," Callie said, taking in the pink-silk draped walls, the pink bridesmaids, even the pink tuxedoed band. The silverware had, as promised, been bedecked with tiny pink bows. "But overall, it's not too bad, and I'm glad Marsha and Samuel worked everything out."

"Thanks to you, I hear." Audra gave Callie a curious look. "Since when did you become a card-carrying promarriage cheerleader?"

Callie grinned, as if this was nothing unusual. "Just doing my job."

"Uh-huh," Audra said, with a knowing smile. "Sounds like more than doing your job, but I'm not going to argue with you. Though, I am starting to buy into your theory about there not being enough Mr. Rights. Especially since my Mr. Right turned out to be Mr. Totally Wrong."

"I'm sorry about that, Audra. I really am." Sympathy shimmered through Callie. How she would have rather seen Audra celebrating a happy ending, rather than herself. "I wish it had worked out for you."

"I'm okay with it. Better to know now than ten years down the road." Then Audra smiled, and Callie knew, as she had known the day of the botched wedding, that Audra would be okay. "And to know before our next poker game."

"Seriously, Audra, don't give up. There's still a perfect ending in store for you. I'm sure of it."

Audra stared at Callie. "You've changed."

"Me? No, not at all." Then she let out a nervous laugh, as Audra continued her suspicious perusal. "I'm just trying to win a bet."

Audra dug in her purse and pulled out a quarter, placing it in Callie's palm. The metal was cold, oddly heavy for such a small piece. "You did win, didn't you?"

It had started out as a joke, and now, Callie regretted ever agreeing to the silly bet. How weird was that?

She stared at the silver coin, an ordinary quarter. She should have been happy. She had, after all, won. This was what she'd wanted. To prove, once and for all, that putting stock in such a ridiculous notion as a perfect man for every woman was crazy.

She'd won.

But won what?

The proof that she would end up unhappy and alone? If that was the prize, Callie didn't want it. She turned the quarter over in her palm, heads, tails, heads, tails.

Neither side seemed to offer a win.

She went to pocket the coin, then changed her mind and dropped it back into Audra's hand. "No. I can't take it."

Audra's brows arched. "Why?"

"This sounds crazy, but for some reason, I just can't give up that last little bit of hope." She gestured toward Marsha and Samuel, dancing cheek to cheek, appearing now like the world's happiest couple. A rumbling of envy tightened in Callie's gut. How she wanted that for herself, even in its pink-wrapped bubble. "Call me sentimental, but I guess I still want to think that maybe…"

"Maybe it's possible. For you," Audra drew in a breath, "and me?"

Callie nodded, meeting Audra's gaze with a shared connection of understanding. "Maybe. Just maybe."

"I understand," Audra said softly.

For a long time, they just watched the happy couple, two friends who didn't need to say a word to know what the other was thinking.

Then Callie spotted her mother across the room, chatting up an older man. Scoping out husband number five? Already? "Or maybe not. Excuse me, Audra. I have someone else I need to talk to."

She rose and crossed the room, reaching her mother just as Vanessa was accepting a glass of wine from the older, distinguished looking gentleman. "Mom. Want to get some air?"

"Sure. Have you met Samuel's father?"

"The groom's father?" Oh, this went too far. Callie opened her mouth to protest, ready to haul her mother out of there when Vanessa waved over the man's wife and completed the introductions.

"I was just telling them what a wonderful thing you did yesterday when you talked to Marsha and calmed her right down," Callie's mother said. "It was just so sweet of Marsha to invite me to the wedding, too. Now there's a girl who knows the importance of mothers."

Callie blinked in surprise. She'd thought her mother was flirting with Samuel's father when in fact she'd actually been singing her daughter's praises? That was a change of pace Callie hadn't expected. The band announced the beginning of the *hora*, so Samuel's parents said their goodbyes and made their way over to participate in the event.

"Let's go outside, Mom," Callie said. A pair of French doors beside the bar led to a private outdoor patio, which Callie had decorated earlier with swooping garlands of stargazer lilies, Gerbera daisies and ivy, matching the table arrangements. The afternoon sun had released the heady perfume of the flowers, giving the air a sweet scent. Callie paused, drawing in the fragrance of her work. "I love flowers. Something about them just makes me…happy."

"Then why are you thinking about quitting your job?"

She turned toward her mother. "How did you know that?"

"I didn't spend all those years with your father and not learn a thing or two about learning to read the signals, Callie." Vanessa took a seat at one of the wrought-iron tables, then waited while her daughter sat in the opposite chair.

"To be honest, I didn't think you paid all that much attention to what I was doing."

Her mother sipped at her wine, watching the sun for a long moment, as the golden orb started its descent toward the horizon. "I haven't been so good at that, have I?"

"No."

"Maybe if I had been…" Vanessa shook her head. "Well, if I'd concentrated more on what had been going on at home, maybe your father might have been more interested in hanging around." Her eyes met her daughter's, and in that moment of connection, Callie realized they had each lost something every time Joseph Phillips had walked out.

"Do you think we shut him out? Weren't there for him?"

"Callie, we stayed. We kept trying." Vanessa snorted. "I don't know why. He was the one who left us. Over and over again."

Callie fingered one of the delicate stargazer lilies, running a fingertip along the deep pink valley of the blossom. "Do you know why I love stargazer lilies? Because they don't conform. They're one of the most fragrant flowers available and that drives growers crazy."

If her mother found the turn in conversation odd, she didn't say anything. Instead she rose, crossed to the flowers and bent to inhale the scent of the lily. "They're heavenly. Why don't growers like them?"

"The more scent a flower has, the more energy it uses up producing the fragrance. Scent, though, is only good for pollinating. There's no need for that in commercial growing, and when a flower like this lily has used up most of its energy to smell pretty, that means its beauty won't last as long."

"So it's not as profitable."

Callie nodded. "It's a square peg in all those round holes. But to me, it's perfect. Bold and dramatic, and so beautiful."

Vanessa cupped a bloom in her palm, studying the delicately dotted petals. "They are beautiful. And what you do with them, honey, is amazing."

"Thank you," Callie said, a smile curving across her face. Her mother had noticed her work, maybe for the first time ever. Joy soared in her heart. Such a silly thing, really, especially at her age, but she supposed a child never really grew too old for a mother's praise.

"You know," Vanessa said, returning to the table, retrieving her wine, "I've been thinking a lot about what Jared said the other night. About chasing after men. And I realized I've been chasing after things all my life. Running, like you."

"Like Dad."

Silence extended between them, as the truth sank in between mother and daughter. "That is what we did, isn't it?"

"It was a lot easier than trying to figure out why he kept leaving us, wasn't it?" Tears filled Callie's eyes, tears for unanswered questions, ones that might never be answered, because the man who held the answers never sat still long enough to tell either of them what they so desperately wanted to know.

A single tear ran down her mother's face, then another, belying all of Vanessa's bravado. She, too, had been hurt by Joseph's continual departures.

"Why did he do it, Mom? Weren't we good enough?" Callie's voice broke, the last syllables shredded in the question she'd never spoken aloud before.

It was the one question she'd never asked her father. Never asked her first husband.

Hadn't she been good enough? Good enough to stay home for? Good enough for forever?

Good enough to love?

Vanessa reached forward then, gathering Callie into her arms. "Of course you were, baby, of course you were. We both were, even if we didn't think so." She wrapped her comfort around her daughter, soothing and saying everything that Callie had needed to hear, but still, she wondered, still, she needed to know.

"Why?" Callie asked. "Why did he keep leaving?"

"I don't know. I asked him, Callie, every time, and he just said that staying around wasn't for him."

The words blasted Callie like ice water. How many times had she said that herself? To landlords, bosses, Tony?

Jared?

Had she turned into the very person she didn't want to be? The one who'd abandoned her over and over again? And all under the guise of wanting to have fun, take risks, live life by her own rules?

"I've looked for Dad, everywhere I've gone," Callie said after a while, the words taking their time to make their journey from her heart to her lips. "And I even found him once, in Mexico City. He seemed so glad to see me, and said he wanted to get to know me, spend time with me again." She remembered how hope had fluttered in her heart like a butterfly, so fragile and new, how she'd gone home to the apartment she and Tony had been renting, bursting with joy that this time, this time would be different with her father.

But Tony hadn't been there to tell. He'd been out with someone else, as usual. And when she'd gone that night, hurrying so she wouldn't be late, carrying pictures of her trips, a pile of letters that had been sent and returned to sender, and most of all, hope in her heart for a connection that had always been as fragile as dried baby's breath, to meet with her father again—

He'd been gone.

"But he didn't stay, Mom. He left." Callie's voice broke, and she hung her head.

Her mother's arms went around her again, drawing her daughter in, the years of distance melting in that moment, of one woman telling another she understood her pain, and wanted so badly to take it away. "I think he was afraid. Afraid that he couldn't close the gap anymore." She tipped Callie's face up to meet hers. "I've done the same thing, Callie. I'm so sorry."

"We both did." Tears slipped out of Callie's eyes, marring her makeup, but she didn't care. She let them come. They were too far overdue. "I'm sorry, too."

"*Is* it too late?" Vanessa asked, her gaze watery, her voice shaky. Her hold on her daughter tight, yet tenuous. "Too late to close the gap? With you? And me?"

Callie couldn't answer her. The words lodged in her throat, stuck behind the lump. Instead she shook her head, whispered no, then wrapped her arms tight around her mother.

And didn't let go for a long, long time.

"Darlin', you are either completely crazy or totally in love," Belle said. She shook her head, laughed again, then waved Jared on in. "If Callie finds out I had anything to do with this, she's bound to start telling people my real age."

Jared chuckled and put up his right hand. "I'll keep your name out of it. Scout's honor. Do you have what I needed?"

Belle nodded then turned and reached into her bag and handed the small black object to Jared. "You're definitely crazy, darlin', but the kind of crazy I like. You'll find Callie outside, on the patio. You go get her and I'll set everything else up." Belle caught his arm before he walked away. "You're sure you can get her to do this? She's one determined filly."

"Well, I'm not planning on taking no for an answer." He gave Belle a grin, then headed across the room. He didn't see the bride, the groom, the crowd of guests, any of the busy reception. He had one destination in mind, and one person.

He found her, as Belle had said, on the patio, with her mother, the two of them talking about the flowers draping the wrought-iron fence. When he stepped through the doors, the two women stopped midsentence and pivoted toward him. "Jared," Callie said, surprise rising the pitch in her voice. "What are you doing here?"

"Looking for you." He had to take a breath, as his gaze swept over her and the impact of seeing her again slammed into him. She was dressed in a simple cranberry-colored dress with a scoop neck, leaving her arms bare, outlining her waist, her hips. The skirt swung around her legs, allowing him a delicious peek at the curve of her calves, enhanced by a pair of high heels with tiny rhinestones marching across the ankle. She'd swept her hair up and tucked it back with little sparkly combs, exposing the graceful swoop of her neck.

But it was her lips—always her lips and the crimson lipstick—that drew his attention again and again. He wanted to draw her to him, feel her in his arms again, and kiss her until everything that stood between them had melted away.

But even Jared knew it wouldn't be that simple. If it were, then the last few times he'd done that would have solved everything.

"I'll leave you two alone," Vanessa said, giving them a

smile before slipping back in to join the wedding. As she passed him, she gave Jared a pat on the shoulder.

"We settled all this earlier, Jared," Callie said. "I don't have anything to say to you."

He grinned. "I expected that argument. And I came armed with a rebuttal."

"A rebuttal?"

"Yep." He took a step closer, the fragrance of the lilies and daisies wrapping around her, as if the flowers she worked with were a part of her. Jared trailed a finger along the neckline of her dress, watching as her eyes widened, her breath quickened, and knew that no matter what Callie said, nothing was settled between them. Not by a long shot. "I'm not here to argue with you, to dance with you or to kiss you, as much as I want to do that."

She didn't answer and a part of him wondered if she was thinking about kissing him, too.

"I'm here to make sure that you take a walk on the wild side tonight. Well, maybe not the wild side, but a definite walk into unfamiliar territory."

"What are you talking about?"

He reached into the breast pocket of his suit and pulled out the item Belle had given him earlier and placed it in Callie's palm. "Get up on that stage, Miss Callie Phillips, and sing."

She stared at the microphone in her hand as if it might bite her. "Sing? Are you crazy? Why would I do that?"

"Because all you ever do is run away, Callie. You're planning on doing it again, you told me so yourself." She looked away and he could tell she hadn't changed her mind. Disappointment slammed into him, but he pressed on. "You can go ahead and leave, but before you do, I want you to do one thing. Tonight I want you to stay and actually *tackle* your dreams instead of leaving them behind."

"I don't—"

He put a finger over her lips, tension coiling in his body, the need to kiss her so real and tangible, Jared felt like he could pluck it out of the air. "I know you do, because I've been doing it myself, too, all my life. And I'm tired of it. In fact, today, when I turned in my research project, I quit my job."

"You did what?"

"I gave my two weeks' notice. And I applied to work at one of those think tanks. But in a way, I kind of hope I don't get the job."

She gaped at him as if he'd grown three heads and a unicorn horn. "You, Mr. Dependable, actually want to be unemployed?"

He grinned. "Yeah. A wise man I know told me it's fun to skate on the edge of life. I think I might try it. At least until the rent's due."

Callie laughed. "So you're skating, but wearing a helmet?"

"Exactly." He chuckled, then sobered. "Tonight, though, isn't about me, it's about you. Go on out on the stage and show everyone what you can do."

Callie shook her head, trying to hand back the mike, but Jared wouldn't take it. "I can't do that. Belle would never—"

He cut off her objections by spinning her toward the reception and pointing at the stage. "You can. I already talked to the band and Marsha and Samuel know all about it, too. Everything is all set up. The only missing ingredient is you."

"You set this up?" She veered back at him. "How did you know I'd even say yes?"

"I didn't." Jared shrugged. "But I wasn't going to leave here until you did. And if worse came to worst, I'd have gotten up there and sung until you came to put me out of my misery."

"Why? Why would you do this for me, Jared?"

"Because—" But before he could get the words out, the leader of the band announced Callie's guest appearance and the wedding guests swiveled their attention toward Callie, erupting into applause. Her friends rushed over, calling her name, waving her on. And Callie was gone, heading toward the stage, the microphone in her hands, and her dream underway.

Jared stayed long enough to watch Callie sing her first song. He stayed at the back of the room, allowing the notes of the song, the sweet melody of Callie's voice, to wash over him, treasuring every note that slipped from her lips. At first, she stood stiff and nervous, but with each stanza, Callie relaxed, falling into a rhythm with the band.

She was a natural performer, just as Jared had known she'd be. He stayed until she reached the last notes of the chorus, then he headed for the exit.

"Jared," Vanessa called, catching up to him. "Where are you going?"

"I did what I came to do," he said, taking one last look at Callie and hoping like hell it wouldn't be the very last one. "The rest is up to her."

CHAPTER TWELVE

"How'd it go last night, man?" Pope asked when Jared returned to the office.

"It didn't." Jared grabbed a small box off the shelf and began loading in the few personal possessions he'd kept on his desk over the years he'd worked at Wiley Games. A Caffeine Stimulates Deep Thinking coffee mug. A suspense novel he'd been meaning to read and never had. A Dilbert stress ball Pope had given him as a joke, probably because of the resemblance. And a picture of him and Callie, a decade old, that he'd tucked into the bulletin board when he'd first moved to Boston. He stared at the image for a long time, then slipped the photo between the pages of the novel.

"So you're just quitting?"

"Yep. As of yesterday, I'm finished." Jared looked over at Pope. "Oh, I'm not quitting on her. The job."

Pope sank into a chair. "Phew. Good thing. I was getting worried about you, dude. Glad to see you got your priorities straight. Unemployment is way easier to take than a broken heart. I know, because—" Pope looked away.

Jared lowered the box to his desk. "You okay, bud?"

"Yeah. Me and my girl, we had a fight and she broke up with me." Pope heaved a sigh and Jared could swear he saw a tear in the eyes of the guy who also sported an earring.

"Well, maybe the, ah, Lethargio approach is not the best one. Perhaps you should step it up." Jared gestured to the report he'd compiled from the data. "According to my research, what women want is a man who keeps pursuing them, no matter what. Who won't give up, even when it seems as if all is lost. Sort of like passing a test…" His voice trailed off and he stared at the green folder holding all the answers. He should have hit himself with all the numbers he'd been compiling, instead of shoving them into the computer. "I'm a complete idiot."

Pope popped out of his chair. "No, dude, you're brilliant. That's exactly what I needed to hear. That's the perfect answer. I'm heading over there right now, to show her I'm a total warrior dude in love."

Pope ran out of the room, as full of fire as an ancient Scotsman on the battlefield. Pope may have been younger, but Jared was more motivated and he passed him easily in the hall.

Jared had some statistics to prove and this time, he didn't care one whit that his hypothesis was based completely on a personal theory.

And that the only possible outcome was marriage.

"Girls, we have a wedding to plan."

Belle stood in the middle of the reception area of the offices for the Wedding Belles, her face lit with a massive smile. She held a bottle of champagne in one hand, a half dozen champagne flutes in the other. "This one is going to put the Wedding Belles on the map. And then some."

Audra, Regina, Natalie, Julie, Serena and Callie gathered around Belle, the six of them pausing in their work, confusion on their faces. "What wedding are you talking about?" Audra asked.

"Does the name Liz Vandiver mean anything to you gals?" Belle beamed. "As in *the* Vandivers?"

"Oh my gosh!" Serena gasped, putting a hand to her chest. "You mean the really, really wealthy Vandivers? The ones that are always in the gossip columns?"

Belle nodded. "Yep. Apparently their daughter was a guest at one of our weddings and she wants the Wedding Belles to put her dream together. Us. Can you believe it?" Belle laid the champagne flutes on the coffee table, then unwrapped the foil and popped the cork on the bottle of bubbly. The cork exploded off the top of bottle, pinging off the armchair. Champagne flowed in a stream of gold from the neck. "Whoops!" Belle laughed, then filled each of the glasses and dispensed them to the Belles. "This is a great thing for us. It's a huge wedding—a big bucks wedding at that—and we need to celebrate!"

The women cheered and toasted, laughter pouring out of them faster than the champagne. "Oh, what a great financial boon this will be," Audra said, clearly mentally calculating the profit margin. "And think of the word of mouth we'll get."

"When the pictures of the wedding get into the newspapers and magazines," Regina added, walking around the room, seeming to frame the images already in her mind, "it'll give us even more exposure. I can only imagine how much this will do for the Wedding Belles business."

Serena nodded. "It's great to see everything looking up for all of us, for a change."

Julie raised her glass. "Hear, hear. I'm all for an increase in business."

Callie had stayed silent, though she was glad for the news. She sipped at her champagne, smiling with her friends. But her mind was on Jared, on last night. After the Vandiver wedding news celebration had died down and the rest of the women had left for a group consultation with another bride and groom at the Marriott Hotel, Belle pulled her aside.

"You were awfully quiet, darlin'. Everything okay?"

Callie nodded, avoided Belle's inquisitive gaze by plucking dead leaves off one of the plants in the entry room. "Just tired. Late night last night."

"I'll say. How many songs did you sing with the band? A dozen?" Belle gave her a wide smile. "You have quite the talent, my girl."

"Thanks." Callie grinned. "I don't know why I was so afraid to show you. It was a lot of fun. And you, I hear, were in on the conspiracy."

"I'm not above a little conspirin', when it's in your best interests." Belle grinned. "Seems that Jared knew you better than you knew yourself. He told me that if I was smart, I'd add a part-time wedding singer to my operation." Belle cocked her head and studied Callie. "You interested in the job?"

Callie opened her mouth, closed it. "Well, I...I never really thought about doing that."

Belle laid her champagne flute on the table and began circling the perimeter of the room, straightening pillows, acting nonchalant. "You know, this Vandiver wedding will be a lot of work. It'll require all of us to pull together. I can't take this one on, if I'm going to be a woman short. Can I count on you to stay?"

Hidden meaning—was she still going to leave town?

Callie stood in the room that she had grown to love over the past three years and considered the woman who had become a second mother. She thought of the future that lay ahead of her here. A future filled with flowers, and with a little bit of singing, if she wanted it.

To have those things meant permanence. The very thing Callie had shied away from for so many years.

"If you're going to stay, you might even want to think about buying a little house," Belle said. "Maybe planting some of those flowers you love so much."

"A garden, huh?" Callie grinned. "Are you trying to convince me to put down roots?"

"Is it that obvious?"

Callie laughed. "Yes."

Belle returned to Callie's side, her touch gentle on Callie's arm. "It's not so bad, you know. Roots hold a person firm; give them something to stand on when a storm rolls in."

Callie thought about that. About all the times when she'd turned tail, instead of staying in one place when her life got hard, then thought of how much easier it had been to go through her divorce because she'd stayed here, stayed with her friends, her job.

Where would she want to be the next time a storm rolled in? Some distant land? A foreign city? A strange town? Alone?

Or right here, surrounded by the people who loved her, the things she loved?

"Stargazer lilies," Callie said finally, thinking of the way her mother had cupped the blooms, the risk growers took with the delicate, short-living plants. Wasn't that what life was about, though? Taking a risk, while living loud and vibrant, like the lilies did? "That's what I want to plant. They're not so easy to grow out here, and they'll take a lot of care, but—"

"You like a challenge," Belle finished. She smiled, then gathered Callie into a hug, one that was as comforting as peach pie and ice cream. "I'm glad you're staying, darlin'. The place just wouldn't be the same without your sunshine."

Callie held onto Belle long enough to savor the sweet moment. Then she heard the roar of a familiar motorcycle engine. Callie broke away from Belle, dread multiplying in her stomach.

She drew back the curtain, peeked out the window. When the motorcycle's rider swung off the bike and Callie saw who it was, she realized that sometimes you couldn't run from your problems—

Because they showed up on the front porch instead.

The motorcycle sitting outside the Wedding Belles shop should have been Jared's first clue that disaster loomed. But he walked right past it, a spring in his step, the song Callie had sung the night before still playing in his veins, his mind entirely focused on finding Callie.

Once he'd talked to Pope, he'd turned off the analytic side of his mind, so Jared didn't process the Harley. He was too wrapped up in his internal speech, how he intended to tell Callie he was done researching their relationship. No more testing the hypothesis of love, stacking the statistics and weighing the facts.

From here on out, he was leaping off the bridge of taking chances. Love was a risk—

One Jared was willing to take. Consequences be damned.

He opened the door to the Belles, a ready smile on his face, a smile that died, falling from his face the second his gaze connected with—

Tony's.

"Well, hey, what a blast from the past." Tony rose from the settee, sticking out in the elegant room like tumbleweed in a rose garden and crossed to Jared, clapping him on the back. As if they were still best friends, as if not a day had passed since they'd last seen each other. "How you been, pal?"

"Fine. You?" Jared couldn't manage any more. Couldn't think of what would possibly be polite, socially correct to say, in this situation.

Had Callie invited Tony here? Had he simply shown up out of the blue?

Whatever the case, Tony hadn't aged a bit. He still had that daredevil glint in his eye, the rugged looks of a man who lived by the seat of his pants. Leather jacket, low-slung jeans, a faint growth of beard, a trim, neat body. The scent of cigarettes hung in the air around him. "I'm the same as always. Trying to get into as much trouble as possible without getting caught." Tony laughed. "Came by to see my girl, see what she's up to."

His girl. They were divorced, and yet Tony still laid claim to Callie. Because there was still something between them?

As if drummed up by his thoughts, Callie rounded the corner and came into the room. She stopped cold when she noticed Jared and Tony, together. "Oh, Jared. I, ah, didn't expect you today."

"Apparently. I thought I'd surprise you. I guess I did." He looked from her to Tony, seeing the past replay itself all over again. What did he need to get the hint that she wanted the opposite kind of man to what he was? A billboard? A tractor trailer truck full of signs? "I can see you're busy. I'll talk to you later." Or never.

Jared turned to go. There wasn't any point in staying. He knew that from past experience. Whenever Tony walked into the room, Jared became invisible. Mr. Cool versus Mr. Straight-and-Narrow. Leather won out every time.

Jared made it as far as the door; even let it shut behind him.

Then he wondered what the hell he was doing. Inside that room was a woman he cared about. A woman who was talking to the very man who had broken her heart. A man who had jerk written all over him. If Jared let her stay there and talk to him—maybe even fall under Tony's spell again—what kind of man would he be?

Even if she didn't care about Jared, *he* cared about her, and he owed her a warning, protection from a man like Tony. That much at least.

Who was he kidding? He'd walked out of that wedding last night, thinking he was doing the best thing for her—

And cursing himself every step of the way.

He wasn't going to do it again.

Jared spun on his heel, flung open the door and nearly collided with Callie. "Don't do it," he said.

"Don't do what?"

"Don't get back together with him. He's no good for you. Hell, he's never been good for you and you know it."

She put her hands on her hips. "Are you telling me what to do?"

"Yeah, I am. And I'm telling you that you should start thinking with your brain and look for a man who actually treasures you and won't crush your heart like a used soda can."

She glared at him. "Who do you think you are?"

"Someone who cares about you. A good friend."

"That's all?" Her eyes sparked like firecrackers. "A good friend?"

"Isn't that what I've always been to you?" He let out a frustrated gust. "A good friend?"

"Well thank you for the advice, Jared, but I am fully capable of making my own decisions. I don't need you to rush in like Sir Galahad. And I don't need another *friend*."

What was it with this woman? She made him completely insane. He'd come over here, intending to tell her how he felt, to ask her to take that risk with him, and now here she was, reinforcing the whole argument they'd had nine years ago. "You're not seriously considering getting back together with Tony, are you?"

"Last I checked, I didn't have to run my love life decisions by you." She pursed her lips, her gaze sweeping over him. "Unless that's part of your research project, too."

"No, I'm done researching love. I've drawn all the conclusions I need. Some that I'm not too happy about, but that's how it goes with research. Sometimes, the results aren't what you'd expect."

"No, they're not. And you know, while we're on that subject, you didn't quite turn out the way I'd expected, either."

He jerked back, surprised. "What do you mean?"

"What happened to the Jared Townsend who had dreams and plans? Because he seems to have disappeared as far as I can tell. I remember that conversation we had the morning after we made love. Do you?"

"Of course I do." He remembered everything about that night—and the next morning.

"You were filled with ideas for your future," she went on. "It was a lot more than the talk about wanting to get married, buy a house, with a garden and a dog. But then you just assumed I wouldn't be interested in that kind of life, Jared."

His mouth opened, closed.

She went on, barreling forward, not waiting for a response. "Maybe I would have said no. Maybe I would have run for the hills. The point is you never gave me a chance to make that choice. But you went on and on, saying you wanted to travel, to jump out of airplanes. To try new things. In the end, you didn't do any of that. You criticize me for running, but at least I'm moving. All you've done is stagnate."

He turned away from her. "I had my reasons."

"Like what, Jared?" She took a step closer to him, coming around to face him again, confronting him. "Why didn't you ever tell me what they were? Why keep it all locked inside?"

"What good was that going to do?" he asked. "Are you going to suddenly change how you feel about me because you found out that I grew up with an alcoholic father? A mother who spent more time with her boyfriends than with me? That my father died when I was seventeen and all of a sudden I was the man of the house? That I became super responsible because I had no choice?"

Her jaw dropped. "I never knew. I'm sorry."

"That's why I needed you as a friend," he said softly, realizing now how much he valued her friendship back then, her quiet presence. Maybe he should have opened up all those years ago. "That's why you were so important to me."

"But why not say anything? That's what friends are for."

"I didn't want your pity, Callie. And besides, I didn't need to tell you," he said, his voice a raw thing that scraped past his throat. "Just having you there in school, and on campus, was enough. You were this…wild thing that gave me hope that someday, down the road, maybe I could do those things, too. To take chances, answer to nobody's clock but my own."

"But you never did."

He sighed. "My mother got sick. Cancer. I needed a dependable job with benefits and a regular paycheck. I ended up becoming your neighborhood bedroom game researcher. Nothing to brag about, but it paid the bills. And after she died last year, it was easier to stay than to jump off the bridge and take a risk." He tipped her chin, studied the green eyes he had known so long, the eyes that both drove him wild and made him want a life he had thus far denied himself. "Until I saw you again."

A smile curved up her face, one filled with understanding, compassion. "Kind of like handing someone a microphone and then leaving them?"

"I was giving you what you wanted, Callie." He inhaled the scent of her perfume, its intoxicating scent driving him crazy at the same time it made him want her in ways he couldn't even count. Damn. How could he walk away? "A way out."

"An escape, you mean."

"The last thing you ever wanted was someone tying you

down, isn't that right?" He waved toward the shop. "Isn't that what Tony's all about? No real ties, no real commitment? That's why you chose him over me. Then and now."

"So you were just going to let me go? Be the big sacrificer again?" She let out a gust. "Is that what you wanted? This time, too?"

"Hell, no, Callie."

"Then stop being so damned nice and noble, Jared." She stepped back, away from him, threw up her hands.

Everything within him rose to a boil, not in anger, but in a heated rush of want. He could barely hold back from the desire to swoop down and kiss her, hold her to him and not let her go until the heat had subsided.

She didn't want him to be nice, to be noble. And yet, those were the very qualities in a man that she deserved. The very kind of man that the Callie he knew and loved should have.

The man she'd once married—the man she'd chosen over him time and time again—was mere feet away. Jared knew that given half the chance, Callie would choose him again. She'd already made that clear by reminding him of their friendship.

She didn't need another friend, she'd said.

Another friend.

No, she didn't need another friend, damn it, and neither did he. He was done being Callie's friend, and if he destroyed that friendship with what he was about to do, then so be it.

"What *are* you really here for, Jared?" she asked.

"This," he said, and he stepped forward, crushed her to him and kissed her more thoroughly and deeply than he ever had before in one long, hot second that took his breath away. His tongue slipped into her mouth, invited hers to dance, and she did, her arms going around his body, her mouth opening wider, a slight moan escaping her throat, and she seemed to go liquid in his arms. Their kiss deepened, and he cupped her jaw, tracing the delicate outline of her face with his thumbs, memorizing every inch of her. When the fire in his gut reached a roar, Jared stepped back, the world spinning for a second, then let her go.

Callie blinked, then drew in a shudder of a breath. "What was that for?"

"An experiment," Jared said. "To test my hypothesis about friendship."

"Friends don't kiss each other like that."

"I don't want to be your friend. Not for one more day, damn it. In fact, we are officially done being friends."

Her mouth opened in surprise, but he cut off her words by trailing a finger along her jaw. Every touch of her silken skin made him want her even more now than he had five seconds ago. "I've wanted you from the first moment I met you, Callie. But I lied to you about what I wanted you for." He cupped her chin, his gaze meeting hers. "I want it all, Callie. I still want the house, the picket fence, the kids, the Labrador. But I want *you* in that house with me. Because I love you. I have always loved you. I loved you when you were making those aprons in home ec. When you were quoting Macbeth, when you were singing Madonna songs, when you were arranging tulips. I love you, Callie, and I want more than friendship."

"Jared—" Her eyes widened, and he knew he'd pushed it too far, too fast.

Damn, he'd done it again. He should know better. Should have learned from his mistakes. Nine years ago, he'd said nearly the same words and Callie had bolted from his bed like she'd been on fire. Running straight into Tony's arms.

But if he stopped now, where would that leave him? Going home to an empty apartment, wondering what if. With a bunch of regrets, and another nine years ahead of him without her.

Nope. Not this time. Jared was getting on the Tilt-A-Whirl and not getting off until he had the answer he wanted. And if he didn't get it, at least he'd know he'd jumped.

He reached into his back pocket and pulled out the plane tickets he'd bought a few days earlier. "Here are two plane tickets to Mexico. I paid for one of those adventure weekends in Cozumel. Skyline riding, ATV rentals, snorkeling, jet skiing, you name the adventure, it's on the ticket."

She stared at them, then at him. "What is this about?"

"I want you to go with me, Callie. Not to run away forever, but for a vacation. The way normal people do it. Then, we come back here, go to work. Well, I start looking for work," he chuckled, "and then we start planning our wedding."

He'd already given her the big scare. Might as well go all in.

She gasped. "Are you…asking me to marry you?"

"Yes, I am." He reached up, loosened his necktie, tugged it off and threw the slip of silk to the ground. "I am tired of being dependable, predictable, nice Jared. I want to be the man who sweeps you off your feet and surprises the hell out of you." Then he dropped to one knee, fished the ring he'd bought the same day as the plane tickets out of his pocket and flipped open the velvet box. The marquis-cut stone and the two smaller stones on either side winked back the sun's reflection. "Callie, I'm asking you to take the biggest risk of all. Will you marry me?"

"You making a pass at my girl?"

Tony's voice was all joke, but the underlying meaning was not. Callie knew that tone.

She spun around, angry at the intrusion, the implication. "Tony, I'm not your girl anymore."

He trundled down the stairs, shot Jared a glare, then slipped in beside Callie. "Sure you are," he said, his arm curling around her waist with a possessiveness that she hated. "You always have been."

Jared rose, the ring box closing with a snap. "Tony, Callie and I were talking."

"Yeah, well I was here first. And she is my wife."

"Ex," Callie stressed. She stepped out of Tony's embrace. "I'm not your girl and I never was. You cheated on me, Tony. Remember? Not just once, but dozens of times. You had all the loyalty of a stray dog."

"Callie, we might have had our disagreements—"

"Disagreements?" Her voice rose. "You left me the minute we moved to Boston to go live with your girlfriend. A girl-friend who *followed* you to Boston, if you remember correctly. Because you asked her to. That was a nice little surprise for me." She shook her head, the familiar disgust returning. How could she have been so stupid, so blinded to a man who had said all the right things, but done all the wrong ones behind her back? "I don't know why I stayed married to you as long as I did. Why I even fell for you in the first place."

But she did know. She'd kept hoping that the words he'd spoken would be true. That the lies would somehow turn around. That someday, Tony would turn into the hero she'd made him out to be in her mind. The bigger than life guy on the motorcycle, Mr. Wild, who would take her away from the upside-down life she'd hated so much. If he had become that man, she wouldn't have had to face the fact that she had made one colossal mistake with her life.

Tony scowled. "Jared, give us some privacy, will ya? Me and Callie, we have things to work out." Tony arched a brow. "If you know what I mean."

Jared looked at Callie, standing his ground. "Do you want me to leave?"

The fact that Jared was willing to stay was enough. But she

was a big girl, and she had to settle this with Tony once and for all at some point. It would be easier to do it without a third party around.

And, she needed time. Time to consider the question Jared had asked her. A question she didn't know how to answer. "Can I call you later?"

Jared looked from Tony to Callie, then back again. "Sure. I'll be at O'Malley's."

Jared walked away, and Callie knew she'd done something wrong. Hurt him again. Somehow it seemed no matter how she handled this situation, she did it wrong.

Damn.

But what was she supposed to do? She hadn't been expecting Jared to whip out two plane tickets and a marriage proposal. Her mind was a whirlwind. What did she want? Should she even marry again? Considering she was standing beside her biggest marital mistake?

Tony shrugged, nonplussed by Jared's departure. He crossed to the building's stoop, sat down on the step, laid back, arms outstretched, legs crossed. "So, babe, I'm back in town," he said, talking as if nothing had happened, that they were just picking up after a day apart, "and I'm thinking of going down to Mexico. There's this guy down there, runs a fishing operation. Has a hut on the beach, easy living, easy money. Drinking margaritas all day. And I need a partner." Tony gave her the familiar grin that had talked her into everything from spending a year living out of an RV to six months of backpacking through the Sierras. "What do you say? One more adventure for you and me?"

She considered Tony, and wondered what she had ever seen in him. Once, he had been handsome to her. But now all she saw was a cocky grin and brown eyes with lonely depths. "That life isn't for me anymore."

"What, you like this nine to five grind?" He let out a snort. "Or with these wedding people, I bet it's more like every weekend, too. They're demanding as hell, from what I see on TV. That's gotta suck."

"Actually it's fun. I really enjoy it."

"Right. You told me once that staying in the same place for more than a few months makes you crazy. You're made for the open road, baby. You're not a stick-to-anything kind of girl."

She shook her head. "I am now, Tony. I like it here. I have a career. A life."

Tony's brown eyes studied her for a long time, then his gaze narrowed. "Oh, I get it. The professor there, he's the kind of guy you want? You throwing me over for the old friend, is that it?"

"I might."

Tony scoffed. "Come on. Five minutes of 'How do you want your eggs?' and 'Pass me the Sunday crossword' and you'll be out of there. I know you, Callie, and I know Jared. That kind of thing—his kind of dull—drives you crazy." He mocked a yawn and shook his head.

"No, it doesn't. Maybe in the old days, but not now." She thought of the Jared she'd gotten to know lately and knew there hadn't been anything dull at all about the feelings he'd awakened in her.

In fact, he had been a grown-up kind of relationship, one where she'd been able to talk, to share her dreams, her work. She'd never done that with Tony, never had him listen to anything that interested her. Instead it had been her following him on one crazy idea after another, thinking that she was happy.

When all she'd been doing was searching for happiness—and never finding it.

Tony popped forward on the step, his eyes bright. "Tell me you haven't gotten the itch lately. Tell me you haven't thought

a hundred times about ditching this place and running off to
Tahiti or Alaska or San Tropez."

The places rattled off his tongue with the tempting whisper
of a man who had been to those exotic locales, a man who
knew which buttons to push in Callie's psyche.

For a split second, the wanderlust roared inside her, the
images of the places popping up like slides on a screen. Tony
may have been a horrible husband, but he knew her well.
Knew the constant craving for something new that ran through
her veins, like a third blood cell. "They need me here, Tony.
I can't just up—"

Tony rose, crossed to her, taking her hand. "Screw those
people. Come with me. I need you, too."

Come with me. I need you. A hundred times before, those
were the words that had convinced Callie to take one trip after
another, brought her from city to city, tagging along with Tony,
talked her into dropping out of college, leaving her hometown,
never buying a house—never signing anything more permanent
than a month-to-month lease. She'd never owned a dog, a cat
or even a potted plant. Not until she'd started working for Belle.

But now she wanted to stay, wanted to plant that garden,
those lilies. Running had never gotten her anywhere but away
from a home.

"Come with me," Tony whispered again, his mouth nuz-
zling along her neck.

Callie jumped away. "No. I don't want that life. I stopped
loving you a long time ago and I stopped loving living like that."

Shock widened his eyes. "You're serious, babe?"

"Yes. All these years, I kept holding the idea of leaving
Boston like a trap door I could slip through when things got
too scary. And here you come along, offering me that door and
guess what? I don't want it. I like what I have here. I can go
to Tahiti and San Tropez. On *vacation.*"

He snorted. "Are you kidding me? You're seriously going to stay here?"

She nodded, grinning like a fool. "Yep. But first, I have to buy a leash."

"A leash?" Tony stared at her. "What the hell do you need a—"

But Callie was already gone.

CHAPTER THIRTEEN

"YOU missing something?"

Jared looked up from the beer that had been sitting in front of him for a good ten minutes and had yet to be touched, to find the bartender at O'Malley's grinning at him. "Missing something?"

O'Malley leaned over the pint glasses before him, gesturing at Jared. "You're the clipboard guy Callie was with, right? Women find statistics sexy and all that?"

"Oh, yeah." Jared toyed with the rim of the mug and shook his head. "But I'm done with that job."

"What was that all about anyway?" O'Malley stood up, then swiped at the counter, cleaning up the circular imprints left by earlier drinks. Even though it was midafternoon, the bar was quite busy, a low hum of conversation carrying across the room from the several filled tables. An Eagles song played on the jukebox, and a couple slow danced to the tune in the middle of the floor.

"Love. I was researching love."

"You learn anything?"

Jared snorted. "Given the results? I don't think so."

O'Malley laughed. "I don't know about that. I think you did pretty good, actually, at least when it comes to relationships with people." He jerked his head to the right. "Have you met my new short-order cook?"

Jared followed O'Malley's direction, then sat back in surprise. "Sam?"

The older man crossed the room, a smile taking over his face, lighting up his clear, bright eyes. No longer drunk, but sober and neat as a pin, wearing an apron, jeans and a denim shirt. "Hey, Jared! I've been hoping you'd come back in. Been wanting to thank you."

"You're working here?" Jared couldn't have been more surprised if Sam had knocked him over with a keg.

Sam nodded. "I took your advice. Cleaned myself up, got a job. Thought I'd start here, since this is kind of where I found my miracle, and a Help Wanted sign." He chuckled.

"Best thing I ever did, hiring him," the bartender said. "Who knew adding spaghetti carbonara and grilled chicken sandwiches to my afternoon menu could boost business so much?"

"I did," Sam said, shooting O'Malley a grin, before turning back to Jared. "We jazzed up the menu, tweaking a few things here and there. Nothing motivates a man like feeling useful again. I missed my restaurant and it was sure nice to get behind a stove again."

"I'm glad for you," Jared said.

Sam studied him, turning the dish towel in his hands over and over. "Why did you help me that night? I was just a sloppy drunk sitting at the end of the bar."

"My dad," Jared began. He paused for a second, then continued. "My dad had a drinking problem. Maybe if someone had talked to him, he might have…"

"Wised up before it was too late?"

Jared nodded.

Sam slipped onto the stool beside Jared and laid a hand on Jared's shoulder. The older man's touch offered a balm that seemed to reach across the years, as if soothing a wound left over from Jared's childhood, and Jared knew why he had helped Sam. Why it made him feel so good to see Sam sober, working. "I'm sorry for you, son," Sam said. "But if it's any help, because of you, I'm mending the fences with my kids and my grandkids."

"It does," Jared said. "More than you know." It might be too late with his parents, but at least he could see one happy ending here. "Thank you, Sam."

"Thank me? For what?" Sam laughed. "I didn't do anything."

"Oh, you did," Jared said. "You did."

The bartender cleared his throat. "Guess you didn't need the clipboard after all. What is it with you professor types? Is it the glasses?"

Jared looked up at O'Malley, then saw that he was pointing toward the door.

"I heard there's a man in here who knows what makes a woman's heart sing."

Jared turned at the sound of Callie's voice, his pulse going from zero to sixty in the time it took him to make the half circle spin. Part of him hadn't expected to see her, and the other part—

Well, it had been hoping like a five-year-old at Christmas.

"I was in the neighborhood," she said, a smile playing across her lips. She crossed to him, looking beautiful, as always. "Want to get some sun, Dracula?"

He grinned, slipped off the stool. "Sure."

Sam and O'Malley exchanged smiles. Jared went to pay his tab, but O'Malley waved it off. "You're welcome here anytime," O'Malley said.

A moment later, Jared and Callie were outside, enjoying a warm April day. They strolled down the sidewalk, faces upturned to the sun. He took her hand in his, the feel of her palm as natural as anything he'd ever known. "Where's Tony?"

She shrugged. "Halfway to Mexico, I guess."

"And you're not?"

"I have better things to stay for."

Hope soared in his chest, but he tamped it down. Jared had always been a realist, and he wasn't about to change today. Not yet. "Are you going to keep working for Belle?"

Callie paused on the sidewalk, swinging into Jared's arms. She shook her head, teasing him. "Are you going to keep talking around the subject?"

"What subject would that be?"

"If I remember right, you asked me a question. A very important, life altering question. And I didn't answer it."

He grinned, felt the smile reach all the way through his veins, down into his gut. "No, you didn't."

"First, I have something to tell you." She took a step closer, grasping his other hand with hers. Her green eyes met his, clear and direct. "All my life, I've been afraid of really committing to anyone, so I did the next worst thing. I married a man who was just like my father. A man who wouldn't stay committed. Of course I didn't realize it at the time, but now that this particular scarecrow got some brains, I see my mistakes a little better."

"In science, we don't call them mistakes. They're part of the learning curve."

She laughed. "Well, it took me a long time to go around that curve. I was so afraid of what might happen if I screwed up again, I just…didn't get involved. Didn't fall in love." She tiptoed a finger up his lips. "Until now."

He swallowed, dared to allow hope to rise even higher. "Until now?"

She nodded. "I love you, Jared. I think I always have, I've just been too afraid to admit it. I love the way you look in a tie. I love that you fiddle with your glasses when you're nervous. I love the way you try to sing. And I especially love the way you kiss me."

He grinned, then lowered his mouth within kissing distance. "You do, do you?"

"Uh-huh."

So he kissed her, just to make sure that she loved that particular kiss, too. Given the way she reacted, he'd say he'd struck gold again. He took his time savoring her lips, tasting the sweetness of her, enjoying every moment of her touch. He'd never imagined there could be anything as wonderful as kissing a woman he had known for so many years.

Maybe that was what gave it the sweetness. Knowing her so well, being able to predict the movements of her lips, her head, her hands. He knew the curve of her jaw, the touch of skin, the scent of her perfume, as well as he knew his own hands.

"Oh, Callie," he murmured, then pulled back, thinking there was nothing more beautiful than the emerald depths of Callie's eyes. "So, now that you've found your Mr. Right, what are you going to do with him?"

She grinned. "Oh, I'm going to marry him. But he'll have to wait a little bit. Someone has to get housebroken first so we can go on our honeymoon and not worry about the carpet."

Jared arched a brow. "Housebroken?"

Callie laughed, then stepped out of Jared's arms and over to her car. She thumbed the remote, unlocking it. Jared noticed the windows were slightly open and a…whimpering was coming from inside the vehicle. "I decided you might want a little proof that I'm here to stay." She opened up the passenger's side door of the Toyota, and out bounded a golden retriever puppy, whose massive paws scrambled across the sidewalk, then up Jared's pants, leaving a dusting of fur. Callie grabbed the leash attached to the dog's collar and got the puppy to halfway sit. "We can't settle down unless we have a house, a garden and a dog."

That had been exactly what they'd talked about all those years ago in her bed, when he'd told her his dream of the perfect life. A house. A garden. A dog. And a wife.

This wife, in particular.

Happiness erupted in Jared's chest, and he took her hand, then pressed a kiss to Callie's lips. "Training a puppy might put a serious crimp in our travel plans."

"I know," Callie said, laughing and smiling. "And I don't care. I have everything I need right here." Then she curved into Jared's arms, finding home right where she stood.

* * * * *

The Heir's

Convenient Wife

MYRNA MACKENZIE

Myrna remembers her own wedding through the photos that mean so much to her:

"When I realised that I would be writing a story about a wedding photographer, I felt a special connection, not because I'm a photographer, but because wedding photographers record stories much as writers do.

Of course, I had to pull out my own wedding photos and live the story over again. There we were, my friends and I, getting ready for our walk down the aisle, pulling out cans of hair spray and fastening each other into our dresses. There's my husband with his brothers, clowning around for the photographer. There he is playing tennis that morning. It's a day that's frozen in time, caught on film forever, the beginning of a story. There we are, my husband and I, smiling as we begin our new adventure together.

Not everyone in those photos is still in my life, of course. Lives change, people move and sometimes we just forget to stay in touch. But during the course of writing this book, an old friend I hadn't seen in a long time, who had been my maid of honour (and I hers), called me out of the blue. It was coincidence, but it made me think about my wedding and the turns our lives had taken since that day (my husband and I happily continue the adventure, but I don't use hair spray any more. He still plays tennis.).

Wedding photos do tell stories, and now and then it's good to look at them and remember how a fairy tale begins. *Once upon a time there was a man and a woman who met, not realising they would get married, but did…*

Or…in the case of Regina and Dell, the hero and heroine of my story: *once upon a time there was a man and a woman who never thought they would stay married…*"

**For Myrna's latest news,
visit www.myrnamackenzie.com**

Regina is the photographer at The Wedding Belles. Here are her tips on how to get picture perfect memories from your big day:

♥ Shop around. Photographs are more than a simple record of an event. Different photographers have different styles, so visit several and examine their work to make sure that your wedding day images will be all you want them to be.

♥ Plan ahead. Photographs are the story of your wedding. Where do you want that story to begin? The shower? The rehearsal dinner? A wedding breakfast? Be clear and make your needs known.

♥ Your photographer will probably have ideas for places to take shots of the wedding party, but consider scouting out areas on your own. Think of places that have special significance to you and your groom, especially places you might want to return to on subsequent anniversaries for an annual photo to chronicle your special relationship.

♥ In this digital age, it's possible to choose only perfect photos, but consider the fact that some of the less-than-perfect moments may be the most precious. So don't discard a photo just because it's not a flawless moment. Look for the real and heartfelt shots, not just the pretty ones. This is the story of your day, and you'll want to cherish every tear and every smile.

♥ Take lots of photos, even more than you think you'll want. If you can't afford all professional shots, enlist friends. There is so much that you, as the bride, will miss, that you'll want tons of pictures to record those special times that may slip your notice. A wedding day is a one-time opportunity, so this is a case of more is better than less.

CHAPTER ONE

I<small>T WAS</small> a hot day in Boston when the curtain finally lifted from Regina Landers O'Ryan's eyes and she realized that she had made the biggest mistake of her life nearly a year ago. Now, because of her mistake, marrying the wrong man—or rather allowing him to marry her—her husband was paying the price. That had become clear this past week.

"Well, no more," she whispered to herself as she watched the clock hands move forward. Dell would be home soon. Normally she wasn't here when he arrived. She usually stayed in the darkroom developing photos for The Wedding Belles, the business where she and her friends worked making wedding dreams for other people come true.

The irony of the situation didn't escape Regina. Her business dealt in the kind of romantic dreams she no longer believed in. Still, *she* wasn't the one at issue.

Dell might still find the woman he would have chosen had he been given a choice. It was long past time to free her husband from his bonds.

Regina sat down to wait.

* * *

The minute Dell walked through the door of the tasteful mansion where he'd lived his whole life, he knew that something was different. And it wasn't the ghosts of old O'Ryan aristocrats that were raising the hair on the back of his neck.

Regina was perched in the hallway on a Victorian settee that had been in his family for generations and was just as uncomfortable as it looked. That in itself set off warning bells. Regina was never waiting for him when he got home. She rose to meet him now.

He looked into her concerned brown eyes. She was holding a sheath of papers.

"What's wrong?" he asked.

"We need to talk." Her soft voice came out unevenly. "We need to talk now," she repeated, clearing her throat and managing to sound firm and determined though she was clearly on edge.

"I see."

She shook her head. "No, you don't, but I do. Finally."

Regina held out her hand and he saw that the top sheet was a page torn out of a local magazine. "Have you seen this?" she asked.

He hadn't. The publication masqueraded as an event guide for the city of Boston, but the real draw was the bits of gossip sprinkled throughout its pages.

Dell lifted a brow. "Not my usual cup of tea."

She blushed slightly, and Dell realized that he'd rarely seen her blush. But then, he didn't really know Regina all that well. Their brief marriage had been entered into hastily for the sake of convenience, and they had spent very little time together. Like his parents had, they occupied this house as virtual strangers. But the delicate pink that tinted Regina's cheeks and dipped into the shadows at the vee of her pale yellow blouse definitely made him aware of her in ways he hadn't been when he'd entered the room. That was a surprise. It was also obviously bad timing.

Regina nodded, and for a moment Dell wondered if she had read his mind. "No, I suppose this wouldn't be the kind of thing a man like you might read," she said, "but I've verified the facts. They're true."

She turned away, her voice muffled, but she held her head high, her straight brown hair brushing her shoulders. Regina was a woman with generous curves, but she seemed thinner than he remembered her being when she'd fallen into his world just over a year ago. Was it any wonder? She'd been through a lot these past few months.

Dell rubbed a hand over his jaw. If Regina had suffered unhappiness, the blame was partly because of events that he had unintentionally set in motion. "You've verified the facts? So, tell me what they are, Regina." His voice came out too rough, and she turned to face him again.

"You were well on your way to marrying Elise Allenby when you—when we—"

"When we wed," he offered.

"Yes, but you did that to help me. You were supposed to marry Elise. Everyone was expecting an engagement announcement from the two of you. I didn't know. If I had, I wouldn't have—at least I *hope* I wouldn't have said yes." Distress filled her voice.

"Don't do that, Regina," he commanded. "You didn't destroy my love life if that's what you're thinking, and Elise and I hadn't even discussed marriage. I'm not a heartbroken man." But she was right in a way. Before the events of the past year had changed everything, he had wondered if he should deepen his relationship with

Elise. It had been a purely practical consideration. Dell had never been a romantic man. His life revolved around the O'Ryan empire, and Elise came from a highly respected family and was an intelligent and beautiful woman. She knew how to conduct herself at events and would have graced his table admirably when he had to entertain. He hadn't done any entertaining since his marriage to Regina.

But that had been his choice and not Regina's fault. He hadn't wanted to make demands given the circumstances. He hadn't felt he'd had the right to demand anything of her.

"Is she a heartbroken woman?" Regina asked, lifting her chin.

He blinked. "I don't know." What he didn't tell her was that Elise had come to his office the day after he'd married Regina in a private ceremony. It was the most emotional he had ever seen Elise. It was, in fact, the only time he'd seen Elise give vent to her emotions. But that had been almost a year ago. Still, it rankled that in trying to keep from hurting one woman he might have inadvertently hurt another.

Dell grimaced. "Why is this rag writing that kind of story now?" he demanded, taking a different tack. "It's old news."

"It's not old news to me. I don't want to think that I might have been the cause of another woman's pain."

"You weren't. It wasn't like that." Dell took a step toward her. "Elise might have thought we would eventually marry—others might have thought that as well—but I never suggested that to her. And if there had been reason…if I had made promises or if she'd been pregnant, I would have done what was right, Regina."

Regina sank back down on the hard mahogany of the settee, her breath *whooshing* out on an audible sigh. "I know you would have. You're…you believe in duty. You rescued me."

But it hadn't helped, Dell realized. Regina was no longer a woman in sudden desperate need, as she had been when they had wed. She had security and work that she enjoyed. But her eyes didn't light up the way they had when she'd shown up on his doorstep with some of his mail that had mistakenly been delivered to her house almost eighteen months ago. Unfortunate things had happened to her since that day, and he had been the unwitting author of some of those things.

"You know I haven't always done the right thing where you're concerned."

Regina's soft brown hair slid against the pale yellow of her blouse as she shook her head. "I haven't always done the right thing where you're concerned, either. Last week—" She frowned and began to pace.

Dell walked toward her, blocking her progress. He tilted his head, trying to see her expression, hidden as she refused to look at him. "What happened last week?" he asked.

Crossing her arms, Regina blew out a deep breath. "I was shooting a wedding when one of the guests, an older woman named Adele Tidings, noticed my name tag. She wanted to know if I was related to you, and once she knew that we were married, she wondered why she hadn't seen me around when she'd been at several functions lately which you had attended, alone. I realized how awful the truth would sound, and I didn't know what to say, so I just…lied. I told her that I'd been horribly ill for a long time."

"Regina, Adele is nice but nosy. She had no business asking you personal questions. Don't worry about it." But Regina shook her head.

"No, you and I both know that I wasn't sick. You helped me out when we wed, but I never even considered accompanying you to any of your social functions, even though I knew they were a part of your business. I didn't hold up my end of the bargain."

"We didn't make a bargain, Regina. We got married for good if unconventional reasons, and this year hasn't been your happiest. You have nothing to apologize for."

But the look in her eyes told him that she wasn't buying his argument.

"You never mentioned anything," she said, "but this article was written because there's a rumor that you've been approached to open a new store in Chicago. I assume it's true that one of your wealthiest customers is petitioning you to expand into her area and that she's started a campaign with her friends to entice you into moving. They're willing to wine you and dine you, to provide you with free advertising and do whatever it takes, but you've resisted even though it's a great opportunity. The city of Chicago would consider it a coup to get you, and the article says that people at the highest levels are wondering why you haven't at least looked into the matter."

Dell blew out a breath. "People often wonder about things that don't concern them."

"They're saying it's because your wife has a business in Boston and you don't want to upset her with a move."

She looked so deliciously miffed that Dell almost wanted to laugh.

"Maybe I should remind them that I have a business

headquartered in Boston and a fine old family home. Perhaps I simply don't want to expand to the Midwest."

She frowned, her nose wrinkling in that cute way it had. "Is that why?"

It wasn't. He loved Chicago and he had been thinking of expanding there for a while, but it would have been unconscionable to desert his new and fragile bride in her hour of need while he left town for the long periods of time that would be necessary to embark on such a venture. The gossips were right, at least partly right. No matter the circumstances, O'Ryans took care of their families and they took care of the family name. Leaving a wife alone so soon after they had wed would have stirred up more gossip than breaking it off with Elise had.

"I'm just pointing out that there's often more than one reason for doing or not doing something," he said, evading the question. "And I don't want you to worry about this. I'll handle it."

Regina stood suddenly and took a step toward him. "When I was ten and you were six, we didn't know each other, but like everyone else in the area, I knew who you were. One day I was walking past this house and your father was explaining to you why an O'Ryan couldn't run around barefoot in the summer the way the rest of us did. You had this longing look in your eyes and, not realizing that we lived in vastly different worlds, I felt sorry for you. I think I just saw a fleeting glimpse of that same look. The gossips are right. You'd like to pursue the Chicago connection, but you feel responsible for me. Well, no more. I don't want to continue our marriage, Dell."

Dell had been opening his mouth to dismiss her arguments, but that last sentence caught him by surprise.

As if someone had unexpectedly punched him square in the chest with a jab that was sharp and surprisingly painful. He blinked. "Excuse me?"

Then her words caught up to him. "Why?" he asked.

A sad smile lifted her lips. Her brown eyes looked equally sad as she held out her hands, then let them fall to her sides. "We married for the wrong reasons, ones that seemed important at the time. Partly it was because you wanted to protect me. And I—" She shook her head. "I was scared and lost and it was too easy to say yes, to want to be protected. I appreciate all you've done for me, all you've given up. You can't know how grateful I am. But I'm not lost anymore, and I'm not the type of woman who was made to be protected. Dell, we don't have a thing in common."

"We have a marriage in common." He didn't know why he was arguing. They *were* completely different kinds of people.

Regina laughed, a soft, pretty sound. "You know that's not enough. You're old money, good family, following the rules, doing what's required, what's right, while I'm a bit of a wild and fluffy mess and always have been."

He opened his mouth. She put up her palm to stop him.

"You don't need to defend me. I spent a lifetime trying to be what my parents expected and then finally realized that I was different. What's more, I'm good at being different, and I like the fact that I've finally accepted my creativity and my tendency to be unpredictable, but I don't fit into your world at all. I may be four years older than you, but you've always been the grown-up while I'll always be…I don't know. Me."

"There's nothing wrong with you."

"You're right. There isn't, but I'm not right for you, and—"

"I'm not right for you," he said, completing her sentence.

Dismay crept into her expression. "I didn't mean it that way. I'm not looking for romance. I don't even want it anymore, so you're not interfering with my love life."

"I'm just interfering with your life?"

"No!" Her voice was a bit too vehement, Dell couldn't help thinking, and he did smile then, even though he didn't feel at all like smiling.

"Liar. Being an O'Ryan probably isn't fun if you're not used to it."

She looked down at the magazine she still held. "People judge you, and I'm not helping your standing."

"Regina, I'm not worried." At least not about that. There had been good reasons why Regina hadn't appeared at his side this year. But theirs had not been an ordinary marriage. It certainly hadn't been what either of them would have chosen. And it hadn't been rewarding.

A pained look came into her eyes. "Every day women come into the shop. They're happy. They're marrying because it's what they want above all else, and that's as it should be, but it's not us. Admit it, Dell. This isn't working out. We're not a real couple. We don't even touch."

She muttered the last part, and Dell's senses began to sizzle. "We could touch," he told her, even though he had touched her only as a friend before their wedding night and never since. She had cried that night—long silent sobs she had tried to hold back. He had stopped. Since then he'd concentrated on just being a provider. He'd been willing to wait and be patient.

"No, we can't," Regina said softly. "It would be a lie. It wouldn't work."

He studied her. She'd obviously thought this through. "How do you know it wouldn't work?" he asked.

She blinked, clearly startled.

"The marriage, I mean," he continued. "Not the touching. How do you know the marriage wouldn't work?"

Regina's gaze met his. "It hasn't," she said softly, and he was pretty sure she was remembering the past months.

So was he, and what he was remembering was that Regina had been happy until she fell into his life and things had gone awry. He'd spent a lifetime learning to be a proper O'Ryan and protecting the O'Ryan reputation from any hint of scandal. But after he had married Regina and scandal had been averted, he had abdicated his responsibility as if his duty had been done. There had been no satisfaction in this marriage and yet…

"We haven't really tried to make our marriage work, have we?" he asked. "You mentioned that Adele wondered why she hadn't seen you around, but very few people have seen us together. Our marriage has been solely on paper, hasn't it?"

"There were reasons for that. You were practically forced to marry me."

Somehow Dell kept from reacting to that. "I *chose* to marry you, Regina." But he knew deep down that he was lying, at least partially. There had been numerous reasons why he had married Regina, but guilt, duty, honor and the need to protect the family name—and her—had been supreme.

But had he really protected her? Had he done anything right where she was concerned?

Maybe. After she had delivered his mail that day, they had become distant friends of a sort. She was nothing like the women he saw socially, nothing like the women he bedded and nothing like the women he considered as the ones who might produce the next O'Ryan heir. But he had liked her. She had been warm and refreshing. They hadn't known each other well, but they might have become friends if he hadn't made a single wrong and hasty decision that had turned the world upside down and had, ultimately, led to them becoming man and wife.

And now here they were, on the verge of another hasty, reckless decision. But he had never been a reckless man. Reckless actions were usually the result of messy emotions and he had spent years learning the ways emotional slips could ruin lives. Haste and recklessness fostered failure, and he didn't like failure.

"I *chose* to marry you," he said again. "But I've been a poor excuse for a husband, Regina. And I think that before we give up on this marriage, we should give ourselves a chance to turn this thing around."

Regina took a deep, audible breath. She paced a few steps, clearly agitated.

He followed her. When she turned suddenly, they were closer than they had been since their disastrous wedding night. Dell breathed in her light honeysuckle scent, and felt a small rush of attraction. Carefully he controlled his reaction.

"You don't love me," she said. "Elise—"

"No," he said. "I don't love you, but I don't love Elise, either. I'm not interested in love and would never have chosen that as a rationale for marrying. You just said that you didn't want love, either, so there are no impediments. I think we should begin again. Why shouldn't we stay married since we're already here?"

"Because now that I've had a chance to think rationally, I realize that I'm not O'Ryan material."

"Too late. You're already an O'Ryan."

"Only because of a few words in a ceremony I don't even remember."

"That counts."

She gave a cute little grimace, and Dell fought some primal male instinct to lean closer.

"Dell, this hasn't been a good year, but I'm—finally— regaining my sense of independence and balance. Help me out here. I'm trying to do the right thing."

He shook his head. "You're trying to do me a favor by setting me free to continue on my previous course, but divorce is the wrong thing if we haven't even tried to succeed. We're married, Regina, even if we didn't get here via the path your clients take. We should at least give ourselves a true trial run and get to know each other before we decide to divorce. There's a chance we might make a success of this situation, after all. We could save ourselves a lot of trouble and the kind of unpleasant publicity that comes to those in the spotlight who marry and then divorce too quickly. Does that make sense?"

She looked a bit unhappy but she nodded. "I guess so. Yes." Why did Dell feel that it was Regina doing him the favor now?

"How long a trial period?" she asked.

He considered. "How about two months? Long enough to get to know each other and become a couple."

"I don't know," she began. "This still seems unfair to you."

But Dell was warming to the idea. O'Ryans never did things impulsively. In fact, marrying Regina had been his only true impulse. His failure there was proof enough that slow and steady was best. For months she had been a silent stranger in his house, and he had accepted that. Now time was healing her, and there was renewed life in her eyes, vibrancy and spunk in her attitude and a woman emerging from the ashes. Yet he barely knew who she was. If they were going to end things, then he darn well wanted to know who he was divorcing. And if they were going to stay married, well…it was time to backtrack and uncover what had been covered. Methodically.

"If you're still worrying because we're not an ordinary couple, don't," he told her. "Not being in love is the best way. Love would only introduce complications and lead to possible rash mistakes. Emotional attachments would make it more difficult to end this later if that's where we finish up."

She had blanched when he had used the words rash mistakes and he cursed himself. She was probably thinking about her own past mistakes. He reached out and tucked a finger beneath her chin to distract her. "Let's give our marriage a fair chance," he urged.

Slowly she nodded, her soft skin sliding against his finger in a way that made him want to curve his palm against her jaw. "If that's what you want," she whispered.

He had no idea what he wanted, but he knew that when he decided, he wanted that decision to be based on logic.

Still, when he looked down at Regina rational thought slipped a bit. She had lifted her chin, and his finger had slid slightly down her throat, over silken skin that was made for a man's caress.

"How about the touching part?" she asked in a choked voice, as if she'd read his mind. His body tightened. But her deep brown eyes were genuinely concerned.

He cleared his throat. "We'll wait on that," he assured her, hoping his voice sounded normal. "At the moment we're just taking some time to make an effort and see if we're going to stay together."

"Or if we're going to part," she added, but he had the feeling that she had already decided that she wanted their marriage to end.

Maybe it would. They might be too different to make things work. But never let it be said that an O'Ryan walked away from a challenge or left a marriage before it was time.

Or left a bride unkissed. The phrase seemed to come out of nowhere. Just as Regina's newfound spirit had. Now that he acknowledged that he was attracted to this reborn Regina with the soft skin and berry lips, he was going to have to stay more in control of himself. This time they would do things right, by the book. Letting his impulses run away from him where his wife was concerned was not a good idea.

Especially since neither of them was certain if they would still be husband and wife by the end of the year.

But a vision of those full lips still lingered after she had gone.

CHAPTER TWO

REGINA was at her desk at The Wedding Belles late the next day pretending to review her week's schedule while she tried not to think about her future or the fact that it would soon be time to go home. The conversation with Dell yesterday had made her jumpy. Tall and dignified with that chestnut hair always in place and those unreadable amber eyes that seemed to measure everything, he was the picture of the elite male. Once again she had felt how ridiculous it was that a man like him should have been forced into marriage with a train wreck of a woman completely unsuited for him.

And that deep aristocratic voice of his always messed with her respiration and reasoning and made her feel as if she were babbling. She hated that. It reminded her too much of how her parents had always admonished her to be more normal and take the time for logic to kick in before she reacted to situations.

"If it were only that easy," she muttered. She wanted to be the type of sophisticated woman who knew how to talk sensibly to a man like Dell without feeling dizzy, but that didn't seem to be possible. Yesterday's meeting with him hadn't turned out at all the way she'd planned.

Suddenly she remembered that moment when he had suggested that they resume their role as man and wife and try touching each other...

Regina jerked at the thought and the pencil she was holding slipped out of her fingers. She lunged for it and knocked a photo album off the desk. It landed with a loud thud.

"Are you all right?" Julie's voice called from the reception area.

Not even close. Two days ago she would have honestly been able to say that she felt fine, but this new situation with Dell made her heart positively race.

"I'm great," Regina called, her voice muffled as she bent to pick up the album.

"Good. Could you come out here?" Julie's slightly tense voice had Regina hurrying past a cabinet filled with frame and matting samples and rushing into the reception area.

Late afternoon sunlight spilled through the tall windows, onto the golden-yellow walls and oak flooring, turning everything bright. It was closing time and most of the customers had gone, so the usual bustle of the shop was missing. Other than that, however, things looked pretty normal. Except for the dozens of containers of yellow daisies just inside the door.

"Where did those come from?" Serena asked, coming out of her own space, carrying a length of satin ribbon from the dress she had been working on. "Callie, did you order daisies for a wedding? I don't have any dresses on my list that would go well with that particular shade."

"Don't look at me. They're not mine," Callie said, her green eyes widening as she came out of the area where she created floral masterpieces and saw the mysterious display. "No orders for daisies lately."

"Nope. They're all for Belle." Natalie slipped some sample pictures of her cakes into her pocket as she bent down to look at the cards.

"You should have seen what it looked like when the delivery guy showed up with his arms full." Julie's reddish-brown curls bounced as she spoke. "I felt guilty sitting at the reception desk, it took him so many trips. Where should we put them?"

"I don't know, but Mr. Right must have been trying to create an impression." Audra gave a low whistle. "I've never heard Belle express a weakness for daisies, but as an accountant, I suppose I should admire the man's thrifty ways."

"So, the date went well, I take it," Regina offered. Belle had been introduced to the man through a mutual friend over the weekend and all of them had been hopeful that she might fall in love again.

"Maybe he *is* her Mr. Right," Callie said. The subject of whether there was a Mr. Right for every woman had come up lately at their weekly poker games. They'd all been friends for a long time, much longer than they'd worked together, and men were often a topic of conversation. And not always a comfortable one, Regina admitted. The friends were divided on their opinions, and some of them, herself included, had engaged in disastrous relationships. Was there a Mr. Right? It was possible. It was also possible that he might live on another planet and never show up, she conceded.

The click of a door sounded just then, and Belle came down from the apartment she kept upstairs, probably drawn by the chatter. The hard-to-ignore daisies and last night's big date in everyone's mind, the women couldn't help but look up. Not that that was unusual. Belle, an ample and gorgeous curvy woman with shining silver beautifully coiffed hair was a presence. She commanded attention without even trying. She was also the most generous, kind person Regina knew. She had inherited this building, she owned the shop and she cared for the Belles as if they were her daughters. They loved her, and it was only natural for them to wonder about the flowers.

"So…he's Mr. Right?" Audra asked, her blond hair sliding across her cheek as she tilted her head.

Belle gave a big sigh. "Hon, I'm afraid I've had my Mr. Right, and when my Matthew died that was it for me. I'm just looking for Mr. Maybe-We-Could-Keep-Each-Other-Company, but not with this man. He seemed nice at first, but then he got too grabby. He almost pulled a button off the sleeve of my best rose silk blouse."

"Well then, he's history," Regina said, giving her friend a hug. Belle loved nice things, especially clothes. "I take it he didn't ask first."

Belle returned the hug, her comforting scent surrounding Regina. "I almost had to damage him for other women," she said. "But I let him off easy by showing him the door and just giving him a quick wallop with my bag."

Julie chuckled. Belle's bag, a work of art, was huge.

"Looks like he's sorry." Natalie gestured toward the flowers. "Or maybe not. Those are some pathetic daisies."

"Sweetie, it doesn't matter." Belle's delicious Southern drawl stretched out the syllables. "That was the last straw. It wasn't even fun and it was downright embarrassing. Imagine a woman of my years having to wrestle with a man! Despite the fact that my friend Rae Anne keeps calling me to encourage me to hop back in the marriage market, I'm through dating, and I'm just going to sit back with those of you who are married or almost married and let the rest of the world look for love."

A chorus of objections echoed through the room. Regina and her friends might each have her own love or lost-love stories, but all of them wanted Belle to find a man who would appreciate her.

"I've got the shop, a good life and all of you girls for family," Belle insisted. "That's all I need. So, stop worrying about me. We've got weddings to plan and you have your own happily-ever-afters." She cast a maternal glance around, letting her gaze rest on each woman. When she came to Regina, Regina wanted to squirm. Everyone had been so worried about her this past year, and these were her best friends in the whole world. They cared about her. But revealing the details of her personal discussions with Dell would feel too much like betrayal of a man who had bent over backward to help her when she had desperately needed help.

"Dell might be opening a store in Chicago," she said instead. What was that surprised look on everyone's faces? "What?" she asked.

Audra shook her head. "Nothing. It's just that you tend not to volunteer information about your husband. Not without a lot of prodding."

"I know. I guess I'm just…" Not myself after the way that conversation went yesterday.

"I'm just excited," she finished, somewhat lamely. "Dell is very good at what he does, and it's—it's nice that his business is going so well."

Heavens, why was she babbling so much? Probably because she had just agreed to try to be something resembling a real wife to Dell, and she didn't have the vaguest idea how to go about that. Trying to transform herself into a genuine wife meant seeing him a lot more than she was used to, being near him all the time and considering the possibility that they might actually touch now and then.

The mere thought of that made her feel much warmer than the day merited. The memory of Dell's finger brushing her chin slid right into her mind. Where was a fan when a girl needed one?

"Regina, you're trembling," Natalie said.

"You must be really excited about Dell's new business venture," Callie added, one eyebrow raised.

"Yes, and Dell must be really excited, too," Serena said.

"What do you mean?" Regina asked, but her friend was staring out the window.

Startled, Regina looked out the window to see Dell, a stern, handsome figure in his black suit, headed toward the shop. Her heart began to trip in a ridiculous fashion.

"I—maybe he has some business with the shop," Regina offered, realizing how ridiculous that sounded. She knew why he was here. Their trial marriage was beginning in earnest.

"Hmm, powerful as he is, you don't exactly think of business when you look at the man," Belle offered.

Definitely not. Even wearing that serious expression, Dell was gorgeous, and several passing women stared at him as if they were about to melt right on the spot.

Regina frowned, even though she couldn't quite figure out why. "Well, yes, Dell is attractive."

Natalie raised an eyebrow. "You say that as if you've never noticed it before."

"Of course I've noticed." Even though that wasn't

strictly true. She had done her best not to notice, probably because their marriage hadn't seemed real.

"I don't think I've ever heard you say anything like that about Dell before," Audra said.

"Well, I should have. He's my husband and he does have a great body. I've thought it." The words came out so stilted and unnatural sounding that Regina half expected the ceiling to crash in on her.

For almost a year she had avoided even thinking of Dell as a husband. When they had wed, she'd been pregnant by his cousin who had deserted her, leaving Dell to save the day. He had, of course. After all, family honor and a baby's future had been at stake. Given the circumstances, it had been easy to think of Dell as a savior rather than a husband. Marriage had simply made them housemates, not more. And after her miscarriage—Regina struggled to breathe—she had ceased to think at all for a long time. But now…

"He's my husband," she said again. *At least for two more months.*

"Yes, we know that, sweetie," Belle said. "Apparently he does, too, since he's here."

Regina took a deep breath and looked down at her feet clad in eye-popping, chili-pepper-red espadrilles. Even after their talk about trying to have a real marriage, she had expected things to simply fall back into their former distant pattern. She would wait out the two months, living mostly in the shop where she felt free to be herself, and Dell would occupy his mansion and downtown office.

Obviously she'd miscalculated. Here he was in all his masculine glory, tall and powerful, the picture of a man of consequence. And here she was, slightly plump, less than willowy, a very ordinary woman who only exuded confidence behind a camera. They were so mismatched. This arrangement could have such dire consequences for her. But she *had* agreed to the plan.

"Regina? You're looking a bit dazed. Are you all right?" Julie asked, moving closer as if to protect her.

Regina nodded. "Oh, yes, I'm great. Just caught a bit off guard."

But there was no more time to prepare herself. Here he was, pushing through the door, causing the little bell to tinkle brightly as if to say, "Dell's here! Every woman in sight, start acting like an utter fool!"

Not me, not me, Regina told herself. She pasted on a smile, remembering their plan.

"Dell! How very nice to see you!" she said a bit too forcefully. Purposely she avoided looking in her friends' direction. She tried not to think about the fact that they would surely wonder why she had gone from a never-comment-on-your-husband woman to an idiotically smiling wife.

A look of mild amusement crossed Dell's face. "How very nice to see you, too," he agreed.

"I—is there something you needed?" she asked. "That is, I—what a surprise to have you show up here!"

Again, that look of barely concealed amusement flashed over his features. "We're married," he reminded her.

Regina looked up into his eyes even though she knew the danger of that. "I know." Actually she felt a bit like a newlywed today, a bride who barely knew her husband.

His gaze met hers, direct and unflinching and intense. "I thought we might go out to dinner together," he said.

His voice dipped low, and despite the fact that she knew that this was just Dell's way of making a concerted effort towards their trial marriage, Regina felt a little queasy at the thought of people watching her with Dell. What if she looked as besotted as every other woman and someone caught that look on film? How utterly embarrassing and humiliating would that be?

She tamped down her reservations and nodded. "Dinner together? That sounds…nice."

He laughed. "You needn't make it sound as if I'm forcing you to watch ten years of home movies."

Regina couldn't help it. She laughed, too. "Dinner *would* be nice," she agreed. It wasn't Dell's fault that he had such presence. "Let me get my purse and camera and we'll go."

As she passed her friends, they gave her questioning looks. Regina knew she'd been acting flustered, but to their credit they didn't appear to have interrogated Dell when she returned and were simply quietly chatting about Chicago. The Belles were protective of each other, but they also respected each other's boundaries. She loved that about them. They obviously realized she didn't want to discuss the details of her marriage.

Which was good, since there wasn't anything to discuss.

Until now.

Trying not to think about that, Regina headed for the door, calling goodbye. Dell slipped around her and held the door. He followed her outside into the fading sunshine, then handed her into a limo that seemed to appear by magic. But then, Dell had always been a man in control of every situation. Unlike herself.

"Thank you for taking me to dinner," she managed

to say. "I have to say, though, that it was unlike you to just show up." Dell was a man who always lived on a schedule.

He nodded. "Yes, but then we're in somewhat un-charted territory right now, aren't we?"

"What do you mean?"

"I've never been a real husband," he said in that deep, low voice that made her think about what real husbands did. *All* the things real husbands did. Like sleeping naked with their wives.

Okay, she was definitely going to have to stop those kinds of thoughts. "Well, I've never been a real wife."

"That's why we're going to talk. We left things rather open-ended last night. We need a plan."

Dell's deep voice rolled over her and Regina's palms began to tingle. She had never been good at plans. That was part of the reason she had done stupid things and Dell had been forced into marriage with her. Dell was very good at plans. He was the one who had proposed that they marry.

Unable to stop herself, Regina folded both palms across her heart, trying to calm herself down.

"Regina?" he asked, his voice filled with concern.

"We'll make a plan," she agreed.

"Good," he said with a smile that did awful, wonder-ful things to her insides. "I'm going to do my best to be the perfect husband."

Oh, no, don't do that, she wanted to say. This is a marriage of convenience. I don't even want to risk feeling more, a move that could be disastrous. But...

"I'll try to be a model wife, too," she said weakly. If only she could figure out how to do that while keeping this marriage risk-free. "Dell?"

"Yes?"

"What exactly *is* a model wife in the O'Ryan world?"

A look of dark amusement filled his eyes and he took her hand, running his thumb over the gold and diamond band that circled her ring finger. "Let's go to dinner," he said.

But he hadn't answered her question, had he? Maybe her answer wasn't important. He probably knew she wasn't capable of being a true O'Ryan. He had wed her out of pity and duty and honor and now he was stuck with her, a poor substitute for Elise Allenby who really would have been a model O'Ryan wife.

A slim and unfamiliar thread of pain ran through Regina followed immediately by a very familiar sense of indignation. She had spent her life trying to please and falling short, and had promised herself never to go that route again. Yet she hadn't said no to this marriage or this plan.

Well, Dell was the one who had opted to extend their wedding. He knew what he had for a wife.

Or did he?

Maybe I can be the perfect O'Ryan bride, Regina thought. But she didn't pursue that thought any further. Some things couldn't bear up under too much scrutiny, could they?

Sometimes a woman just had to fly on faith and hope for a miracle.

CHAPTER THREE

DELL watched Regina pick at her food. Had he been bullying her? Probably. He'd spent a lifetime learning to be an O'Ryan and sometimes it was difficult to remember that he didn't have to be that way with his wife.

His wife. How had that happened?

"Regina, before we begin, I want to say that I'm sorry for everything that's happened."

She stopped toying with her food and looked up, those deep caramel eyes studying him carefully. Regina had the most amazing eyes, clear and utterly transparent. He had startled her and now she was nervous. "I shouldn't have thrown you together with Lee," he clarified, then realized that it was the first time his cousin's name had been mentioned in a long time.

She shook her head. "What happened wasn't your fault."

"And if I insist it was?"

"You don't get to say." Regina speared a piece of asparagus. "What happened with Lee is on my head."

But she was wrong. That day when Regina had shown up with his mail had happened at a time when he was worrying about Lee, because Lee, orphaned young and raised with Dell, had been like a brother, a wild and socially awkward brother who had not been a hit with women. Regina's unexpected appearance and cheerful disposition had seemed like a gift, a woman who could give Lee the confidence he needed to take his place in the O'Ryan empire. So Dell had sacrificed her to his cousin, and everything that had happened afterward was on his conscience.

He opened his mouth to tell her so.

Instantly she leaned closer. "Don't do that O'Ryan thing," she told him.

Dell blinked. "Excuse me?"

Regina placed her palms on the burgundy tablecloth. "Dell, I know how much responsibility you have. The O'Ryan Gemstone Gallery is only one arm of O'Ryan Enterprises and it must take an amazing amount of work to manage something like that. You don't have to take responsibility for my problems, too. What happened to me this year wasn't your doing."

He drew his brows together, preparing to object.

"I need to get past it myself," she continued, not allowing him to cut in.

"All right, we'll drop that subject." Dell blew out a breath and sat back in his chair. Not that he was agreeing with her, but if she needed to claim responsibility, he would allow her to do that. This time.

Silence set in. Regina looked around her, surveying the elegant surroundings, the tapestries on the walls, the string quartet playing softly, the tuxedoed waiters. She fidgeted with her spoon and squirmed on her chair. "This is nice," she said.

Dell noted that she still hadn't eaten much. He smiled. "Not your style?"

"It doesn't have to be my style. It's your style. I don't really have a style, so at least one of us should have one," she said.

Dell couldn't help chuckling at that.

Regina smiled. He realized then that he hadn't seen a genuine smile on her face since their whole fiasco of a marriage had begun. And it had been her sunny disposition that had first told him she would be right for Lee.

Dell brushed that thought aside, but his gaze drifted to her lips nonetheless. She had pretty lips, plump but not overly so. The kind of lips a man would like to feel beneath his own. He could see why Lee had let things get out of hand.

But his staring was making her uncomfortable. A trace of delicious pink climbed up her throat.

"You should smile more," he said, almost without thought.

She gave an almost imperceptible nod. "I'll try to remember that. Smiling at each other should be part of our plan, shouldn't it?"

Oh, yes, the plan.

"I suppose we'd better start brainstorming," he agreed, glad that she had been thinking straight while he had been ogling her mouth. He reached into his jacket pocket and pulled out a small black notebook and a pen.

Her eyes widened.

"What?" he said.

"You're really very good at what you do, aren't you?" she asked. "I mean, of course, you are. You run an empire, you hire and fire people, you date fabulous women and command the attention of important people. Politicians and lawyers and media types and such."

"All that because I took out a pen and paper?"

"No. It was more the way you did it. You're going to make a plan and we're going to carry it out and you have no doubt that everything will go according to that plan. It comes naturally. You're an O'Ryan, and controlling the universe is in your genes." She said that as if it were a new discovery she had just made after having been married to him for many months.

"You seem concerned. Am I pushing you?"

She studied him for a minute, then slowly shook her head. "No, it's more a matter of you being so sure that things will turn out a certain way and me being nervous that I'll mess it up. I tend to just let loose and do things and sometimes that doesn't work so well. Although—" she lifted one shoulder in a shrug "—I'm not sure even I could mess up your game plan once you've set the course."

Ouch. He had worked hard at learning to be organized and in charge. Barreling through with a logical plan had helped his parents' disaster of a marriage survive, it had enabled him to overcome an early heartbreak and had kept him ahead of his competition in business, but he supposed that to someone like Regina he might appear overbearing.

"You're frowning. I'm sorry. I shouldn't have said…whatever I said." Regina's voice was soft.

He held up one hand. "You should say what you think. That's part of being married."

"How do you know?"

He smiled and shrugged. "I'm guessing."

She returned his smile. "Well, you probably *are* right about us needing a blueprint. And…everything."

He raised a brow.

"Okay, almost everything. I'm sure you're not perfect."

Dell's smile grew.

"Well, you must have *some* flaws," she reasoned. "Doesn't everyone?"

She looked so deliciously flustered at her frank words that he couldn't help chuckling.

"*You* are amazing," he said.

Pale pink tinged her cheeks again. Why had he never noticed that she was a blusher before yesterday? There was something wickedly delicious and erotic about a woman who blushed. "Amazing? Maybe your judgment isn't as good as I thought," she said, still visibly flustered. "Take your pen. Let's get to work. How do we go about trying to get started on our marriage plans? What should we do?"

Kiss was the first thought that came into his mind, but he quickly squelched it. This had been a difficult year for Regina, including an unexpected pregnancy, the betrayal of a man she had trusted, a hasty wedding and a devastating miscarriage. The two of them had started married life in a rush. He knew the mailman and the valet at the parking garage better than he knew her. When they finally touched, if they ever touched, he wanted her to know who she was kissing. Trust had to be established, and given her past, that would be impossible if he pushed her too fast. They needed time and more.

"I'd like to visit you at work again," he said, scribbling that down.

She looked startled. "Why?"

Because she had friends there who cared about her and would protect her even if he did something foolish. "I've never seen you at work," he said, and that was the truth as well.

"I've never seen you at work, either."

Dell thought of his office. Sophisticated, expensive,

oppressively dull. He loved his work, but the offices were the same as they had been in his father's time and his grandfather's before that. They reeked of the O'Ryan legacy and would be considered stuffy by modern standards. Regina was the epitome of modern with her cute little shockingly gaudy shoes, her digital cameras and her creative spirit.

"You might find it boring," he said, surprised that it mattered to him what she thought. He'd never cared for people's opinions before.

She crossed her arms, obviously trying to look firm. Instead she looked like an adorable kitten trying to wield control. "Fair is fair," she said. "If you visit the Belles, I should visit O'Ryan Enterprises."

"You're right," he conceded.

"What else should we do? I suspect that being a normal, married couple in my world and yours is a bit different. What do normal, married people do in your world?"

They sleep together, he thought. *They make love.* The thought brought instant heat to his body, and he forced himself to push it aside. "I think we should make our own rules. We've both agreed that we don't have a conventional marriage and what we're each looking for is…a partner?" he said.

She nodded. "A companion?"

"Of sorts."

"And you would expect…what?" She looked a bit nervous. His heart ached. Dell was willing to wager that when she had delivered his mail that day she would have never guessed that she would end up here today, in this way, with him, a man she would not have chosen to spend her life with.

"Relax, Regina," he said, reaching over and covering

her hand with his own. "I won't make you meet the queen."

Her eyes widened momentarily and then she laughed. "Good. I won't ask you to come with me to the seamier places I sometimes travel to when taking photos."

Dell let that sink in. Interesting and alarming. Had has wife been spending time in dark alleys and he didn't know about it? Was she safe? And could they bridge their gaps and make this marriage work?

He hoped so. It had been difficult enough dodging bad publicity when they had gotten married. Divorcing so soon afterward would only make the gossips and the media gather. They would dig deeper. The O'Ryan name would be smudged and Regina would be gossiped about. Her experience with Lee would no doubt be discovered and made public. Some might accuse her of being a gold digger, and that kind of thing couldn't help The Wedding Belles, the business that was Regina's life. So, if they could avoid divorce they should.

"All right," he said, just as if she hadn't mentioned the words seamier places. "Now that we've set a course, I'll want to meet the people you spend your time with." *And I'll want to make sure you're safe,* he thought.

"Dell, the shop isn't exactly a male kind of place. Are you sure?"

He smiled. "I'll be brave, and I'll stay out of your way. Let's just call this a beginning. Now about those seamy places…"

Frowning, Regina looked up at him. "I don't go there to embarrass you."

"I didn't say that."

"And I don't end up there often, but…"

He waited.

"In my spare time, I freelance, and I'm doing a pictorial on Boston. I cover a lot of territory and a variety of settings. Businesses, bridges, landmarks, artists, executives, homemakers, museum curators, hot dog vendors, homeless people and yes, sometimes prostitutes or addicts. I interview them. I listen to their stories. They let me take their pictures. It's my work," she explained solemnly. "It matters to me."

"Understood," he said. "But it's your safety I'm concerned about. I can hire people."

She considered that. "I don't think I'd feel comfortable with that, but I'll be careful. I always am, and since night photography isn't my specialty, I'm out in daylight, usually on Sundays. The risk is slight."

Their gazes met, held. Dell couldn't help thinking that their ideas of what constituted a risk might be different...

But she was already uncomfortable now, practically squirming from all his questions. He would file the subject away for later.

For now, he made a few more suggestions about things they could do and gatherings they might attend together. He'd make sure there was good publicity surrounding these events. Then, if things fell apart and she still wanted out once these two months were up, at least the world would know her as a real and valuable person, not just as the whirlwind wife of Dell O'Ryan.

"Dell?" Regina suddenly said.

He looked at her. She was clenching her water glass.

"I'm sorry. Have I overdone things? Is there anything we should change or omit?" he asked.

She sat up taller and took a visible breath. "I just want you to know that I'm going to do my best and give this a solid effort, no-holds-barred. In the end…we'll at least be friends, won't we?"

Their eyes met. "I hope we will if it comes to that." Maybe it would. No doubt this marriage had been far less than the salvation he had planned. She had obviously once wanted something with Lee that she had lost, and marriage with Dell O'Ryan hadn't been it. "You're sure you're all right with this plan?" he prodded gently again.

Regina looked slightly shaken but she nodded, her silky hair sliding against her shoulders. "Absolutely."

"All right then. We're on," he agreed.

"What do we do now?" Regina asked, looking around the rapidly emptying restaurant.

"We go home," Dell said simply, but as he stood to pull out her chair he realized that there was nothing simple about it. Beginning tonight they were moving down a new path, one that would lead them into the spotlight they had avoided thus far. As a prominent Bostonian he was used to having private moments showing up in the newspapers. Now that he and Regina would be spending time together, they would be on display. It wasn't the first time. When they had first gotten married, there had been photographers hovering, but after the two of them had failed to make public appearances together, the interest in them had tapered off. It would resurface, and there would be questions about why they were a couple again. The fact that Regina had suffered a miscarriage might come up.

Dell tried to block the automatic ache that assaulted him at that memory, but it was difficult. He concentrated on the fact that he would do what was necessary to protect Regina and to distract reporters from that topic.

That meant giving them something else to concentrate on. And now was the time to begin setting the stage with the media should there be any gossip miners around.

"I should—" *Put my arm around you,* he thought, but given their circumstances and the newness of all this, that seemed intrusive. Instead he reached down, his fingertips sliding against her palm as he folded his hand around hers.

She was warm, smooth, soft. His skin tingled. All he was doing was holding her hand, yet it felt like an intimate caress.

Regina looked down to where their hands were linked. "Of course," she said. "A married couple would do this. We'll go home." Where they would not be on display.

Where they could be private, Dell thought, then immediately pushed the vision of Regina in his arms away. She had just asked him for a divorce yesterday. She had agreed to a plan to get to know each other and nothing more. This marriage wasn't real yet, not in the true sense of the word.

And it might never be.

For the first time in a long while, Regina dreaded seeing her friends. The Belles loved her and knew her so well that they were practically mind readers. And the truth was that when she and Dell had arrived home last night, she had been painfully aware of him as a man in a way she hadn't been before.

That was risky. She'd been hurt by men who wanted to be friends but not more. And then there had been Lee who had left her pregnant and—given the fact that she'd funneled most of her money into The Wedding Belles business—with almost zero funds to raise a child. The whole scenario had been utterly demeaning and frightening.

"Now, I'm…"

Better, she wanted to say, but the truth was that she was a mess, she admitted, struggling into her jeans and slipping on a pair of electric-blue clogs with silver lightning bolts on the sides. This business with Dell was making her feel weird and uncomfortable. Even physically they were night and day, him being the tall, gorgeous, lean one and her being the ten extra pounds one. Moreover, she was socially not of his class, and their basic life philosophies would appear in two different volumes if there were encyclopedias that tracked such things.

The fact that they were now trying to think of each other as an actual husband and wife was making her crazy. He had held her hand, and her body had tightened in response. They had entered the house together, and all she could think of was what he must have done with other women in bed.

And then she had realized that he had probably been forced to give up sleeping with other women this past year and she hadn't been sleeping with him, either. It had been impossible not to wonder if he was feeling sexually frustrated or if she even made him think of desire.

"Agh!" she yelped, pulling on a powder-blue bell-sleeved blouse. "Don't even think such things."

Instead she should think about today and plan ahead the way Dell would.

"Okay, then," she said to herself. "When Dell shows up at the shop, the Belles are going to notice a change in the way we're interacting."

That was bad. She had been distraught for so long,

especially after she'd lost her child. Now that she was coming back to life her friends might think that she would do something foolish, like fall in love with another man who really didn't want her in the ways that counted. So if Dell brushed against her or took her hand and she trembled, they would definitely notice. That was how well they knew her.

Regina groaned. Her plan crumbled. She had agreed to give them a try, but she didn't think this new, shaky marriage could hold up under too much scrutiny, especially not the scrutiny of the people who loved and knew her best. Dell had saved her when she'd needed saving. He wanted a real marriage. She couldn't betray him by telling her friends the truth but she couldn't lie to her friends, either.

What if they asked him what was going on?

He's an honorable man. He'll tell the truth, she thought. He might even mention how practical they were being by pursuing a marriage devoid of love.

Then her friends would hate him. And if her friends hated Dell...

"Things will be beyond uncomfortable," she muttered. "Even a good marriage would suffer under those circumstances."

There was only one option. Keep Dell and her friends apart as much as possible until the marriage was either seriously settled or dissolved. But for today...

CHAPTER FOUR

"JUST so you know, Dell's stopping by today," Regina told her friends fifteen minutes before the shop was due to open.

Her friends all turned to look at her. "Wow, twice in two days after never having been here before. Anything you want to tell us about?" Julie asked.

Regina struggled for words.

"I mean, besides butt out of my marriage?" Callie asked.

That brought a round of laughter and helped Regina relax a little. "I know you're just curious because you care about me, but he's a good man," she said simply.

"All right, I understand," Audra said, which was saying a lot. After having been left at the altar, Audra had issues. "I do know there are some worthy males out there. Look at Julie's Matt or Callie's Jared or Serena's Mr. Perfect."

Julie smiled. The love she and her fiancé shared made her glow. Serena didn't glance up from the adjustments she was making to the dress on the mannequin, but lately Serena had been rather quiet about her own blossoming love life. Regina could identify. Some things were meant to be hugged to yourself.

But Callie openly grinned. She was well on the way to marrying Mr. Perfect and it was no secret. "All right, sweetie. You can't blame us for being curious about Dell's suddenly sociable ways, but it's your marriage. We'll back off. And actually, just having him here is a bit of a coup. He might be a draw to business and might create even more of a sensation than the Vandivers." The Vandivers were the Belles' big chance, a celebrity wedding, the biggest they had ever planned.

"At least he won't be as difficult as the Vandivers," Julie said. "Dell's always polite. Not like Liz Vandiver. What a temperamental bride."

"Yes, she's changed her mind four times about what kind of cake she wants," Natalie said.

"Five times on the flowers," Callie offered.

"But at least we've got the account," Serena added, and everyone agreed. The Vandivers were spending a lot of money and the very fact that the Belles had scored them as clients was attracting more business.

"Enough about the Vandivers," Regina said. "Their wedding may involve the most money but it's not the only one in town."

"Well, that's a relief, because we'd be out of business if they were," Julie remarked, earning a laugh. "But the Vandiver affair *will* be the most special one we'll arrange this year."

The rest of the Belles exchanged looks. "It's going to be impressive," Regina agreed, but Julie was going to have the most special wedding of the year. She just didn't know it yet. She and Matt couldn't afford all the trimmings for a wedding, so the rest of the Belles had decided to surprise her and give her a fairy tale send-off.

Regina tried not to remember how rushed and emotionless her own brief civil ceremony had been. At least her friends would have fairy-tale weddings. Callie, Julie and soon, hopefully, Serena.

Regina would never live the fairy tale. She didn't want to anymore. In fact, what she wanted...well, she didn't really know what she wanted. It wasn't her husband. It couldn't be her husband. Falling for a man like Dell when their marriage was only one of convenience would surely go down as the most foolish thing she could possibly do.

Still...he would be here any minute. Why was she so nervous when she hadn't been nervous around him mere days ago?

Probably because then Dell had only been part of the backdrop of her life. Now, she couldn't help thinking of him on more intimate terms and she had promised to show him her studio, a room that was very small and cozy.

Regina nearly groaned, but that would have attracted attention. Instead she went to her studio to try to create some more space.

"All right, tell me what's wrong, Regina."

Regina paused in her explanation of the difference between photographing wedding parties and other subjects and glanced up into Dell's eyes. Bad mistake. He had moved closer while she wasn't looking. She had to tip her head up. His lips would be within reach if she rose on her toes just slightly. The very thought made her feel warm and vulnerable.

"Why do you say that?" she asked.

He smiled. "Other than the fact that you're engaging in what I can only politely describe as speed-talking and the fact that you keep looking at me as if I intended to pounce on you?"

She grimaced. "Was I really doing that?"

"Am I making you uncomfortable? Should I leave?"

"No. No, it's not you. It's just…"

He waited.

"It's just, well I *do* feel self-conscious. This can't really be interesting to you."

Dell's amber eyes narrowed. "I thought we agreed to get to know more about each other. Your work is a big part of your life, isn't it?"

Regina looked around the room that had been her salvation many times in the past year. "I pour myself into it," she admitted. "Sometimes I probably get carried away."

"Then if I'm going to know you, I need to know… this." He held out one hand.

She understood. He had a list and a method. Making their marriage work was a business of sorts. Somehow that made her feel more comfortable, even though she knew it would distress her friends.

Just business, she thought. It's a simple plan. We get to know each other, we start to be seen together. We become a couple and make this marriage work. It made sense.

And yet when she looked up into his eyes to smile her agreement, she realized again just how close she was standing to him. His height, the breadth of his shoulders…her body felt too aware and sensitive.

She spun away. "All right, well, here we have some backdrops and I keep a few props for the brides. Sometimes I borrow things from the other Belles. Flowers or maybe a veil. Lighting is always important, and obviously the cameras and the computer are key. I still do some old-fashioned shots and use a darkroom but most of my work is digital these days. It's just more versatile and I don't have to worry about losing any shots, something that's very important for a wedding. Brides get very upset when there are gaps, but with digital cameras I can take pictures of everything, more than will ever be needed. I can take risky shots and cover the entire day. Sometimes I'm asked to be there for every aspect of the wedding, including the fittings, the bachelorette party, the shower, the rehearsal—"

"You didn't have any of that, did you? None of the things a bride should expect."

His voice broke in and cut her off. Regina glanced up from the piece of pink tulle she had draped across a backdrop and was fidgeting with. Dell looked concerned. He was studying her too closely. "That's what you wanted with Lee," he said quietly, "and it's what you should have had."

Okay, yes, she should have, but she was happy to be done with wanting the unattainable, and besides, Dell wasn't responsible. He might have introduced her to his cousin, but he was not the man who had deserted her. He was the man who had stayed, despite having no affection for her at all. He was also the man with a sense of duty so strong that he was here now making an effort.

She could do no less in return. So, ignoring the fears and warnings coursing through her, she smiled. "I got a lot more than I ever expected, Dell. I mean, have you seen your house?" she said, trying for a light tone. "It's absolutely gorgeous. I certainly never expected to live in a mansion like that."

He smiled a bit, but she could tell that he wasn't convinced or playing along. And her reference to the difference in their stations had obviously sent his thoughts elsewhere.

"I never even asked if I could help you with your

business," he mused. "I have plenty of money. You should have the best equipment, the newest cameras." He looked toward the area where she kept her cameras.

Any shyness or discomfort fled. Regina walked up to her husband. She tilted her head and gave him a stern smile. "No insulting my cameras. This ancient Nikon is war weary, but it was my first love. This Canon is beat up from use, but it signaled my first sale. They're special. They're almost like people to me."

He raised one wicked brow, and Regina melted. She remembered why women fell all over him. "People?" he asked.

"Good friends," she said, remaining firm. "Sacred stuff."

"Interesting." He stared at her, and Regina felt a low hum begin to run through her. The small room felt cramped. Dell seemed to fill the space. She had a terrible urge to step closer to him. This had to stop. Now.

"But if you really want to know what being a photographer is about," she rushed on, her words tripping out breathlessly. "I'll have to take you out in the field." Where there's open space and room to breathe, where she could not think about the power of the man she was married to.

"Out in the field?"

"You don't have to go," she said, wondering if she sounded hopeful. A woman could only take so much proximity to this man in one day.

"I don't want to make you change your plans."

But he already had. Her original plan had been to end their relationship and go back to her poor but comfortable existence where there were no devastating men making her feel flustered. Still, the kind of marriage

Dell wanted could be a kind of protection. Once she got past the achingly obvious virility of the man and got used to it, they could, hopefully, become friends.

A new friend might be nice. A male friend, that was. Love would never be an issue or a threat in her life again. Being married to Dell would protect her from all that. And, in that moment, Regina finally fell into the plan. She and Dell *could* make this work. They could really have a marriage without love but with companionship. That could be a very good thing, couldn't it?

She grinned at her husband. "I know how you love plans, but they don't always work. Today, for instance. No matter what you say, this can't be interesting to you. I can putter around here all day, but that's because I'm not seeing a vase of roses or a brass bowl." She motioned to two props on a table.

"What are you seeing?" He looked at the roses and the bowl and seemed genuinely interested.

She tilted her head. "I'm seeing a young bride throwing the petals in the air so that they flutter around her, brush her eyelids and rain on her shoulders as she smiles up at the man she's going to marry. I see a woman holding up the brass bowl like a genie's lantern, her heart full of wishes."

"I see."

His words seemed a bit cool, and Regina glanced at him, startled out of her reverie. "What?"

"Those are a girl's romantic dreams. The kind you gave up."

She felt her face growing warm and felt embarrassed. "No, they're not," she said, staring directly into his eyes. "They're stories, the kind a photographer weaves with her subjects. I happen to write love stories. That doesn't mean I'm interested in a love story of my own any more than a mystery writer is looking for the opportunity to go out and commit crimes. It just means I'm good at my work. And I am," she said, tilting her chin high.

He stared at her solemnly, and then he smiled. "I believe you. And I think I do see…a little," he said, staring at the roses. But now, with her admission and his, the room really did seem too intimate.

"Anyway, I do have to get out into the field," she said. "I need to scout out some new locations for group photos." And if we leave, we can go somewhere public, she thought. Not a place infused with all the signs of love and marriage. It was probably the atmosphere of the shop that was making her look at Dell as some sort of a romantic figure. "But I don't want to push you," she added.

Dell grinned, those amber eyes lighting up. "Now there's something few people attempt with someone like me. So…go ahead. Push me," he ordered.

She blinked. And then she grinned. "All right."

Quickly she turned to go with Dell right behind her, but just before they opened the door, she thought of something and turned again. "Dell?"

He looked down at her, his face only inches from hers. "What?"

She swallowed. "My friends…I haven't told them about our trial marriage. I don't want them to know. There's pressure enough without everyone waiting to see what happens and…"

His jaw tightened. His look was grim. "You think it won't work?"

"No, it's not that." But, it was, partly. "The thing is that we've given ourselves a trial of two months. If our marriage doesn't work after that, I don't want anyone to blame you."

An incredulous look came over his face. "Are you telling me that you're protecting me from your friends?"

Regina didn't answer at first. The utter ridiculousness of the situation hit her. Dell was probably invulnerable to anything her friends might say, but that wasn't the point.

"This place," she said, indicating the building, "reeks of romance. We see it every day. I just don't want anyone to expect that with us. My friends worry, and if they see us together all the time and know what we've planned, they might think that I'll end up in the same situation I was in before, falling for a man who doesn't love me. I'm trying to prevent that from happening."

"All right," he said, and she could almost see the wheels turning in his head.

She thought back over her words and moaned. "I meant that I'm trying to prevent them from thinking I might be in danger. I'm not trying to prevent myself from falling in love with you."

For a second she thought he looked amused. She knew she was blushing.

"Because there's absolutely no danger of that ever happening," she continued, babbling on. "I've explained that before and I just don't want them to look at you with expectations. Our marriage is…private, don't you think?"

For a second the look he gave her was searing hot. She remembered how he had come to her on their wedding night. She swallowed.

"Absolutely. Private. What happens in our marriage stays in our marriage," he promised. "And, Regina?"

"Yes?" Her voice felt weak and too soft.

"Thank you for worrying even if it was completely

unnecessary. I'm glad that your friends care about you
and that they've been there for you this year when I
haven't been. But I'm here now."

Somehow she managed to nod.

"Now," he continued. "Where are you taking me?"

"Oh, no," she said. "You'll just write it down in your
plan book, and this is a surprise. No plans. We're going
to wander."

"You can do that? During the workday? Just wander
off and not know where you're going?"

She wrinkled her nose at him. "Some days I can.
Scouting locations is an important part of my job, and
I won't be gone all day. I have an afternoon appointment. It's one I can't miss because we really can't afford
to lose the account. Especially with so much on our
plates these days." The shop had finally turned a corner
after three years and was doing well, but the added
expense of Julie's wedding was going to cost the Belles
some of their not yet comfortable cushion.

"What do you mean? What's on your plate?"

Regina recognized the calculating look in her
husband's eyes, and remembering his comment about
giving her the best cameras, she realized that she had
made a tactical error in hinting at the shop's financial
obligations.

"Never mind," she told him.

"Never mind what?"

"You don't get to dress up as the rescue squad for me.
You've already done your part. Marrying me was enough."

Dell frowned.

"And anyway," she told him. "Everything is just
great. We've got plenty of business and we've recently
snagged a very big client in Liz Vandiver."

"Liz Vandiver? Daughter of Ephraim Vandiver, one of the biggest, most temperamental asses in the corporate world?"

"Yes. Don't worry. Everything's fine. The Belles and I just have to provide them with a totally scrumptious wedding, something unique and elegant, and our reputation will be made. Pulling off this wedding will be a coup that will attract other lavish wedding parties."

A frown marred Dell's gorgeous forehead. "Be careful, though, all right? Ephraim's a jerk, a powerful jerk."

Regina turned to Dell right in front of his car. "There you go again. Trying to protect me from life. You can't do it, you know. Life just keeps doing what it's going to do. Besides, the Vandiver wedding is my problem, not yours. By the time it takes place, two months will have gone. If this doesn't work, you and I might already be..."

He placed two fingers across her lips, stopping her. "Shh," he said. "I'll bet the D word is never used in a place like this," he said. "There might be customers nearby."

"Then I guess you're turning out to be pretty useful as a husband," she whispered against his fingertips. "How did you know we didn't use that word?"

"I read it in an article a local paper did on the shop."

She groaned. "Not the one where they ran a picture of me looking like a wild woman with my hair all out of place? I'd been down on my hands and knees arranging a bride's dress when they came in."

"You looked artistic," he said.

"Oh, you *are* learning to be good at this husband stuff," she said. "Because I know that you're the only person who would have looked at that picture and called me artistic. Even the other Belles called me maniacal."

Her words made him smile and she couldn't help

smiling back in return. The movement made her mouth slide against his fingertips, creating a deliciously erotic sensation.

Regina fought not to let him see her reaction. She pulled back. "We'd better go. I have a lot planned for us today."

"Then let's go, my maniacal, artistic wife. Your wish is mine to obey."

But Regina didn't even want to think about wishes, because for a moment there she had wished that Dell would kiss her. What a crazy thought. Because this trial marriage was all about being practical and friendly. Kisses weren't part of the plan.

At least not yet.

CHAPTER FIVE

FOLLOWING Regina rather than leading left Dell out of his element, but that couldn't matter. In the short time he had spent with his wife at the shop he had learned a lot about her. Even nervous and uncomfortable, her enthusiasm for her subjects had come through. And her photos, ranging from classic black and white studies to a playful picture of a bride crushing her new husband to her by pulling on his lapels, were works of art.

Amazingly enough, he'd seen little of his wife's work during this past year. She had none hanging at home. No doubt she considered the mansion too austere. The only photos were somber portraits of dead O'Ryans. At least he assumed that was her reasoning. He didn't actually know how she felt about much, not even about her miscarriage.

Dell pushed away his black thoughts and turned them to the future. Two months wasn't a long time to get to know a stranger and to try to craft a working relationship from air. If they didn't suit...failure was a possibility. He frowned.

"Are you okay? This is probably boring you," Regina said, flinging out an arm. "But, of course you've been here already, haven't you? You're the quintessential Bostonian."

Dell shook his head, stopping her. "I'm sure I haven't seen things in quite the way you have," Dell said, looking at the sculptures placed outside the Quinn cafeteria at the University of Massachusetts. The large pots and kettles looked like comic figures in a play.

"I love using sculpture as a backdrop for wedding parties. Here you have these sculpted figures with their slightly open lids, facing each other as if they're squabbling, and interspersed between them I get to place all these fabulously dressed and starry-eyed members of the wedding party who are so obviously bent on the harmony of beginning a new life together. Great contrast, and I think it might actually work, even though you can't hear the recording that accompanies the sculpture."

"Might be quirky," he agreed. "It might appeal to those looking for something different."

"I love different," she agreed, her eyes lighting up, and Dell just had to laugh. What would his parents have said if they'd been alive the day he brought her home? No need to wonder. They would have had plenty of criticism for anyone stepping outside the bounds of the conventional. They'd even be appalled at the way Regina eschewed traditional fashion.

She was practically dancing on her toes as she darted around looking at the sculpture from all angles. She was like tempting sunbeams, peeking out from the shadows of the sculpture and urging a man to see what lay underneath. The sun suddenly felt much more intense than it had only moments ago.

"Dell? Is something wrong? You're staring at me."

He'd never met anyone like her. The woman was practically electric. If he touched her…

Dell cleared his throat. "So you're a sculpture aficionado?" he said.

His mundane question must have reassured her. She took a shot of the kettle. "Oh, yes. It's big, it's bold, it makes a statement. What's not to like?" she said with a laugh. "But don't let me drag you around. You're free to go, you know."

"Trying to get rid of me, Regina?"

She blushed. In fact, Dell thought, he might have said it just because he had known she would blush and he was fascinated by the way it transformed her face into something out of the ordinary.

"No, but are you sure you want to be here? You're not just humoring me?"

"My choice," he insisted.

"No Chicago meetings?"

"Later."

"No major social events?"

"Not today, although there are some things coming up." He studied her. "In fact, I'd like it if you would accompany me."

"Oh boy, you don't really want me to put in an appearance at one of your social functions?" She sounded a bit breathless. Dell watched her with interest.

"I do. Will that be a problem?"

She considered it, practically wincing. "I'm not sure I would show well with the kind of people you're used to socializing with. I'm not exactly…"

He took her hand. "You're my wife, Regina O'Ryan, and you show quite well from my viewpoint." Too well. He was having to force himself to keep his hands off her, even though he knew that wasn't at all what she had meant.

"But…"

"Shh," he said, stopping her for the second time that day. "Don't criticize my wife. It's not allowed. She's rumored to have some very good friends who wouldn't like it, and neither would I," he teased.

She opened her mouth, then closed it again. "I don't think you were quite this bossy when you were young. At least you didn't seem like it from what I could tell the few times I saw you."

"You're right," he said. "I wasn't like this. I changed."

"What changed you?"

"My family. There were expectations. The O'Ryan heir must take charge. He has to be bold and forceful," he said.

"Well, you are," she said quietly.

"Yes, I am, I think. But, as I said, I don't want to push *you* around."

She shook her head. "You're not. We both agreed to try this and I knew that would mean occasionally being out of my element. So, yes, I can do wifely, I suppose. Just don't expect elegance. I wasn't bred to it."

"I'm not worried," he said, but he could see that *she* was.

As they continued on their tour of local sculpture, she barely spoke. Standing on the arched blue metal waves of the sculpted walkway at Constitution Beach, Dell watched her. He had said he wanted this marriage to work, but…what if it didn't? As a businessman, he'd learned to be prepared for all possibilities. Taking Regina into his world would be a good move on both counts. If their marriage worked, she would already have been introduced to his world, and if she still wanted

a divorce when the two months were up—he frowned—
well, knowing influential people would be good for her,
business-wise. Their patronage would help set her
business on solid ground.

"There's a charity ball in two weeks," he said.
"Would you go with me?"

"A ball?" She croaked out the words.

He chuckled. "Yes, you know the kind where you
dress up and there's lots of dancing and conversation?
They're considered pleasurable by some people."

But not by her, he could tell. Panic was written in her
eyes.

"Not a problem," she told him. "I'll be there."

"Spoken like a woman scheduled for a chat with the
Spanish Inquisition," he said lightly and with a smile.
"Don't worry. I'll stay right by your side."

But if anything, that only made her look more
panicked. Dell had to face facts. There was something
about him that made his wife uncomfortable. What was
he going to do about that?

Regina stared at the dress lying on the bed. It had been
two weeks since Dell had told her that he'd like her to
attend the ball with him. The good part was that he had
spent a lot of time in Chicago scouting out locations for
his new store so that she didn't have to worry about him
noticing that she found him attractive. The bad news was
that because he had been away she hadn't been able to
chicken out. It hardly seemed fair to leave him in the
lurch after she had already agreed to go.

Besides, she wasn't backing out now. During the
time they had been married Dell had asked nothing of
her. That article about Dell and Elise had only dredged

up the things that people must have been saying about
him all year long, the things that Regina had, in her confusion and grief after losing her baby, been unaware of.
Dell had no doubt appeared at numerous social functions this past year. It was part of his job and his
heritage. People must have wondered what kind of wife
he had married. They might even have questioned him
as to why she was never at his side.

That must have bothered him. When he had talked
about the O'Ryan expectations yesterday, she was sure
he was merely scraping the surface. He was a prominent figure. As a married man his wife should have
been with him.

Regina let out a long, deep sigh. "I'll be there
tonight," she said. But she wasn't sure her being there
wouldn't be worse than her not being there.

When she'd told her friends that, Audra had scowled.
"That just doesn't make sense. You know how to talk to
people. You do it every day in the shop. You deal with
customers who have money."

"Yes, but that's just it. They're customers. I'm providing a service. These people tonight will expect an equal.
I don't want them to think less of Dell for marrying—"

"If you say a nobody, I'm going to have to shake you,
hon," Belle had said. "There's nothing at all wrong with
you. I'm sure Dell doesn't think you're deficient, either."

Thinking about that conversation now, Regina sat
down on the bed and pulled on stockings. She reached
for the dress. *Dell thinks I'm a responsibility.* He had
matched her up with his cousin, thinking he was helping
the two of them. Then, when things hadn't worked out,
he had become her rescuer. Now she had the feeling that
she had become his obligation, his next O'Ryan project.

He had married her and, darn it, he was going to make a go of the marriage, no matter what. Defeat was not an option for an O'Ryan.

And she, fool that she was, had agreed to go along with the whole thing. Two months, he'd said, and most of that time was still ahead. They were supposed to be getting to know each other, but…

"I'm afraid," she finally admitted out loud. Dell didn't want love, *she* didn't want love, but Dell was a very potent man. He was hard to ignore. Despite her goal of a friendly arrangement, his presence made her think ridiculous, giddy thoughts. Lately she'd awakened from dreams of wedding nights…and heat, satin sheets, a man's strong, naked chest, things that went on in the dark between a man and a woman and…

"Agh! Stop it," she ordered herself. This trial marriage was purely practical and quite possibly temporary, and sleeping with a man who might be gone in two months would only complicate matters in dangerous, emotional ways. Hadn't she learned her lesson?

Yes. And what she knew was that she had better stop letting her thoughts fly off to fantasyland and start being the kind of logical, exemplary, helpful wife a man like Dell had a right to expect. Right now.

She took a deep breath and concentrated, but what she heard was her parents' voices. Try to be the right kind of wife tonight, Regina. Try to change who you are, try to be more like our friends' children, try to pretend you're not different. Try to finally make us proud and be a credit.

But later when she looked in the mirror, she didn't feel like a credit. The dress, an ivory strapless affair, looked elegant enough on its own. But her too ample curves at the bust and hip turned elegance into something more earthy, possibly even crude. She just hoped she didn't jiggle out of the top of the dress.

Or drop food on the skirt or laugh too loud or…

"Just stop it and go," she muttered to herself as she fastened on her own worst nightmare—strappy spiked heels she was forcing herself to wear but that she was afraid she wouldn't be able to walk in. Still, they were on her feet and they looked good. Slowly she moved out of the room and to the head of the stairs.

Dell stood at the bottom of the stairs and watched Regina descend. Out of her usual eyebrow-raising, bright-colored but practical flats, she was a bit awkward, tottering on heels. He should have told her she didn't have to subject herself to such torture, but when she lifted her dress to negotiate a step and he caught a flash of exposed ankle and leg, heat pooled in his body. The pale, slender dress and the shoes were the epitome of elegance, but Regina's lush curves and long, shapely legs gave her attire a highly sensual tone. Some might even say there was something erotic about her appearance.

And if anyone even hints that to Regina, there's going to be hell to pay, Dell decided. She had not wanted to come tonight. She was only here at his behest, and he would be damned if he would allow anyone to make her feel uncomfortable.

He smiled and held out his arm as she reached the bottom of the stairs. "You look lovely," he told her. Immediately he saw that it was the wrong thing to say, but he didn't know why.

"It's just me," she said softly. "You don't have to be *The O'Ryan* with me or say all the expected things. Time enough for that when we get there."

He growled. The woman had actually induced him to growl. Him. Dell O'Ryan.

"You *do* look very nice," he said, toning it down a bit.

She patted his arm as they moved forward. "I have a very clear full-length mirror, Dell, and the truth is that I look a bit like a stripper trying to play at being a duchess."

Dell stopped in his tracks and looked down at her.

"But a really nice stripper," she said, amending her comment. "And don't worry. I won't use the word stripper at the ball. I hardly ever use it at the shop anymore." She opened her eyes wide, feigning innocence, and Dell couldn't help laughing.

But despite her attempt to lighten the mood, Dell could see that she was still very nervous. He wanted to tell her to just be herself, but he was afraid of what would happen if she did that. Like it or not, he had been raised to a crowd that punished those who didn't follow the rules.

"I won't embarrass you," she promised.

"I'm not worried," he assured her, taking both her hands in one of his. And he *wasn't* worried about her behavior. What he was worried about was whether anyone would say something hurtful to her.

Regina had grown up only a few blocks from him, but it might as well have been a different universe. She was from a blue collar crowd where survival and financial security often depended on living by one's wits, and where the rules changed from day to day. He was from a slightly inbred group where the rules had barely changed in his entire life. Presentation was all, so when his mother broke his father's heart right after their wedding, that had been ignored. When she had cheated on her husband, she was ostracized by him in private but smiled at by him in public. The truth was that his kind sometimes ate their young if they didn't conform to the mold or learn the rules, Dell admitted. He couldn't imagine what they would do to someone like Regina. She roamed the streets with her camera and asked people about things few woman of this group would even admit to knowing, but she didn't know the secret born-into-wealth handshake. She had no knowledge of the rules that had been drummed into people of his ilk.

Still, if she could keep her secrets and charm this crowd, they would accept her as his wife. And later, even if she chose to give up being his wife, doors could open for her, and that was a good thing, too. If they stayed together when their two months were up, they would be on companionable and convenient terms and if they parted…well, he wouldn't have to worry that she would be inconvenienced or shunned. Her business, which meant so much to her, would thrive if she made connections tonight. So yes, there was a great deal riding on tonight, but there was no way he was going to tell her so.

"Just relax, and let the games begin, Mrs. O'Ryan," he said.

"Relax. Okay," she agreed, taking a deep breath that lifted her bodice and made his body tighten. Tamping down the sudden taste of desire was so difficult that Dell almost saw stars and he once again doubted the intelligence of his decision to do this, but then she smiled up at him innocently and nodded.

"All right, I'm ready," she said. It was so obvious that she knew she was going into the lion's den and that she considered this far more stressful than wandering the tougher areas of Boston. It was also clear that she believed she was doing this for him. Could he do any less for her?

He held out his arm and she wrapped her palm around it. Dell drew her forward into the night. They were strangers, and yet, tonight, they were companions on an adventure of sorts.

It had damned well better be a good experience and a rewarding adventure for her, he warned himself.

The room was all gold and cream and sparkling chandeliers with women swishing by in their long, tasteful gowns on the arms of men clad in severe black tuxes. A small orchestra played in the background, the champagne was flowing, jewels glittered in the women's upswept hair. Some of those women looked at Dell and gave Regina speculative or even evil glances as they passed. She tried not to squeeze his arm or cower. She hoped she didn't trip in these dratted shoes or breathe in too deeply and split the seams of her gown.

"I'd like you to meet my wife, Regina," Dell was saying, presenting her to a short balding man and his statuesque wife, the Nedlinsons.

Regina dipped her head. "I'm very pleased to meet you," she said, politely.

"Edward is in shipping," Dell explained. "He and Mary have three daughters in their twenties. Regina is in the bridal business. She's a wonderful and imaginative photographer," he continued.

Mary smiled. "It's so difficult to find a good photographer. Do you do portraits as well as weddings?"

A small bell went off in Regina's head as she answered the question. She was beginning to see why Dell had insisted on coming to her shop to learn about what she did. He was doing what might have been called "bringing her out" in another time and place. Once again, he was being responsible for her.

Part of her subconscious told her she shouldn't let him do this. She was capable of standing on her own two feet and even if they stayed married she still needed to do that. She could never be one of those wives who relied on their husbands to take all the responsibility for the family's future, but Mrs. Nedlinson was being so nice that it would have been rude to turn away from the introduction.

"I have to say I was surprised when Dell got married," Edward was saying. "We all thought—" He stopped midsentence and looked at his wife as if she had pinched him. Maybe she had because soon after that, Edward and Mary moved on.

"They seemed very friendly," she offered, thinking that she should say something positive. She looked up, right into Dell's intense amber gaze.

"Yes. They're some of the friendliest," he told her. And they had those three daughters in their twenties, she remembered. Marriageable age. Of course. Now she understood that Dell was handpicking the people he was introducing her to. They had to be kind and they had to be potential clients for her business.

This scenario was repeated over and over again with Dell's polite introductions, the other couple's equally polite responses and Regina struggling to maintain an air of worldliness she didn't actually feel. Everyone was on their best behavior, but she could sense their underlying curiosity. "How did you and Dell meet?" one woman finally asked.

"I just showed up on his doorstep one day," she said instantly, then realized how strange that sounded. "With his mail. I was delivering his mail," she explained.

The woman in question frowned, and Regina realized what she was thinking. "I wasn't his postal carrier," she clarified. "Not that there's anything at all wrong with postal carriers." She was beginning to babble.

"Regina and I were neighbors," Dell said gently.

Under normal circumstances that might have sufficed, but Regina could see the wheels turning in the woman's consciousness. Dell's house was magnificent and historic, but the O'Ryan mansion was an island unto itself. Sitting on several acres of land, the rest of the more elegant neighborhood surrounding it had been sold off and rebuilt. Consequently his palatial estate, once neighbor to other estates of its ilk, now sat in the center of a very blue collar area, its wrought-iron fence a barrier that had separated the O'Ryans from the riffraff.

"A neighbor," the woman said. "I see." And what she saw, Regina knew, was that Dell had married beneath him.

"But she's no longer a neighbor," Dell was saying, and there was a trace of dark, warning fire in his eyes. "Regina is my wife. She's an O'Ryan now."

And that was that, it was clear. Regina saw the startled look in the woman's eyes…and the acceptance. The great Dell O'Ryan had spoken. Arguments were futile, but she doubted that the woman had changed her mind about anything. In fact, Dell's insistence that everyone climb on board the respect-my-wife train had probably only verified what the woman already believed. Regina was a lowly beetle trying to mingle with the butterflies.

Dell instantly realized the futility of his comment. He might as well have announced that Regina was no longer a money grubbing opportunist. But there was little to be done about that now. Trying to explain any further would only make it look as if they were trying to hide something.

Besides, he knew the rules. This was a crowd where position had to be earned, even if a person had married into the group. One was accepted either with the passing of time or through action. But time wasn't an option, because if he didn't make this work in the next two months, Regina would move on. She would insist on going. He would no longer have the right to protect her. Tonight he had insisted she come here, but what if she ended up getting hurt from this encounter?

The very possibility made him angry...at himself and at his world. Now Dell was even more determined to protect Regina from harm, even though this wasn't achieving his goal. If he scowled at anyone, that wasn't going to help Regina. It was a dilemma.

She plucked at his sleeve and he looked down at her. "Great party, huh?" she asked with a too bright smile. "You know, I'm really starting to enjoy myself."

Not knowing whether to howl with frustration or laugh at Regina's obvious attempt to soothe him and convince him that she was fine with all this, he chose to smile. "I shouldn't have brought you here."

She stilled. Then she lifted her chin. "You know, if you were here without me, I'll bet you would be off chatting it up with the guys, talking major business deals or sports or whatever it is that you wealthy, old money types talk about. You should go do that. Now."

He blinked. "I'm not leaving you."

"No, really," she said. "I'll be fine. And I promise not to say anything too embarrassing. I do know how to conduct myself in public, you know. I do it every day."

"Of course. I know that." But he didn't want to leave

her alone. He didn't trust people not to attempt to weasel information out of her.

"And you're looking a bit bearish. People are going to think that we really must have some pretty big secrets to hide. Or maybe even that we've been fighting."

Okay, she was right…or maybe she just wanted to be rid of him. He couldn't quite blame her. The fact that he had dragged her to such a stuffy formal occasion as her initiation into his world, even if his intentions had been good, nagged at him. It was a bit like throwing a fluffy little lamb into a bunch of hungry wolves and asking the lamb to just try to fit in.

"You're sure you want this?" he asked, gazing at her intently.

She lifted those long lashes and stared straight at him. "I'll be fine. I promise not to hand out business cards or tell rude jokes or be ungrammatical."

He chuckled. "You wouldn't be the only person handing out business cards. Half the people here are making deals."

She wrinkled her nose and smiled. "Then I'll be on the lookout for promising subjects. Or I'll at least think of everyone as a photo op. It's pretty much what I do anyway. Don't worry. I'm not even nervous anymore."

No, she was tired of him hanging around her as if she might do something embarrassing, Dell could see. Or maybe she was just tired of him hanging around her.

"If you're sure," he said.

"I am. Have fun." She gave him a cute little wave and he reluctantly moved off.

He just hoped he was doing the right thing.

CHAPTER SIX

REGINA was petrified. This ball and these people…she was so out of her element. But she'd had to ask Dell to go. The more people had come up to check her out, the more he had looked like some delicious dark guard trying to protect her from snotty comments.

He'd been nearly irresistible. It had gotten so bad that the thought of trying to converse with people she had absolutely nothing in common with was less daunting than the sensation of standing next to Dell. She wasn't used to having anyone look out for her well-being, and she certainly wasn't used to being near a man like Dell. He made her want things she had no hope of attaining. In that respect this whole plan was probably unwise, but Dell had been so good to her and she had agreed to this trial period. She could at least make an attempt to fit in and be a credit to him. He probably hadn't known he'd married such a social misfit on their wedding day, but she knew that he would have gone through with the ceremony even if he had known. So, darn it, for once she was going to follow the rules and try to be something close to the type of wife Dell should have had. If he needed her to fit in here, she would fit in the best she could.

Just think of everyone as subjects, she told herself. *This is all one big session.* Dredging up a brilliant smile, she pushed her shoulders back, smoothed her hands down over the ivory silk of her dress and sallied forth to meet Dell's crowd.

She didn't even have to introduce herself. Apparently word had spread that Dell's wife was finally out in public with him, and the curious practically lined up to meet her. In a most polite way, of course. There were no lines. Everyone waited his or her turn. There was no pushing or shoving the way there was sometimes in the real world. No actual name calling. Maybe a sneer here or there, or a twitch, a shoulder raised haughtily or a cold tone. Eventually order prevailed.

Regina tilted her head. "How nice to meet you," she said to a woman whose name she immediately forgot. "Yes, I am a photographer. You would make a wonderful subject. You've got the perfect smile."

One down, she thought as the woman went away happy. Regina found Dell in the crowd and gave him a reassuring smile. He studied her as if he were checking for bruises and she shivered slightly. How could a man stare at a woman from twenty feet away and make her feel as if her clothes were too tight?

More people came by. She tilted her head, using her photo shoot technique to find the humanity behind the façade of each person. *A kind smile. Old, sad eyes. A wise expression. A jaw that would demonstrate a resolute personality. A face that would fade in group photos.* And while she took pretend photos she talked, just the way she did with her clients. "Tell me about your hobbies." "I'm afraid I haven't traveled all that much. Have you?" "You have a look in your eyes that makes me think you've lived an interesting life." "Your name is Angelique? I love that name! It's so exotic."

Between faces, she looked up to see that Dell had moved around the room engaging in discussions, but he was always turned toward her when she glanced his way. And he always looked up, straight into her eyes. The man had obviously learned the art of conversation as a baby. He could carry on his side of a discussion while staring at his wife as if he knew the intimate details of her conversation as well.

Sometimes Regina had a hard time looking away.

"A glass of champagne, madame?" a server asked her, holding out a tray.

"Oh. No. She might be pregnant," a silky feminine voice said, shooing the man away before Regina could tell him no, thank you. She hadn't been drinking tonight. A single glass could make her dizzy, but she liked the taste and occasionally drank socially or at dinner. It was a habit she'd cut out completely when she was pregnant, and tonight she had simply been concerned that if she used alcohol to brace herself, she might inadvertently say something that would embarrass Dell.

But this last decision that she shouldn't be drinking had not been her choice.

Regina looked at the woman. Slender, tall, blond, with eyes the shade of violets and a figure that was displayed to advantage in a peach halter gown that hugged her curves and displayed lots of perfect skin. In a most tasteful way, of course.

"Elise Allenby." The woman held out her hand. "You're Dell's current wife."

Regina felt as if she were suffocating. She resisted the urge to raise her eyebrows. Out of the corner of her eye she saw Dell and knew that he must have miscued in the conversation he was having because the man beside him stiffened and looked this way, too. She knew he was going to come over to attempt damage control, and she also knew that nothing good for Dell could come out of that kind of a scenario. As discreetly as she could, she gave a small shake of her head and hoped he understood.

"Yes, Dell and I are married," she said as airily as she could. Her earlier concerns about the woman's emotional state seemed to have flown out the window. With the words "current wife" Elise had signaled that she wanted a catfight. She wanted Dell and she didn't like the fact that Regina had him.

But I might not have him long if things don't work out, Regina thought. And in that case Elise might be Dell's "current wife" by this time next year. *So, smile,* she told herself. *Be nice. Do it for Dell.*

"I'm sorry. I probably shouldn't have made that comment about you being pregnant," Elise said. "I'm sure you know that Dell never was the type to like kids."

Touché, Regina thought, even as her heart cracked painfully at the thought of the child she had lost. Someone must have told Elise that she had been pregnant on her wedding day. Had it been Dell? If she knew that Regina had been pregnant, she must also realize that she hadn't had a baby. The coldness of her comments seeped in, making it difficult for Regina to even think or breathe.

But "No, I'm not pregnant," she somehow managed. Was it true what Elise had said about Dell not wanting kids? And yet he had married her because she was pregnant. If what this woman had said was true then he had sacrificed more than Regina had realized in order to marry her.

"I'm sorry to slip up on you in this sudden way. I know we haven't met, but I'm an old friend of Dell's," Elise was saying, her voice turning from harsh to slightly choked. "I've known him a long time. A very long time." And then Elise's face seemed to transform. She stopped speaking. She blinked. A look of horror came over her. She blinked again, and a tear ran down those beautiful cheeks, leaving a dark streak of mascara. "I'm sorry," she said. "I'm sorry I'm being so intrusive and mean and disgusting and crudely emotional."

Ah, she loved him after all, and she was horribly jealous.

So, despite Elise's harshness a moment ago, a part of Regina felt guilty. Had Dell given Elise up for the sake of a pregnant woman and an unborn child? Maybe not entirely, since he'd been raised to protect the family name and divorcing his wife so soon after marrying would certainly raise some eyebrows. But if their trial marriage failed and he wanted to marry Elise...

"Don't worry," Regina said softly. "You haven't hurt me." *If I'm hurting, I'm completely responsible for everything myself.* "Come on. I'll walk you to the ladies' room and you can repair your makeup."

Immediately Elise touched her hands to her face. "My makeup. Oh, as if I haven't been idiotic enough." She turned to flee, just as a very pregnant woman in a gorgeous gold gown came up to her.

"Elise! It's been so long since I've seen you," the woman said.

Elise shook her head. "Not now. Change of plans,"

she croaked. She rushed off, blotting at her cheek with a handkerchief she had pulled from the tiny bag she was carrying.

The very pregnant woman and Regina were left standing alone. The woman looked at Regina as if she wasn't quite sure what to say or do, but all Regina could do was stare at the woman's clearly pregnant state. She looked as if she should have delivered the baby yesterday. While Regina watched, the woman's belly undulated, a small lump making a gliding motion beneath the surface of the gold of her gown as the baby moved.

An arrow of hot, sharp pain shot through Regina. She felt achy and faint and frightened at the intensity of her emotions.

Change of plans, Elise had said. This meeting had been deliberate and cruel.

Regina struggled for breath. She felt rather than saw people looking their way. No wonder, with Elise the former almost-fiancée rushing away from the "current wife" with a tearstained face. Dell's friends were watching. Decorum was necessary.

Struggling to somehow smile just a little, Regina lifted her eyes to the woman's beautiful face. "I'm Regina O'Ryan," she said. "How wonderful about your baby. Will it be soon?"

Was that wrong? Was it a faux pas to ask about a woman's pregnancy when she was so clearly on the verge of delivering a child any second? Regina couldn't think. Memories and hopes and dreams kept pushing at her.

And words. Dell wasn't the type to want children, but he had married her. She wasn't what he'd wanted. Her baby wasn't what he'd wanted. Duty was all. He was the epitome of what this group stood for.

But he had been good to her. So good. She had to reciprocate.

"I hope I'm not being too bold or making you uncomfortable," she said, hoping her voice was strong and her expression friendly. "I'm just…children are so special."

The woman smiled gently. "I'm lucky," she said. "Thank you for asking. I'm Tonya Deerfield. And…I'm sorry." She touched Regina's arm just as Dell came striding up to them.

He gave the woman a strained smile and a curt nod. "Tonya," he said. "Excuse us. The dancing is beginning. I'd like to dance with my wife."

"Of course. Very nice meeting you, Regina," she said, moving away.

Dell said nothing. He simply took her hand and started leading her toward the ballroom. She was aware of whispers as they passed. It was clear that Elise's emotional exit had been witnessed by a large number of people.

"I'm sorry," she said.

Dell's steps faltered and she in turn stumbled slightly. She would have fallen if he hadn't swept his arm around her waist and steadied her. The iron strength of him and the warmth of his palm made her shiver.

"We'll talk later," he said, his voice low and tight. He was obviously angry. Her heart sank. None of this might be her fault, but she had told him she wouldn't embarrass him and now everyone was talking. She should have moved away when Elise approached her, she realized now. Who would have blamed her? But it was too late now.

"Smile," Dell said as he looked down at her and swept her into the dance. He, in turn, gave her a look that, under other circumstances and with another man, would have made her think that she was the most important person in his life.

He was pretending. Could she do any less? She smiled as brightly as she was able. And she did her best to dance, although the darn shoes kept betraying her.

Her heel turned, but Dell lifted her, bringing her closer to him, his chest nearly touching hers.

Regina's head began to spin at his nearness. She struggled for breath and hoped he didn't realize how he was affecting her. He was her former neighbor, her friend, not her lover or her love, despite their legal connection. She had to remember that. She and Dell were married but not in the usual sense. Still, she had promised to give this relationship, platonic though it might be, a chance. How could she do less when Dell had given her security and the opportunity of a normal life after Lee had deserted her? Taking a breath, she made more of an effort to stay upright.

"Look at me, not at your feet, Regina," Dell ordered, and she did. She gazed right up into his fierce eyes and found her balance.

Her gown was thin, and the warmth of his hand at her waist felt like a caress against her skin. But it wasn't. This was just a dance. This was how it was done. Dell had danced with hundreds of women just like this before.

Still, she didn't allow herself to look away. She smiled up at him, her gaze linked with his. For a moment, she forgot that other people were watching. For the space of a dance, the world held only her and this man who was keeping her upright by the sheer force of his personality. Her heart beat more strongly, her senses were heightened. She was so close to him that she could rise on her toes and kiss him if she wanted.

That thought caught her off guard. Emotion seeped

in, but…emotion wasn't part of this marriage, was it? Dell didn't want that. Of course he didn't, and it would be totally unfair of her to inject that element now. She had to look away from him, and only with great effort did she maintain her balance. But the music was ending. The dance was over.

"It's time to leave," he said.

She understood. Now they would talk. And it would not be good.

The ride home was silent and strained. Dell didn't trust himself to speak. Because once he began to talk, all the emotions that had been roiling through him tonight might come out, and it wasn't safe driving with that much explosive energy blowing up in both their faces.

So he tried not to think about how small and tense Regina seemed on the far side of the passenger seat. She was almost wedged up against the door.

No wonder. He must look like a thundercloud. He was certainly feeling like one. And the storm was about to hit.

Somehow, someway, he got them home. He handed Regina out of the car and led her to the door.

He opened it and followed her inside, sliding the lock into place behind them. The outside light's glow filtering through the fanlight window cast an eerie shimmer of pale yellow light framed by dark shadows in the high-ceilinged entranceway.

Regina held herself rigid, almost as if she were waiting for him to strike. And then she did a very brave thing. She turned and faced him.

"I shouldn't have gone there," she said.

"I shouldn't have made you go," he countered.

"I told you I could handle myself, but speaking to Elise was a foolish move. I…I guess I wasn't thinking straight."

Dell wanted to laugh, but it would have been an ugly, harsh and sarcastic laugh. *He* hadn't been thinking straight for a very long time. Certainly not tonight.

"Do you really think I believe any of this is your fault? Regina, I as good as pushed you into that appearance. I didn't even stop to think that Elise might be there."

"Do you think *I* believe that you would do anything that would intentionally hurt her?" Regina asked.

Dell scowled. "Of course not, Regina. You wouldn't hurt anyone. I led you into a risky situation and then left you there alone to fend for yourself."

"I'm not spineless or helpless. You know that. I made you go away and leave me alone at the ball. It was my decision."

Now, he did smile. He couldn't help himself. "Regina, do you really think you could make me do anything I didn't want to do?"

A look of intense concentration came over her face, wrinkling her nose in a delightful way. "All right then, I *asked* you to go."

Ah, she had him there. He had left her side tonight because she had asked him to. "Maybe that's true, but if I had known you would be subjected to Elise Allenby, the meeting would never have taken place."

"Dell, you can't stand between me and life. You've already done that. Elise said you didn't want children."

"Did she now?"

"So you sacrificed yourself by marrying me."

"Really?" He seemed less than convinced. "The ranking O'Ryan needs an heir."

She blinked. "Oh. Yes. So, are you actually trying to

tell me you married me because I was pregnant and you needed an heir?"

No, he'd been trying to bluff.

"How *do* you feel about children?" she demanded.

"I don't know much of them." He sidestepped the question. Obviously not adroitly enough. He saw the accusation in her eyes. It was valid, too. He knew nothing of children, and given the fact that he was too much like his father, he doubted that he would be good with them. Still, he knew Regina would have been good with children. And the child she had been carrying…

"I might not have been the best choice for your child's father, Regina, but I would have welcomed your baby. In the end, I wanted to see your child born. I wanted to be a father." His voice cracked on the words. He tried not to think back to the day when he had come home to find her as pale as winter snow and as silent. She had allowed him to take her to the doctor and then she had retreated. So had he. "I—your child would never have been a burden or an obligation," he said, "if that's what you were thinking."

And just like that, those pretty brown eyes filled. She closed her eyes and swayed slightly. He caught her, his palms closing around her arms, her skin yielding beneath his touch.

He felt her tremble. He breathed in her scent and desire swept through him. Unfair. He couldn't treat her this way, not after all the pain his actions had caused her. It wasn't her fault that he was having trouble controlling his reactions.

And yet, he was having *so* much trouble.

"Regina." She opened her eyes.

He slid his hands beneath her hair. "Promise me…" He pulled her closer.

"What?" she whispered, looking up into his eyes. Such warm caramel eyes.

"Taking you to the ball this evening put you at risk. Promise me you won't let me nudge you into any more situations where you'll feel uncomfortable." And he knew as he held her here that he wasn't just talking about events like this evening.

"I won't," she said.

"I mean it. Don't do something just because you think I want it or because you think it's part of our plan. If I'm out of line, in any way, if you feel I'm pushing you, I want you to push back."

He took her hands and placed them palm down on his chest as if to demonstrate.

Big mistake. The warmth of her hands resting against him was too much. Slick desire coursed through him. He placed his palms on the curve of her waist, his actions belying his words. Her dress was thin. She felt so right. And soft. In just a second, if he didn't stop, he would crush her to him. He would taste her, push her, break his promise about not touching her before their two months were up and again risk rushing her into something she might not really want.

Dell ordered himself to step away completely.

Regina stared at him as if she had known what had been going through his mind.

"If I do that again, I want you to stop me. Tell me no," he said.

She raised her eyes to his and said nothing.

He groaned. "Regina. Please."

She nodded hard. "Yes. I will. I'll stop you. Next time."

The words "next time" hung between them like a threat. Like a promise.

He slugged in a deep breath of air, trying to pull it together. "Good. I think…good night." It was time to get away before he changed his mind and touched her again.

He turned, headed toward the stairs.

"Dell?" Her soft, sad voice stopped him cold and he turned back to her. He waited.

"You didn't hurt me tonight. It was difficult talking to Elise, but I have to learn how to handle those kinds of situations. I need to be strong. No, I *am* strong."

"I know. And you handled it well, but that doesn't mean I would ever drag you through something like that again." And then because she looked so small and alone and pretty, he smiled.

And got a tremulous smile in return for his efforts.

"Sleep tight," she said.

As if that was going to happen. Tonight he had done what he had never considered doing since the night they had wed. He had touched his wife.

It couldn't happen again. At least not yet. If this relationship was ever to be forged, it had to be built on steel, on trust. It had to be proven to be something that could last, not a thing of heat and passion that might die out and leave only ashes and the need to dissolve their union as quickly as possible.

He would not be just another man taking advantage of her warmth and her giving ways, he would not follow the path his cousin had taken with Regina. Only when she had decided that she could be his partner forever would he allow himself to claim her body.

CHAPTER SEVEN

REGINA was jumpy and tense at work the next day. No question why. She was lusting after her husband.

Please don't do something stupid, Regina, she told herself.

But it was too late. She and Dell had overstepped the bounds last night. There had been touching. Not just platonic touching, either. She knew that as well as she knew that her heart was hammering out of her chest. He had wanted her.

And oh my, she had wanted him. The longing had been deep and strong and almost overwhelming. It was a wonder that she hadn't pressed up against him. She had almost not been able to stop herself.

Thank goodness he at least had stopped, because she had a bad feeling that physical contact between them might lead to longing on her part and that was just…so wrong. If she started wanting more than Dell was offering, she would get seriously hurt.

"Regina?"

Regina looked up, confused.

Belle was staring at her. "Are you all right?"

Giving herself a mental shake, Regina nodded. "I'm perfect. Why?"

"You've been staring at the appointment book for three minutes. Was there something you wanted to record?"

Trying to remember, Regina finally frowned. "Yes, the Vandivers want to expand the number of places where I'll be taking photos. An engagement party, two showers, a bachelor and bachelorette party as well as a complete pictorial of the entire day from the time the bride and groom arise to the time they leave for their honeymoon. They want everything bigger and better. We're to spare no expense."

Regina felt a brief moment of panic. "I'll have to hire another photographer for the separate locations, but I suppose that won't be a problem. It can't be. What the Vandivers want, the Vandivers get, right?" She looked at her friends.

"Right," Natalie said. "I got a call, too. More tiers on the cake and an expanded dessert table for those who don't want cake. I'm sure I can do this. I'm even working on a special cake. I'll need all of you to taste it, so get those taste buds in gear. You're all so good at making helpful suggestions." But she sounded a little flustered herself and it wasn't just the fact that Natalie was diabetic and had to have her friends do her cake tasting. That was part of her everyday existence. The Vandivers were being more than unusually demanding.

Regina looked toward her other friends. "Anything else?"

"Lots more beads on the dresses," Serena said. "All the dresses."

"Flower arrangements for every location they visit on the wedding day." Callie smiled tightly. "And for special guests. There are quite a few special guests."

"We're going to have to ask for a bigger deposit,

Belle." Audra looked worried. "Extra people and mate-
rials are going to stretch our budget. I mean, we'll get
it all back the day of the wedding, but we might have to
be careful until that day."

"I don't want anyone having to beg Liz Vandiver for
money," Julie said suddenly. "She's being disagreeable
enough as it is and changing her plans five times a day.
You can just…I don't want the Belles to go under
because you're spending money on my wedding."

Everyone froze. "How did you know?" Audra asked.

Julie looked around the room. "None of you are very
good at keeping things from me. All those furtive looks
you've been exchanging. Besides, I found some notes
that had fallen next to a trash can when I was emptying
it yesterday. It must have been from a brainstorming
session you were all having. I'm not going to let you
sacrifice anything for me."

Regina forgot her own problems. "Julie, we're fine.
Your wedding to Matt is a gift to ourselves as well as
you. We love planning every detail. Don't make me tell
you this again. We have money, and we're using it.
You're going to have the perfect wedding and marry the
perfect man. Okay, sweetie?"

Julie's eyes teared up. "I love all of you so much."

"We love you, too, darlin', so don't worry about the
Vandivers," Belle said. "They're pompous, but they
know business and they know that when they want
something extra, it costs. I'll handle them and I'll be so
delightfully charming they'll fall over their feet to throw
bushels of money at us."

Finally Regina smiled. "You're always charming,
Belle. That's why everyone loves you. By the way, Rae

Anne called. She wanted to know if Charlie Wiley had come in to see you."

Instantly Belle frowned. "I wish she would stop trying to fix me up. Charlie Wiley called yesterday while I was out, but I'm not interested in another new man trying to frisk me. If he comes in or calls again you can tell him that."

Immediately everyone looked a bit uncomfortable. "That wouldn't feel right, Belle," Julie said.

"I know. I'm just mad. I'll tell him myself. Now, you girls get going. Isn't it your weekly poker night?"

It was. But Regina couldn't do it. Yesterday evening was too much on her mind. If she socialized with her friends tonight, she didn't trust herself not to open up and relate her fears. And if she went home…

She couldn't go home yet. Not until she'd had time to work off some of her fears and inhibitions and get back on track. Today's crop of sparkling-eyed brides hadn't helped. She needed something rougher. A good dose of reality.

"I'm sorry guys. I have work to do," she said, grabbing her camera bag. "If I'm lucky I can catch Edna before she goes to work."

"Regina…"

Regina whirled around, walking backward toward the door. "You know I hate missing poker night, but I have to."

"And you know that's not what Audra is worried about," Callie said.

"I know, but there's no need. Edna's a good person."

"I'm sure she is, but…"

Regina smiled and waved. "I love you guys, and I appreciate your concern, but there's absolutely no reason for you to worry," she said. And she hurried out the door.

Of course, she was wrong. There was a lot to worry about. Mainly how she was going to keep from thinking about the way Dell's hands had felt against her skin and how she was going to manage to pretend she hadn't felt a thing. The time until the end of this trial period seemed longer than ever.

Dell hung up the phone and swore. That had been Belle.

"Dell, I wouldn't have called under normal circumstances. This feels a bit like a betrayal, and my concerns are probably unfounded. It's most likely just me doing that mother hen thing, but Regina's gone out on a photo shoot and…I don't know. She's used this woman and place as a subject before, but she doesn't ever miss the girls' poker night for something like this. Besides, this time she seemed a bit distracted," the woman had said. "I'm sure the neighborhood's fine if a person is with someone, but alone…a woman needs to stay alert. Regina doesn't like anyone going with her because she says it breaks the trust of her subjects, but if you could just keep a distance, make sure she's all right and give me a call when you get back, I'd really appreciate it."

His temper had started to rise. "She shouldn't be going anywhere even remotely questionable. Couldn't you stop her?"

Silence had ensued. "Regina is an adult. She's a professional and she's exceptionally good at what she does. She's also smart and fiercely independent and she needs to be that way. So if you're going to lecture her or treat her like a child I'll look elsewhere. That girl has had enough lecturing to last her a lifetime. Her parents did it every day of her life, and some of the men she's known—"

He swore and ran a hand through his hair. "No

lectures. But I have to know she's safe. Can you give me an address?"

"I can give you an area. It's all I know."

But when she had named the region, Dell blanched. "I'm gone," he said.

"You'll call?"

"When I deal with my anger."

"Dell…"

"I'm her husband, Belle. I have a right to be angry."

"If you hurt her…"

"Never. She's always safe with me. I promise you that. You'll just have to trust me." He didn't wait for an answer. In ten seconds flat he was out of the door and headed into one of the few dubious areas of the city. He had no idea what he was going to say to Regina when he found her. Somehow, he hoped he would find the right words.

The best of the light was starting to fade when Regina peeked out from behind her camera and noticed that Edna was staring at a point somewhere behind Regina's shoulder. The woman was frowning.

"What are you looking at?" Regina asked. "Is something wrong?"

"Time for you to be going, I think, sweet pea," Edna said. "There's a man sneaking about. A pretty young thing like you shouldn't be here at this hour. I tried to tell you that earlier."

"I know, but I had time today, and I wanted to finish your part of the story. You're so unique, Edna. Thank you for taking the time with me."

The older woman nodded. "You're always welcome, Regina, but now you really need to be going. I don't like this at all." An edge crept into Edna's voice.

Regina's heart began to pound a bit. With the late summer sun it wasn't even close to dark but she was usually here only during the busy part of the daytime. Now the streets were becoming deserted, and if there was trouble…

"I'm not leaving you to fend for yourself," Regina said.

The woman cackled. "Honey, I've been fending for myself all my life."

And she had paid a high price many times, Regina knew. "I'm not leaving. We'll go somewhere else. I'll call the police if I have to." But she knew Edna wouldn't want her to do that unless she really had to. There were good people in this neighborhood who nonetheless had shady pasts.

Still, when two men started walking toward them from the other direction Regina's heart fled into her throat.

Edna growled. "Look out. Here comes trouble. You go home now."

"Edna," one of the men called. "Who you got there with you? She's pretty."

"She's nobody," Edna said. "Get out of here."

"Oh, no. I don't think so," the man said, continuing to advance. "I want a better look. Maybe a taste. I definitely want me some of this."

"You don't want none of this," Edna said. "She's sick."

"You're lying. I can tell. That woman is soft and stacked and—"

"And she's most definitely mine," a low, deep voice announced, and Edna's eyes widened. Regina whirled to see Dell walking toward them, fire in his eyes. "Furthermore, if you come even one step closer to her, I will hurt you beyond repair," he promised the man.

The man hooted. "With what? You got a gun?"

"Much better than that. I've got a cold, hard direct line to the police chief on my cell. He's an old friend. If you want to meet him just take one step closer to my wife."

"Wife?"

"Absolutely." He pulled out his cell, flipped it open and pressed a couple of buttons. "What is the closest intersection? Oh, yes," he said, naming the two nearest streets. "What are your names?" he asked the men.

"Yeah, like we're gonna tell you that."

"That's Bodie and Reg," Edna said. "I can tell you where you can find them most of the time, too."

A slow, lethal smile turned Dell's grim expression into a dark mask of satisfaction. Someone must have answered the phone. "I've got a situation here I need an assist on," he told the person on the other line. "Good. How long? Ten minutes? Make it five."

One of the men let loose a string of curses. The two of them started to back away. "We're gone, man. Never even saw your woman. She's safe. Got a hands-off perimeter around her."

"Yeah, that's right. It'd be real smart to go home right around now, Bodie," Edna said.

"Shut up, old woman. You and me will meet later," Bodie said, but he pulled the other man away and together they retreated down the street.

Regina looked up at her husband, who was canceling his order. He wasn't looking any more cheerful. She raised her chin and took a deep, shivery breath.

"I—Edna, I'd—I'd like you to meet my husband," she said, turning toward the woman. No one was there.

"She slipped around the corner," Dell said.

"You scared her away."

"I don't think she was scared. Not of me."

He was most likely right. Edna wasn't scared of much, and the look in her eyes when she'd realized that Dell was Regina's husband had been much closer to admiration than fear. Knowing that, Regina felt a deep sense of relief slide slowly through her. Bodie had scared her. She wasn't going to admit it.

"Maybe she wasn't exactly scared, but Edna wouldn't want to meet the police chief any more than those two men would," she explained. "She has…a background."

"And this neighborhood isn't the safest, yet you're here. Without adequate protection." His voice was low and soft and disappointed. It was worse than having her parents chastise her, even though no true words of criticism had left his lips.

"Edna's special," Regina explained. "There are those here who have hard lives. Now that she's old and not able to work anymore she helps those who need it. She takes care of them when they're sick. She runs errands. She writes letters for runaways so their families won't worry."

"She could let their families know where they are."

"If she thought it was right, she would. Every case is different. Edna is different."

He was advancing, still with that look of utter frustration on his face.

"Damn it, Regina, *you're* different. I don't want you hurt on my watch."

The words sank in. *On his watch.* A finite period. He was conceding that this marriage might not work. She gave a quick nod. "I know. I'm sorry. I just…"

He shook his head. "Don't explain. I know this is your work, your life. I know how important it is, but…"

She waited.

He blew out a breath. "I can't be the way you are. I have to know you're safe."

There was an edge in his voice but also a note of defeat. Pain bit at Regina. She had broken trust today and all because she was trying to stay away from home to protect her heart.

Giving a quick nod, she moved a step closer. "Remember how I said that I hoped we could be friends eventually? I still feel that way, and friends don't ignore friends' concerns. Today, someone had to have called you. That means I worried the Belles. You, too. That's not right. I—" She tried to find the words.

"I'm not asking you to give up your work, Regina. I would never do that, but I can hire people to come here with you."

She gave a tight nod. That would never work, but it would probably only be for a short while.

"Good people," he amended, watching her. "I can afford the best. Former Navy Seals, the top detectives in the country, people who know how to disappear into the brickwork. They won't interfere unless you're in danger."

Gratitude filled her soul. She fought the hot tears that threatened. "Thank you," she said.

"Let's go home," he said, holding out his hand.

And though touching him was even more of a danger than Bodie had been, Regina took his hand.

CHAPTER EIGHT

Two nights later, Regina lay in bed staring at the ceiling, the memory of Dell walking toward her saying "She's most definitely mine," in a continuous replay, and every time that deep baritone sounded in her memory, she shivered with awareness. Her husband was a very commanding, very physical man. He had ridden to her rescue no questions asked when Belle had called.

For the moment it didn't even matter that he considered her an obligation, a bit of family duty. At least, she wasn't going to let it matter.

Dell had saved her skin. What's more, he had most likely saved Edna's. She knew because she'd received a phone call from Edna today.

"Guess where I am?" Edna had asked. "I'm on the street, talking into my bodyguard's cell phone. Isn't that a hoot?" she asked with a trill of laughter. "Me, Edna Dooney, with her very own personal bodyguard to keep the Bodies away. Doesn't talk much, but he's sure handy at carrying things and frowning. You tell your man thank you, all right? You sure got lucky, girl."

"Yes, I sure got lucky," Regina whispered in the

dark. Dell was rock solid, a good man. He had helped her so much.

And what had she done for him? Other than bringing him his mail one day and giving Lee enough confidence to disappear off on his own personal quest?

"Not a thing," she muttered. "What could I do for someone like Dell?" She'd been mulling over that question for two days. And she had no answer other than the subliminal *Sleep with him* that kept creeping into her thoughts.

"Just stop it!" She moaned, turning over. "That's not the way I want things to work." If they ever did sleep together, it had to be because they both wanted it and the time was right. What she wanted to do for Dell had to be different. Out of the ordinary.

She threw off the covers and paced the room. Flipping on her computer, she pulled up one of the few pictures she'd taken of Dell. He was turned to the side, his jawline a blade. The photo had been taken back when she'd been dating Lee, and Dell had been happy then. Less tense. He was smiling at something in the distance. He was…impressive, very aristocratic, very Boston.

Regina frowned at that. She clicked onto the Internet and typed Dell's name and the word Chicago into the search engine. One small page came up, the same passage she had mentioned to him that day she had asked for the divorce.

She typed in jewelry stores and Chicago and a host of them came up. Obviously Chicago was a competitive market. Despite the fact that there were those who wanted him to set up shop in the town, expanding there could still be a risk. A new enterprise would need to stand out from the crowd. A major public relations push would be necessary.

"Which Dell knows and which he can well afford," she whispered. No doubt he had the best agencies available at the task right now.

But they don't know him personally. They don't know what makes him tick, what makes him stand out as a man and what makes him interesting.

"You don't, either," Regina told herself. At least she didn't know enough to approach him with the idea that was forming in her head. But then she hadn't known Edna, either, at one time. Or Lyle, the doorman who serenaded the people in his apartment building. These people were Boston, Regina thought, opening up the files she'd made for the book that was almost completed.

And so is my husband. There's no one more Boston than he is, she thought, thinking of this old mansion and the weight of the history lining the walls in those old, somber photos of former O'Ryans.

Regina smiled. A plan swirled, began to take shape and solidified. "I think my book needs another chapter, maybe an excerpt that might be sent out as a teaser. Maybe even some people in Chicago might find that interesting."

She flicked the computer monitor off and lay back down, but she didn't go to sleep. It didn't matter. Excitement filled her soul. There was one thing she could give to her husband. It might be the last and only thing she ever did for him.

That thought stung, but she did her best to ignore it. Nothing, not even painful thoughts, were ever allowed to interfere with her work, and this was definitely work.

Her troubles with Dell were over. Now he was a subject, and that was so much easier than having him as the man she desired night and day.

* * *

Dell was pacing the floor of his office, his phone up against his ear when a knock sounded on the door. Since only he and Regina and a few servants occupied the house, Regina had left for work hours ago and the servants always waited until his door was open, there had to be something wrong. He tried not to remember how he'd felt the other day when he'd seen that jerk leering at Regina and holding out his hand as if he intended to touch her.

A muscle in Dell's cheek twitched and he quickly excused himself to the associate on the other end of the line, rounded his desk and reached the door in two strides. When he pulled it back, Regina was there. And so was Edna. His wife looked a bit guilty.

"I'm sorry if you were working," she said.

"Something's wrong. Bodie?" he asked Edna gently, turning to the woman who bore the scars of a hard life on her wrinkled face.

"No. Bodie tried to come around once and Samuel scared him away. That man you sent me is something," Edna assured him.

"I don't understand, then. Do you need something?" he asked.

But already Regina was slipping into his office. "Just a few minutes of your time, Dell. Hardly anything, really." She pulled out a camera that was the equivalent of a photographer's phallic symbol. Dell knew powerful men who would covet that camera. But, he thought, remembering the photos he'd seen on the walls of The Wedding Belles, they wouldn't be able to make use of it half as well as his wife did.

Then, as Regina began to set up, the reason for her visit hit him. "You want to take my picture? Why?"

His wife gave him a patient smile, although he

detected a slight shift to her eyes. Was she about to
lie to him? "I told you about my pictorial of Boston.
It's almost done. Edna and I are pretty much through,
and I have lots of other Bostonians, the meat of the
city, but...it occurred to me that I'm missing something. I have hardly any old school types, not many
wealthy people and no blue-bloods to speak of. You
could really round out the last chapter and help me
sell the thing."

She was still smiling but not exactly looking at him.
Interesting.

He glanced at Edna. "She wants to take our picture
together, so she can have a caption about how you
helped me," the woman told him.

Dell was taken aback. "Not necessary. That wasn't
meant to curry favor with the public."

Now Regina had one hand on her hip and she was
looking at him dead-on. "I know that, Dell, but putting
something like that in a public record could help Edna
and others as well. It might help raise awareness of
those who have limited resources and might bring in donations. I intend to list a couple of organizations Edna
has worked with which provide medical care and social
services to the people who need them but are afraid to
ask for them or can't afford them."

Her expression was earnest. He fully believed she
meant what she said and he knew she cared about Edna,
but...

"You already have a segment on Edna."

Ah, the evasive look again. "But not one of someone
like you who can actually help. Besides, you're making
this move to Chicago. If I send out some complimentary
copies to the right people, it could be a bridge between

the two cities. For Edna, I mean. That is…people might mail in donations even from that far away."

A smile played at his lips. "Edna doesn't look too bothered by the lack of donations flowing in from Chicago." He looked at the woman. She shrugged.

Regina's shoulders slumped. "You've hardly said anything about the Chicago connection. Some targeted publicity would be a good thing for you and your business, wouldn't it?"

Undoubtedly, but he wasn't concerned about his slow start. He'd held off on some things so that he could concentrate on his marriage. "I'm not worried about Chicago," he told his wife.

That seemed to worry her even more. "See, you're taking care of the rest of us, fussing over me and not tending to your own needs."

He chuckled. "Regina, relax. I'm not going to go broke."

Uh-oh, now she had that offended look in her pretty brown eyes. "Do you think I don't know that, Dell? Heavens, you must have more money than—I don't know—pretty much anyone I know. That makes it really hard to do things for you."

Her meaning became even clearer. Dell tilted his head. "Does it matter? Doing things for me?" A slow thread of interest wound its way through him. Was there more to this marriage than he had thought? He studied his wife carefully.

"Yes," she said as if that didn't make her happy. "You've done so many things for me. What have I done for you?"

Answers flowed into his consciousness. She'd brought the element of charming surprise into his life but he knew from experience that Regina considered her tendency to do the unexpected a detriment. She'd shown him how important a smile and compassion could be, but again, he didn't think she would believe him if he told her that. And besides, he wanted her closer than this when he whispered that to her. He wanted to be touching her, and they weren't alone right now.

"You married me," he said simply, and that, too, was obviously the wrong response. He could see that she wanted to counter his suggestion, but with Edna in the room she probably didn't want to go into details.

"I want to do something real and meaningful," she said, clearly unhappy. "To use my skills. Dell, I need to contribute and I haven't. I can't clean your house or help you in your work or…anything. I can't save you from the bad guys and the bad parts of life the way you did me. Let me do *something*. I'm a really good photographer."

"You're the best. I've seen some of your work," he agreed. And if he didn't let her do this, he would be devaluing her talent. "What do you need me to do?"

Instantly that miracle smile lit up, bathing her face in pure, beautiful seductive light. "Just let me shadow you a bit, ask questions, take some pictures. We would have to be…together a fair amount."

"Yes," he answered immediately, and he knew it wasn't the pictures or the interviews he was saying yes to. In spite of their plan for a trial marriage, they had danced around each other, even avoided each other at times. Because there was such a strong urge to touch her, to make love with her. He knew that, and he knew that the choice to stay married or not to stay married couldn't be complicated by lust that might fade away in time. If they stayed together it had to be for solid reasons. Otherwise, like his mother who had withered away an unhappy woman, their marriage might destroy Regina. Or, like his father, who regretted marrying the wrong person every day of his life and took it out on others, the two of them might grow bitter. They would hate each other.

He never wanted Regina to hate him.

"Let's do it," he said again.

Regina grinned. "Edna, we're on," she said, but it was Dell she looked at with total excitement in her eyes.

Immediately his body tightened and desire filled him. Sometime soon, he promised himself, he was going to kiss his wife. Probably just as soon as he got her alone.

Talk about burning the candle at both ends! Regina had been rushing from the shop to Dell's side for three days. Where he was, she was, and she was amazed at some of the places her husband showed up at.

"The bird house at the zoo?" she'd asked, trailing her husband through the gates.

He'd laughed. "I know, but the client is a world famous ornithologist proposing to his lady love. The ring is a custom job and he insisted that I transport it myself. It's shaped like a rare hummingbird from Peru, one he's spent his life studying." He'd flipped open a ring box and Regina had stared down at the most exquisite little ring she had ever seen. Diamonds and sapphires and amethysts made up a perfect miniature bird nesting on a delicate gold band.

"It's beautiful," she'd said with awe. "You?"

He'd shaken his head. "I didn't design it. I just made it happen."

That was what he appeared to do, she realized the more she followed him around. He made things happen.

In the short few days since she had started this project, Dell had appeared at the mayor's office donating money for a green project several businessmen were sponsoring, he'd handled an emergency with his housekeeper, providing her with a car and driver, money and lots of reassurance so that she could visit her daughter who lived in Iowa and had delivered triplets three weeks early. He'd fielded calls from his office and soothed ruffled feathers when there had been a mix-up in accounting and his employees had been pointing fingers at each other. He was a man in control and on top of things at all times.

And today they were about to attend a late meeting followed by a cocktail party with his associates regarding the progress of the Chicago expansion.

"I'll just stay near the back," she whispered to him as they entered the room.

He smiled and slipped his arm through hers. "Be my wife tonight," he urged. "Not my biographer."

Regina glanced up into Dell's amber gaze. She needed to answer but her breath felt shaky. She realized that she'd spent days focusing on him, learning about him. It was all impressive, but she had been-mostly-able to lock it away in her mind as work. This would be different.

"I'm not dressed for this."

He glanced down at the plain, sleeveless black dress she was wearing. It was one she had owned years before she had met him and it was not O'Ryan quality. The other women in the room were suited and coiffed, perfumed, bejeweled and expensive.

"I look like someone you picked up at the discount

store," she said, intending to step away and hide behind her camera.

He smiled and her heart did that flippy thing it had been doing for three days. "Then I got a bargain," he said. "Even rich people appreciate bargains. There isn't a man in the room who hasn't given you an appreciative glance."

Okay, now she was out of her element. "I—you're kidding me. I—"

"I meant that as a compliment, Regina."

"I know." Her voice came out a bit mortified. "I don't handle compliments well."

He shrugged. "You don't have to say anything to me. With other people, a simple thank you will do."

She nodded. "Okay, what do you want me to do?"

"Be here. Next to me."

Oh my, she felt suddenly warm. "All right."

But within a few minutes of the presentation beginning she was fidgeting. She felt conspicuous. It was stupid, she knew, but she felt as if she needed a reason to be here and she didn't have one. She wasn't really a part of the company or of Dell's world.

"Mrs. O'Ryan," one man finally said, interrupting the procedures. "That's a gorgeous Hasselblad you're carrying," he said, pointing to her camera. "I understand you're a photographer. Why aren't you taking pictures?"

She opened her mouth, but didn't know what to say. Her fingers plucked at the camera, a familiar object she trusted. "I—" Regina turned to her husband, and a resigned smile of defeat came over his gorgeous features.

"She was just waiting until we were done with the boring part," he said, giving her an encouraging smile. "But I'm sure she'll take your picture now if you're nice to her. She *is* a very talented woman."

With a relieved grin, Regina turned to her husband and mouthed the words "thank you" just before she raised her camera. For the next forty-five minutes, she shot photo after photo, but found herself returning again and again to her husband. Here was Dell with a woman coated in diamonds; here he was with his arm reassuringly on the shoulder of a man wearing a worried look on his face.

"It's time to strike in Chicago," the man said. "If you delay any longer, you'll lose the opportunity. Already some of the people who were trying to coax you to come are moving along to the next new thing. They loved your rare creatures collection and the fact that you try to be socially responsible, but they're fickle. You need to make a move, find a location."

Regina took a photo, but she said nothing. She was listening intently, taking shot after shot of Dell. The look in his eyes, the deft way he handled the man's concerns, the very shape of his hand and the lines of his body were an aphrodisiac for her camera.

Soon she had forgotten what she was doing. In fact she had forgotten everything except making love to her husband with the camera. When she suddenly dropped to her knees and panned her camera upward, taking a series of shots ending with a close-up of his face, she heard a gasp behind her.

Immediately Regina was back in the here and now. She blinked, then frowned, wondering why everyone was staring at her. A woman came up behind her. "Dell, you could at least have leaped in here and done the honors," the woman said as she drew Regina up and draped an arm around her.

The movement upward revealed a flow of air over

Regina's back. "Oh my goodness," she said, realizing that the thin, aging fabric of her dress had given way with her athletic movements.

She glanced up at her husband, whose hooded gaze was fierce. "You're right, of course, Lisette. I should have been the one to tend to my wife."

And in one swift, graceful move he slid into place, replacing the woman, leading Regina toward the ladies room. Once inside the empty room, he whirled her around and pressed her up against the wall.

"I'm sorry," she said. "I'm so embarrassed. All your friends saw, and darn it, I wasn't even wearing my best underwear. Don't people always say to wear good underwear in case you have to go to the hospital? But this isn't the hospital. It's worse. The cream of Boston society saw my faded pink bra with the stretched out strap and the hole in the nylon and—"

"Shh," Dell said, and then his lips came down on hers.

Sensation claimed her. Dell's lips were magic. She was sinking, reeling, aching, mindless. She wanted more.

Her arms came up around his neck. She rose on her toes and angled closer.

When he finally released her and pulled back a bit for air, Regina blinked to get her bearings. "I'm so…I don't know," she said.

"Regina, you're driving me absolutely insane," he said. "You and your camera, all this concentration on me, all this closeness. Did you really take a picture of my pants?" He tilted his mouth over hers, caressing, licking, driving her mad.

"I—I might have," she said when she could speak again. "I don't know what I was doing. I wasn't thinking."

"Mmm." He kissed her again. He ran his hands up

her sides, and she shivered. Somewhere in the back of her mind a voice reminded her that a roomful of elite Bostonians had seen them come in here together and that she had been half-dressed.

Alarm bells rang in her head. She pushed at Dell.

Instantly he released her, although his hands were still lightly resting at her waist. "Dell, you're not thinking straight, either. That man was right. You're supposed to be working on Chicago, but you've stayed here because you feel some sort of obligation to me and our plan."

He frowned. He opened his mouth, no doubt to deny it. She placed her fingertips over his lips. "Admit it. You should be in Chicago."

He didn't say a word, and he didn't look happy.

And she knew the truth. For both of them. "Dell, you said I was making you insane. I feel the same way. I *have* been taking too many pictures of your body. I *am* lusting after you, if you couldn't tell. It's only natural. We're a man and a woman and we spend a lot of time together. But what's going on between us…it's lust," she said. "That's what was between Lee and me. Lust." Although it had never been like this. Nothing like this heat and need and fear of tipping over the edge. Fear of feeling more. "I don't want that to happen to me again," she whispered.

Immediately, without another word or touch, Dell removed his hands from her waist. He turned her around, reached for a bowl of safety pins kept on the counter and deftly pinned her dress closed.

"I'll go to Chicago," he told her. "I'll give us both a break."

When he turned her back to face him, she nodded.

He forced a smile. "But do not get rid of this dress. I love this dress," he told her.

Her own smile was tremulous. "Thank you," she whispered, and she knew that he understood that the thank you wasn't for the dress. It was for allowing her to save herself.

CHAPTER NINE

REGINA felt as if she had run Dell out of town. It was one thing to take pictures of the man. It was another to forget what she was doing behind the camera. If she hadn't been so pushy, she and Dell wouldn't have ended up in each other's arms, forgetting their surroundings, and he wouldn't have gone away.

The truth was that she missed having him around. Trying to fill her time so she wouldn't wonder how he was or what he was doing, she devoted herself to working on his section of the book. She cruised the Internet looking for background information on the O'Ryan empire and located an old box of O'Ryan family photos, a pitifully small collection. All of them were professionally done and painfully posed. No pictures of Dell with chocolate on his face or skinned knees. His smiles were television, public-eye smiles. Where was the real Dell?

Regina frowned. She chose several, then moved on to Dell's downtown store and office. Despite her "three days of Dell" as she was beginning to think of it, she still hadn't visited his offices. As she did for all appointments she called ahead, but even being married to

Dell she felt a vague discomfort explaining to the management just what she wanted to do. No doubt they couldn't be too careful when a place loaded with jewels was at risk, but a part of her wanted to keep saying, "I'm really his wife. It's okay for me to come down and take photos, isn't it?"

Instead she gritted her teeth and ignored the disapproving glances of the personnel when she finally showed up to take pictures of the lavish, gold and silver and white establishment that was a perfect backdrop for all the diamonds and rubies and emeralds. Her feet sank into the plush carpeting as she visited Dell's office and ran a finger over the massive mahogany desk that must have been in the family for generations.

"It's lovely," she told the frowning woman who had led her there.

"Of course," the woman said. "But, this is highly irregular, Mrs. O'Ryan. Mr. O'Ryan is not a rash man or one who does things without telling me. He sticks to a schedule, he comes to work precisely at nine and leaves precisely at five and he always gives me his agenda and his list of daily contacts."

Ouch! Clearly a wife wasn't on the list of today's contacts, Regina thought. She wondered if Dell had chosen Louella or if he had inherited her with the company. The woman's description of his life seemed so harsh and sterile, so devoid of fun or spontaneity.

"Dell won't mind," she said, hoping that it was so. He had always been kind to her and he had okayed her project. But then she had never invaded his workplace or messed with his agenda before and she hadn't informed him that she was coming here.

The woman frowned harder.

"Why don't you call him?" Regina asked.

"I already have. I also checked your background on the Internet, Mrs. O'Ryan, long before you married him. Doing background checks on all employees is part of my job."

Regina opened her eyes wide at the implication that she was no different than an employee. Darn. This woman thought she had married Dell for his money. Regina had a terrible urge to try to explain that money wasn't the issue here, but that would only have sounded pathetically conciliatory.

"Then everything is all right, I suppose," Regina said, brazening it out. Louella obviously didn't agree. She opened her mouth to speak just as Regina's eyes lit on a glass case in which an exquisite emerald necklace was displayed.

"Oh, my." Regina practically breathed the words. She had never really owned jewels, but she knew that these were out of the ordinary.

As if she had threatened to steal the woman's child, Dell's secretary moved to stand in front of the case, a human guard. "These have belonged to *the O'Ryan Bride* for the past five generations." Her implication couldn't have been clearer. Regina didn't rate. She had not been given the jewels.

But Regina wasn't offended. She wasn't really Dell's bride, and the tense pain that coursed through her had nothing to do with her need for the man. It simply reflected her regret that she would never understand a relationship so strong that it would inspire a man to want to give her such gems.

She smiled at the woman. "They're lovely."

Then she brazenly took a step to the side, raised her

camera and fired off a shot. She might never use this photo, she certainly would ask Dell's permission first, but for now she was married to *The O'Ryan* and she would not be treated as an interloper by anyone other than her husband. Only Dell had that right.

Thanking the woman, Regina took a few more photos and left. A sense of loss and loneliness overtook her. It was probably just because when she looked at the photos and at the text she had included so far, there was still something missing. She didn't know what, but she would have to keep following Dell until she got the magic element she needed.

That fact weighed heavily on her. Those comments she had made to him about lust had not been the whole story, either. The more she knew of her husband the more he fascinated her. Edna had contacted her and told her that she now had more helpers. Besides protecting her and some of her friends, they were making city gardens for the local residents, giving them access to healthier food and sunshine. All of this was, of course, Dell's doing. He felt that promoting his wife's causes was part of his duty. She was his responsibility. And yes, he was her fascination. But fascination, especially toward a man like Dell, could be dangerous to a woman's heart.

At home, she stood outside the door to the room he used as an office. She had been inside before but the details eluded her. It was the man who had caught her attention. She wanted to go inside, but…she had already gone too far. She wouldn't invade without him being here. As for entering his bedroom…

Regina closed her eyes. She had been inside. Once.

The memory was a blur. So soon after Lee's humiliating desertion, she had been desperately unhappy and ashamed. She hadn't even really been aware who had been touching her when Dell had put his hands on her body. All she had felt was that she was a throwaway, a second best. She hadn't believed in Dell's passion and so she hadn't wanted it. But that was before these last few weeks, before she had gazed up into those fiery amber eyes, felt his heat, had his mouth cover hers and fill her with mindless desire.

"Mrs. O'Ryan?"

Regina raised her head and looked up to see Janice, one of the maids, staring at her with a concerned expression. She realized that she had stopped outside her husband's bedroom and that her forehead was resting against the wood. She was remembering Dell's scent and wishing that he were here.

An automatic urge to press her palms to her cheeks and scurry away, embarrassed, came over her. It was what she might have done a few weeks ago before the trial period had begun. But would an O'Ryan wife do something so pathetic?

Regina raised her head and gave Janice a big smile. "My husband is a compelling man, Janice. I miss him," she confessed.

And Regina realized that it was true, a distressing fact she refused to examine. If she was starting to miss him, a man who felt strong emotions were a serious mistake in a marriage…she couldn't complete the thought.

"It's good that you're feeling well enough to miss him, ma'am," Janice said. "I know you were sick for a while. Mr. O'Ryan told me you needed quiet and time to recover. I'm sure he's happy now that you're feeling so much better. I'm glad you're much improved, too," Janice added. "He's a good man and he deserves someone who cares."

The two of them exchanged a meaningful look. Dell was obviously of importance to both of them.

Regina knew then that this private woman-to-woman exchange wouldn't go any further. The maid wouldn't feel compelled to share this with Dell the way she would if she had thought her mistress was looking ill again.

A small sense of satisfaction filled Regina. She had taken a step closer to being something akin to a true O'Ryan bride who was beginning to feel comfortable in her adopted home.

Her satisfaction lasted until the morning when she went down to breakfast and found her husband sitting there.

There was a look in his eyes that seemed to see right through her clothes to her skin, even to her soul.

"You're…Dell, you're home," she stammered like an errant child caught in a fit of misbehavior.

His laugh was delicious and bold and sexy. Sitting there in his white shirt that showed off his tanned skin with the black pants that fit him to perfection, he looked like an unattainable piece of temptation. Man candy dangling before a woman who really needed to stick to her diet.

"I'm home. I hear you've been visiting."

Regina's jaw dropped. "Louella called you to tattle on me."

Dell's amber eyes gazed into her own. He grinned. "Louella is a tigress where my office is concerned."

"Tell me about it," Regina said. "She didn't want me there. But I'm not apologizing. I wasn't doing anything wrong."

"You're right," he agreed.

"And I was working on the chapter for the book. It's supposed to help you, not hurt you."

"I know that. I told her that."

"But you came back to check up on me."

Slowly he shook his head. "Not in the way you mean. I came back to reassure her, yes, and also because when I reprimand an employee I like it to be face-to-face."

Shock filled Regina's consciousness. "You don't have to reprimand her."

"You're my wife."

He had said that several times, but what did it mean? Regina knew. It was a matter of duty, of position, of protocol. She had married into the O'Ryan clan, taken the family name and that alone afforded her a certain measure of consequence. It had nothing to do with how he felt about her.

A slow ache surprised her. She forced it away.

"Don't reprimand her," she said. "Louella is prickly but she cares about you. I'm sure she thought she was protecting you."

"I'll be gentle," he promised. "But I won't have anyone criticizing my wife. Especially not my employees."

"She was probably worried that I was trying to use you or that I wanted your money. Besides, I don't want her to dislike me," she beseeched. "That would make our marriage more difficult."

He frowned and started to protect.

"Please," she said.

Dell blew out a breath. "All right, but only because you requested it."

Regina nodded. "I got the feeling Louella was, I don't know, rather maternal about you."

Immediately he looked wary. "I suppose she is. Most of the people who were around when my parents were alive tend to be that way."

It was one of the few personal things Dell had ever

told her about himself. He knew a lot about her background. She knew very little about his.

Without thought, she sat down at the table. "Are there very many of those people around now?"

Dell's hands folded around his coffee cup as he shook his head. "Most left during my father's last few years. He was…difficult. Partly I think it was the fact that he was ill, but he was also an intensely bitter man."

She wanted to ask why but that seemed intrusive, too nosy. "He seemed distant the few times I saw him when I was a child."

"He was. Always. That wasn't the illness or age." Then Dell reached across the table and took Regina's hand, lightly caressing her fingers. "My parents had an unfortunate marriage. My father fell head over heels for my mother when she was only nineteen. She was very beautiful, exotic, highly emotional and impulsive. He was rich. She became pregnant."

A deep sense of dread came over Regina. She struggled to battle her emotions.

"He married her, of course, and things should have been all right."

"But they weren't."

"No. Not at all. He loved her. But for her, he had merely been a lark, an impulse. Even worse, she fell in love with someone else—my father's valet. It was…ugly."

"Why didn't they divorce?"

"Pride. The desire to avoid scandal and…in the end, they made it work. It wasn't pretty but over time they developed a respect for each other."

"And you?"

He shrugged. "They pinned their hopes on me, that I would be smarter, handle things better."

And not get involved in a messy emotional relation-ship, Regina assumed. "And everyone else pinned their hopes on you, too? Louella?"

"As you said, she cares in her way. I've disappointed her before, so she's touchy."

Regina assumed that he was talking about a woman. That made breathing difficult, but she couldn't think about that. With great effort, she managed a smile. "Well, we'll have to prove to her that you're acting smart now."

But his gaze locked with hers. "I'm not sure I am."

What did that mean? Regina didn't know, but it was obvious that it wasn't making him happy. What would make him happy—or at least distract him?

"Edna sends her thanks. I think she's driving Sam nuts. He says she's giving him silly jobs."

He smiled. "Good. Sam needs to be less serious sometimes." But Dell still didn't look totally relaxed.

"Did something go wrong in Chicago?" she asked.

"Everything's fine," he assured her, but his response was too quick, too casual. Something was wrong.

"Are you going back after you speak to Louella?"

He slowly shook his head. "I would have had to come back in any case. When I spoke to Louella, she reminded me that I had appointments and obligations."

Regina nodded. She was pretty sure that some of those appointments and obligations were social. Yet he didn't request her presence. No doubt after the last fiasco, he had decided he would be better off without her help.

In the past, that might have been a relief. For some reason it wasn't today. Which was totally ridiculous. He *was* better off going without her.

"Well," she said, backing away. "It's good to see you."

"Off to work?"

"No. It's my day off. You?"

"Louella. Then work." He rose and came up behind her, putting his hands on her shoulders. "Thank you," he said.

Regina frowned. "For what?"

"For holding back and giving me the chance to have a heart-to-heart with Louella this time. But I intend to let her know that you have full access to the office and make it clear that as my wife, you have the right to do as you please. And in the future, don't be afraid to speak your mind."

She grinned. "I didn't. I took a picture of the bride emeralds, even though she didn't want me to."

"The bride emeralds?"

"Yes. You know the ones."

His hands tightened on her shoulders. "I should have already given them to you."

"No. You shouldn't. It's a love gesture. That's so not us. And besides, I might be gone soon. You have to keep the emeralds in case there's another Mrs. O'Ryan."

Silence settled into the room.

Dell's hands loosened slightly on her shoulders, and Regina thought he was going to let her go and leave the room. Then he bent nearer, swept her hair back and kissed her neck. So lightly his lips barely made contact.

But she felt it. So deeply. With a shiver of anticipation and desire.

"I'll see you later," he whispered as he whisked out of the room. It was a simple statement, the kind people make all the time to the most casual of acquaintances.

But Regina's heart began to racket around in her chest with an eagerness for him. That was regrettable. She couldn't start needing to see him all the time or someday she would be the one he was reprimanding and explaining things to. Things like "don't expect love. That's not what this is about."

But at least you already knew that, she thought. At least you can insulate your heart.

And at least for today she wouldn't have to worry. It was her day off and she had plans that didn't involve having to steel herself against desiring her husband.

CHAPTER TEN

HE WAS supposed to be staying away from his wife today, Dell reminded himself. This was her day off and she was probably looking forward to some alone time, free of the restrictions of being his wife.

He frowned, thinking of how uncomfortable she had been at that gathering last week and how shabbily his office staff had treated her. It was a reminder that not all women were dying to be Mrs. Dell O'Ryan. The truth was that if this kind of thing kept up, Regina might be happier without him. He should give her another day off before they tried again.

Yes, here he was walking into the garden. He stopped just inside the gates. Regina was down on her hands and knees pulling out a weed next to a white petunia. She hadn't seen him. There was still time to be smart and retreat. But there was also that old line about meeting challenges head-on. He and Regina had been apart for days, and time was passing. If they continued keeping their distance, where would they be when this trial was over?

He drew nearer to his wife. "I have gardeners to do that."

No startled look. All right, she had obviously already realized he was here.

"Yes, I know you do," she said, "but I talked Fred into letting me have my own little plot of land. I like gardening. Callie's been teaching me some stuff."

She liked gardening. He had been married to her for almost a year, so why did he not know that?

"Show me," he said suddenly. He dropped to one knee beside her.

"Dell, your pants. You're not dressed for this."

"They're only pants, Regina." The soap clean scent of her invaded his senses.

"Only pants. They're probably designer or something like that."

They were an exclusive Italian brand. But she didn't have to know that, and it wasn't important. His clothes were expensive but they were just clothes. They were replaceable, not like time missed with a woman who might decide to leave soon. In that moment, his decision about whether to stay or go to the office was made.

"Stop complaining about my pants and show me what you're doing," he teased. "Maybe you can teach me something and I can impress Fred with my extensive knowledge of soil types. The man has considered me a hopeless case ever since I rode through his prize rosebush with my bicycle when I was twelve."

Finally she laughed. It was such a lovely, unfettered sound that he couldn't help moving closer. "I'm just tending them so they can keep growing, and there's not much to say. These are simple gerbera daisies, nothing exotic," she said, moving to another mound of bright pink, white and yellow flowers. "But they still need to breathe. It just takes some simple get-your-hands-dirty work."

He leaned closer and plucked out a weed, his body close to hers, the warmth of the sun and her nearness incredibly soothing and…something else. Exciting? "You think I can't get my hands dirty, do you, Mrs. O'Ryan?" he asked, trying to keep his tone light.

She waved her hand airily. "*You're* an O'Ryan and as you mentioned, you grew up with gardeners to handle the messy stuff."

And she hadn't. It occurred to him that despite their proximity he had little experience of the world she'd grown up in. Whatever had happened to her had made her strong, but she was fragile, too. And, he reminded himself, for the time being, at least, she was still his.

"It's your day off," he remarked. "Are you going to spend all of it in the garden?"

She turned toward him and now her face was only inches from his. "No." And for a second he wasn't sure if she was telling him not to get any ideas and lean closer or if she was answering his question.

"Care to elaborate?"

"I have plans. Not gardening plans."

Okay, this was his cue to leave. She wasn't volunteering what she was going to do, so she obviously didn't want him to know. Maybe there was even a man involved.

"Mind if I tag along and shadow you?" he asked, to his own and obviously to her surprise as well. Those caramel eyes opened wide. She seemed incapable of speech.

"But then, I might be intruding," he offered. "In which case, I'll withdraw that suggestion. Pretty rude of me anyway."

"No." She paused. "I mean, no, you aren't being rude and you wouldn't be intruding. I just, well, of course you can come. We're supposed to be getting to know each other. I want us to be friends. And after all, I've spent plenty of time following you with my camera. Fair is fair."

Which meant she really didn't want him along but she was going to put up with him.

Dell felt a slight sense of annoyance…and a decent measure of satisfaction.

"It's part of our trial period, part of the plan, after all," she added.

His satisfaction faded. He was beginning to be tired of the plan as the main reason for their every interaction. But then it was, wasn't it? If he hadn't insisted on a two-month trial to try to save their marriage, she would have already filed for divorce. Perhaps he should have let her do that.

"Regina, maybe—if I forced all this togetherness on you, you can say no to more of it."

She rose to her feet suddenly. "Is that what you want?"

"No, but I don't want you to be unhappy or to feel trapped."

"Then we'll go on," she said, raising her chin in a haughty, pretty way. "I think…we're making progress, and besides, I have plans of my own. I want to write your section of my book."

All right, so he was a subject now. Someone she could photograph. Irritating as it was, he could live with that, he supposed.

"I'll meet you back here in twenty minutes, all right?" she said, moving toward the house. "Wear something you can burn later."

And with that intriguing comment, she left him. There was a spring in her step. Dell realized that that was a new touch. Just two weeks ago, she hadn't looked nearly so perky. And now his wife got all excited at the prospect of using him for a pictorial subject and also at the prospect of getting dirty.

A chuckle slipped between Dell's lips. He took the stairs two at a time.

"You call those casual clothes?" Regina asked, eyeing Dell's obviously expensive and pressed khakis.

"They'll burn as well as any I've got."

She sighed. "You're probably right. It would be too much to expect an O'Ryan to have blue jeans in his closet."

"I have them. They're nicer than these."

"Let me rephrase that. It would be too much to ask to expect an O'Ryan to have *normal* blue jeans in his closet. Like these," she said, pointing toward her own well-worn jeans with a hole in the knee and another enticing place high on her thigh where a few remaining strands of denim crossed her pale skin, revealing more than they covered. The jeans fit her as if they had been made to her exact measurements, cradling a slender waist and the flare of her full hips.

"Very nice," he said, his voice thick. He couldn't help examining that bit of naked skin at her thigh.

"Come on," she said, blushing as she turned and showed him her delicious backside. "I'll drive."

Dell groaned.

"Hey, I'm a good driver," she said.

"You are," he admitted. "I've seen you drive. But I'm a tall man."

She studied the little red subcompact. "I love my little car."

And what was he to do? He folded himself inside. Now they were in this tiny space together. His knees were jammed to his chest. His head was against the ceiling. And his arm was almost touching hers. Suddenly the car seemed much nicer.

Regina looked at his pretzeled body. "Oh, you poor man. What am I thinking? You're right. We should take your car."

"No. I'm good." He turned and looked at her and realized that he really was good. She looked perfect in the car. It made her happy.

"You're not good. Your poor knees." She leaned closer to get a view of his position and her body brushed his thigh.

Oh, yes, he was very good. He had an ache, a physical ache, one he couldn't assuage without being a jerk. But that was his own problem.

"Drive, Regina. I'm fine."

"All right. It's not far." But she didn't tell him where they were going.

"You might change your mind, and now that I have you, I've decided to use you."

Interesting. He stared at her.

She blushed. "Your muscle power," she explained.

Even more interesting. "You'll see," she added lamely.

But he still didn't understand when she pulled up in front of the local animal shelter.

"Muscle power?" he asked.

"I take pictures of them," she explained. "Sometimes they're rambunctious. There aren't enough volunteers and the animals aren't used to so much individual attention. And if there's someone who can hold them and pet them while I take the shots, it's easier to make them look cute and lovable and help them find homes."

Her voice was matter-of-fact, but he could see by her

expression that there was nothing matter-of-fact about her reaction. And once inside he saw even more evidence of how much this meant to her.

"Hello, Maynard," she said to a little Airedale with a body that wriggled uncontrollably when he saw Regina. "Still here, sweetie? He has issues," she told Dell.

"Issues?"

"He was mistreated by his owners. Can you imagine? Who would hurt a creature with eyes like this?" she asked, her soul in her own eyes.

He *could* imagine. She had been hurt, and he knew that. It killed him that people—Lee—had hurt her, but…had he been any better? Lately he had been asking himself how he could have been married to her and known so little of her.

She looked up at him and now she was wary. "Don't do that," she said. "Don't look that way."

"How am I looking?"

Regina glanced away. "Like there's something about me that makes you feel guilty. All the time."

"No. That's not how I feel about you all the time." But he wasn't sure what he did feel. Barely controlled lust of late. But he wasn't about to tell her that.

And anyway, just then Maynard whimpered. Regina bent over the little creature and stroked his wriggling body. "I'm going to do my best to find a place for you, Maynard," she said. "A safe place. I'm going to make some lists of possible owners. I'll be like Dell here. You'll be part of my big plan."

When she looked up, she was wearing an impish smile.

"Are you teasing me, Regina?"

"Yes, but you're an O'Ryan. Teasing is probably bred out of you."

"Maynard, the woman is incorrigible," Dell said. "I hadn't realized."

She laughed. "Come on, Mr. O'Ryan, we have work to do."

For the next several hours, she put Dell through his paces. "Yes, hold him just like that. You look good with a dog. Oh, yeah, this man is going to sell you to the public, Phoebe," she told a flirtatious white poodle. "Women will take one look at him holding you and say, 'I have to get me some of that.'"

"Phoebe, I feel exploited. I'm nothing to this woman but a backdrop."

"A sexy backdrop," Regina insisted.

"Well, that makes it so much better," he agreed, and actually it did. He was having the time of his life. Regina was in love with these poor creatures so in need of a home.

"They haven't measured up. In some way they've all been considered deficient," she explained later when they were on the way home, tired and wrinkled and with tears in their clothing where dog and cat claws had occasionally broken through. A black lab named Sandy had been especially enthusiastic about meeting Dell and had bowled him over, ripping his shirt and giving him a tongue washing.

"You were good with them," she said. "Thank you. I was teasing earlier but it really could make a difference to have you in the shots. I want them all to be saved, to find good homes, and frankly, I don't care if it takes a gorgeous man in the picture to do the trick."

Her tone was so fervent, so poignant that Dell couldn't look away from her. A sudden thought came to him. His cousin Lee had been a lot like a lost puppy.

"Were you trying to save Lee?"

The sudden change in topic and the personal nature of the question had been unfair, Dell conceded. Regina's hands tightened on the wheel. She went silent for five whole seconds. "No," she finally said, her voice not much more than a whisper. "I don't think so."

"I was."

She nodded. "Why? He was an adult."

They were just outside the gates to the house now. Regina stopped the car and turned to look at him. As if she didn't trust his words to be true and had to see his expression.

Dell held out his hands in a dismissive gesture. "Lee was an adult but he came to live with us as a broken child. His father, my uncle Jack, had been wild and rebellious, and my grandfather had disinherited him. Jack married a woman just as rebellious. It wasn't a good relationship, and they were abusive parents, I think. By the time they overdosed and Lee came to live with us, he was nervous and awkward and a bit wild himself.

"Still, we were cousins, and I grew to care about him. My father was impatient with him. He never felt that Lee could represent the family in a good light and he didn't mince words. I became Lee's protector. I tried to teach him things so that he wouldn't make my father angry. Lee wanted to be accepted in the worst way. He always told me that he wished he were a true O'Ryan."

"Wasn't he?"

"Of course. But my father wouldn't let him forget that his parents had created a scandal. Lee wanted to escape that bad boy image so much."

"So you tried to help him become a true O'Ryan." Regina's brow furrowed. "Was I a part of that plan, then?"

"At some point you *were* the plan. Nothing else had worked."

She shook her head. "I don't understand. I don't meet any of the O'Ryan requirements. I was never a debutante."

The more she spoke the more Dell realized how much he had wronged her, used her. Not that he hadn't already flayed himself with that whip when Lee had deserted her. "A debutante would have been more of what Lee had been handed all his life. He wouldn't have met expectations; he would have been hit with criticism. Not because he lacked breeding or money. What he lacked was confidence. He needed kindness, someone who would give him stability, stroke his ego, make him less anxious and help him come into his own."

"And I was to do that for him?"

"Yes." His answer was terse. "I didn't know he would hurt you, Regina. It never occurred to me that that might happen."

He gazed into those clear, kind eyes of hers and found that she was looking back at him, full of pride, her chin held high. No tears, no accusation in her expression.

"I knew that you thought I would be good for Lee. Why else would you have introduced us? But I never knew you expected me to be able to do so much, that you had that much faith in my abilities. And see, you were wrong. I didn't do any of the things you thought that I could. I failed."

A rush of anger and frustration rose up in Dell. He leaned across the small confines of the car and reached out. Sliding his fingers into Regina's hair, her cupped her face, staring down into her eyes.

"Regina, you didn't fail. I was unfair, and I am so incredibly sorry."

She was shaking her head. "Don't be. I was old enough to know what I was doing. I got sucked in."

"Because you loved him, and I let that happen."

Gazing up at him, she stared directly into his eyes. He could feel her pulse beneath his fingertips. "I don't think I did love him. That is, I cared about him immensely and I just…you're right. He was like a puppy, and that kind of wide-eyed loyalty and neediness can be very appealing."

Her lips were so close, so full, her words so soft.

Dell swallowed. "Do you still miss him?"

"I only miss what I thought he was, and…"

"What?" His voice was a harsh whisper.

"I love the fact that you cared about him so much, that you wanted to help him fit in so he wouldn't be hurt."

"Don't make me out to be the good guy. I was raised to follow my duty, to know what a good O'Ryan should be. That was my goal, to turn Lee into a good O'Ryan."

But that look in her eyes, those luminous, lovely eyes…

He leaned closer and covered her lips with his own. He tasted her fully, deeply, sipping at her lips. She was soft, giving, sweet and moist. Desire spiraled, and he pulled her closer, his palms skimming down her arms to her waist.

Regina shifted and slid her long fingers into his hair. She kissed him back.

He leaned into her touch, bending her backward.

The small, shrill horn of the little car went off as they leaned too close. Dell jerked and banged his elbow against the dash.

Regina shrieked.

The sound of voices sent them both turning. There were people across the street taking pictures. Not of them but of the estate. It wasn't unusual. The house was on the

National Register of Historic Places, and sightseers were fairly common. What wasn't common was him making out with his wife in broad daylight in a too small car.

Not that he minded. At all.

His wife clearly did. "Dell," she whispered in his ear, urgently, pushing at him. "Dell, people are watching us."

"Not us. The house."

"But we're here. If they take a picture and you're in it, sooner or later, someone might notice that it's you…and me."

"We're married."

"I don't feel married right now."

Something hot and fierce lanced through him. He pulled back and stared at her. She didn't seem to notice. "I feel like some teenager having sex for the first time in the back of a car."

Which only made Dell more aware that he hadn't yet made love to his wife. At least not fully. And he wanted to badly. Right now.

"What would we say if they recognized you?"

"Regina, not everyone knows who I am. They're just interested in the house."

But the group was coming closer. "I feel conspicuous," Regina said. "I'm going inside."

Without another word she got out of the car and started toward the house. *What was a man to do?* Dell thought. He followed his wife.

"Excuse me," one member of the tourist group said. "Do you know anything about this house? Who lives here?"

Dell watched as a very pretty blush climbed his wife's cheeks. "The O'Ryans live here."

The people shook their heads as if they didn't know

the name. They probably didn't, and, bored, would leave soon, move on to the next mansion.

But to his surprise, Regina suddenly looked indignant. "Of the O'Ryan Gemstone Galleries? They make jewelry for the stars."

Now the group was interested. "Do you two know them?" one man asked, indicating the path Regina was taking.

His wife looked delightfully flustered. Dell held back a grin.

"No," she said suddenly. "That is, not personally. I just—clean their house and my husband, Donald, is the gardener. He weeds the flower beds."

"So…you get to see the inside?"

"Every day," she assured them, but Dell couldn't help noticing the tension around Regina's eyes.

"Well, it's certainly beautiful," the woman said as she snapped a photo that took in the house as well as Regina and Dell. Then she waved and the group moved away.

When they had gone, Dell studied her. Her cheeks grew pinker. "I'll bet you were a pistol when you were a kid. Probably gave your teachers a run for their money."

Regina groaned. "I did tell a white lie or two."

He grinned.

"But only in emergencies," she said. "I would never lie about anything important. And I wouldn't have lied now except I was worried. You're an O'Ryan. I'm working very hard on this pictorial. You're making a big move into an unknown market. You don't need bad publicity or to have your picture in the tabloids, especially not with the notation that you were making out in a car in broad daylight."

He tilted his head and couldn't stop smiling. "It might improve my snooty reputation."

"You're not snooty. You're reserved and refined."

"And as Donald the gardener I bet I'm good at pulling weeds, too," he reminded her.

"Agh!" she groaned. "Don't remind me. I don't know what came over me. I just…you were talking about what it takes to be a good O'Ryan. I'm sure that dignity is a part of the O'Ryan credo. I just didn't want anyone to think I had brought you down to the level of a common…man. If we were going to make out, we could at least have had the good taste to do it in the limo."

Dell wanted to smile. She was so cute in her distress. But she *did* sound distressed, and he knew she felt somehow responsible for what had happened. Heaven knew why. He had barely been able to keep his hands off her all day and this wasn't the first time he had kissed her. If anyone was responsible for that hot, sizzling kiss, it was him. And he wasn't ashamed. Right now he wanted nothing more than to taste those lips again. The limo would do. So would any available space where he could hold her, slide his hands over her skin, peel back her clothing and find the treasure that lay beneath. White-hot desire raged through him, but somehow he managed to ignore it. Instead he reached out and gently cupped his palms around her waist.

"Regina, hush," he said, pulling her into his arms. "Don't look like that. You're my wife, and what you and I do together is nobody's business but our own. Kissing my wife is not a crime." Although he knew how ill-advised it was given the tentative nature of their relationship.

But Regina was still staring up at him, uncertainty in her eyes. He couldn't blame her. Things were unsettled and she had already been hurt by a seemingly settled relationship. She was worried. He couldn't have that.

"I told them you were a gardener," she murmured as she leaned against him, her lips moving softly against his chest and driving him mad.

"I know. Do you think I'm a good gardener?" he mused, trying to tease her into a happier mood.

His plan worked. She ducked her head, then leaned back in his arms and looked up, giving him a sheepish smile. "I'm sure you're…at least adequate. But Dell?"

"What?"

"You're a really great kisser." Then she pulled away and hurried into the house.

Dell's eyes widened as he watched her disappear. He couldn't help chuckling. His wife had had the last word in the teasing game. And now he wanted her even more.

CHAPTER ELEVEN

DELL stared at the appointment sheet Louella had given him as if he had never seen an appointment sheet. He was obviously not himself today. And no wonder. All his thoughts were starting to focus on Regina.

Some people might say that was a good thing. A husband should be attentive to his wife. But that wasn't the problem. This wasn't about attentiveness. This was about the fact that she was becoming the driving force in his day. And he very much doubted that she felt the same way.

Especially now that she had confessed that she hadn't really loved Lee but had thought of him as a needy puppy.

Something unpleasant slipped through Dell. He remembered how diligently Regina had been working on this pictorial to promote him to the Chicago prospects, he remembered her work with Edna, her charitable acts with the animal shelter.

He had the very bad feeling that he, Dell O'Ryan, a man who was a mover and a shaker and a powerhouse among the upper echelons of Boston society and Boston businessmen, had become one of his wife's charitable projects. Why else did she keep talking about becoming his friend?

And she didn't want his jewels, Dell reminded himself, remembering their discussion of the Bride Emeralds. Swearing beneath his breath, he stared down at the list of things he had to do, people he had to see. He didn't want to see any of them. He wanted to be with Regina. Too darn much.

The fact that she had admitted enjoying his kiss didn't make it any easier, because now he knew that he could force the issue and she would probably play along.

He didn't want her playing along or taking care of him, but keeping himself from taking things to the next complicated level was becoming more difficult. He needed a good distraction.

Picking up the phone, he made a few calls. Then, with a growl, he picked up the list Louella had given him. Work had always distracted him from his troubles in the past.

Anticipation grew in Regina the closer she got to the door of the mansion. And it was a good anticipation, the kind that left her breathless and aching and…

Stop it, she told herself leaning against the door. The day had been mostly awful. Despite a good early beginning with a shy, glowing bride, it had gone downhill after that with the Vandivers changing half their plans and making more demands, forcing the Belles to redo work and rearrange schedules. Then, while Belle and Julie had been trying to manage the rescheduling, Charlie Wiley had called again, flustering Belle and forcing Julie to tell him Belle was unavailable.

Only one good thing had happened after that and it

had to do with Dell, Regina was sure. Almost against her will, her heart flipped, and the bad day seemed to fade away. That man…

No, not that man. Dell, who was starting to mean too much to her. Just the sound of his name had started to conjure up unwelcome images, desires. That kiss the other day…

Regina shivered in response. She was starting to feel things for her husband, to want to be with him. Which was so wrong. Longing had never been a part of the plan. This whole arrangement was supposed to have been practical. Dell would have a wife and he wouldn't have to worry about the whispers and the media circus of an O'Ryan going through a divorce. She would have a secure and calm existence.

Companionship was allowed. Desire of a sort was to be expected. If they stayed together it would be a real marriage with nothing too far out of the ordinary, but…what was going on inside her wasn't ordinary at all. When Dell had kissed her, she had quite simply lost herself. All that had mattered had been touching Dell, feeling his lips caress hers.

Panic gathered in Regina's stomach. If she continued this way, she was going to get hurt.

"I won't let that happen," she whispered. Somehow, she would have to find a way to protect herself. Still, Dell needed to be thanked for the news she had gotten today.

She climbed the stairs to his office. He wasn't there. That was odd. Dell was almost always home by now. But then for the past two days he'd been spending an amazing amount of time working. The Chicago project, she assumed. Of course. With things heating up after his last trip, he would be too busy to do much else.

A tiny sliver of longing shot through her. *Irrelevant,* she thought. And then Dell appeared in the hallway behind her. He looked tired. His tie was slightly askew, his hair looked as if he had run his fingers through it. He was delightfully rumpled and sexy and far too compelling in spite of it all.

Her first thought was to get closer to him. "Long day?" she asked instead.

His amber eyes turned dark. "Standard," he said, but he had a look in his eyes that told her he would like to come closer, too. But he didn't.

"I had a call from Jaz Ezland who runs the shelter. Phoebe has a new home, a very nice one," she offered. "So do a lot of the dogs we saw the other day. An unusual number of them."

To his credit, he didn't blink. "I'm glad." His voice was warm.

"Dell?"

He waited.

"Thank you. This means so much to me," she said, taking a step closer, her hand outstretched.

In two long strides, Dell was across his room. He dropped one hard, quick kiss on her lips, hesitated, then kissed her again. Longer, deeper.

Her mind sizzled. She rose on her toes. A moan escaped hers.

Immediately Dell froze. "I'm trying very hard to keep from touching you," he said. "Until you're ready for more."

Her immediate thought was that she *was* ready for more. She wanted it all, but she'd spent a lifetime following impulses and this time, a wrong impulse could leave her irreparably damaged. What if things didn't work out? What if he left her? Didn't people always leave?

Dell, took a deep breath. He brushed his fingers lightly

across her cheek, then turned. "Work," he said, and the word sounded more like an order than an explanation.

Within five minutes she heard his office door close. He didn't come out before she went to bed.

Regina lay on her bed that night, wondering what on earth she was doing. That kiss…every kiss they'd shared…

Oh, my word. Dell's lips, his hands…no wonder women wanted her husband so badly. And no wonder Elise Allenby was so heartbroken. Had he kissed *her* that way?

Regina covered her face with her hands. That was none of her business. It was before her time, and it was with a woman…

A woman he had chosen.

Abruptly Regina sat up.

What am I doing? It was true that she'd had doubts earlier about her relationship with Dell, but she had offered him a divorce and he had turned her down. He was the one who had suggested the trial marriage and he was fulfilling his bargain. Hadn't he been doing all that he could to get to know her, even going so far as to go to the shelter with her that day? And he had tried to help her at the ball by extending her business connections.

If things had stalled just because there was a little heat flaring between them, the kind that was bound to appear between any man and woman who had shared living space, surely she could get past that. She hadn't taken a single picture of Dell in days or finished the chapter on him, and time was running out.

You've never been a shy little weakling, Regina, she told herself. *Don't start now.* In the end, this union might not work, but it wasn't going to be because she hadn't done her share. Dell might have money and position and a body that made her shiver. He might be the world's greatest kisser, but she had some skills, too. And tomorrow she was going to get back on the horse…er, back behind the camera and do her part.

Just don't start thinking all this togetherness and touching means more than it does, she reminded herself.

Because despite the heat that flared between them he had already told her multiple times that this would never be a marriage based on love. And if a woman kept that in mind and just did the smart thing, surely she would be okay. Wouldn't she?

Doubts assailed her. *Time to squelch those and take a stand,* she thought, picking up the cell phone lying by her bed. She punched in a number.

"Dell O'Ryan," came over the phone, his voice deep and low and husky. Had he been sleeping already?

"Dell, it's Regina."

A pause followed. "Where *are* you?"

"In bed," she said automatically.

She heard his swift intake of breath. "All right, forget I asked that. Is there an emergency?"

"Not exactly."

"You're calling me from within the house. You could have come to see me."

No, she was brave but not brave enough to go to his room while her emotions were still racketing around inside her body like explosive ping-pong balls.

"Tomorrow, I'm going to finish the photos," she told him. "All right?"

Again, a hesitation. "I'll be ready," he finally said.

For some reason, getting that settled didn't make it any easier to sleep.

* * *

Dell was lifting weights in a private training room in the gym and Regina was taking photos when a news crew from a local cable television station showed up. Apparently his recent excursions with Regina and the fact that she had been following him all week with a camera had come to the attention of a local station that was low on news for the day. Before either of them was aware what was happening the cameras were turned on him and Regina.

"Mrs. O'Ryan, can you tell us how exactly you met your husband?"

Regina's eyes opened wide. Clearly startled and uncomfortable, she hesitated.

Dell frowned. He was just about to tell the man to get lost when Regina shook her head. "We were neighbors. I've known who he was most of my life." Which left a lot out but satisfied the reporter. Dell was proud of his wife for fielding that one so deftly.

"And is it true that Mr. O'Ryan has taken up one of your favorite causes? I understand that a number of pets at a local shelter have suddenly found homes in elite neighborhoods." The man shoved an eight-by-ten of a cute little dachshund into Regina's hands. The dog had melt-your-heart soulful eyes and suddenly Regina looked up at him, wearing a soft, grateful look that would have been a threat to the most icy of men's hearts.

"Trixie. I didn't know she was one of the ones chosen, Dell. And she had that lame leg, too." Regina looked up at him as if he had given her a priceless gift.

He took a step toward her. She took a step toward him, too, but then she seemed to catch herself. She gave him a quick shake of her head. Ah yes, they weren't alone.

"My husband is a very fine man," she said. She looked

up at Dell, and the cameraman turned the lights and camera on the two of them. Regina blinked from the glare.

"I—" she continued, but caught in the whir of the video camera, she looked suddenly self-conscious. "I know this sounds strange coming from a photographer, but I don't wish to be interviewed on film. I'm not—I don't think—" She looked down at her favorite ripped jeans and loose white blouse. She'd been down on the floor only moments earlier taking photos at knee level, and her hair was mussed, strands of the silken stuff kissing her cheeks and temples. She looked a bit wanton, and Dell had a sudden urge to step in front of her and shield her from the view of the other two men.

Instantly he turned to the crew, adopting the icy hauteur he'd learned from a master at the game, his father. "I don't recall okaying this interview."

"You're a public figure, Mr. O'Ryan."

"But this is a private club."

"Yes, but—"

"There are rules, and they're enforced." He had no idea if such rules even existed, although there were people milling about outside this door who probably did know. He didn't bother asking. These two men were not seasoned reporters, and they probably didn't know protocol here, either. From the uncomfortable look the two men gave each other, neither of them wanted to risk a visit from management or the local authorities. Good, they were on the verge of deciding to leave.

But then…

"Excuse me, but I'm in the middle of doing a major photo shoot of my husband. Your cameras are wreaking havoc with the lighting." Regina had apparently found her voice and her resolve. She stood as tall as Dell had ever seen her and faced the men. "If you don't mind, I'd like to finish my work."

Her brown eyes were flecked with gold, he realized, and when she was miffed, they appeared to flash. Her normally creamy complexion turned a dusky rose. Her chest rose and fell with every deep, irritated breath.

With her tousled hair and her fervor, she was mesmerizing. Dell didn't know whether to applaud or to groan. The men turned their attention from him. They forgot about his implied threat.

"We apologize for the lighting, but this is for television," one man argued. "Don't worry, Mrs. O'Ryan, we'll get out of your way soon, and we'll do your husband justice. We'll send you some really nice pictures. Professional quality."

Regina froze. She looked down, her hair covering her face, and when she raised her head again that pretty little chin had come up, she drew her shoulders back and turned her full attention to the intruders. They were twice her size, taller, broader and beefy where she was delicate, but she placed one hand on her denim-clad hip and stared them down as the gist of the man's words settled in.

"If you're trying to imply that I'm merely playing at being a professional or that your credentials and expertise outweigh mine, then you're wrong. In fact—" Regina whirled to turn her Hasselblad on the camera crew "—it occurs to me that the pictorial of my husband should engage *all* aspects of his life, including the media's attraction to him. Would you mind moving a little closer and looking as if you're having a conversation with Dell? Yes, both of you." She didn't wait for a response. She just started snapping shots.

"What? Whoa, wait a minute," the clearly startled

men objected, but Regina kept shooting pictures. "Tilt your head slightly," she ordered. "Yes, you know the routine and the importance of setting and contrast and mood. Try to catch that beam of light filtering in through that skylight. Ask my husband a question. Any question. The answer doesn't matter, only the realism of you looking as if you're actually talking to him. Oh, yeah, that's it exactly. I love this!"

Her camera clicked off shot after shot. Although she had started off insulted, Dell could tell that she soon forgot her pique. She was thoroughly enjoying herself, losing herself in the moment. And in almost no time the men began to join in, infected by her enthusiasm and technique, suggesting shots. By the time she was done, they were both looking at her as if they'd been given a rare gift. They'd obviously never met anyone quite like Regina, and when she finally lowered her camera and sighed with satisfaction, they were half in love with her, Dell thought. And who could blame them?

"Mr. O'Ryan, your wife's something else. She flipped that camera like a juggler at the circus, but we can't go back to work with absolutely nothing to show. Come on, give us a break. How about a couple of answers and a newsworthy moment here?" one of them coaxed. "We'll make it good."

And, Dell thought, they were sure to mention that his wife was a very talented woman. After the last few minutes, he had no doubt that they would paint her in a highly flattering light. All of that would be a definite boon to Regina and the Belles. What was a man to do?

Give in, Dell thought. Promote and protect his wife. No question.

"All right, here's a bit of truth, gentlemen," Dell

said. "My wife, Regina, grew up not far from me, almost beneath my nose, in fact, but I never knew she existed until recently. I must have been blind, because anyone can see that she's both talented and lovely and that I am an incredibly lucky man to have found such a treasure." And with that, he stepped closer to Regina, tilted her face up and dropped a kiss on her lips. Her eyes drifted shut and he tasted her sweetness. She rose ever so slightly on her toes. Her palms pressed against his chest. Then she curled her fingers into his T-shirt and pulled just a touch closer, returning his kiss.

Dell's world began to tilt. He slipped a hand beneath the silk of her hair as he deepened the kiss.

"Oh, yeah," the cameraman said. "That's perfect."

As if he had shot her, Regina's eyes flew open. Warm color drifted up her cheeks and she leaned back. Instantly Dell released her.

"That's off the record," she stammered to the men.

One of them saluted her as they gathered their equipment. "I can't wait to see those pictures, Mrs. O'Ryan. Will you e-mail a couple to the station?"

Then they were out the door. Dell was left standing there with his wife's hands still bunched in his shirt. And then in the next minute she had backed away and turned all business. "I really have to get to the shop. And I have to see what I can do with these pictures. This rounds things out nicely. I think we're almost through," she said.

Dell nearly swore. He had embarrassed her publicly, and she was going into hiding. He could tell. Which couldn't mean anything good. The look in her eyes was unhappy, and there had been too much unhappiness in her life this year. His plan to make this marriage of convenience truly convenient for him might not work for her, he finally acknowledged. She had had a terrible year. She had lost so much. A child.

And if the child had been born they wouldn't be considering whether to stay together or not. Their daughter would have bound them.

The thought slipped in, but Dell discarded it. A child should never be given the burden of maintaining his parents' marriage. It didn't work that way, as he well knew. If a couple was going to stay together, that should be a choice built on reason. Not on necessity, not on love and certainly not on the mere flash and fire of passion.

But he didn't say any of that. It brought the tentative nature of his relationship with Regina under the microscope and he wasn't ready to examine it right now.

"I should have sent them away," he said.

She shook her head. "No, it made sense. We're trying to be a couple. That means appearing as a couple, united, normal, even touching at times.

"But...I don't think I'm very good at this, Dell. As you know, I tend to be impetuous, but I can't be impetuous now. I can't afford any more drastic mistakes, especially not when I've made so many already." She looked up at him, uncertain.

"Regina, I didn't mean to upset you."

"No, it's not you. It's me. I..." She leaned closer as if to tell him something, then blanched and quickly whirled away. "I'm sorry, but I really have to go to work. I'll see you later."

And without another word, she hurried out the door. Dell was left there standing in the silent and suddenly empty room. He felt like kicking himself. What had he said or done?

A lot, and obviously one or all of those things had spooked Regina and pushed her farther away. Once again he had handled things all wrong with his wife and now she was on the run.

A desperate need to get things back on a comfortable level took hold of him, and that in itself was alarming. He didn't want to feel so much or so strongly about a woman.

So what was he going to do about that? This sweet, impetuous woman was feeling as if she had to put reins on herself in order to make this trial marriage work.

That was something to think about…

CHAPTER TWELVE

"You're looking pale, Regina," Serena said. "Is everything all right?"

"I'm just a bit tired." Which was as close to the truth as Regina could get. She was also scared. Positively petrified in fact. This trial marriage had seemed so simple at first, and now…she didn't want to think about the now or what had been happening to her heart lately.

Serena looked concerned. "It's not your husband, is it?" she asked.

Regina wondered how Serena could always see right through to her fears, but she shook her head. "Dell is great," she answered, and it was the truth. That in itself was alarming. She didn't want to start thinking of him in superlatives or begin to feel emotions that could never be returned. What was she going to do? How was she going to get past this?

Her thoughts were interrupted by a bell jangling over the door.

Belle smiled at the man who entered. Probably a salesman, but Belle knew how to handle salesmen so that they left without feeling they had been kicked out.

"May I help you?" she asked the man who appeared to be in his mid-fifties with salt and pepper hair.

"I sure hope so," the man said. "I'm hoping to find Belle Mackenzie. I was here once before but missed her. Would you happen to know where I might find her?"

Immediately Belle looked wary. Regina's attention went on full-alert.

"I'm Belle. You're Rae Anne's friend, aren't you?" Belle asked. Her tone seemed a bit chilly.

"Yes, ma'am, I am. And so are you, I understand." There was a tone in the man's voice that snagged Regina's attention. The man was looking at Belle as if she were the last piece of chocolate cake on the plate.

"Yes, Rae Anne and I go way back. She thinks she knows me." Her tone indicated that Belle disagreed and that she was not happy that her friend had sent this man around.

The man, however, grinned broadly. "So, you don't want to sell your car?"

Belle blinked. "My car? The Rolls?"

"I hear she's a real beauty. A vintage model and the prettiest shade of forest-green a man has ever seen."

Instantly Belle looked even more flustered. "Oh, yes, Rae Anne said you were interested in my car."

For the first time all day Regina wanted to smile, too. Belle had been very upset that Rae Anne had been trying to set her up with this man, but now maybe that wasn't true? Regina wondered how any woman could understand anything that went on in a man's head. No wonder women got hurt so often.

"I'm Charlie Wiley," the man was telling Belle. "And yes, I'm very interested. I hear you've got a 1930 Rolls-

Royce Phantom II. I've been looking for one like that. Could I see it?"

Unfortunately the bell clanged again and a customer came through the door looking for Callie. With Julie on her lunch break, Belle took over the task of meeting and greeting and getting the woman back to where she needed to be.

Regina gave Charlie a smile and went back to her task of changing the photos she had hanging on the wall. Serena worked on the dress on the display mannequin. By the time Belle finished and turned back, the customer had been tended to and Charlie was studying Belle as if she were some strange sort of wonderful exotic creature he had never encountered before.

"About the car," Belle was saying.

"The car? Oh…yes, the Rolls Phantom II is sure a beauty." But he was looking at Belle as if she were the beauty.

And Belle was looking a bit flustered. Regina could relate.

"I'm sorry. I can't do this," Belle said suddenly.

"You don't want to sell your car," he said sadly.

"It was my late husband's."

Regina raised a brow. Belle's words made it sound as if Belle had undergone a recent loss, but Matthew had been gone many years.

Now, Charlie was looking sad and concerned. He looked as if he was going to go over to Belle and hug her. He even took a step forward. "I understand. I lost my wife. It's difficult to give up the things they loved. It's just that when I talked to Rae Anne she seemed to indicate that you might be interested."

"Interested?"

"In selling the car. I really want that car." But he was looking at Belle's lips.

She licked them. "I'm afraid I can't do that. Not yet."

"All right then," Charlie said. "Thank you for talking to me, at least. But, if you change your mind, let me know." Then he walked out of the shop.

When Charlie was gone, Belle seemed to deflate. She started fanning herself. She looked at Regina and Serena with a frown. "If you tell anyone I made a fool of myself, I will flatly deny it."

A tiny sympathetic smile lifted Regina's lips. "You were just fine, Belle. But…you know it wasn't the car. He liked *you*."

"Chicken feathers. He's younger than me, he's thinner than me and I am going to have Rae Anne's head on a platter. With gravy. I actually thought for a while that she was trying to fix me up with the man. But he was only after my car. You don't think he saw what I was thinking, do you?"

But she didn't wait for an answer. Belle walked away fanning herself. "I have got to go call Rae Anne and give her a piece of my mind before the next wedding party comes in."

Regina and Serena exchanged a look. "It's never easy with men, is it?" Serena asked.

Regina didn't answer, but she totally agreed. It was her last coherent thought of the day. Customers began to swarm. One of the senior Vandivers called with even more changes. Regina, who took the call, could hear Liz Vandiver screaming at someone in the background.

"Just let me get through a few more weeks," she told herself. "Let everything turn out all right." But she knew that it wasn't the Vandivers she was thinking about.

* * *

Dell hesitated outside his wife's door. It was early, but then early was a necessity. If he didn't catch her now, she would be gone for work. Raising his hand, he rapped on the solid mahogany, then waited and rapped again.

Ten seconds later, the door opened. He looked down at Regina. She was wearing a cropped, red v-necked T-shirt.

His mind began to short-circuit but he stopped himself. That was not what this was about. Instead he looked down at her feet.

"You have kittens on your feet," he said.

Immediately she looked down, too. "Oh, yes. Dell?"

"I know. What am I doing here? What do I want?"

What he wanted was to kiss her. "I'm taking you out for a day on the town," he said.

Those caramel eyes opened wide. "I have work."

"I know. Me, too. But…"

She waited. "Yesterday," he explained. "And all the days that have passed…I think we're losing sight of something important. We were once friends of a sort. We should try for that again. At least one day to be sure."

Of whether we're going to make it or not, he added to himself.

Suddenly she smiled. "You're kidding, right? Take a whole day off when it wasn't in your appointment book? I'll bet you've never played hooky once in all your life. You can't make me believe that Louella would have approved."

"Louella would be appropriately horrified." His parents, too.

Regina patted his arm. "Then it's good that you have me, a woman with some experience in these matters. I'll call in sick for you."

"Excuse me?"

"You know, like when you're in high school and you

want to go to the beach but you need a parental excuse, you have to get an adult, or at least someone who sounds like an adult to call in sick at the school."

"You did that?" He chuckled.

"Once or twice when I was younger. Nowadays, hardly ever. I'm good at my job, I'm needed and I enjoy it. But after yesterday when the Vandivers were acting up, I could use a few hours of freedom. Today was supposed to be a prep day, not a photo day, so I can swing some time off. Tomorrow I'm booked, so if I'm going to play it has to be now."

And what man could turn away from that?

"I'll leave you to get ready," he said.

"Where are we going?"

Dell blinked. "I have no idea."

Her laugh caught him square in the gut. "I'll bet that's another first for you. No plan. Leave it to me. I know the perfect places for friends to hang out together. You don't have to worry about a thing."

Except for keeping this platonic, he reminded himself.

Regina couldn't stop smiling. She had dragged Dell all over the place today. They had visited a park where she'd fed him popcorn and cherry slushes and asked him to push her on the swings and then had offered to push him because she was pretty sure that he hadn't had a lot of opportunity to spend time on swings. Playgrounds probably hadn't been approved recreational activities by his parents. They'd walked part of The Freedom Trail and taken a side trip in order to walk through the Mapparium, the three-story stained-glass globe at The Mary Baker Eddy Library. She had even taken him on the MBTA blue line down to the waterfront and he hadn't complained a bit about the pace or the way she was charging ahead and leading him around. Dell had lived in Boston all his life but he had never ridden the subway. O'Ryans didn't. That hadn't been a surprise. What *had* surprised her was that he had never taken the ferry over to the Boston Harbor Islands.

Now they were on Georges Island having a picnic. "You haven't taken many pictures today," he noted.

She laughed. "Yes, it's hard to believe, isn't it? Most people who know me think me and my camera are joined at the hip."

"You're not?" he teased.

"Okay, most of the time I am. Taking photos is almost like talking, to me. It's a form of communication, but today wasn't for taking lots of pictures. It was for fun."

"It *has* been fun. Still I wish you'd show me more of your work. I've seen some of your shots, of course, the ones on the shop walls and the few you have at home, but you don't have many at home."

She shrugged. "It didn't feel right, but I'll show you the ones I've taken of you."

"That's work, though."

Regina crossed her arms. "It was not work. I did that out of…"

Love. The word just floated right in there. "Marital responsibility," she said. What a dry-sounding phrase.

Dell didn't look as if he liked it, either.

"Maybe friendship, too," she said, using the word she was beginning to hate. This day had been fun and wonderful, but there was just something about her husband that didn't make her feel friendly. She felt more.

Ugh, was she pathetic or what? The man had practically offered her the world; a marriage, a mansion, his name and protection, his friendship, even passion. To ask for more would be so wrong. Not to mention impossible, since it wasn't at all what he wanted.

Don't think about that. Don't think about that, she ordered herself. *Don't mess up the day.*

"So...friend and trial husband," she said, trying to keep her tone light, "you're Mr. Competitive, aren't you?"

"Hmm, that sounds like a trick question, but I'll bite," he said with a smile that practically stole every breath in her body. "Yes, friend and trial wife. My Mrs. O'Ryan," he added, and it was almost all Regina could do to keep from launching herself into his arms. "I've been told that I'm competitive."

"Good. You'll need your competitive spirit for the next half hour. Otherwise, I'm going to beat the pants off of you at Frisbee." She stood and pulled an orange disk out of the bag she had brought with her.

Flopping onto his back in the grass, Dell groaned. "I just ate and you want me to run and jump?"

"And catch," she agreed, placing a hand on her hip. "You grew up in that great big house with all those rules and expectations. I'll bet you never even played this before."

"I'm an O'Ryan, not an alien from another planet." He rose and moved out and away from her.

"Hmm, that might be close to the same thing." She tossed the disk his way.

He lunged, catching it with ease, then twisted and whipped it back her way.

"Very nice, Mr. O'Ryan."

"My father didn't take us on family outings or feel that common playgrounds were classy enough, but he felt it was important for O'Ryan males to have some athletic skill. There were goals to be met. Achievement was stressed."

"Achievement is great, but it's not fun." She flipped the disk high so that it looped back toward him lazily.

"Fun is overrated, young lady. The most common person can have fun, but an O'Ryan sets the bar for achievement and success," Dell said with such an imperious tone that Regina could almost hear his father lecturing a young and still wide-eyed Dell. It was no wonder her husband spent so much time working and so little time playing.

"Your father said that?"

Dell didn't question her assumption that the quote had been his father's. "Don't worry. I survived childhood, Regina," he said. "And I grew up to marry a woman who knows the value of cherry slushes and playgrounds and play," he said. "And who was willing to spend a day teaching me all the things she thought I needed to know."

He released the disk, sending it her way. Unfortunately Regina was so choked up by Dell's heartfelt assessment of her that she failed to reach out quickly enough. She leaned too far the wrong way and the disk nearly hit her in the head, leading her to duck backward and fall right onto her back. She lay there, dazed.

Dell came running up. "Regina, are you all right?" He leaned over her, his amber eyes worried.

Her head was still spinning and with the sun behind him, her husband was so dazzlingly gorgeous. No wonder Elise Allenby wanted him.

"Regina?" Dell held up three fingers. "How many?"

She giggled. "I'm fine."

"How many?" he ordered.

"You're pretty good at all this lord and commander

stuff," she said. But Dell looked ready to explode. "Three," she said primly. "And thank you."

"Good," he said in reference to her finger counting. "And thank you for what?"

"I don't know. For suggesting this day and for going along with my version of what you had planned. I know all of this—" she held out her hands "—is outside your comfort zone. And it was nice of you to agree to take the subway instead of bringing the limo."

His smile was mischievous. "Yes, it was a terrible sacrifice. We O'Ryans have to have our comfort or we throw tantrums."

"You know what I mean." She sat up and hit him lightly on the arm.

"I do. And…this is nice."

"I can't believe you haven't been here before. There's so much history in these islands. I mean, the only manned lighthouse remaining in the States is on the island, and here on Georges Island there's supposed to be a ghost. Prisoners from the Confederate Army were kept here and the legendary Lady in Black was a prisoner's wife. Thirty-four islands right outside your home and no one ever took you here. That's so…"

He smiled.

She frowned. "What?"

"You don't have to be indignant for me, Regina. I'm not a poor-little-rich-boy anymore. I'm a man and I don't have to conform to the rules. I can do whatever I like."

She looked up at him to see if he was telling the truth or just trying to make her feel better, but kneeling beside her, he was so close…so warm, so Dell…

He leaned down and kissed her. Slowly. Thoroughly. She surged up, grasping his biceps to keep from falling backward, but there was no need. Dell had wrapped one strong arm around her. He was holding her close. *I can't let myself fall any further than I already have* was her last coherent thought as she lifted her face and returned his kiss. His lips were warm, his touch was magic; the air around them sizzled.

Dell kissed her again, more deeply.

"Look, Mommy, those people are kissing," she heard a child's voice say.

Immediately Regina sat up and pushed away. She stared at her husband with regret and desire and a hefty portion of guilt. So much for not being able to fall. All she had to do was get too close to Dell and she did all kinds of stupid things.

"Well, that was very nice," she said primly. "A nice way to top off the day." She tried to rise.

"Regina." Dell's voice was stern. "I—"

"If you say you're sorry or try to take some sort of responsibility, I will hit you very hard. This was supposed to be a day of play and a day of no regrets, and we were playing…sort of, so don't regret. At least there were no camera crews this time. No harm done."

He studied her for a moment silently, but then he moved aside, rose and helped her to her feet. When she dared to look up at him again, he was wearing a speculative look.

"What?" she demanded.

"You taste like cherry slushes," he said.

"Well, that's good then. I like cherry slushes."

"And so do I. A lot more than I want to."

Which was a totally depressing thought, since it was obvious they weren't talking about cherry slushes at all. He wanted her but he didn't like it one bit. It didn't fit in with his plan for this marriage. But when they got back to the house and she turned her phone back on and picked up her messages, all thoughts of plans fled.

She turned to Dell and she knew that her face was ghostly white. "The Vandivers have canceled. We're out money, but worse, they were going to be our ticket to success and lots more business. Instead once word gets out that they've canceled our contract, the lemmings will start to flee."

All that work, all her friends, all their dreams…

"Regina," Dell said gently. "Come here."

That was all it took, that deep voice laden with complete sympathy. Without another word, Regina threw herself into her husband's arms.

CHAPTER THIRTEEN

DELL caught Regina and pulled her close. "I'm so sorry, Regina, but please...don't worry. I can help you."

"No."

"The Vandivers are asses, and they shouldn't be allowed to harm you this way just because they're selfish. You know I have the means. I won't even feel the dent, and—"

Immediately she pulled back. "No," she said again. "No, please. I appreciate your offer so much, Dell, and I know you don't understand, but I can't take your help. All my life, I've struggled to prove that I'm good enough, that I can do things, that I'm not a screw-up, and if I take money from you for this, then I haven't done anything."

He opened his mouth to object but she shook her head. "Don't mouth the usual platitudes. I know what I am and what I'm not. Believe me, I know my strengths, but this business with the Vandivers...it hurts the people I care about. I'm so angry and disappointed, I can barely think straight. I just need time and I need...I don't know, but I know I can't take your money to fix things. Through thick and thin, dis-

appointments and trials and years of work and friendship, the Belles have come together on this and it's
ours, mistakes and all. I can't inject you into this. I
can't become indebted to you. If you and I end…
feeling that I owed you money…if we end our
marriage, it has to be clean."

Her words lashed through him. "And if we don't?"

She hesitated. "That has to be clean, too. Nothing
messy. No complications."

But what Dell saw in her eyes, that hesitation, told
him that she was thinking of ending things. She needed
to be able to walk away totally free. Something dark and
hot and wrong ripped at him, but he fought to contain
it. She was hurting right now. Scared. And she wouldn't
let him help her. What could he do?

Nothing. Apparently absolutely nothing. So, he
pulled her closer into his arms and just held on. That was
all he could give her, all she would allow. His strength.
His comfort.

When it grew dark and she was still wide-eyed and
in pain, he carried her to bed and lay her down.

"Don't leave me," she whispered. "Stay. I don't want
to be alone with my thoughts."

He nodded and lay down next to her, pulling her
body up against his as he rested his chin on the top of
her silky hair and stroked one hand down her back. "Do
you want to tell me your thoughts? You don't have to."

"I know." And she didn't say anything for long
minutes. He listened to her breathing, felt her shudder
when he shifted her to pull her closer still.

"My parents wanted me to be an accountant," she
finally said. "Something practical. They were so disappointed when I insisted on becoming a photographer. It

was there in every look, every word. They had only one child, one shot. They had hoped for someone they could brag about to their friends, not someone who at times ended up praying that the jar of peanut butter would hold out until she sold something."

Her words echoed through his body, a soft whisper. "Didn't they ever see your work and how good it is?"

She pulled back in his arms and a hint of a painful smile flickered across her face. "Well, they did try to smile politely when they realized that they weren't going to be able to change me, but to them it was just irresponsible to try to sell people pictures. I was just playing at being an adult in their eyes. And now they're gone, swept away in a boating accident before I had a chance to make them proud just once."

"Maybe now they understand," he whispered. "Maybe wisdom and true appreciation comes with dying and they're looking down seeing what they hadn't seen before."

Even in the dark he could see that she didn't believe him. "You obviously never met my parents."

"I've met you, and you really are incredibly talented."

Regina leaned forward. He felt her small smile against his chest. Her muffled thank you warmed his skin. Against his will, desire shunted through him. He started to turn away slightly.

But in the dark she caught at him. "No. It was inevitable that we would do this, finally. I've wanted it before and I want it more now. Tonight, I need to touch you and have you touch me. I am, after all, the woman who lives for today. Can't be an artist without that attitude. Maybe tomorrow will never come or it won't be the tomorrow you want, so take today. I think maybe

I forgot that in the past year. Today is important. Maybe it's more important than yesterday or tomorrow."

With that, she pulled herself up and slid her arms around his neck. She kissed him and gave him what he'd been dying to have.

Dell gave up the battle he'd been fighting for too long. He swept his wife beneath him. He kissed her the way he'd been wanting to for weeks, tasting her, savoring her, plunging his fingers into her hair.

She rose to meet him, tearing at the buttons on his shirt, a participant, not a mere recipient. Together they undressed him.

"You're beautiful," she said. "You've always been so beautiful."

"I think those are my lines," he said, reaching for her.

"No. They're not. They're definitely mine."

"I'll show you," he argued. With only the rising moon for light, he found Regina, slipped her out of her pretty little shoes, her blouse and jeans. He removed the tiny, pale blue scraps that remained, shielding her from him.

For half a second, with moonlight in her eyes, he saw the self-doubt in her expression.

"You're incredibly lovely," he said fiercely. "And you're driving me mad with the need to touch. So, my pretty little wife, if you're going to change your mind, then—"

"And miss this? That's so not going to happen," she said, cutting him off and giving him a beautiful smile. "I'll even agree to let you tell me that I'm lovely if you'll touch me, Dell. Right now. Please."

"You can't know how much of a pleasure it will be." He traced his fingers over her sensitive lips. He kissed her eyes, her cheeks, her throat. Then together he and his wife found each other in the dark. He lost his legendary self-control. She enchanted him more than any princess could. They touched in ways they had never touched before.

And when he entered her, he knew it had to be right. It had to be special for her, because she was special.

It was. He loved her into the night, reveling in her softness and breathing in the scent of her hair. His fingertips learned the contours of her body. He discovered that what he'd thought of as ecstasy was only a shadow of the real thing. And, when the morning came, and he looked over to see Regina sleeping peacefully, her dark hair against her pale skin, he knew he might never know a night this magical again.

Because the sand was almost out of the hourglass. A decision would be made soon. What if it were the wrong one? She still hadn't told him that she would stay. A silent protest roared through his brain.

The stark light flowed in through the window, illuminating everything. It woke Regina. When she opened her eyes and looked at him, she smiled at first. And then he saw it. Just a hint. The smallest trace.

Regret. Cinderella's magical evening had flown, and unforgiving reality reined once again.

He had just made love to his wife for the first time and it had been earth-shattering. But now it was morning, and she was remorseful.

"Good morning," he said and gave her a reassuring smile she didn't return. "Don't be sorry," he said.

"I'm not. I'm happy."

Had a woman ever sounded less happy? What was he to say to that? "Good, because I don't regret a minute," he said and kissed her softly. Then, sure that she wanted to forget and aware that she had important matters and work she had to tend to, he climbed from bed and went to get dressed and face the day. There was something he absolutely had to do and it wouldn't wait.

Regina came home from work not sure what to expect. The shop had been too silent. Whether that was because the word had already spread that they had lost their biggest account or just the result of an unusually hot day didn't really matter.

"It's probably better that we don't have too much business," Julie had said. "With expressions like ours, anyone who came through the door would most likely run away."

But Regina knew that her own woebegone expression had less to do with the Vandiver cancellation than what had happened last night. What had been a possibility before had turned into a reality. She had lowered her defenses and made love with Dell. It had been wonderful, blissful…devastating.

Because now she had no protection remaining. She was falling in love with her husband when he had specifically told her not to expect love.

Would she never learn?

She was still asking that question when she warily pushed open the door at home later that evening. In an eerily familiar scene, Dell was waiting for her much like that day she had asked him for the divorce.

Regina's heart hurt. It wasn't that she thought he would ask her for a divorce. Rather, it was that she knew he never would. He would be content staying married to her without love.

Could she do that?

"Is something wrong?" she asked.

"Not at all. Everything's going according to plan," he whispered, dropping a light kiss on her lips. But there was a slight tension in his stance. Did he suspect that she felt more than he did? Was it a burden?

"Regina, I have a dinner party tonight at seven. If you're willing, I'd very much like you to come." His manner was so formal, so very Dell as she had known him from afar once, so solicitous of her. What could she say?

"Of course. I'll just get ready."

"Thank you," he said. There was a hint of regret in his eyes, but he gave her a smile as she left. A short time later when they walked out the door, he handed her into the limo.

The drive was quiet, the house they pulled up to imposing but not as imposing as Dell's mansion.

"Regina, I'd like you to meet Mr. and Mrs. Roger Stanson, and this is their daughter Jennifer. This is my wife, Regina," he said as smiles and polite greetings were exchanged. Regina didn't fail to notice the appreciative glance the young woman gave Dell. For half a second, she was tempted to move closer to him, but that would have been juvenile, wouldn't it? And she would never want to embarrass Dell.

"My wife is a talented photographer for The Wedding Belles, a wedding planning service," Dell volunteered as dinner progressed. "She and her colleagues offer only the best."

"Oh, that's so nice to know," Mrs. Stanson said with a smile.

Regina wasn't sure what to say. It certainly wasn't the first time Dell had promoted her, but he'd never mentioned the Belles before. He was obviously trying to be helpful.

He might not believe in love, but he was an incredibly generous person. If only she could settle for that…

Tears gathered in her throat, but she choked them back. Steadfastly she kept her eyes off her husband, afraid her feelings would be too obvious.

"Dell is an incredible catch, my dear. I can't believe a woman ever got him to settle down. He'd been dodging marriage for a long time," Mrs. Stanson said. She obviously meant it as a compliment to Regina, but all Regina could think was that she had entrapped Dell by getting pregnant.

"I'm very lucky," she admitted as Dell's hand covered her own.

"Not as lucky as I am, sweetheart," Dell said, taking her hand and placing his lips against it. Instantly her body was on full-alert. What was going on here? What was Dell doing?

"You two are so romantic," Jennifer said with excitement in her eyes.

"It's probably Regina's work," Dell said. "When a woman and her friends spend all day turning girls into princesses and making magic for brides and grooms, that tends to rub off. My wife knows how to make romance come alive."

A slight bit of tension crept into Regina's soul. What *was* Dell doing? But then she knew. He was selling her.

"Jennifer's getting married soon," Mrs. Stanson said. "As she's our only child, of course we want the very best for her."

What could Regina say? "She should have the very best. Every bride should. Every woman should have that special day when everything that happens is a re-flection of the love she and her groom feel for each other." Which was, indeed, what Regina believed. *But I would never have brought it up,* she thought, *without Dell steering the conversation in that direction.*

"I like that," Mrs. Stanson said. "It sounds as if you really care about your clients."

"I do. I really do," Regina told her. Which was of course the truth, and seemed to make Mrs. Stanson positively glow.

The rest of the evening passed in polite conversation, but when they finally left to return home and climbed into the limo, Regina turned to her husband. "Dell...I'm so very grateful for what you're trying to do, but you can't save me every time I fall. It doesn't work that way. I'm not Lee."

"I know that, but I couldn't not do this."

In that instant, she knew that that was the relationship they would have. She would fall more in love with him. He would be kind and gallant and wonderfully passionate. He would make love to her gently, sending her to heaven and beyond and every day she would be more distressingly, hopelessly in love. Sooner or later she might let the words slip out in the night.

He would know, and though it wouldn't be the kind of marriage he wanted he would still never desert her. He would stay. Out of duty and honor and because he wouldn't want to hurt her.

And it won't be him hurting me, she thought as they came to a halt. *It will be me. I'm hurting me. I'm the one in love here. I'm the one who stepped out of line and who didn't obey the rules.* Just like always. Only, unlike her parents, Dell would never reprimand her. He would just never love her.

Her heart was shattering. The truth was damning.

When the car arrived at the mansion, she turned to him. "I'm very tired," she said apologetically, even though she wanted nothing more than to throw herself into his arms and make love.

He stroked her cheek gently. "Get some rest then. Everything will be fine, Regina."

But it wouldn't be. There never had been a chance of it working.

She went upstairs, but she didn't sleep. Instead she dragged out everything she had for the book. She worked through the night filling in the missing pieces that completed the project and presented a true picture of Dell the man, not just Dell the millionaire. When morning came at last, she was done. An electronic package went out to numerous locations with a few clicks on the keyboard.

Carefully she packed, choosing only the things she needed most. Then she went to Dell's study, her bag in hand.

He took one look and rose from his chair. Rounding the desk, he started toward her.

She took a step back and held out a hand.

"Is it because of last night, because you asked me not to help you and I ignored your wishes?" he asked.

"No," she said, shaking her head vehemently. "Courting the Stansons wasn't like handing me money. It was a nice gesture. I just…" She looked up at him and fought back tears. "We just don't suit, Dell. I like you. I've always liked you." Which was so far from what she felt it was just totally inadequate as a description. "But…I can't be happy here."

And that was the complete truth.

"Forgive me," she said. "I never meant to bring

scandal or notoriety to your family, and I'm sure the divorce will at least bring you some negative attention."

The word that fell from Dell's lips was one she'd never heard him use, but he quickly composed himself. He advanced with his hand out.

"You didn't bring scandal," he said. "I wish you could be happy here, but if you can't…"

He took the hand she had held out to meet his and pulled her close, snaking his arm around her. For a few seconds he held on tight and Regina thought he would surely see her heart breaking to bits. Then he pulled back, gave her a quick kiss and said goodbye. He turned back to his desk.

Regret filled her soul. He might say that she had not brought scandal to his life, but she had obviously disrupted his life. He had been on track to a bright future with no shaky spots when she had come along.

At least his future will still be bright eventually, she reassured herself as she left the house for the last time. When the truth became known, when the women of his world discovered that Dell O'Ryan was a free man again, there would be celebrating in the streets.

Eventually there would be another Mrs. O'Ryan, one who fit the mold.

And I—

Regina couldn't finish her thought. Thinking of a world without Dell was too hard to bear. And there was still so much to do before she left him forever.

CHAPTER FOURTEEN

DELL had never been an emotional or demonstrative man. He had lived most of his life completely in control of his emotions, but these past two days…

Had he really thrown a glass against the wall in his office?

He rubbed a hand back through his hair and forced himself to try to concentrate on work and on forgetting. But it wasn't working, and he knew why. He had fallen in love with his wife, and she didn't want to be married to him anymore.

Every impulse in his body screamed at him to go to her and ask her to give him more time, but he knew that wouldn't work. Somehow he had to get through this.

"And I will just as soon as I make sure she's all right," he promised himself.

He picked up the phone and dialed. Within seconds, a voice answered.

"Belle? It's Dell O'Ryan."

Was that a gasp? "You have a lot of nerve calling here."

A thousand questions ran through his brain, but only three mattered. "Why? Where is she? How is she?"

"She's here." Was that Natalie? Had Belle put him on speakerphone?

"As in listening?"

"No. We wouldn't let her talk to you. She's in her studio with a client." That was most definitely Audra.

"But we know you hurt her."

Pain exploded in Dell's brain. He didn't even know who had made the comment. He didn't care. "How do you know she's hurt?"

"She slept at the shop two days in a row and she looks like hell," Belle said. "I don't know what's going on between you two. Even as close as we all are, Regina would never discuss her marriage. She'd feel it was a betrayal of her vows, but…"

"I would feel the same way," Dell said, "but in this case I'm too worried about Regina to keep quiet any longer." He explained what had been going on between him and his wife, her request for a divorce and the agreement that had followed.

"She wants out," he said, not bothering to keep the despair from his voice.

A long silence ensued. "No, she thinks she broke the pact." Serena's voice was unmistakable.

Slowly a tiny thread of hope slipped through Dell. "I don't understand. Explain that."

Someone gave a long sigh. "Regina has never been the type of woman for a practical marriage. It just isn't possible in her world. She's emotion personified. If she decided she couldn't stay, it was because she loves you."

Dell wasn't buying that. "Or because she realized that I love her and she didn't want to hurt me."

Now the silence lengthened. "But which one is it?" Belle asked, her voice less accusatory now. "You'll never know if you just leave things the way they are, will you?"

Doubt assailed Dell. He didn't want to make things

more difficult for Regina by making her listen to his declarations. The thought of her having to spell out the fact that she could never love him was like a thousand knives in his heart, but...

"I'll tell her the truth," he said.

"That could work. Or she might believe you're just humoring her and being gallant. Regina has said more than once that you're a good guy."

Callie was right. Words weren't enough, not for someone as amazing and complex as Regina.

"Thank you," he told them and started to hang up.

"Wait! What are you going to do?" Belle demanded.

"I don't know. Just don't tell her that I called."

Dell hung up the phone, no plan in sight. He waited. He thought. He took a pen and paper, but for the first time in his life, no plan emerged. How did a man try to win a woman who had been hurt by so many people all of whom should have been on her side? What could he do? *And what if she still turns me down?*

Dread seized him. Trying again with Regina was a serious gamble and he had never been a gambler. What if he lost? And what should he do?

He sat there for a long time, uncertain where to turn. The sun began to sink. The sky turned rosy and purple, and as if the heavens had heard his questions, the answer finally dropped in from nowhere. *What would Regina do?* What would his flamboyant, fiery wife do?

The answer was so obvious. *Something big. Something risky and unexpected.* He might have to connive a little, play hooky, tell a few white lies and throw caution and dignity out the window.

In six seconds flat he had Louella on the telephone, firing off instructions.

"She's changed you, I see," Louella said, giving a sniff.

"Yes, she has," he said with a smile.

"And you don't mind that she's practically papered Chicago with stories about how you have been helping former prostitutes?"

Dell raised a brow. "Excuse me?"

Was that a yelp of delight from Louella? "I knew you didn't know about it. I've been keeping tabs on your wife. The word hit the Internet today. She wrote a big article, lots of pictures. Most of it good, she probably thinks, but that picture with the prostitute is all over the image searches. If you don't believe me, look it up yourself."

He did. There he was with Edna. And there he was with Maynard. With the two cameramen. The captions were all glowing. And only one person was missing. Regina herself.

"Your father wouldn't have approved of some of that stuff," Louella said. "And he wouldn't have approved of that picture those two cameramen put on the Internet the other day, either. Your wife looks like a prostitute herself. I think her tongue might have been in your mouth."

"You don't say." Dell did a new search and there he was with Regina, locked in each other's arms. They looked...right together.

"Your father—" Louella began again.

"Is no longer your boss," Dell said. "I am. And actually, my wife is, too. If you have a problem with that, Louella, I'm sure we can make some sort of early retirement arrangement."

She sputtered. "I—"

"I believe the words you're looking for are 'I apolo-gize, Mr. O'Ryan and I will never insult your wife again.'"

Louella muttered the words but Dell knew they would eventually have to work something different out. He didn't care about that now. But there was one thing more.

"Don't bother with those instructions I gave you earlier," he told his secretary. "I've decided that this requires my personal attention."

He hung up the phone, took a deep breath and thought of the woman he adored. Today he was going to risk everything he had ever been and said and done. If he failed, he would look like a hopelessly pathetic chump in the eyes of the world. That kind of attitude could even affect his business. It was almost akin to leaping off a cliff onto the rocks. Not the type of thing an O'Ryan did, ever.

Dell pushed back from his desk…and leaped.

Regina felt as if her feet were made of lead. Each day was more difficult than the one before. Being without Dell was like no pain she had ever felt. It was more intense, more disorienting. She wasn't even doing her job well, the one thing she had always been able to count on in the past. It was as if a part of her had been ripped away.

It's not fair to my friends, either, she reminded herself as she got in her car. Things were picking up here. Belle had even invited Charlie over and let him see the car. Callie was singing, everyone was smiling and an excited hum had begun to thrum through the shop again. Probably because the upcoming Stanson wedding had brought in more business. Once again, Dell had bailed her out. She would have to write a thank-you note. The thought of doing something so formal with Dell made her spirits sink. But she really had to at least pretend to be happy. Her sadness was affecting her friends. That was probably why Callie had sent her on a flower run.

"Nothing like a whole carload of pink roses to cheer a person up," Callie had said, all but pushing her out the door.

Regina had smiled obediently. Now she made her way down the street. It was lunch hour and traffic was heavy. Stalled, Regina looked around her. A billboard high above the street caught her eye. Was that Dell's face?

Her heart began to race, but then she chastised herself. She'd grown used to seeing Dell in her dreams. Now, distraught and lovesick, she was seeing him everywhere. But she shaded her eyes and looked again.

No, it was Dell and in big red letters the sign proclaimed, "Please come home, Regina."

A car honked its horn behind her. She continued down the street. A mobile billboard crossed the intersection in front of her. "Meet me at the mansion," it said.

Someone must be having a joke at her expense. An O'Ryan would never do something as public as this. But as she turned the corner, determined to keep her mind on her task, she got stopped at another street corner. A trio of musicians was singing, nearly blocking traffic. "I'm so sorry if I hurt you, Regina," the man sang. "Please come back and let me tell you how I feel." The sad words and the plaintive melody would be considered sappy and silly by some, but as the singer sang the words, "Come back, Regina," tears began to slide down her face.

A knocking sounded on her window. She looked up to see a police officer outside her car and realized that the light had changed, but when she rolled down the window, the man smiled sympathetically. "He said to tell you that he needs you and that he's sorry if that hurts you. Oh, and he also said to hurry."

Regina blinked and nodded, but she didn't move.

The man tilted his head. "Hurry," he repeated, then nodded toward the line of cars behind her.

"Thank you," she whispered.

The man winked. "Dell's a good guy. Maybe a little crazy today, or maybe a lot crazy, but a good guy. Better hurry before he really gets desperate and calls out the marching band."

Regina swiped at her tears and obediently turned the car. *Dell needed her.*

It wasn't the same as loving her, but…

"I have to see him," she said out loud. She must have messed him up in some way if he was doing something so out of character. At the very least she could explain why she couldn't stay and accept the generous offer of his name. She had wanted to protect her heart, but he deserved to at least know that she wasn't rejecting *him*.

All the way to the mansion, she saw the signs. On billboards, on bicycles, on buses. There was even a blimp.

"Oh, Dell," she whispered. What had she done to him? For the first time ever, she could sympathize with Louella. The man was just too caring for his own good. She should never have allowed him to marry her in the first place. Look what she had driven him to do. Every O'Ryan in history would sit up in their graves and scream at the top of their lungs at the indignity of it all.

With a squeal of tires, Regina pulled the car up in front of the mansion. She ran from the car and threw open the door to the house.

Everything was silent.

"Dell? Dell, are you here?" Her heart was pounding,

racing, practically thumping its way out of her chest. She hadn't seen him in three days but it felt more like three hundred days.

A whimpering sounded.

Regina looked down to see Maynard running toward her. She bent and scooped him up and he began to wag his tail and wriggle and lick at her chin.

"Lucky dog." Dell's deep voice sounded, and Regina whirled to see him leaning casually against a wall at the end of the hall.

"You have a dog," she said, as if her brain had suddenly ceased to function.

He slowly shook his head. "No, you have a dog."

"Oh, yes, your staff doesn't like dogs."

"To hell with my staff. They'll learn to like them. We might end up with two or three or more...if you come back."

Regina closed her eyes. "Dell..."

"I know," he said, his voice harsh. "I know. You can't stay. You told me so."

Her heart was hurting so much. Everything in her soul was hurting. She wanted to stay...so much.

"Just tell me this," he said. "The reason you can't stay, is it because you don't love me?"

He took a step closer, and her mind ceased to function. What was he asking? And how much could she reveal without being irreparably damaged. But wasn't she that already? Shouldn't there be truth among them.

"It was never because I didn't love you," she said, her voice coming out thick and broken.

He took another step closer. "Then is it because you know that I love you and that scares you?"

Her eyes opened wide. "Don't say things that aren't true. You said emotions were too messy."

"They are," he agreed, drawing close enough for her to touch him now. "I've been dying inside since you left. Can't get much messier than that."

"Dell, I—"

"I would never hurt you, Regina."

And then she broke. "Do you think I don't know that? You would never *want* to hurt me, but you couldn't help it. Feeling about you the way I do and knowing that you would just be so darn nice when you didn't feel the same way at all…"

He cleared the small space between them. "How *do* you feel about me?" he demanded.

She stood there, struggling with her pain.

He shook his head. "No, you're right. It's not fair to make you answer that when I all but kidnapped you to get you here. Regina, I love you, heart and soul. I miss you every minute we're apart. I'm not sure if I can live without you, but if being with me hurts you, I—"

His words broke through her pain. She all but flew forward, rose on her toes and kissed him. "That wasn't what was hurting me. It was loving you so much and thinking you could never love me."

Dell's smile was instantaneous and incredulous. He spun her around and planted a hard, demanding kiss on her lips. "I couldn't help loving you. You're everything."

"A friend?" she asked.

"Oh, yes, and a conscience and a lover and the most wonderful gift of a wife a man could ever have."

Regina felt something against her ankle. Maynard was rubbing up against her.

"The dog has taste," Dell said.

"Where did you find him? I know he was already adopted."

He shrugged. "I signed my life away to the friend who had him."

"Oh, Dell, you shouldn't have done that."

"Do you want to give him back?"

"Never. I want to keep him."

"And me?"

"I gave you your chance. Now I'm not letting you go."

Dell's laughter rang out, the most wonderful sound in the world. "That makes me the luckiest man in the world."

Regina smiled and she and Dell came together again, but a rumbling in the street caught their attention. They went to the door and opened it. A crowd had gathered there. A news helicopter was flying overhead. The Belles were at the front of the crowd.

"What's this all about?" someone called.

"Kiss her already," another one called out.

Regina blinked as the cameras snapped and flashed. "Dell, all those signs," she said. "Not an O'Ryan thing to do. It looks as if you got all of Boston's attention."

He wrapped his arm around her waist and pulled her up against him. "I don't care about Boston or the world. Just you. Do I have your attention now?"

"Oh, yes," she said. "Most definitely. Now, did you hear what the man said? It's past time for you to kiss me."

Dell grinned and followed his wife's instructions to the letter, scooping her up against his body as his lips met hers. "I love being married to you," he said when he finally released her.

The crowd went wild. Dell pulled something from his pocket. He bowed to the crowd. He turned to Regina. Obediently she turned and lifted her hair.

"Don't ever leave me again, Regina," he said as he fastened the O'Ryan bride emeralds around her neck and kissed the spot where the clasp rested.

Regina shivered and turned in his arms. "Never again, Dell. Now, can we go inside and begin our marriage again?"

"You have the most wonderful ideas, love," he told her as he closed the door on the cheering crowd and gave Regina his heart forever.

* * * * *

SOS Marry Me!

MELISSA McCLONE

For my own Belles: Shirley Jump, Myrna Mackenzie, Linda Goodnight, Susan Meier and Melissa James. Talented Harlequin authors and amazing friends!

Special thanks to: Missoula County Detective David Brenner, Idaho County Sheriff Larry Dasenbrock, Virendra Gauthier, John Frieh, Virginia Kantra, Michael Leming, Dru Ann Love, Mike Mooney, Anne Ryan, Tiffany Talbott and last, but not least, Carol Hennessey, Jen Hensiek and Le Ann Martin with the Clearwater National Forest.
I take full responsibility for any mistakes and/or discrepancies!

Melissa spills the beans about her own wedding dress:

"I was a practical bride on a budget – a mechanical engineer who couldn't conceive of spending tons of money on a dress I would wear only once. But there was a secret romantic in me, a woman who wrote romance novels on her lunch hour and dreamed of feeling, for one special day, like Grace Kelly or Princess Diana or Cinderella.

Never mind, I told myself firmly as I went shopping. It's only one day. It's only one dress.

I visited store after store. I found practical gowns. Budget-priced gowns. I tried on dress after dress. And staring in the mirror, I never saw the bride of my romantic longings smiling back at me.

Nearing desperation, I went to a bridal boutique a colleague had recommended. The gowns I tried on were far from practical, and not one was on sale. But finally, as I was zipped and hooked and buttoned into what must have been my hundredth dress, I turned to the mirror and saw...a bride. Me. The girl of my romantic dreams. The woman who was ready to pledge her life to one special man.

Only one day. Only one dress.

I bought it.

As I wrote *SOS Marry Me!*, I thought about the friend who helped me find my gown and the woman who designed it. She knew what was important to brides. And so does my wedding-dress designer heroine, Serena James."

**Hear all about Melissa's latest news at
www.melissamcclone.com**

Serena is a top wedding-dress designer for The Wedding Belles. Here are her tips on how to pick the right dress for your big day:

♥ Don't visit too many bridal boutiques on the same day. Trying on wedding gowns should be a fun experience, not a chore! Do invite a trusted friend or your mother to go with you to offer opinions and support. But try to discourage the entire bridal party from trooping along. Too many opinions may only confuse you. Ultimately it's your day, your dress and your decision.

♥ Stark white, diamond white, ivory and champagne are a few of the "whites" used for wedding-dress fabrics. Try on different shades of white to determine which one flatters your skin tone and hair colour best.

♥ Discuss the type of wedding you are having and your dress budget with the sales consultant before she brings you dresses to try on. If money is an issue, ask about bridesmaid dresses that can be worn as wedding gowns. They can be quite lovely, but less expensive.

♥ Try on all the gowns the sales consultant suggests. Dresses look very different on the hanger than on a bride. Don't forget that your dream gown might not fit your body type, so it's a good idea to try on a variety of styles to see how they look on you.

♥ Take at least two pairs of comfortable shoes with different heel heights to the final dress fitting. If the hem isn't exactly right, you won't freak out and you'll be good to go for your wedding day.

CHAPTER ONE

"I'LL go to the bridal show," Serena James announced. "I've always wanted to visit Seattle."

Not that she cared where she went as long as she could get out of town.

Four of her coworkers at The Wedding Belles, a Boston-based full-service wedding planning company, turned surprised looks in her direction. Oops. Serena tried not to grimace. Had she sounded too enthusiastic for a woman with a devoted boyfriend?

"That is, if no one else wants to go," she added with a forced smile.

"Well, darlin'," Belle Mackenzie, owner of The Wedding Belles, purred in her distinct Southern drawl. A beautiful woman with coiffed silver hair and a generous glossed smile, she gave the best hugs this side of the Mason-Dixon line. "That's sweet of you to offer. We do need a little positive publicity after the Vandiver wedding cancellation fiasco, and the show's sponsors would be delighted to have one of the country's up-and-coming wedding dress designers fill in at the last moment."

This was going to work. Satisfaction filled Serena.

"But you usually avoid bridal shows," Belle continued. "Are you sure about this with all you have going on?"

"I'm sure," Serena answered, hoping to sound willing but not desperate. "Besides, there really isn't anyone else."

Belle drummed her French-manicured nails on the mahogany table. "That's true. We all seem to have an extra serving or two on our plates."

"Well, whoever goes to Seattle—" Callie Underwood, florist extraordinaire, brushed a lock of dark blond hair off her face "—I want them to take my wedding gown to the show."

The other women gasped.

"You're getting married in just a few weeks," Belle said.

"November 22 to be exact, as Jared keeps reminding me, but we need to show brides that The Wedding Belles is still one of the premier wedding planning companies in the country, if not the world," Callie explained. "That means showing off what we do best, everything from Natalie's delicious cakes to Serena's stunning designs. Serena's entire spring line is beautiful, but my custom gown is her latest and most exquisite creation."

"But it's your wedding dress," Serena said. "I made it to fit you, not some size zero model. Anyway, I wouldn't want to risk getting makeup or runway stains on the silk."

"That doesn't mean you couldn't display the gown on a mannequin in the booth."

"What if something happens to the dress?" Regina O'Ryan, a gifted photographer, asked.

"Nothing will happen to it." Callie winked across the table. "Isn't that right, Serena?"

"Not if I'm the one who goes to Seattle." Serena appreciated her friend's vote of confidence. She wouldn't let Callie down. "I'll make sure the dress comes back."

"Seattle is on the other side of the country." Regina, her

brown eyes as bright as the flash on her ever-present camera, leaned toward her. "Did you and Rupert have plans for that weekend?"

Serena gritted her teeth at the mention of her boy-friend's—make that ex-boyfriend's—name, but her smile remained steadfast. "He's been traveling a lot himself. He won't mind."

At all.

She hadn't spoken to him in months. Not since he'd dumped her in April after The Wedding Belles' assistant, Julie Montgomery, had announced her engagement to Matt McLachlan. Serena still hadn't figured out how to tell people.

Things like this didn't happen to her. Serena lived a charmed life. She was used to getting what she wanted. She'd wanted to get married and start a family. She'd thought she'd found the right guy except that she'd been too focused on the end result to realize he hadn't been so right after all.

"We don't have any plans," she added.

"You got the last good man, Serena," Natalie Thompson, a young widow with mischievous eight-year-old twin girls, said. The petite blonde sighed. "After Julie, Callie and Regina. Pretty soon, we'll have another Belle's wedding to plan. I can already guess the cake you'll want. Chocolate with orange-flavored fudge filling."

The baker, who called herself a cake fairy, brought in slices for the Belles to try every time she made samples for brides to taste. That Natalie remembered her favorite flavor touched Serena.

"And I know the flowers." Callie's green eyes twinkled like the white mini decorator lights she used with yards of tulle and garlands of blossoms. "White dendrobium orchids, green roses, green cymbidium orchids and white and green parrot tulips."

White and green. One of Serena's favorite color combinations. She shouldn't be surprised. Callie knew her tastes so well.

A cake. Flowers. Serena's friends had her perfect wedding figured out. The only thing missing was…the groom.

A weight pressed down on the center of her chest. She thought of the nearly completed wedding dress hanging in her hall closet. Okay, she had been foolish, tempting fate by starting on the gown before she had a ring. But who could blame her?

Her relationship with Rupert Collier had proceeded right on schedule. They'd dated a year, met and liked each other's families and talked about the future, about creating a family together, which was what Serena wanted most of all. Becoming engaged had been the next obvious step. She'd started work on her wedding dress because she'd wanted time to get every stitch and every detail exactly right. She'd chosen the fabrics and design with the same care with which she'd chosen Rupert Collier. Not only smart, gorgeous and rich, but also ideal husband and father material. Everything she'd been looking for in a man, everything her friends expected her boyfriend to be, everything her parents wanted her to marry.

Until, impatient for a ring after dating exclusively for so long, she'd brought up the *M*-word. *Marriage*. And suddenly her perfect boyfriend wasn't ready for a serious relationship. He'd accused her of being too selfish and too self-reliant to make a permanent commitment. Oh he'd wanted to keep seeing her, she remembered bitterly. They looked good together and his boss liked her. But he'd wanted to take a serious step backward in the commitment department. Maybe, he'd suggested, they should start dating other people, too. Serena had said no, thinking he only needed a push to get their relationship back on track. Rupert had said goodbye. Proving once again that if she didn't do what others wanted, she wouldn't get what she wanted.

His parting words had stung.

You don't need me, Serena. You don't need anyone.

In the months since, she'd come to realize he was right. They were better off without each other. She didn't need him. She hadn't loved him the way a woman should love the man she wanted to marry. She hadn't wanted him as much as she liked how he'd fit into her plans. So much for her perfect dress. Her perfect groom. Her perfect life.

She forced herself to breathe. A setback, yes. A total failure, no. Serena James didn't fail.

Regina grinned, as if she'd found the perfect Kodak moment to capture with her camera. "Rupert will have to adjust his travel schedule once you get married."

Serena's stomach roiled. Her temples throbbed. She hated keeping secrets from the women she cared most about in the world, women who were more like family than coworkers, but what else was she supposed to do?

Julie had been thrilled about getting engaged. The other Belles were excited to be giving her a dream wedding. Serena couldn't let her bad news affect everyone else's joy. When Callie had fallen in love with Jared, Serena hadn't wanted her breakup to take anything away from the couple's happiness. And after Regina and Dell's marriage had become a love match, Serena couldn't find the right time to tell everyone she'd been dumped.

Now wasn't the right time, either.

Natalie and Audra Green, the company's accountant,

were down on men. Telling them the truth about what had happened would only reaffirm their belief that Mr. Right didn't exist. Serena wouldn't do that to her friends. They'd already faced too much disappointment and heartache.

Besides, her friends expected more from her. Everyone did. Serena worked hard on her polished image, kept a positive attitude and was always there in a pinch. People counted on her. They expected her to find Mr. Right.

That was exactly what she intended to do—find someone to give her the perfect love, family and life she dreamed about. Just because she'd been wrong about one man didn't mean her one true love wasn't out there somewhere. Maybe even in Seattle.

"So about the bridal show—" Serena leaned back in her chair "—what else do I need to bring with me in addition to the wedding dresses?"

Kane Wiley ducked around the business jet's engine to place his bags in the plane's exterior storage compartment. His breath steamed in the November air.

"Is that all you've got?" his father, Charlie, asked.

"Yep." Not only for this flight. All Kane owned—besides the business jet itself—could fit into two bags. He traveled light. And liked it that way.

"I appreciate your making the trip, son." Wearing faded jeans, a black turtleneck and down vest, Charlie looked younger than his fifty-six years, even with his salt-and-pepper hair.

"Just hold up your end of the deal, Dad."

"I will." Charlie picked up a box containing soda, water, ice, boxed lunches and a plate of cookies and brownies. "I will leave you alone. No more questions. No more badgering you to come home."

Home. That was a good one. Kane nearly laughed. There hadn't been a real home to come back to since his mom had died suddenly from a heart attack three years ago and his dad had quickly remarried...and divorced. Now his father looked poised to make the same mistake again.

"But—" Charlie pushed the box of food through the doorway of the cabin "—I still expect a card or e-mail or phone call at Christmastime."

"I can manage that." Easter and Father's Day, too. Even his dad's birthday. Kane would do anything to get away from Boston and never have to return. He didn't want to watch his father woo and wed yet another woman who could never take the place of his mother.

"Just remember, I love you, son. I'm here if you need me. For anything. Money, whatever."

Kane nodded once. He glanced at his watch. Damn. "Where is she?"

"Belle?" Charlie asked.

Kane fought the urge not to wince at his dad's newest "friend's" name. "The one I'm flying to Seattle."

"Serena will be here," Charlie said. "Traffic is always bad at this time."

Norwood Airport was twenty-five miles north of Boston. That meant she could be really late. Kane wanted to get in the air.

"Try smiling, son," Charlie said. "You might have fun. Serena James is a beautiful young woman."

"There are lots of beautiful women out there. No need to settle on just one."

Though a cross-country romance might not be too bad. As long as it was over by the time they returned home.

Charlie shook his head. "You just haven't met the right woman to love yet."

"I meet lots of women." Kane grinned. "Love them, too."

Charlie frowned. "I mean the forever kind of love. The kind I had with your mother."

And with his second wife.

And with what's-her-name. Belle.

Forever was a joke. And love—the kind his dad was talking about—was nothing more than a pretty word for convenient sex and companionship.

A white van pulled through the gate and honked its horn.

Charlie turned toward the sound. "They're here."

"Great." Kane had been hoping "they" would be a no-show.

A woman with silvery-blond hair and a beaming smile drove. She waved. Her passenger held a cell phone to her ear and wore dark, round sunglasses that hid much of her face.

The van stopped. The driver's door opened. The older woman, wearing brown pants and a colorful jacket, slid out gracefully.

"Good morning." She greeted Charlie with a handshake. The woman stepped toward Kane, extending her arm. "You must be Kane."

He shook her hand, noting her warmth and strong grip. She was different from his mother and his ex-stepmother. Older. Maybe even older than his father. That surprised Kane. "You must be Belle."

"I am." Her voice sounded like honey. Deep South honey. Slow and sweet. "I appreciate your flying Serena to Seattle."

Of course she did, especially with his father picking up all the associated flight and fuel costs.

"Kane's happy to do it," Charlie answered. "Aren't you, son?"

Kane nodded. He would be very happy once this trip was behind him and he'd be flying away for good.

"Well, we'd better get busy then." Belle opened the van doors and pulled out a box. "We have boxes to load. Brochures, favor samples and portfolios. Plus linens, flower arrangements, a cake and gowns."

Belle's eagerness to help surprised Kane. "O-kay."

"You still have to meet Serena James, our wedding dress designer," Belle said. "She's finishing up a phone call. No doubt talking to Rupert."

Kane bit. "Rupert?"

"Her boyfriend." Belle's ever present smile widened. "The two are practically engaged."

So much for a little romance in Seattle. Ring on the finger or not, Kane didn't mess around with another man's girl.

The passenger door opened. He focused on the woman exiting the van. She was, in a word, stunning. Long blond bangs fell over her forehead, but her hair didn't touch the collar of the jacket in the back. The short cut looked hip and trendy, just like the woman herself.

She wasn't tall, five-six if he was being generous and subtracted the heels on her brown leather boots. Even with her long wool coat, he could tell she had curves in all the right places.

He liked what he saw. She was exactly his type. Kane blew out a puff of breath that hung in the cold air. Old type, he corrected with a frown. He'd given up on blondes.

Her hair color coupled with the way she dressed reminded him of a former girlfriend, Amber Wallersby, who had been sexy as hell, but also a spoiled, pampered prin-

cess. She'd wanted him to stop flying his grandfather
around on his private jet and take a boring desk job at one
of her father's companies so he could pamper her in the
manner to which she'd become accustomed. Kane had
almost agreed, almost been taken in, until he'd seen that
she might have been gorgeous on the outside, but was all
show and zero substance on the inside.

Was Serena James the same?

Not that he was in any position to find out. Or care. Still
they would be spending several hours flying west together.
No sense starting off on the wrong foot.

"Hi," he said. "I'm your pilot. Kane."

Serena didn't extend her hand. She removed her sunglasses and glanced up at him. Clear, sharp eyes met his.
He hadn't expected such directness or such stunning blue
eyes.

"You're Kane Wiley?" Serena sounded surprised, almost as if she disapproved. "Charlie's son?"

"In the flesh."

"Do you see a family resemblance?" Charlie asked.

She glanced between the two men. "Not really."

"Oh, I do," Belle said. "Like father, like son. Both of
you are quite handsome."

Charlie beamed.

Kane rocked back on his heels. He wasn't anything like
his father. He didn't need a woman in his life—not on a
permanent basis, anyway. And unlike his father, Kane's
loyalty was hard to earn and his disapproval slow to fade.

"The eyes are the same," Serena conceded. "Maybe the
chins, too."

The way she studied him made Kane uncomfortable.
"We're running late. Let's get your stuff on board."

Serena glanced at Belle.

"Is something wrong, darlin'?" the woman asked. "Did you get a chance to say goodbye to Rupert?"

"Um, no."

Pink tinged Serena's cheeks.

Interesting. Kane wouldn't have thought her the blushing type. She seemed too cool and collected, but maybe leaving her "practically a fiancé" had rattled her.

"Would you mind if the gowns went in the cabin, Mr. Wiley?" she asked.

"It's Kane, and no, I don't mind."

The relief in her eyes was almost palpable. "I'll put them in the cabin."

"I'll load them."

"I don't mind doing it," she said.

"That's okay. I'd rather do it myself."

Serena eyed him warily. He waited for her to say something to challenge him. He was surprised when she didn't.

"You can put the food in the galley if you want," he offered. "It's in a box near the door."

"Fine."

Not fine if the tightness around her mouth was anything to go by. At least she didn't pout like Amber. Though he'd bet Serena could work wonders with that full bottom lip of hers.

As he removed several long, bulky white dress bags from the van, he heard his father.

"Kane prefers doing things on his own," Charlie explained.

"So does Serena," Belle added. "She likes being in control."

"Then the two of them should get along fine."

Nope, Kane realized. The exact opposite. Flying with

two captains in the cockpit was a recipe for disaster because neither wanted to give up control. And that meant one thing. It was going to be a really long flight to Seattle and back.

Serena had a checklist for her Mr. Right: polite, attentive, articulate, smartly tailored. All qualities her parents had taught her to value. All qualities Rupert had possessed in spades.

All qualities Kane Wiley lacked.

She unfastened her seat belt and moved back to where he'd secured the gowns.

What had Belle gotten her into?

Serena checked each of the dress bags. She repositioned three of them. Not much, but she felt better taking control. That is, taking care of her dresses. That was her job even if Kane didn't seem to realize that.

The man was arrogant and rude, the polar opposite of his kind and generous father, who epitomized a true gentleman. If not for the price of the flight—free, thanks to Charlie—and the ability to personally oversee the transport of the gowns, Serena would have found another way to Seattle. But any extra money The Wedding Belles had was going into a fund to pay for their cherished assistant, Julie's, wedding next June. They couldn't afford to be too choosy after losing money on the Vandiver cancellation and the negative publicity that had followed.

She thought about how much Julie and Matt were in love. Her other friends, too. Serena would find the same kind of love, the same kind of forever love, they had found. All she needed was her Mr. Right. One who didn't just look good on paper, but whom she could love, too.

Looking out of a window, she caught a glimpse of Kane

as he performed his preflight walk-around. Light glinted off his sun-streaked light brown hair that fell past the collar of his dark leather jacket. A jacket that emphasized his broad shoulders.

Talk about Mr. Wrong.

Some women might find him good-looking. If they liked tall, classically handsome guys with chiseled jawlines, square chins, sharpened noses and intense brown eyes.

Serena didn't object to any of those things, exactly. She just preferred them packaged in a suit and tie, and paired with a short, styled haircut and clean-shaven face. She didn't want a man who looked as if he'd rolled out of bed, bypassed the razor and brushed his fingers through his hair as an afterthought.

He glanced up at the plane, at the window she stared out of to be exact. His gaze met hers. His eyes, the same color of her favorite dark chocolate, made her heart bump.

Uh-oh.

She hurried back to her seat, sank into the comfortable leather club chair and fastened her seat belt. The temperature in the cabin seemed to rise even though the door was still open. She removed her coat, picked up her sketch pad and fanned herself.

What was the matter with her? Of course, she hadn't been sleeping well lately. Or eating, either. One good meal, and she'd feel better.

She'd like to take a bite out of Kane.

"Hot?"

Her sketch pad fell onto her lap. She looked up.

Kane stood at the entrance to the plane. The interior suddenly seemed smaller. He appeared larger. She gulped.

"Excuse me?" Serena asked.

"Are you hot?"

"I—I…" Something about him made her flustered and tongue-tied and heated. She didn't like the feelings, either. "I'm a little warm."

"I'll take care of it." He closed and latched the door. "Are your dresses okay?"

Serena heard the challenge in his voice. She raised her chin. "They are fine. Now."

The intensity in his dark eyes sent heat rushing through her veins. She sucked in a breath. Looked away.

"Seat belt fastened?" he asked.

Not trusting her voice, she nodded.

"The same rules apply on this flight as your typical commercial flight," Kane explained. "When we reach cruising altitude, you can visit the lavatory or help yourself to whatever you would like in the galley."

"No flight attendant?"

"Not unless you want to fly the plane while I serve you lunch and a beverage." He pointed out the exits and where the oxygen masks were located. "If we lose cabin pressure, place the mask over your nose and mouth and breath normally. Did you bring a laptop?"

"No." She'd wanted to escape from the constant pretending of her life in Boston. Her prying friends, her fake phone calls…even e-mail was a hassle these days. "Just my cell phone. I know not to use it during the flight."

"Even if you miss your boyfriend?"

She tried not to cringe, but the thought of lying to a total stranger left a bitter taste in her mouth. "It won't be a problem."

"Not using your cell phone or missing him?"

"Either."

At least that was the truth.

"If you need anything," he said, "let me know."

Serena could just imagine his reaction if she asked for, oh, a bag of pretzels and a fiancé. She bit back a smile.

No matter how desperately she wanted to maintain her image with her friends and family, she would never ask someone like Kane—someone so obviously wrong for a woman like her—to help in her quest to find a new Mr. Right and one true love.

That was something she could do on her own. And would.

CHAPTER TWO

"THE doors will open in ten minutes," announced a feminine voice over the convention center loudspeakers.

Ten minutes? Kane scanned the large hall, balancing the gold-wrapped box he'd promised to deliver to Serena. He'd thought he had more time.

Little-Miss-I'm-In-Charge Serena had sounded really upset when she'd called and asked if the box was still on the plane. When Kane had finally found the package in the tail-cone baggage compartment and brought it over, she'd told him she'd be right out. But he was already there, wasn't he?

And—admit it—he'd been curious to see the blonde in action. Curious enough to volunteer to deliver the box himself.

Man, was he sorry now. This wedding stuff gave him the heebie jeebies.

He might as well be standing in the middle of a wedding nightmare. Instead of fire, heat and screams, this place reeked with flowers, tulle and as much pipe organ music as the soundtrack of some cheesy Dracula movie.

A woman dressed in black with spiked red hair, flushed cheeks and a clipboard in her hand raced up to him. "Are you a fashion show model?"

"No."

"Where could they be?" Her face scrunched, then, as she studied him, brightened. "Would you want to be one of the models?"

Kane pictured himself dressed up like a penguin and escorting models in white dresses down a runway. He didn't mind models, but the other stuff... Not his thing. "No, thanks."

With a frustrated sigh, she ran down the aisle and disappeared out of sight.

She wasn't the only one in a hurry. Exhibitors rushed around, putting finishing touches on their booths and applying their lipstick. Kane didn't see many men, not like yesterday when he'd dropped off Serena to set up, but a few guys remained. This seemed like the last place any male would choose to spend an hour. Let alone a day. Or two.

Once, he might have thought about settling down someday, but now, after all he'd seen, Kane knew better.

As he searched the booths, every company seemed to have the word *wedding* somewhere in its name and everything looked sort of similar. He felt lost and out of place.

"Kane." He turned to see Serena waving at him. "Over here."

Relieved, he walked across the aisle to her booth. Whatever panic he'd heard in her voice wasn't visible on her face, looking fresh and rested with expertly applied makeup.

That's right, dummy, look at the lipstick. Keep your eyes on her face. She is so not your type.

But man, she looked good in that dress.

Her gaze was intent on him. "You made it."

"With minutes to spare."

"Minutes?" Serena asked.

"A few. Were you getting worried?"

Kane already knew the answer was yes. She seemed to keep a tight hold on her responsibilities, on pretty much everything within her sphere of influence. He happened to be the exact opposite, taking things as they came. It was probably a good thing she had an almost-fiancé. Because the way she looked, he could have been tempted into a fling. And the last thing he wanted or needed in his life was a cool blond control freak with a thing for weddings.

Serena took the box from him. "I wasn't worried, but I was getting a little impatient."

"Not the patient type?"

"Waiting for someone to come through can be hard."

"Sometimes."

But he wouldn't mind waiting right there. He didn't have to want to spend the rest of his life with her to enjoy the view. What man with blood running through his veins wouldn't want to look? Her brown and blue dress clung in all the right places. The hem fell above the knee, and her high heels made her legs look long and sexy. She defined "it" girl.

He didn't know whether to envy that Rupert fellow or pity him. Serena James was the type who knew how to make a guy roll over and beg. And Kane didn't sit, stay or play dead for any woman, no matter how hot she looked in heels.

"I do appreciate your bringing this over." She walked toward a linen-covered table with one of the elaborate floral arrangements she'd brought with her in the center. Candles in silver holders sat on either side. She tossed a smile his way. "Thank you."

Her gratitude sounded genuine. Kane couldn't tell

whether she was sincere or not, but he was willing to play nice. "You're welcome."

The gentle sway of her hips and the swirl of her dress hem around her legs captured his attention. The lingering scent of her light floral perfume filled his nostrils.

Serena opened the box. "Now all I have to do is set these things out and the table will be ready."

The table already looked finished and fancy enough to him. A little too fancy, but probably what the monkey-suit, bouquet-tossing set expected. "What's in there?"

"Chocolate." As she unwrapped each item, she placed the pieces of candy on an oval beveled-edged mirror setting on the table: three chocolate truffles shaped like three-tiered wedding cakes, small gold and silver boxes tied with ribbon, oval and heart-shaped engraved chocolates packaged in a gold base and wrapped with tulle and a ribbon, gold and silver engraved foiled coins. "No wedding is complete without something chocolate."

"I don't care much for weddings, but I like chocolate."

Her eyebrows rose at his not-so-subtle hint, but she tossed a coin his way.

He unwrapped the gold foil and took a bite. Good stuff. "Aren't you having any?"

"I don't sample the merchandise," she said in her cool, controlled voice.

Yeah. Right. Probably one of those salad-and-rice-cake types who wouldn't let herself eat a piece of candy. Too bad. She had a sweet little body, but he'd rather see a woman enjoy a meal with dessert than starve in order to fit into a smaller size.

She hid the box underneath the linen tablecloth–covered round table displaying a four-tiered white-iced wedding cake decorated with real flowers cascading down from the top like a colorful pink and white waterfall. "All done."

He'd say so. Judging by this booth, The Wedding Belles was a high-class, high-end operation. From the neatly stacked full-color brochures to the maroon leather embossed photo albums, everything shouted "money." Including Serena herself.

Kane leisurely finished his chocolate, surveying the booth. He noticed a stack of boxes. Board games, actually. Who would have thought to make a game out of getting married? Playing that sounded more like torture than fun.

A burgundy upholstered chaise longue sat at a right angle to a row of headless mannequins in white—the Wedding Shop of Horrors. "Looks like someone went furniture shopping last night."

"We contracted with a rental store here in Seattle who delivered all this yesterday."

"You must have worked all night."

She pushed a strand of hair back from her face. "Just doing my job."

"Don't you design the wedding dresses?"

"Each of us helps out where we can," she said. "That's why working for The Wedding Belles is such fun."

Fun? Serena never seemed to stop working. She moved through the booth adjusting swags of rich yellow fabric draped on the boring white panels separating each of the exhibit areas.

Didn't she ever slow down or rest? Even sitting on the flight she'd been working on something. He didn't know how she did it.

"Everything looks good," he said.

"Good won't cut it. Brides are the pickiest people on

this planet, next to their mothers." She straightened a stack of brochures. "Everything needs to be perfect."

"Nothing's ever perfect."

"Then you've never attended a wedding put on by The Wedding Belles." Kneeling, she realigned the hem of one of the wedding dresses. "Or worn one of my gowns."

"No offense, but I don't look my best in a train and heels."

She smiled up at him.

He smiled back.

Now this was more like it.

"Do you need anything?" he asked. "Breakfast? Coffee?"

Me.

"Thanks, but I already ate and my coffee is stashed where I can get to it easily." Standing, she peeked at her watch. "You might want to get going. The doors are going to—"

"Welcome to the Northwest Fall Bridal Extravaganza," the voice over the loudspeaker announced.

"Uh-oh. You didn't make it out in time. Watch out." Serena smoothed the skirt of her dress. "We're about to be overrun by the bridal brigade commanded by mothers and supported by best friends, sisters and cousins."

Within seconds, chattering, laughter and even shrieks filled the large hall as if someone had turned off the mute switch on the remote. Packs of women ran past him.

"Where are they going?" he asked.

"The first fashion show."

Had he agreed to model, all those women would have been running to him. Wonder what Blondie would say to that? A smile tugged on his lips.

Two young women walked up to her with questions about the cake on display.

The once empty aisles and booths were now crowded with women lugging ten-pound bags of bridal literature. Lots of women. Young ones, old ones...mostly young ones. Good-looking, too.

And engaged, Kane reminded himself. He didn't do engaged women. Or even almost-engaged women, like Serena.

"Mom." A twenty-something woman with chestnut hair wearing a green baby-doll style dress rushed into The Wedding Belles' booth. "This is it. I have to have this dress."

"We've been here two minutes and that's the third dress you've said that about," the mother said.

"Mo-om."

Serena was speaking to two other women, but that didn't stop the mother from interrupting the conversation.

"How much is this wedding gown?" the mother asked.

"I'm sorry, but that dress is not for sale," Serena explained. "It will be worn at a wedding on November 22."

The daughter's collagen-injected, shimmery pink lips puckered like some kind of bizarre human-hybrid fish. Kane grinned to himself. Maybe this was the Northwest version of bridezilla.

"Could you make one like this for my daughter?" the mother asked, not-so-subtly showing off her designer purse and iceberg-sized diamond ring.

Despite the interruptions, Serena smiled pleasantly. "I can create something just as beautiful for her. With your daughter's lovely figure, an asymmetrical A-line gown would be stunning. A cutaway skirt, even. And champagne embroidered lace would be a wonderful accent with her coloring."

The bride tossed her artfully streaked hair. "We'd pay you extra for that dress on display."

Kane would have told the mother to take her money and... Well, go someplace else.

"If you are interested in our gowns, we have a couple of samples here that can be sold off-the-rack." Serena's smile never wavered as she motioned to the photo albums on the table. "You might also want to make yourself comfortable and glance through the portfolio to get a taste of all our designs."

"We might come back later." The mother looked down her surgically designed pert nose. "Or not."

The words didn't seem to faze Serena. "I'll be here."

The way she handled herself with the appearances-are-everything, I-can-buy-whatever-I-want attitude impressed Kane. He only hoped she wasn't cut from the same cloth. Not that it meant anything to him if she were.

As the bride stomped away, more women fawned over the dresses. Serena answered their questions not only promoting her gowns, but the services provided by The Wedding Belles, especially when it came to full-service destination weddings.

She was in her element. Glowing, sparkling, radiant.

Kane slowly backed away. He liked watching her, but this wasn't the place for a single guy intent on remaining that way.

Serena gave a quick nod his way. He was surprised she'd noticed him leaving. He was also surprised he liked her noticing.

Uh-oh. Not good. Very bad actually.

Serena James might not have a ring on her finger, but

avoiding her was the smart thing to do. The right thing to
do, even if he spent another night in his hotel room alone
watching television. On second thought, maybe he could
find a bridesmaid, sprinkled among the brides and their
mothers, here with something on her mind besides marriage.

Maybe all the shiny fabrics and chocolate would put her
in the mood for satin sheets and room service. And maybe
that would get his mind off a certain "practically engaged"
someone.

He glanced back at Serena.

Or…maybe not.

"Thanks for dinner, Malcolm." Malcolm Rapier was
Serena's friend and former classmate from design school.
She kissed his cheek, expertly avoiding his twist to meet
her mouth. "It was great catching up with you."

"Sure you don't want to go to the party?" With his
boyish grin, he looked more like one of his models than
the rising star of men's formal wear design. "I'd love to
show you off."

Serena was tempted. Talk about a looker in a stylish
black suit he'd designed himself and multicolored silk tie.
Almost as handsome as Kane. Where had that come from?

"I usually enjoy being shown off, but I didn't sleep
much last night." Going out wasn't a good idea when she
wanted to yawn. Not to mention her feet ached.

"Understood. Return of bridezilla tomorrow." He laced
his fingers with hers, his hands warm and smooth like the
fabrics he dealt with every day. "But if you change your
mind, call me. I'll send the limo back."

"You're too sweet."

Unlike her pilot. *The* pilot, she corrected.

"No, you're too sexy and look great on my arm." Malcolm twirled her to him as if they were dancing and pulled her against him. "Any chance you'd leave Boston for Seattle?"

Serena knew exactly how the game was played... Normally she would concede, but she didn't like the way Kane kept intruding on her thoughts. She wanted to prove to herself the pilot had no effect on her.

She looked up at Malcolm through her eyelashes. "Why would I want to do that?"

"Oh, Serena, my muse, can't you imagine the beautiful formal wear we could create together? Paris, Milan, New York. Nothing could compete with us."

"You're right about that." But Serena wanted more than that kind of partnership. She wanted true love—marriage and children. She eyed Malcolm subjectively, as if inventorying the pieces of her next design. "Would this be strictly a business arrangement?"

He lowered his mouth to her ear, his warm breath tickling her skin. "Do you think I'd ask you to relocate across the country just for a job?"

Maybe she was going a little too far here. Okay, Malcolm and she would make a stunning pair. They shared common interests and enjoyed each other's company. Yet if she were at all interested in pursuing a relationship with him, why couldn't she get Kane out of her mind?

His smile widened. "You're thinking about it."

Not really. At least not with him. She shrugged.

"You are." Laughing, Malcolm caressed her cheek with his fingertip and kissed her forehead. "Until tomorrow, my soon-to-be Seattle love and partner."

With that he walked out of the revolving door to hit whatever hip parties were happening that night. She wasn't sad to see him go.

Serena's heels clicked on the marble floor of the hotel lobby. Even after the long day at the bridal show, she felt reenergized though her body's internal clock was running three hours ahead.

The first day of the Northwest Bridal Extravaganza had been a hit, an "in the park home run" to quote one of the Seattle show's organizers. Tomorrow might just be a grand slam. Serena already felt like an all-star.

"What would Rupert say?"

She recognized the voice and stopped, annoyed that Kane had not only been on her mind, but was now here. He sat at a nearby table with a pint of beer in his hand, looking totally comfortable and at ease. In his jeans and long-sleeved black T-shirt, he had that carefree, I-don't-care-what-you-think, sexy style down. Not that she thought he was sexy. Her type of sexy, that was.

Oh, she'd once been tempted by bad boys, but her sister's experience had made Serena immune to their charms. Her sister, Morgan, had fallen in love with a guy who'd had women calling him day and night. He had no steady job nor seemed to want one. Morgan had moved in with him anyway and then married him, claiming he loved her and would change. He hadn't and didn't. Serena had been the one to pick up the pieces when his infidelity destroyed the marriage and left her pregnant sister devastated and alone. Their parents still hadn't forgiven Morgan for falling in love with the wrong man and "ruining" her life.

"What do you mean by that?" Serena asked.

He motioned to an empty seat.

She really shouldn't.

She really wanted to.

Kane pushed the chair out from the small round table with his foot. "You can buy me a drink for this morning."

Her mouth curved. "You already have one."

"I wouldn't mind another."

She did owe him for dropping off the box on time, even if he had waited until the last possible minute. She sat, grateful the moment her bottom hit the leather chair and she was no longer standing.

"Ooooh," she moaned.

His brows lifted. "You're easily satisfied."

She flushed. "I should look into designing a high heel that could be worn for fourteen hours straight without causing foot pain."

"I meant the guy. For a woman who's practically engaged, you seemed pretty chummy with Mr. Suit."

Each time Serena heard that phrase—practically engaged—she felt as if another heavy bolt of fabric had been stapled to her shoulders. And right now she didn't like the judgmental tone of Kane's voice. He didn't know her. He knew nothing about her. "Are you a pilot or a chaperone?"

"Pilot. Unattached. But if you were my girl—" his gaze traveled over her with lazy appreciation "—I sure wouldn't want you having dinner or cozying up with another man."

Tingles shot through her and she sat straighter. Her reaction had everything to do with being tired and nothing to do with him. "Then it's a good thing I'm not your girl, isn't it?"

"A damn good thing."

Serena winced. She wasn't used to such rudeness or honesty. She didn't know what to say. That left her more than a little flustered. She could always be counted on to find the right words or do the right thing.

"Let me guess," he continued. "Your boyfriend is a carbon copy of the guy you were with."

"Malcolm Rapier is the guy's name, and he's a little like

Rupert." Only better. Malcolm was a better dresser than her ex. "He's a fellow designer and a friend."

"Who wants to be more than a friend."

It wasn't a question. "And you know this because…"

"I'm a guy."

"And guys know everything."

"You said it." Kane raised his glass.

"Malcolm likes pretty things," she said.

Kane took a swig of beer. "Things?"

"Women." She didn't know why she was wasting her time explaining things to him. "Malcolm likes to be seen escorting attractive women around. You know, arm candy."

Which was probably why he wanted her to move to Seattle. A built-in date to take to social functions. Not exactly the strongest foundation for a lasting relationship.

Kane's mouth quirked. "Modest, aren't we?"

"You asked."

"I did." A beat passed. "So Rupert—"

"Doesn't worry." The words tumbled from her lips. Not exactly a lie. Her ex-boyfriend didn't care what she did. "There's no need."

"You're a one-woman man."

"Yes, I am." When she had a man. "I've never understood people who play the field."

"As long as the individuals involved know what's going on, I don't see a problem with it."

"That's because you're a guy."

"Women play the field, too," Kane said. "Otherwise, it would get mighty lonely out there."

"Were you lonely tonight?" she asked.

"No." He swirled his glass. "I had dinner with a lovely bridesmaid who had only one thing on her mind."

"What was that?"

"Becoming a bride."

Serena laughed. "You don't want to get married?"

"Nope," he said. "Marital bliss isn't for me."

She wasn't surprised. He didn't look like husband or daddy material. But if a woman were looking for a temporary lover instead of something more permanent…

"What *do* you want?" Serena asked, curious.

He got a faraway look in his eyes. "Freedom."

She'd never known freedom in her entire life. She was always working toward something, fulfilling an obligation or meeting a responsibility. "I'm sure that must be nice."

"You should try it sometime."

Temptation sparked. And then she thought about her parents. She couldn't do anything to upset them. "Not my style."

"Mr. Suit is your style?" Kane asked.

"Pretty much."

"Too bad."

"Not for Mr. Suit."

He nodded then stopped. "Except for Rupert."

"Ah, yes. Rupert."

"Women like you need to open your eyes," Kane said. "The perfect guy could be right in front of you, but if he wasn't your 'style' you'd walk right by and miss your chance."

"Love will find a way."

Kane studied her. "You really buy into all this wedding stuff, don't you?"

"Completely," she said.

"Well, then." He raised his glass to her. "I'm sure you'll find exactly what you're looking for."

"You, too," she said. "A juicy piece of eye candy like yourself must have women falling at your feet."

"Pretty much."

A smile erupted across Kane's face. The effect—devastatingly charming. Serena moistened her lips, trying not to stare.

"Juicy, huh? Thanks." He placed his empty glass on the table. "It's not often I get a compliment from an esteemed piece of arm candy."

"It's not often I give them." Uh-oh. She was flirting. But she kind of liked how it felt. "Do you want that drink now?"

"I'll take a rain check."

A twinge of disappointment ran through her. Ridiculous.

Serena was just having a little fun. Nothing more. She knew what she wanted to find. It sure wasn't Kane Wiley.

CHAPTER THREE

THE next afternoon, Kane eyed the altocumulus clouds to the west. No immediate danger there. The weather service had issued an icing advisory at high altitudes, but they'd be flying below the problem. His plane was only certified to forty-five thousand feet. Still he wanted to get in the air.

As soon as his passenger got off her damn pink cell phone.

"Yes, Belle," Serena said. "Both the local paper and the magazine took photos."

"Hang up," Kane ordered. "Time to go."

Serena held up a single, slim finger in response: One minute.

He'd already given up more than a minute.

Back at the convention center, photographers had swarmed The Wedding Belles' booth, snapping pictures and jotting down quotes from Serena. She really was some kind of hotshot in the wedding world.

Kane had suffered the commotion as well and as long as he could. He could see success was important to her. Anyway, his dad was paying for his time. Complaining wasn't going to get him anything but a headache.

But after the Suit had shown up, eager to shower Serena

with congratulations and kisses and who knew what else, Kane's patience had evaporated. He wasn't a clocks-and-schedules kind of guy, but the weather system pushing down from Canada wasn't waiting while Serena played kissy-face with her designer buddy.

Now Kane was waiting again. The plane had been fueled. He had loaded their food and luggage, filed his flight plan and completed his walk-around. It was time—past time—to go.

"Get in the plane."

She raised her index finger again, like a dog trainer hushing a barking pooch.

Kane bit back a growl and grabbed her phone.

"She's got to go," he said into the tiny receiver. "She'll call you later."

He switched off the phone and tossed it into the plane, onto her seat.

"What did you do that for?" Lines creased Serena's forehead. "I was only on the phone for a couple of minutes."

"Try twenty," he corrected.

Serena opened her mouth then pressed her lips together. She entered the plane. He followed her.

"A couple storms are brewing with a low pressure system off the Pacific." Kane locked the door. "There's weather in Canada that's moving south."

"Why didn't you tell me?" she asked.

"You were on the phone."

Serena removed her coat. Took her a pad out of her bag. Sat down.

Kane recognized the silent treatment. The way her eyes avoided his. Amber used to do that. So did a lot of other women. He wouldn't let Serena make him feel guilty. Not when *she* should be apologizing to *him.*

"The weather shouldn't affect us," he said. "But keep your seat belt fastened in case we hit any turbulence."

She buckled herself up. "Not a problem."

"There's food in the galley, but be quick about it because of the—"

"Turbulence," she finished for him. "I will, and, Kane…"

"Yeah."

"I'm sorry for taking so long." Her gaze captured his, her big blue eyes apologetic. Appealing. Not like Amber at all. Not like any other of the women in his life. "I know you delayed our departure back at the convention center, and I really appreciate that, but I was excited. I wanted to share the news of all the good publicity and photo ops with my friends."

He grunted. "No worries."

Kane lied.

He was worried plenty. Not about the weather. He was a good pilot. Surface wind speeds were acceptably low, and the system coming in was moving slowly enough that it shouldn't be a problem.

His reaction to her, however, was a whole other story.

Kane was upset at her. Serena stared out the small window at the overcast sky.

Even though he'd accepted her apology, she could tell he didn't like being made to wait. She didn't like waiting, either. Time to make it up to him?

Not necessary, a voice in her head whispered.

He'd been a jerk.

He'd grabbed her phone.

He'd hung up on Belle.

Kane had explained all that. She could forgive his impatience to get in the air. She wasn't quite as ready to let go of his brusque rejection last night.

Then it's a good thing I'm not your girl, isn't it?

A damn good thing.

Serena bit her lip. Kane hadn't even let her buy him a beer. He'd wanted a "rain check."

Not that she cared. Not much anyway.

Unless his wanting a "rain check" was his way of seeing her in Boston. Maybe it was time to find out.

They hadn't hit any turbulence. Now that they were at cruising altitude, Serena unfastened her seat belt and went to the galley that reminded her more of a refreshment center than an actual kitchen. Still the efficiently designed space made it easy to pour a cup of coffee, find two freshly baked cookies and put them on a napkin. She carried everything to the cockpit.

Payback? Or peace offering?

Either way, she didn't want to owe Kane anything.

"I brought you a snack," she said.

He glanced back. "What?"

"Coffee and chocolate-chip cookies." He liked chocolate, she remembered. "I, um, owe you a drink, remember? There wasn't any cream—"

"Black is fine." He took the food from her. "Thanks."

Okay, she was done now. "I'll be going back."

"Come on up," he said at the same time.

Kane motioned to the other seat. "Sit up here for a while."

Serena stared at the high-tech-looking instrument panel with a small computerlike device between the two pilot seats. Not a lot of space up here.

She glanced at the cabin. Safer, back there.

"Plenty of room," Kane said. "This baby's simple enough for one pilot, but it can be flown by two."

"I can't fly."

His attractive mouth curved. "But you can sit, right?"

She crawled into the seat and peered out the window. The one-hundred-and-eighty-degree view took her breath away. Clouds blanketed the sky as far as she could see. She couldn't tell where the ground was or where the sky ended. Forget about locating the horizon. "Wow."

The word described how she felt inside. Every nerve ending tingled. Her insides buzzed.

Being up here, cocooned in the small cockpit with Kane and cut off from the earth below, made all her problems seem a world away. A world she wasn't in any hurry to return to.

"Fasten your seat belt," he said.

The harness-style seat belt went over her shoulders and around her waist. She had trouble buckling it. Kane reached over to help her. The warm skin of his hands brushed hers, sending tiny shocks down to the tips of her fingers.

Nothing. It meant nothing. "I've got it."

"Sure?" he asked.

She wasn't sure about anything. Still she nodded and clipped the buckle in.

"Most of the weather is behind us," he said. "It should be smooth flying. We might even make up some time."

"Good."

But it wasn't. Not really.

Serena wasn't ready to return to Boston. She wanted this time, a time with no lies, no expectations to uphold and no responsibility a little while longer. The bridal show in Seattle had been stressful, but also successful. Coming off that high, she was still literally flying, and she'd never felt such freedom as she did now.

Was that what Kane liked? The freedom? The ability to go wherever he wanted, whenever he wanted? She could definitely understand that appeal now.

She glanced his way. "So…do you like to fly?"

He gave her a look.

Okay, dumb question.

Serena would try again. "How long have you been flying?"

"Since I was sixteen. It's the only thing I've ever wanted to do."

"Why did you choose to be a charter pilot and not an airline pilot?"

"I thought about doing the corporate gig, but it's too much like working for a bus company. My grandfather bought a business jet. When he offered me a job as his personal pilot, I jumped at it. I flew for him for six years, until he got sick." Kane's mouth tightened. "He doesn't travel anymore."

Her chest tightened. "I'm sorry."

"Why? I got my hands on this plane for next to nothing and my grandfather's instructions were to make my own way in the wild blue yonder. That's what I've been doing."

Serena envied his go-where-the-wind-carried-him attitude. She'd planned out her entire life. Rarely did she go out to eat without reservations.

"How often do you fly?" she asked, wanting to learn more about him. Something about Kane Wiley intrigued her in a way she'd never felt before.

"All the time." He patted the yoke. "This baby isn't only how I make my living. It's where I call home."

"Home." She thought about her painstakingly decorated flat in Boston. "You and me. We're very different."

"Nothing wrong with that."

Serena nodded.

He was rootless, a wanderer, free. She was tied down by her business, responsibility, expectations.

But at this moment, for as long as it could last, Serena wanted to enjoy the flight and this time with Kane, in spite of their differences and because of them. She wanted a taste—a nibble really—of what his life was like.

"You're such a free spirit," she said.

"I like to go where I want to go."

"And Boston?"

"A layover," he said. "Nothing more."

"Isn't your family there?"

"My dad." Kane pushed a couple of buttons. "We don't always see eye to eye on things."

"My sister is like that with my mom and dad. That's made things…difficult."

For all of them.

"What about you and your parents?" he asked.

"I get along fine with my folks."

She'd made sure of that.

"Lucky."

Serena nodded. But feeling lucky had nothing to do with her parents and everything to do with the sexy man sitting next to her. She held back a sigh.

A button lit up on the instrument panel. Kane immediately noticed it. Sat straighter. Furrowed his brow.

Her heart jolted. "Is something wrong?"

"Nope, but I need to take care of that light." He studied the instrument panel. "Would you mind going back to the cabin and fastening your seat belt?"

"Sure." She unbuckled the harness and squeezed out of the seat. "I'll see you later."

He nodded, pulling out some kind of manual.

Serena returned to her seat and buckled her seat belt. Leaning back, she blew out a puff of air.

What had she been thinking? Doing up there?

That warning light had been a sign, a reminder that she was better off earthbound. She needed to get her head out of the clouds. Being up in the air was a dangerous place. And being with Kane…

She didn't want any turbulence in her well-planned life.

Why was engine number two's damn fuel filter light on?

Kane stared on the instrument panel. He reset the circuit. The light remained on.

Interesting.

He had dealt with this before and knew what to do, but with Serena on board, he glanced at the flight procedure's manual to make sure he hadn't forgotten anything.

Okay. Just as he remembered. One fuel filter light. No problem. He would wait and see what happened next.

The usual chatter filled the radio airwaves. Nothing to worry about.

Kane focused his attention on the instrument panel. Everything was looking good.

The other fuel filter light popped on.

His stomach knotted in about a hundred different ways.

Two fuel filter lights meant fuel contamination. Damn. The plane had been filled with bad gas.

Kane took a deep breath and exhaled.

Okay, he'd trained for this. He knew what to do.

As he ran through emergency procedures in his head,

he flipped to the appropriate section of the flight manual and began the checklist.

Kane radioed his situation to the flight center and was cleared for descent. The only problem would be finding a place to land in the middle of nowhere. If worst came to worst, he could always set down on a freeway or road. Other pilots had done it.

At least the weather was holding. Though the sky had darkened above him. All he needed was clear weather to land this baby. Then the skies could open up with rain, snow, sleet or all of the above.

He thought about Serena sitting in the back by herself. She would be safer back there. Still he needed to prepare her for what might happen.

As the altimeter spun to a lower altitude, Kane searched for a landing spot. All he saw were mountains, trees and canyons. Lots of snow. Not good.

Over the years he'd had a couple of minor incidents in the air and an aborted takeoff, but nothing like this and never with a passenger on board. A big-eyed blonde who looked out of the cockpit like she was tasting freedom for the first time.

Sweat ran down his back and slicked his grip on the controls. Kane flipped on the intercom.

"Listen, Serena," he announced, his voice calm and steady. "You need to prepare for an emergency landing. All items need to be stored securely. That includes the galley. Once you're done, check your seat belt. Make sure it's flat and tight across your lower torso. When I say 'brace,' I want you to keep your feet flat on the floor and bend forward so you're facing down at your lap. Hold on to your ankles or legs. It might be a little bumpy, but everything will be okay."

As long as he could set down before the engines stopped turning, everything would be okay.

Unfortunately with bad fuel, Kane had no idea how long the engines would keep working.

Emergency landing?

Every one of Serena's muscles tensed.

Okay, that explained why they were descending. She glanced out of the window at the tree-covered, snowcapped mountains. Where were they? Washington? Oregon? Maybe even Idaho?

She didn't understand what was going on. She didn't like not knowing.

Except for that light, everything seemed fine. Nothing out of the ordinary, except for an edge to Kane's otherwise calm voice. Something she hadn't heard before.

Worst-case scenarios filled her mind. She tapped her feet. Flexed her fingers. Imagined dying.

Don't think about it. Stay in control. Do what Kane told you.

With a plan of action in place, Serena reached for her sketch pad and pencil. With trembling hands, she shoved them into her bag and placed it under a seat. Next she checked the galley and then her dresses. Everything seemed okay. Secure. Nothing should fly around if they had a rough landing.

Her heart pounded.

She hoped that was all it was.

Focusing on slow, even breaths, Serena sat and tightened her seat belt. She double-checked it, giving the strap one last tug.

Despite that tantalizing interlude in the cockpit, she knew this trip with Tall, Dark and Sexy had been a mistake.

She shivered. She should have stayed firmly on the ground in Boston, where she belonged. Freedom, even a taste of it, wasn't for her. Whether something was wrong with the plane or not, it was too…dangerous.

A strange, whining noise sounded, as if something was winding down. She thought about covering her ears, but clasped the armrests instead, gripping them so hard her knuckles turned white. An image of Kane, so confident and sure, flying the plane popped into her head making her feel safer, calmer.

Suddenly everything went quiet. Too quiet. Her breath rasped in the silence.

Oh, no.

Realization struck, chilling her to the bone. The engines had stopped. Her jaw clenched. She stared out of the window.

The mountains, so beautiful only moments ago, now loomed dark and deadly below. They seemed closer. The trees taller.

Her heart slammed against her chest.

The plane soared down through the sky, silent as a balsam-wood glider.

Fear and panic rioted through her.

Emergency landing? Not crash landing.

Right now Serena wasn't sure of anything. She hated the feeling. The lack of control. The whim of fate.

Tears stung her eyes. She'd planned her entire life out, what she wanted and when, but all of her plans didn't seem worth much now.

Serena thought about her family and friends. She swallowed around the lump in her throat. She wanted to tell them how much she loved them. She wanted…a second chance.

"Brace," Kane shouted.

Her heart pounding in her ears, she bent over and grabbed on to her ankles.

Please let it be over quickly, she prayed.

For a moment nothing happened. The quiet seemed…unnatural.

Then the plane slammed into the ground. The impact sent her forward against the seat belt. Knocked the wind out of her. Jostled her around.

Something hit her in the head.

Serena ignored the ache in her stomach, the pain from her head, the sticky, oozing substance rolling down the side of her face. She concentrated on holding on to her ankles. And breathing. It hurt to breathe.

Kane yelled something. Was he okay? She struggled for a breath. Yelling was out of the question.

The plane bounced like a ball. Metal shrieked and rattled. The sounds, worse than the crunching of two cars in an accident, made her want to cover her ears, but she couldn't let go of her legs.

How much longer?

Make it stop, Kane.

The plane veered, skidded to the right. Serena squeezed her eyes closed and screamed.

CHAPTER FOUR

SERENA'S scream shivered through the cockpit.

Kane broke into a cold sweat.

He gripped the yoke, his muscles straining to regain control of the speeding plane. The plane jostled, skidding and bouncing on the deceptively flat snow. He couldn't worry about what lay hidden underneath that white blanket. A row of trees loomed straight ahead. He stepped harder on the brakes.

Come on, baby. Stop for Papa.

The lights on the control panel flickered. What the…? No engines, no electricity, no control.

And Serena, along for the ride.

Kane swore, wrestling the unresponsive yoke as the forest hurtled closer. Individual trees sprang out of the shadowed mass. Far too little space between the solid trunks. Heavy, snow-laden branches. Sharp, frozen pine needles.

Fear was flat and bitter in his mouth.

A hard jolt knocked Kane to the right. He yelled a single word of warning. "Serena!" His harness held in place. The plane veered, dipped, rolled. The teeth-clenching squeal of tearing metal knotted his stomach.

Time slowed.

Falling sideward, Kane clutched the yoke, his knuckles white, his heart lodged in his throat. The flight manual flew across the cockpit, impacting the window with a loud boom. He expected to be next, but the harness straps dug into his skin, keeping him secured against his seat.

The plane spun, skidding on its side, away from the trees, and slowly, ever so slowly, came to a stop.

"Serena?"

A question now. A prayer. A plea.

His already pounding heart slammed against his chest. He unbuckled his harness, dropping hard against the center console. He lurched toward the cabin, stumbling over cabinets that now made up the floor. Nothing was where it should be. Light streamed in from the windows above him. Cold air seeped inside from a gash in the fuselage.

Had the tanks ruptured? Was the fuselage or wing on fire?

His breath steamed in the freezing draft. "Serena?"

"Here."

Her soft voice brought a rush of relief. She drooped at an awkward angle still strapped to her seat. One side of her face was covered in blood. She clutched her stomach.

But she was breathing. Responsive. And unless she'd broken her neck, he had to move her before the plane caught fire. Or started sliding again into the trees.

Ripping off the bottom of his shirt, he pressed the wadded material to her bleeding scalp. She gasped in protest.

"Where does it hurt?"

"My head and stomach. Ribs, I think." Her voice sounded strained, almost breathless. "Not bad."

Bad enough. "We need to get off the plane. Can you move?"

"I... Yes."

Her quiet voice bothered him, but he had to get her away from the plane in case of a fuel leak and/or fire. "Good. I'll help you."

Kane reached across her. His forearm brushed her stomach.

She winced.

"Sorry." Worry made him brusque.

"It's okay."

Kane released the buckle. "Let's go."

She glanced to the back of the cabin. "The wedding dresses."

"There isn't time, Serena." Kane opened the door and stepped out. His feet sunk six inches through a crusty layer of snow. No way did he want Serena wading through this.

"This might hurt." He placed one arm around her back and the other under her knees. As he lifted her from the plane, she inhaled sharply.

"Don't apologize," she said.

"I wasn't going to." He carried her from the plane, ignoring the soft curves pressing against him, until he felt they were far enough away in case of an explosion. "Can you stand?"

"Yes."

She didn't sound too certain. Carefully, he placed her on her feet, not letting go until he was certain she wouldn't fall or faint.

"I'm fine." Serena crossed her arms in front of her. "Really."

He took a long look at her. No coat, bleeding head,

arms around possibly injured ribs. "You sure have a different definition of 'fine' than I do."

Her gaze dropped.

Damn. That wasn't the reaction he wanted. He wanted to rouse her, to make her fighting mad. She would need all the fight in her, all her determination and vitality and assurance, to survive this.

"I'll bring back your coat and blankets," he said. "Stay here. I've got to check the plane for any fuel leaks."

Holding the cloth against her head, Serena nodded gingerly.

His breath hung in the crisp, pine-scented air. He lingered, oddly reluctant to leave her. "I'll be right back."

She made a shooing motion with the hand protecting her ribs. "Go."

He did.

A quick but thorough walk-around showed no fuel leaks. Kane checked both engines and the aircraft itself.

The plane lay on its side, crippled and crumpled and torn. Had the landing gear broken and caused the plane to roll? With all these trees in the meadow he wouldn't be surprised if they'd hit something. Whatever the reason, the sight in front of him broke his heart.

Everything he had—his livelihood, his home, his love— was gone. Just like that. Just like his mother. He set his jaw.

His life hadn't flashed before his eyes in the damn crash. But now Kane saw her, his mother, lying again on the floor of the kitchen. He'd heard a crash, run downstairs and found her. Unconscious. Her right hand on her heart. A broken bowl of bread dough next to her. He'd checked her breathing. None. Her pulse. None. But that hadn't stopped him from calling for help, applying the first aid measures he'd learned over the years, but nothing he did, nothing he tried, could disguise the fact it was too late to save her.

Just like it was too late to save the plane.

Kane shook himself. He still needed supplies, blankets. Serena needed blankets. He crawled into the plane.

First stop—the ELT, emergency locator transmitter. Not working. Kane tried the radio. Nothing. Not even static.

This wasn't looking good.

Sure, he'd radioed his final coordinates, but the plane had drifted several miles while he searched for a safe place to land. The search would start from the last known coordinates and spread out from there. Even if the weather held off, that could mean a long wait before they were found. Especially with this meadow that wasn't really big enough to land a plane. They were lucky. Damn lucky.

They were also missing. Lost. Screwed.

At least he didn't smell fuel.

They could stay inside the plane until they were rescued. Although that tear in the fuselage meant they were in for a long, cold night. He'd have to fix that, somehow, in the remaining daylight.

Kane scoured the cockpit and cabin, salvaging a first aid kit, flashlight, lighter, food, water, blankets, pillows and toilet paper from where they'd been tossed and tumbled around the aircraft. He found Serena's purse secured cleverly to the bottom of her seat, and then—finally!—her long wool coat, buried beneath another seat. Clutching it and a blanket, he trudged through the snow, returning to the exact spot where he'd left Serena.

Only…she wasn't there.

He gripped her coat and the blanket, looked around.

Panic hollowed his gut. "Serena."

A million and one thoughts screamed through his brain.

Idiot.

He shouldn't have left her alone out here. She had a head injury. Possibly fractured or bruised ribs. Shock. Even the onset of hypothermia.

She couldn't have disappeared on a snow-covered meadow somewhere in middle-of-nowhere Idaho. He noticed a trail of footprints in the snow.

Anger slightly eclipsed his worry.

She could, however, have wandered off.

"Serena?" Kane called her name as he followed her trail to the edge of the meadow where a hillside—more like a mountain—rose up steeply.

No way would she climb up there. In her condition. In high-heeled boots.

But the footprints led upward. Was she disoriented? Confused? A concussion, maybe.

Or maybe she was just plain dumb.

He climbed up after her.

"Serena?" No answer. He hadn't been gone that long. Five minutes. Tops. She couldn't have climbed too high. Unless she'd passed out. His chest tightened. "Serena?"

"I'm right here." Her low voice sounded almost husky. She carefully made her way down the slope, teetering on her heels in the snow.

He climbed to meet her. Relief at finding her didn't appease his anger. Her face was white, her lips nearly blue.

"What the hell were you doing?" His already skyrocketing blood pressure spiked higher. "I told you to stay put not walk into a forest. You could have gotten lost or hurt or—"

"I was trying to get a signal on my cell phone." She pulled the thin, hot-pink device out of her pocket, her hands shaking. He was shaking, too, with reaction. "I wanted to call 911."

As if the local fire department could be here in three minutes to help them out of this situation. Kane bundled Serena roughly into her coat and wrapped the blanket over her, hoping she wouldn't notice his trembling hands. "And what if you couldn't find your way back?"

"I picked two spots and made sure I could always see them so I wouldn't get lost. I'm not stupid, Kane."

"I never said—"

But he'd thought it, he realized, chagrined.

She stared up at him and he found himself…speechless. He'd always been a pushover for big baby blues. Serena James had about the prettiest eyes he'd ever seen. Still he couldn't have her wandering off in the wilderness in her condition. He looked away, checking her head. At least her scalp wound had stopped bleeding.

"You could have gotten disoriented, passed out—"

She arched her eyebrows. "Eaten by bears?"

He scowled. "It's not funny. Too many things can happen out here. We're not in the city anymore. Even if you reached 911, we're a long way from any type of emergency service."

"I just wanted to help."

"Putting yourself in more danger is not helping."

"More danger than, say, being stranded up in the mountains in the middle of a snowstorm?"

"It's not snowing."

She gave him a pointed look. "Yet."

Kane hated to admit it, but she was right. He needed to get them both to shelter before the temperatures dipped further.

"Come on, we'll go back to the plane. The fuselage is

damaged, but I can rig something that will keep any rain out and block the wind some."

"What about the log cabin at the end of the meadow?" she asked.

"What log cabin?"

She pointed. "You can see it from up there."

This could be exactly what they needed. Kane straightened. "Show me."

Tottering on her heels through the snow, she led him a few yards farther up the slope. Visible through the trees, at the other end of the meadow was a small rustic-looking log cabin. The kind hunters or hikers might use. Snow drifted across the doorway but the roof looked secure enough. There even seemed to be an outhouse out back. Finally luck was on their side.

The cabin had to be warmer than the damaged plane.

Especially if those dark clouds now overhead decided to drop rain or snow.

"Looks good," he said. "Let's go."

"You're welcome," she said.

"What?"

"I thought you were thanking me for finding shelter."

"Yeah, I'll be real grateful tonight if the roof doesn't cave in."

"Tonight?" A slight tremor sounded in her voice. Her brows drew together, her forehead wrinkling. "Aren't we going to be rescued soon?"

Not wanting to scare her, he shrugged. "Probably not."

"Aren't you supposed to stay with your vehicle if you're lost?"

"Not if your vehicle won't keep you warm and dry through the night. We can leave a signal," he offered. "An SOS in the snow and an arrow pointing to the cabin in case the searchers arrive at daybreak. The two are close enough together it shouldn't be a problem."

Though the chances of being found tomorrow morning in this kind of weather were slim to none.

The corners of her mouth turned up. Appeased for now. Good.

"So what do we do now?" Serena asked.

"We make a signal, gather supplies and get to the cabin before dark."

Climbing down the hill, Serena struggled in her high-heeled boots, but she didn't complain, didn't sigh, didn't grimace. She trudged downward without saying a word. His respect inched up. She was tough.

More like stubborn, he told himself. What if she slipped? She could hurt her ribs more or something else.

As she picked her way over a fallen sapling, he grabbed her elbow to steady her. "Watch your step."

She snatched her arm away. "I can manage on my own."

"Yeah, until you fall on that cute little ass of yours."

She glared and marched away, her hips swaying under her brown and pink plaid wool coat.

Stubborn, Kane thought again. But the ass was definitely cute.

Serena had already made enough mistakes in the past seven months to last a lifetime. Stuck here in the middle of who-knew-where, she wasn't going to make another. Her boots sank into the snow as she made her way down the mountain. That meant keeping her distance from Kane Wiley.

Being in his arms, feeling the heat and strength emanating from him had been enough to send her senses spinning earlier. Serena turned up the collar of her coat.

Oh, she wanted to blame the reaction on her head injury, on the circumstances surrounding the emergency landing, on the relief of being alive. But she'd felt this way about him before they'd almost died, when she'd been sitting in the cockpit.

The man was as dangerous on the ground as he had been in the air. At least until he started up with all the manly, macho, I'm-in-charge attitude.

…until you fall on that cute little ass of yours.

Some nerve, but he was right about the falling part. One wrong step and she could do more than land flat on her face or bottom. All her plans, so meticulously put together over the years, could literally fall apart. Circumstances could change in an instant. One wrong decision could affect her entire future. Especially when the wrong man entered one's life. She'd seen that happen. She wouldn't allow that to happen to her.

"I'm…" Fine was on the tip of her tongue once again, but a glimpse at the wilderness surrounding her—natural, raw, untamed—made her feel anything but fine. She had never been more scared in her life, but she'd die before letting Kane know that. She looked at him. "I'm…okay."

Or would be, sooner or later.

She hoped.

Right now, she felt like a quivering mass of goo inside. Sheer willpower was getting her down this mountainside. Nothing more. And that was, as she'd just told him, okay.

She prided herself on her self-reliance. Others counted on her, not the other way around. Serena would never forget what had happened to her sister when she'd given up everything, putting all her faith and trust into one man, the absolutely wrong man for her. Morgan had lost everything, including their parents' love and respect. Years later, her sister was still trying to recover and reinvent herself as she struggled to raise a child on her own. Their parents still hadn't fully forgiven her lapse in…judgment.

No way did Serena want Kane's assistance. The only thing she needed was a new plan to get her through this ordeal.

One night in a cabin with him.

No. Big. Deal.

The more times she told herself that, the better.

"Are you warm enough?" he asked.

That depended on the definition of enough. Her feet tingled, the familiar pins and needles sensation after sitting in one place too long, and her fingers ached. She shoved her hands deeper into her jacket pockets. That helped. A little.

"Yes," she replied. "Are you?"

"I'm nice and toasty." Kane's mouth curved slightly, and his smile sent a warm rush through her. Too much charm, too little substance. "This little hike warmed me right up."

She focused on his eyes, serious and intent. "Glad it helped you."

"I'm going to make an SOS and an arrow pointed at the cabin out of rocks and branches. As long as it doesn't snow, someone might see it from the air."

"I'll help," she offered.

"Your ribs. Head."

"If it hurts, I'll stop."

Carefully Serena kneeled, picked up a rock sticking out of the snow and stood. A knife-edged pain sliced through her midsection. The freezing rock burned her already cold hands. She nearly dropped the rock.

"You okay?" Kane asked.

Not trusting her voice at the moment, she nodded. Serena mustered every ounce of strength to carry the rock to where Kane stood without dropping it or crying out.

"Gather tree branches for the arrow." He removed the gloves from his hands. "Put these on."

"I can't take your gloves."

He dropped the pair at her feet and walked away.

Serena stared at the black gloves lying on the snow. She didn't get him. Not at all. She put them on.

As they worked, the temperature dropped. Finally both symbols were finished. Not a moment too soon. Serena could barely catch her breath. She needed to sit.

"Let's get the supplies from the plane. I'll pull out your suitcase."

"Thanks." Serena wished she were strong enough to get her own bag. Not that any of those clothes packed away were appropriate attire for this weather or situation. Nor were any of them clean. Well, except for a pair of panties. She'd packed an extra. Thank goodness. And then she remembered. "We need to bring the dresses."

"No."

"Yes." She pointed out the tear in the fuselage, not that he was looking at her. "If moisture gets inside the cabin, the dresses could be ruined."

"We can cover them up."

"With what?" She mentally counted the days until Callie's wedding. Serena shuddered. "The dresses must come with us."

"We don't need wedding dresses to survive."

"The company does."

"Belle's company."

"Yes."

A beat passed.

"Fine," Kane said. "You want them, you carry them. You'll have to leave your clothes. I'm going to have my hands full with supplies."

"Fine." Serena felt anything but. Why did he have to be such a jerk about this?

Inside the cabin of the plane, she unhooked the dress bags. She moved slowly to keep from aggravating her sore ribs.

A noise caught Serena's attention. She looked over. Kane filled a duffel bag with the supplies.

"We need to hurry." He stuffed blankets into the bag. "The sky looks like it's going to open up any minute."

She counted the bags like a mother hen checking her chicks. Six. "I've got all of them."

"Come on then."

Serena struggled to climb out of the plane with the dress bags in her hands.

Kane snorted in disgust and took them from her. "Go."

When she was on the ground, he handed over the bulky gowns, tossed down the duffel, and jumped after it.

Serena clutched the bags, unsure what to do with them. She struggled to keep them out of the snow. Kane lifted another box through the plane's hatch before closing it behind him. He swung the strap of the duffel bag over his shoulder. "Move it."

He strode in the direction of the cabin, leaving deep tracks in the snow.

Serena stood frozen in place. Between the dresses, her injuries and the distance she needed to walk, she felt overwhelmed. It wasn't that far, but still...

He glanced back. "What are you waiting for?"

Mr. Right.

Someone to take the bags out of her hands, to tell her

everything would be okay and to love her from this day forward no matter what she said or did.

The lump in her throat matched the knot in her heart. Her vision blurred.

Oh, no, Serena didn't want to start crying. That was not part of their deal. And definitely not part of her image. She stared up at the sky, the dark clouds thicker than before, and blinked.

"Serena?" Kane called.

"I'm coming." What else was she going to do? Stay here? That would probably please Kane to no end. Blowing out a disgusted breath, she adjusted the bulky bags in her arms. No matter, she could handle this. She would save the dresses herself. Serena walked toward him. "Right behind you."

And that was where she stayed. Behind him.

Keeping up with Kane wasn't easy. Clumsy and hurting, she struggled to hold the bulky dresses and walk at the same time. She stumbled in the deep snow. Bit back a sigh. Swallowed a cry for help.

And hated every minute of it.

She repositioned the dress bags in her arms. The dark sky overhead looked ominous and threatening.

Kane walked back to her. He swore, muttering under his breath. "I knew this was going to happen."

"I've got them." Well, sort of.

He placed the box on the snow and took the dresses from her. "Carry the supplies."

He trudged toward the cabin without a glance back, the dress bags billowing over his arms, the heavy duffel banging his hip. Relieved, she wiped the corner of her eye and picked up the box.

She still had trouble walking straight, but the box was lighter and easier to handle than the dress bags.

No matter what she might think of him, attractive or not, a gentleman or a ladies' man, a nice guy or a jerk, he had saved the dresses by carrying them. Serena would toast Kane at the upcoming poker and margarita night the Belles held each month. The next one, she remembered with a pang, would also be a surprise bridal shower for Callie at Regina's house.

Callie.

Serena had to keep her gown safe.

Halfway to the cabin, a mix of sleet and snow poured from the sky, stinging her cheeks and chilling her lungs. The scent of ice permeated the air. Forget that it was only November. Winter had arrived. Those dress bags had better be waterproof as advertised.

With each step, the conditions deteriorated. Damp hair clung to her face. Her jacket felt heavier. The box in her hands weighed her down. She had no sense of direction.

"We're almost there," Kane yelled. "Do you see the cabin?"

She scanned the horizon, but all she could see was white in every direction. A burst of panic rioted through her. "No."

"Eleven o'clock."

Serena squinted in that direction. More white. And then the roofline came into focus. Thank goodness. "I see it."

"Don't lose sight of the cabin."

She didn't want to lose sight of him. A bone-deep chill overtook her, made it harder to breathe and walk, but she forged ahead, carried by fear and responsibility. Her numb fingers, in their borrowed gloves, cried out in pain. Guiltily she wondered how Kane's hands were faring, especially carrying the gowns.

The gowns. If Serena couldn't get to the cabin and Kane came back after her with the dresses they would get wetter. She quickened the pace.

And fell flat on her butt.

Just as Kane had predicted she would.

She sat on the snow empty-handed and struggling to breath. "Please don't turn around."

He didn't.

Kane reached the cabin and pushed his shoulder against the door. A banging sound echoed.

If he opened the door, he would look back.

Every muscle ached. Her ribs hurt. She couldn't catch her breath. But her pride was stronger than her physical ailments.

Using every ounce of strength she could muster, Serena stood. Pain radiated through her stomach. She waited for the hurt to subside, then brushed the snow off her bottom.

Thank goodness Kane was still trying to get into the cabin. Each of his attempts boomed through the meadow.

She gathered the supplies that had fallen onto the snow, put them back into the box and marched to the cabin.

By the time she arrived, the door was open. Kane stood outside, brushing the snow and ice off the dress bags.

"The dresses," she said.

"Get inside."

His harsh tone made her wince. The sound matched his dark eyes.

Serena did as she'd been told without a word.

She placed the box of supplies on a wooden table with chairs pushed under it. Her breath hung on the cold, stale air. The temperature inside the one-room cabin was warmer than outside, but not by much. She left her wet coat on.

Kane stepped inside. He hung the dress bags on one of the two sets of metal bunk beds along the wall opposite the door. Four beds but only one mattress.

She gulped. What had she gotten herself into?

"There must be a propane tank somewhere for the two wall lamps, the stovetop and oven." He removed the duffel bag from around his shoulder and picked up some sort of tube that was on the table. "I need to insert the chimney so we can use the woodstove and remove the shutters to get some air and light in here. I'll be right back."

Serena stood in near darkness. She noticed a wood cupboard. She opened it up and found cans of food. Not quite all the comforts of home, but they would be warm here and wouldn't starve. If you didn't mind rustic, the cabin was almost quaint and cozy with its log walls, beamed ceilings and small wood-paned windows. With the right companion, one might even find the place romantic.

She heard noises on the roof and on the two sides of the cabin where the windows were.

Several long minutes later, Kane came back in, carrying a stack of wood. He pulled off his jacket and hung it on a hook behind the door.

"No leaking holes in this roof, unlike my plane." As Kane opened the door to the stove, the hinges creaked. "You done good, Blondie."

Serena swallowed. "You, too."

"We're in this together."

She nodded.

He grabbed a newspaper from the duffel bag, crumpled a few pages up and stuck them inside the stove. Next he added a few smaller logs from the stash of dry wood sitting next to the stove and put them in. He pulled out a lighter from a pocket in his bag. The paper caught fire. A burst of heat warmed her from five feet away. The crackling sound and smell of burning wood filled the air.

Serena would never take domestic central heating for granted again. She removed the wet gloves.

"Stand closer to the stove," he said.

She did, placing her icy hands over the top. As the heat warmed her fingers, she wiggled all ten digits. "Thanks."

Next he lit the two wall lamps, filling the cabin with light. Kane didn't stop there. He poured a bottle of water into a pan and placed the pot on the stovetop. "You'll feel better once you drink something hot."

"What about you?" she asked, knowing he had to be as cold as she was.

He kicked off his shoes and removed his socks. "Let's get you warmed up first."

His concern for her well-being surprised Serena. He didn't seem the nurturing type. Still she hated being forced to depend on him for, well, everything.

A gust of wind rattled the windows. She shivered. If only the storm would go away so they could be found...

"You've done a great job getting us set up here." And she meant that. Serena was relieved he was with her.

Not many men—definitely not Rupert, who watched home improvement shows with her, but didn't own a toolbox, or Malcolm, who got weekly manicures—would know what to do in a situation like this. Rupert would be going crazy without being able to use his BlackBerry or laptop. Malcolm would be so inspired by the surroundings to design a line of casual outdoor wear that he wouldn't worry about anything else, including survival.

At least Kane, the poster boy for Mr. Oh-So-Wrong,

knew how to get them through a white-out, break into the cabin and get a fire going so they would have a warm, dry place to stay tonight and food. Yes, she could be in worse hands. An unfamiliar, yet content feeling settled over her.

"Warmed up enough?" Kane asked.

"For what?"

"To get undressed."

CHAPTER FIVE

SERENA wrapped her arms over her chest. "Get undressed?"

He scowled, feeling like an idiot. "You're not that irresistible, babe. We need to get out of our wet clothes to avoid hypothermia. That's all."

With the caked, dried blood on her forehead and face, she looked as if she'd fought a long, hard battle. Still, she raised her chin. "I don't have any other clothes to wear."

Serena had been polite up until now. Stubborn, yes, but composed. He appreciated that. She'd even tried to lift rocks with her ribs hurting. Kane respected that. But the way she stared down her nose at him like some ice princess irritated the hell out of him. The last thing he wanted, the last thing he needed, was to be responsible for someone else, especially a wide-eyed blonde who reminded him of his worst mistakes.

"You've got six wedding dresses to choose from," he said. "Take your pick."

Her mouth gaped.

"You chose the gowns over your clothes. Someone should get some use out of them."

"Someone will. The very lucky women I designed them

for." Her eyes never left his. "Which is why I'm not parading around a dirty, cold cabin in a couture wedding gown."

"Fine." Kane had just been rattling her chain, anyway. He opened the jam-packed duffel bag, pulled out a blanket and a shirt and tossed them to her. "Here."

"You want me to wear these?"

"It's all we've got. I left most of my clothes in the plane so I could bring supplies." Kane failed to mention he'd only brought clothes for himself. He wasn't used to thinking about someone else. "You can have the pants. I'll wear the blanket."

"That's okay. I don't need to change." She flapped the sides of her skirt like a flamenco dancer. "I'm drying off."

"Yeah, right." Her coat looked like a sopping wet, oversize dishrag. Droplets fell from the hem of her skirt. Her sad excuse for boots were completely water soaked. Not good for warming her up. "Take your clothes off now or I'll take them off for you."

Her mouth gaped. "What did you say?"

"You heard me." He opened the first aid kit he'd packed in the duffel bag. "Hypothermia is nothing to mess around with. Your speech slurs, your breathing slows down, your skin becomes pale and cold, you shiver uncontrollably and you feel lethargic and confused. In its final stages, you feel so hot you rip your clothes off to cool down. But by then it's usually too late."

"Too late?"

"To recover."

A beat passed. She tried to remove her coat, wincing with every movement.

After her third attempt, Kane cursed. He did not need

this. Her. He grabbed hold of the collar. "You're going to hurt yourself more."

Carefully he drew the coat down her arms and over her hands. She didn't grimace, but he could tell she was hurting.

He put the jacket on another of the hooks on the back of the cabin door. "This thing weighs a ton. I can't believe you hiked all the way here wearing it."

"I didn't have a choice."

"True, but you're stronger than you look."

"Thank you," she mumbled.

"Sit." He moved an empty chair closer to the stove. "I'll take your boots off then you can undress."

Serena sat, still and silent, as if waiting for a jury to declare her innocence or guilt. She clutched the blanket and shirt in her lap.

"Left or right?" Kane asked.

She raised her right foot. He pulled on the tall boot. The wet leather clung to her thin calf and didn't budge. She gripped the seat of the chair.

"This might hurt," he said.

"Just get them off." A hint of vulnerability flickered in her eyes. "Please."

Her plea hit him hard in the gut.

"You got it." Kane peeled the leather off, folding it over toward her ankle. He tugged until the boot came off. "Next."

She raised her left foot. Removing that one was easier now that he knew what to do.

"Now your—" he stared at her feet "—nylons?"

As she reached under her skirt, his groin tightened. What the hell was she doing? And how could he get a better look? He tilted his head.

Serena rolled something down her leg. "Thigh highs."

Despite the chill lingering in the air and his wet clothes, his temperature shot up twenty degrees. Time to get back to business. "I need to check your ribs."

"My ribs are better."

"Your breathing's off."

"Do you make a habit of staring at women's chests?"

"Every chance I get," he admitted cheerfully. "Come on, let's have a look."

Her mouth tightened. "You're a pilot, not a doctor."

"Right," he admitted. "But I've played doctor before."

Serena stared at him.

Okay, he'd cut her some slack for having no sense of humor right now. "You like being in control and taking care of yourself, right?"

She nodded.

"I'm the same way. I'm used to being on my own, not having to worry about anyone else, but sometimes life throws you a curveball and you have to make the best of it. I'm all you've got, Blondie," he said. "So lift your shirt."

"Does that line ever work?" she asked.

"You'd be amazed."

"I'd be astonished." A corner of her mouth lifted. "You really need to work on your bedside manner."

Finally a crack in the princess's ice.

He bit back a smile. "You think?"

"Most definitely." Serena raised her blouse enough to show an expanse of smooth skin and a flat belly.

Oh, man. Talk about sweet. The air rushed out of his lungs. His mouth went dry. He focused on her belly button—an innie.

"Kane?"

What was he doing? Staring? Leering?

Talk about a curveball. She was his passenger. His responsibility. He was stuck taking care of her whether he liked it or not. "Where does it hurt?"

Serena pointed to her left side. "Here."

He studied the spot, ignoring her creamy complexion and the curve of her waist. He pressed lightly, her skin soft against his fingers. "Does this hurt?"

"A little."

He moved to a different spot. "How about here?"

She winced. "Ouch."

Kane pulled his hand back. "I—"

"It's okay," she said before he could apologize. "Really."

"You could have fractured a rib, but it's likely they're just bruised. There's no way to tell without an X-ray." He opened the first aid kit. Fully stocked. At least he was prepared. "I'm going to wrap you with an Ace bandage to be on the safe side. Stand up."

She did and raised her blouse higher. He glimpsed the lace edge of her bra—pink, but who was noticing?—and sucked in a breath.

Don't look. Don't think. Just get it done.

Wrapping the bandage around her ribs, he mentally recited the multiplication table for nine, ten and eleven. "How does that feel? Too tight?"

She looked as uncomfortable as he felt. "Just right."

Was it? Kane hoped so. He didn't want to hurt her.

He secured the end. "All done."

"Thanks," she mumbled.

Outside the storm raged, the wind blew and icy pellets hit the cabin. The forced intimacy of the situation only added to the tension inside. The lack of conversation didn't help. The burning logs crackled. The water boiled. The sounds and sight of their breathing filled the air.

It had been a long day. It would be an even longer night.

"Let's clean your cut." He washed away the dried blood with an antiseptic wipe, dabbed antibiotic cream on the cut and placed two butterfly bandages over the long gash. She didn't flinch or complain. "All done. It's not too bad, but you might have a little scar."

"A scar?" She sounded concerned.

"Maybe, right near your temple. It's hard to tell."

She reached up, but he grabbed hold of her hand. "Don't touch."

"But—"

"A little Vitamin E oil can go a long way." He released her hand. "Though guys dig chicks with scars."

"Not all men. Some guys find an imperfection and leave."

"Idiots," Kane muttered. "You'd be better off without a man like that. Scars show a person takes risks and isn't afraid to live. Very cool in my book."

She gazed up at him. "You mean that?"

"Yep."

A shy smile graced her lips. "Thanks."

"No problem." He grabbed the dry pants, a pair of khakis. "You want them?"

"No, thanks," she said. "I'll stick with what I have."

"You can dress by the stove. I'll be over there."

By the bunk beds, he unbuckled his belt and unzipped his pants. As he pulled them off, he heard another zipper—Serena's skirt?—and the rustling of fabric.

"If something's wet, even damp, take it off." He removed his underwear and torn shirt. "We can hang our clothes on the hooks and purlins so they'll be dry in the morning."

"Okay."

Kane almost laughed. Nothing about this was okay, especially standing naked in a cold cabin, miles away from civilization, with a beautiful woman he wanted nothing to do with. He pulled on the dry pants and zipped them. "You dressed?"

The sound of fabric ripping filled the air. "Almost."

The scent of smoke lingered in the air, even though he'd opened the damper to the flue. Staring at the aged, dark wood walls of the cabin, Kane wondered who else had been forced to take refuge here during a winter storm. The items inside—food and firewood—suggested someone used the cabin. Maybe forest service employees checked the place routinely.

"I'm dressed," Serena said.

Kane turned. His mouth dropped open. Unbelievable. She looked like a Grecian princess with the blanket wrapped around her body and tied at the waist and at the top with sashes made from strips of the fabric. Absolutely beautiful.

"Wow." Forget about being cold. His temperature shot into the red zone. He remembered what she'd said about her dresses. "You can even make 'couture' out of a blanket."

"What can I say?" She put on his blue shirt, buttoned the front and rolled up the sleeves. The color brought out the blue of her eyes. "It's a gift."

Seeing her wearing his shirt was kind of sexy, too. "I'd say so."

He smiled at her.

She smiled back.

Time stopped. They could have been anywhere—the cabin, inside the plane, Seattle, Boston. The place didn't matter.

Only here, only now, only them.

The beat of his heart seemed stronger, the blood flowing through his veins warmer. He didn't want to have to take care of her. He didn't want to have to worry about her. But at this moment he wouldn't have wanted to be with anyone else.

The moment lingered.

Kane could have broken the contact, but didn't want to. He hadn't felt this connected to someone in…well, ever.

Finally Serena looked away, her gaze resting on the bunks for a few seconds before focusing on the wood-stove. "I guess now there's not much else to do except hit the sack. I mean, bed. You know, sleep. Somewhere."

She looked cute all flustered with her cheeks pink. Forget the ice princess glare or the Grecian princess attire, she was suddenly natural and approachable.

Too bad she was practically engaged or something.

"You can always make a nest out of those wedding dresses," he said to lighten the mood, to set some distance between them. "Lots of nice, comfy material there."

But instead of getting all prissy on him again, Serena laughed. "Obviously, you don't know much about wedding gown fabrics. Tulle is too scratchy and satin is too slippery. Silk wouldn't be too bad except for all the beading and appliqué. That might be uncomfortable."

His smile widened. "Then we'll have to share the bed."

That was what Serena was afraid he'd say. "I…"

"You have a boyfriend," Kane finished for her. "I understand."

But she didn't. And he couldn't.

"Using our body heat is the best way to keep each other warm," he explained.

The coal-size lump in her throat kept her from answering.

"You can trust me, Serena."

But did she trust herself? That was the real question. One she'd never worried about before. Serena had never understood what unknown trait made a totally wrong man so irresistible to a woman. She'd vowed never to allow herself to be in that position, never to make the same mistake her sister had.

Which meant figuring out how to handle this…dilemma. Serena fussed with the folds of the blanket she wore.

"Hungry?" he asked.

She nodded, rolling up the long-sleeved shirt more. Wearing Kane's shirt felt strange, and she wasn't sure she liked it.

He unwrapped the cellophane from a sandwich. "Turkey and Swiss cheese, okay?"

"My favorite actually." She stared at the sandwich he placed in front of her. "Thanks."

He sat at the table with a sandwich of his own. "We have two more sandwiches, a bunch of fruit and enough prepackaged snacks to last a week."

"Plus all the canned goods in the cupboard. We aren't going to starve."

They ate quickly without saying a word to one another. She didn't mind the silence. Not when she needed to figure out a solution to the sleeping arrangement problem, one that didn't involve a long, cold night shivering on the table or floor. She had to think of something.

The alternative…

Serena didn't want to feel Kane's bare, broad shoulders and chest against her. She didn't want to feel his heart beat. She didn't want to breathe his warm breath. Those things were too intimate, too dangerous.

"What if we slept head to toe, in the opposite directions?" she suggested. "We'd still be able to share body heat, but not…"

Time to stop babbling. The less she said the better. A mouse scurried across the floor. She didn't scream, but she lifted her feet.

"Not a bad suggestion," he said, not seeming to notice the mouse. "But you don't want your nose anywhere near my feet. Besides, our good parts will still be in contact."

"True." She rubbed her hands together. "I'm just—"

"Nervous?"

"A little." More like a lot. "Silly, I know."

He pulled out another blanket. "Once you feel how warm it is when we're both in the bed, all your doubts will disappear."

That's what she was afraid of.

Still Serena knew he was right. Keeping warm was the most important thing.

She crawled onto the lower bunk. The mattress, more like a pad, sank from her weight.

"Give me a shove if I snore," he said.

"Uh, sure." She didn't want to touch him, let alone shove him. "But I'm so tired I probably won't notice anything."

Facing the log wall, she squeezed her eyes shut. She wanted sleep to come quickly and easily tonight.

Something creaked. The floor? The roof? Something bigger than a mouse? She opened her eyes. Black, total darkness as if the moon and stars had been sucked into a vacuum. She couldn't see her hand. He must have turned off the lamps.

Serena lay there. She smelled smoke and heard the burning logs in the stove. She also felt a presence nearby.

Kane.

The mattress sank to the right. He crawled in.

His foot brushed hers and tingles shot up her leg. "Oops," he said.

The tingles didn't stop. "It's a little cramped."

"Better than the floor."

"Or a chair." She didn't want to sound as if she were complaining. He shouldn't have to put up with that after today, even if the only thing she wanted to do was get on a wide-body plane with four engines, at least two pilots and three hundred passengers and fly home.

Far away from this wilderness nightmare.

Far, far away from Kane.

"It could be worse," he said.

She rolled toward him. "What?"

"It could be worse," Kane repeated.

The wind howled, blowing snow against the cabin, the noises outside as unfamiliar as the complete darkness inside. Thinking about the emergency landing sent a chill shivering down her spine. This could not be any worse unless one of them had been seriously injured or worse. "Thank you for landing the plane, Kane, and coming after me and…"

"Just doing my job."

He sounded so nonchalant after saving their lives. "It was more than that."

"You've done well yourself," he said. "Finding this cabin."

"Sure beats the airplane."

"I'll say." He rolled onto his side. The motion sent her falling back against him. She scooted away. Well, as away as she could manage on a twin-size bed. "But you would have managed in the plane tonight if it'd come to that."

"No, I wouldn't," she whispered.

Serena cringed. She couldn't believe she'd said the words out loud.

His body drew closer. "Why do you say that?"

She was afraid to move. Breathe. "It's just—"

"What?"

This was so hard, but after all he'd done for her today she owed him this much. "I'm not exactly the type to just go with it, without quite a bit of…planning and preparation."

"You've been doing okay here with very little prep time."

His compliment pleased her. More than it should. "Thanks."

"You're welcome," he said. "I'm more a seat-of-my-pants type of guy."

I like to go where I want to go.

She remembered what he'd said in the cockpit, about his need for freedom. "We're very different."

"Yes, we are."

His words made her feel sad for some reason. Isolated by the snow and wilderness, cut off from everything and everyone familiar, she wanted to be like Kane. If she could be more like him, this "situation" might not be so hard to handle.

"We'll get through this," he reassured. "Go to sleep."

Not such an easy thing to do when lying next to him felt so good. Better than it should.

His body heat warmed the space next to her. She heard the rasp of his breathing, the beat of his heart. Letting her guard down and drifting off to sleep probably wasn't the smartest course of action.

Not when she felt safe and secure with Kane. Two ways she never thought she'd ever feel with a man like him. They might be different, but those differences made her feel better and more at ease.

Out here where she didn't belong, Serena knew he would take care of her. Make sure they survived. She survived. Whether she wanted his help or not.

And for that she was grateful.

More than he would ever know.

On Monday morning, Belle stepped into the reception area of the shop with anticipation. She couldn't wait to find out more about the bridal show, though she knew Serena was coming in late.

Julie, her auburn hair a mass of corkscrew curls, sat at the front desk preparing for the day. Natalie set out cake samples for the Belles to taste when they arrived.

"Good morning," Belle said. "What are we sampling today?"

"Banana cake with custard parfait filling." Two rainbow-striped pencils held Natalie's blond hair on top of her head. "The girls wanted me to do something with bananas so I figured why not. Of course, they wanted a chocolate filling."

Belle grinned, imagining the eight-year-old twins asking their mom to bake them a special cake. She wondered if they helped or just made a mess with the flour like the last time.

"Things are looking up businesswise this morning,"

Julie said. "We have four appointments scheduled today and a full inbox of e-mail requests for information."

Belle clapped her hands together. "Fantastic news."

"What's going on?" Audra asked as she walked into the shop, carrying a leather briefcase on her shoulder and holding a coffee in her hand. Sleek with long blond hair, she looked more like one of their clients than a certified public accountant.

"Just the usual Monday catch-up." Natalie handed Audra a plate. "Taste this."

"It's not yet nine and already I'm loading up on calories. Not that I mind. No one's looking at these hips." Audra took a bite. Sighed. "This is absolutely incredible. Your best yet."

"I'll remember that when you get married."

Audra set her fork on the plate. "I'm never getting married."

"That makes two of us then," Natalie said. "I've got my hands full with the twins. I couldn't imagine having to add a boyfriend let alone a husband into the mix."

Julie frowned. "Don't say that."

"I agree." Belle wanted each of her girls to have a happy ending. "You never know when love will come calling."

The doorbell rang. The four women looked at each other.

"How did you do that, Belle?" Audra asked.

Belle shrugged. "Probably just an appointment."

"Hmm." Julie checked the appointment book lying on the table. "We don't have any this early."

"I'll answer as long as it's not love calling for me." Audra opened the door. "Charlie?"

Charlie Wiley stood on the front step, looking anxious. "Is Belle here?"

The faint tremor in his voice worried Belle. She had never seen him look so upset, not even when she wouldn't sell him her late husband, Matthew's, vintage Rolls-Royce. "I'm right here. What's wrong?"

His brown eyes glistened with tears. He opened his mouth to speak, but no words came out.

Belle touched his arm. "Are you okay?"

He nodded, swallowed. "Kane and Serena never made it back from Seattle last night."

Julie gasped. "Where are they?"

"Has anyone heard from them?" Audra asked.

Natalie covered her mouth with her hands. "Oh, no."

Panic rioted through Belle. Fear clogged her throat. She loved all the Belles like daughters. "Do you have any idea where they might be?"

"The control center received a distress call. Kane was going to make an emergency landing, but that was the final transmission," Charlie said. "The plane's last known position places them somewhere over Idaho."

Audra's forehead creased. "Last known position?"

Charlie grimaced. "Kane and Serena's plane is officially missing."

CHAPTER SIX

HALF asleep, Kane snuggled against the inviting warmth and feminine softness of the body next to him. He could get used to waking up like this, his legs tangled in hers.

She had her back to him, her feet tucked between his legs.

His hand rested on the curve of her hip, the fabric of her makeshift skirt separating skin from skin. He opened his eyes, but didn't move. Not even his hand.

Serena.

Waking up with her so close in this small bed was…nice.

Yeah, nice.

As if he were sleeping with a cuddly puppy or something. A puppy would be better than an attractive, sexy woman with a serious boyfriend. What the hell was he thinking? Doing?

He untangled himself and crawled off the lower bunk. Faint light shone through the wood-paned windows. Morning already? Kane felt as if he'd only closed his eyes a few minutes ago.

Outside, a blanket of fresh white powder covered the ground, trees and bushes. It looked like a Christmas card.

Pain ricocheted through Kane as he remembered Christmases with his mother. She would have been frantic right now if she'd been alive and he was missing. He thought about his dad. Had his father been notified of the situation? Were people searching for them yet?

The overcast skies didn't fill Kane with much hope for rescue this morning, but at least it wasn't snowing anymore. Their signals could have been covered, though. He might as well take advantage of the break in the weather and head back to the plane.

Kane glanced back at Serena. She slept soundly, a hint of a smile on her face. He wondered what she dreamed about. Shopping and weddings? Or something more, deeper, secret?

A warm feeling settled over him. He shook it off.

He dressed in his clothes from yesterday, now dry, added a log to the woodstove so she wouldn't wake up cold and put on his shoes.

"Where are you going?" Serena asked softly.

"To the plane," he said. "It's stopped snowing. I'm going to check on our signal, bring back more supplies. Clothes."

She sat up on her elbows, looking sleep-rumpled and adorable. "Want me to go with you?"

"Stay here. You can help me later, okay?"

Serena nodded.

"How are your ribs?" he asked.

"Not as sore."

"Good. Probably bruised then, not broken," he said. "Go back to sleep."

She closed her eyes and rolled over away from him.

Kane watched her for a moment, noticing her long, graceful neck, then forced himself out into the cold. He hiked back to the plane, unable to see his and Serena's foot-prints from yesterday due to the weather overnight.

Not a good sign.

At the plane, he couldn't see the SOS or the arrow. He spent five minutes trying to locate the rocks and branches and another ten brushing and kicking off the snow. His effort felt like a lesson in futility given the thick, dark cloud-covered sky above. It was going to start snowing any minute. But if Serena asked about the signals, he wanted to tell her the truth.

Who knew? Maybe a plane was looking for them right now. The thought made him light a fire in the middle of the snow-covered meadow far away from any trees or plants. Smoke might be easier for others to see than the SOS, arrow or plane.

As smoke drifted up to the sky, Kane turned his atten-tion to the plane. He stared at the crippled aircraft covered in white. "Damn."

He'd known the damage had been bad, but seeing the plane this morning… He wanted to punch something. Disappointment crashed into him. Frustration burned. He'd lost everything.

No, not everything.

He was still here. Serena, too. No reason to lose control.

Kane entered the plane and looked for anything that might come in handy, including the clothes he'd removed from his duffel bag yesterday. He found his camera in the pile and took pictures of the plane in case the insurance company needed them. By the time he had finished and closed the door to the plane, snowflakes were falling from the sky and the fire was dying.

So much for a break in the weather.

Kane unloaded Serena's suitcase and his second bag.

He noticed items from the bridal show. He remembered candles from the booth and took out the two boxes. There might be other stuff they could use. Something that might make Serena more comfortable. Besides, he should take all he could. This might be his last trip back to the plane today.

The snow fell faster, harder.

Or tomorrow.

"The weather has grounded the air operation, but they plan to get a land search under way once they determine the search grid," Charlie said later that morning after a telephone conversation with the county sheriff in charge of the search and rescue operation. "I'm flying west."

Belle's insides clenched. She walked to the window of her apartment above The Wedding Belles' shop. On the street below, life went on. A car honked. People hurried along the sidewalks. A taxi pulled up to the curb. Two well-dressed women exited. But inside her building, everything—except hope and prayers—had stopped.

"Of course you're going," she said.

Belle wouldn't expect any less from Charlie. She understood he needed to go, to be closer to where his son was, but a part of her hated to see him leave. His presence at the shop this morning had been a blessing to her and her girls.

"Did you speak with Serena's parents?" he asked.

"Yes. They are somewhere in the Himalayas. They decided that by the time they make it to an airport let alone fly back, this will probably all be over with so they are continuing on their trek." Belle's heart ached for her young designer. Pleasing her parents and gaining their approval was important to Serena. She included them in all her triumphs. And now they were too busy to come when their daughter needed them most? Belle didn't understand that. "They asked me to pass on information as I hear it. Will you keep me updated?"

He walked to her and linked his fingers with hers. His touch comforted. His hand felt warm and strong against her skin. "I want you to come with me."

Her heart bumped. "Me?"

"Yes, you." Charlie squeezed her hand. When he let go, she missed the unexpected contact. "Serena might want a familiar face around when she's found."

"Oh, she definitely needs someone there for her."

"So you'll go?" he asked.

For Serena's sake, Belle wanted to say yes, but she'd heard the anticipation in Charlie's voice and she couldn't forget the way her heart had reacted when he'd invited her. She wanted to go with him for her own sake as much as Serena's. And that concerned Belle. "Let me talk to Serena's boyfriend first. If he can't go, I will."

Serena stared out of the cabin window. With all the white on the ground and falling from the sky, she couldn't see anything. She couldn't see Kane. "Where are you?"

She rubbed her arms to fight a shiver. She'd changed back into her own clothes. Wearing Kane's shirt felt too…intimate, but now she felt like putting it back on. Anything to feel closer to him. She didn't like being left alone out here. She didn't like any of this.

Not that she was throwing herself a pity party. That wasn't her style. She'd managed to do a couple of things this morning: visiting the outhouse, trying to find reception on her cell phone, brushing her teeth and setting out breakfast—fruit, granola bars and raisins.

But with Kane gone for so long and the weather turning bad again, all she could do now was wait and think. What if he didn't come back?

Needing to do something, she forced herself away from the window, organized the food and tidied the cabin the best she could. But thoughts of Kane never left her mind. "Come back, please."

The minutes dragged.

Finally she heard a noise outside. The storm or…

Serena opened the door. A gust of wind blew snow and cold air inside, pushing the door back into the cabin. She didn't care. Not when she saw Kane pulling her suitcase like a sled through the snow. Piled on top were boxes and a duffel bag.

Relief filled her, but she played it cool. Easy to do with the snow falling hard and fast. Goose bumps prickled her skin. She should have put on her coat, but seeing him sent warmth surging through her veins. "Back already?"

"You're going to get cold." His mouth tightened. "Where are your coat and shoes?"

Why had she wanted him to come back? Serena sighed. "I want to help. Hand me something."

He hesitated for a moment then handed her one of the boxes. "Watch your ribs."

"They're not hurting, but I'll be careful."

She helped him unload the supplies. Together they moved everything inside in less than three minutes.

Kane closed the door, shutting out the storm and sealing them inside. "Thanks for the help."

With his rugged good looks, razor stubble on his face and strong body, he looked like a renegade mountain man. Rough, raw, wild. All he needed was a rifle, boots and parka to complete the picture.

"You're welcome." Serena fought the urge to brush off the snow still in his hair. Personality aside, even a casual touch wouldn't be a good idea. He might not be the kind of man she wanted in her life, but she couldn't deny his appeal. "You brought back a lot of stuff."

"It'll save me a trip later."

"Smart thinking." And that would save her from worrying about being alone. "But it's almost like moving day with all these things crammed in here."

"Did you just move?"

"About a year ago," she said. "I have a flat in Back Bay."

He unpacked one of the boxes. "Must be nice."

"It is, but I'd rather have a house. One with a fireplace, a fenced yard, a sewing room and—" *a nursery* "—room for a family."

Serena ignored a twinge of disappointment that her plans weren't looking too good right now.

And hadn't been for a while.

"What about you?" She rummaged through her suitcase for any suitable or warmer clothing. "Where do you live?"

"As of now, here." Kane added a log to the fire. "What's with the food?"

Didn't he like it? Had she wasted their provisions? Or did he think she was trying too hard, like a woman who slipped from her lover's bed to make him pancakes?

Of course, Kane probably liked pancakes.

Serena would have settled for coffee.

She lifted her chin. "While you were gone, Bigfoot made breakfast."

"Looks good." Kane's grin reached his eyes. "Thanks, Sassquatch."

Okay, Serena felt better. And her tummy felt all tingly. Hungry. She must be hungry.

She recognized boxes from the bridal show. "Why did you bring these back?"

"To see if we could find anything useful inside." He bit into a granola bar.

She opened the first box and dug through the contents. Jackpot. "Oh. Wow."

"Candles?"

"Something better. Something you're going to like."

He popped a grape into his mouth. "What's that?"

She raised a small item wrapped in cellophane from the box. "Chocolate."

He wiped his hand over his forehead in an exaggerated gesture. "Now I can last at least another day."

Serena pulled out the pieces and placed them on the table. "We have more than enough for a few more days if worst comes to worst."

"Someone will come for us."

His words reassured her, gave her hope. "As soon as the weather breaks."

A slight hesitation, then a nod.

Uh-oh. "What's wrong?" she asked.

"Nothing's wrong," he said. "But finding us might take a few days even after the weather breaks."

Days, not a day. She chewed on the inside of her mouth.

"It's going to be okay, Serena."

"I'm sure things will be better now that we've found chocolate." She hoped she sounded lighthearted, even cheerful, in spite of the heaviness pressing down on the center of her chest.

"Much better."

Serena nodded. This was so out of her everyday routine, even her not-so-ordinary life. A picnic was about the ⟨

closest she'd come to the outdoors in the last ten years. "And we have plenty of water to drink with all the snow."

"Just remember, don't eat the snow. Otherwise, your body wastes too many calories trying to melt it."

"How do you know all this?" she asked, impressed.

"I was a Boy Scout."

"Interesting." She tried to picture him fresh-faced with neatly trimmed hair and a sharply pressed uniform. Tried and failed. Though she could imagine him being a really cute little boy. "The Scouts seem like they would have been too structured for someone like you."

"Like me?"

"A...free spirit."

"I was just a kid. I didn't know the meaning of the word *free*. Scouting was what my dad and I did together back then."

"You must have had fun. Charlie's a great guy."

"He has his moments."

She thought about Kane's father and him wanting to buy Belle's late husband's old car. Even after she said no, Charlie kept coming around the shop. "We're all hoping Belle will go out with him."

Kane's brow furrowed. "I thought they were already dating."

"Not yet. Although not for your father's lack of trying."

"My father goes after what he wants. No matter what the consequences."

The bitterness lacing Kane's words surprised her. "Charlie doesn't seem so tunnel vision to me. He was okay when Belle wouldn't sell her car to him."

Kane shrugged.

"Either way," Serena said. "He must be so worried about you right now."

"Maybe. We aren't that close anymore. I don't see him much. Sometimes not at all."

She didn't understand. "But he's your father."

"He's done a few things I don't agree with."

Serena got a familiar sinking feeling in her stomach. "So what? You stay away from him because of that?"

Kane nodded. "He made his choices. He can live with the consequences."

Her heart dropped. Not another person, like her parents and others, who withheld love if disappointed. That was so unfair, so wrong. Serena had tried to make her parents see what they were doing, but they wouldn't listen. Maybe she could help Kane see what he was doing by holding a grudge. "I'm sure your father is frantic right now."

With a shrug, he finished his granola bar. "I'd bet Rupert is more worried about you."

Serena stared out the window. The news would only bring relief to her ex-boyfriend. No more bumping into her at the newest café or hippest club with a date by his side and having to deal with the ensuing awkwardness.

"Rupert…" Guilt coated her mouth at the thought of lying again. Her friends, her family, even Kane deserved better.

"What?" Kane asked.

The silence intensified the knot in her stomach. She listened to her breathing, to his, to the logs popping in the wood stove. "We're not… We… Rupert broke up with me in April."

There. She'd said it. And, surprisingly, her world hadn't exploded.

Instead a rare peace filled her heart. Finally someone knew the truth.

His eyes darkened. "Belle said—"

"No one knows," Serena interrupted.

"Why not?"

"Well…not telling anyone made sense at the time." She took a deep breath and exhaled slowly. "I planned to tell people, but I never could find the right opportunity. We decided to throw our assistant, Julie, a wedding. Everyone was so happy and trying to keep it a secret from her. I didn't want my news to spoil the fun. A little while later, our florist, Callie, fell in love and got engaged to this great guy named Jared. After that, our photographer, Regina, seemed to go through something with her husband, Dell, but now they are so happy and in love." Serena watched the snow falling from the sky. Each flake reminded her of the time that had passed. "And now, so many months have gone by, telling them seems like an even bigger deal than before."

"Your friends wouldn't care."

But Serena had cared. She hadn't wanted their sympathy. She didn't want their pity. She only wanted them to see her as a smart, successful woman who was on her way to having it all. "They will be disappointed."

He raised his eyebrows. "All because you aren't practically engaged?"

"Because I wasn't—" perfect "—the person they thought I was."

The person they liked. The person they depended on. The person she had taught and groomed herself to be— bright, capable, accomplished, without needs or flaws.

"What about The Suit?" Kane asked.

"The Suit?" And then she remembered. "Malcolm is a friend who would like us to become business partners."

"But he wouldn't mind more," Kane said. "And you?"

"I…" She thought about Malcolm. On paper she

couldn't ask for anything more, but she really didn't think of him as anything more than a friend. And though he was a great guy, she wasn't sure what kind of father he'd be. Dad-potential was an important quality for her Mr. Right. "Probably not."

"So no boyfriend?"

"No boyfriend." Serena stared at initials with a heart around them carved on the wood windowsill. She traced the engraving with her fingertip. Maybe V and J had found the true love she wanted so badly. "Pretty pathetic, huh?"

"That you don't have a boyfriend?"

Not having a boyfriend didn't bother her as much as how not having a boyfriend affected her plans. She shook her head. "That I lied."

"Not lied. More like withholding information." Kane rose from his chair. "And you had your reasons."

"It seemed so at the time."

He moved toward her, with purpose and intent. "You did it for your friends."

"I did."

"You weren't trying to hurt anyone." He stopped in front of her. "You wanted to help them by making sure they were happy."

"You nailed it." A smile tugged on the corners of her mouth. "And you also made me feel better. Thanks."

"Want me to keep making you feel better?" he asked.

She nearly laughed. Okay, maybe his personality wasn't so horrible. "Please do."

"I, for one, am really happy you're not dating Rupert or The Suit."

"Why?"

"Because if you were, I couldn't do this."

"Do…?"

His mouth covered hers before she could say another word. His lips pressed against hers with an urgency that took her breath away. Hunger, desire, need.

His kiss possessed.

She tasted salt, sweat, male. An intoxicating, addictive combination. One she couldn't get enough of.

His razor stubble scratched her face. She didn't care. Serena wrapped her arms around his neck and kissed him back. The kiss melded into another and another. She wanted to get closer to him.

As if reading her mind, Kane embraced her. He pressed lightly—perhaps remembering her injured ribs?—drawing her toward him. She went eagerly, wanting more.

She'd never known so much hunger; she'd never felt so complete. The emotions contradicted each other as a battle between mind and body warred inside her.

His arms tight around her, she wanted him even closer. But he was oh-so-wrong for her.

His tongue lingered, explored and caressed with such care, she could barely stand. But he wanted freedom at any cost.

His mouth against hers, she felt as if she could fly, soar and never have to come back to the ground. But he didn't love unconditionally.

Nothing made sense. Not him kissing her. Not her response to him kissing her.

But with his lips devouring hers, reason and common sense took a back seat. Nothing else mattered. Nothing except more kisses. She leaned into him, soaking up his strength and his warmth.

Gratitude. That had to be the explanation.

She was kissing Kane back as a way to repay him for all he'd done. But the blood boiling through her veins had nothing to do with thankfulness and everything to do with desire.

Kane kissed her as if she were what kept him alive—air, water, his heart. He made her feel so special. She didn't deserve it after lying about Rupert, but Kane didn't seem to mind.

He showered her with kiss after kiss after kiss as if this were her reward. She accepted. Gladly.

She'd kissed men before, of course, but all of those seemed like practice to prepare her for this…for the main event.

Everything about his kisses was perfect.

Everything except the man himself.

Serena didn't care.

Oh, she should care. No doubt she would care later.

But for now, for this very moment, she wouldn't think so much. She wouldn't analyze. She wouldn't plan.

She would simply…enjoy.

Enjoy the moment.

Enjoy the sensation.

Enjoy Kane.

The kisses continued, on and on. Thank goodness he had his arms around her or she might already be on the floor. He moved his lips from her mouth across her jaw to her ear. He nibbled on her earlobe. Tingles exploded like firecrackers. She gasped. Kane dragged his mouth away.

His breathing fast, his eyes dark, he stared at her. "I'm sorry. I shouldn't have done that. It won't happen again."

Those were the last words her tingling lips wanted to hear.

"But thank you," he added.

Serena hadn't known what to expect, but his saying thanks wasn't it. Granted, a man like Kane probably made out regularly with women. But he didn't even seem to like her much. Not enough to kiss her, but he acted as if she'd held open a door for him, not let him plunder and pillage her mouth. "You're welcome?"

He raised a hand to her face and brushed a strand of hair out of her eyes. "Ready?"

Her pounding heart accelerated. "For what?"

She sounded as breathless as she felt.

"To get to work."

If she had been a hot air balloon, she would have gone splat against the Earth. "Work?"

"We need to unpack, find wood for the stove, a lot of things."

No, she wanted to scream. Her lips felt swollen and bruised. Her insides still tingled. And he wanted to talk about getting to work? Not the kiss?

Serena straightened. If the kiss meant nothing to him, then it meant nothing to her. And maybe all wedding dresses next season would be hot-pink like Marsha Schumacher had wanted her gown to be. "Before we get to work, I have to ask. What was that all about?"

He looked at Serena expectantly.

"The, um, kiss," she added.

"An impulse," Kane said. "I just wanted to kiss you."

"You wanted to kiss me?"

"Yeah, you looked like you needed to be kissed. With no boyfriend in the picture there was nothing stopping me."

Okay. Not. "So is this something you do a lot? Kissing women who look like they need a kiss?"

"Not random women on the street. Well, except for this one time in Paris and another in Rome. But generally, with minor exceptions, the answer is no. I do not make a habit of kissing random women. And I only planned to kiss you once."

"What happened?" she asked.

"You kissed me back."

Embarrassed, her cheeks burned. At least there would be no more kisses. She agreed it shouldn't happen again. Because now Serena knew who she was dealing with.

Forget about being baffled and bewildered any longer. Kane was exactly what she'd known him to be the minute she'd met him. Even though his kiss would have knocked her socks off had she been wearing any, he was the epitome of Mr. Wrong.

In every sense of the word.

Forget about being stranded or the bad weather hanging over them or anything else facing her in the wilderness. The most difficult thing she would have to survive was Kane Wiley. She realized something else, too.

For years she had blamed her sister for lacking good judgment about men. Serena touched a finger to her still throbbing lips and finally understood. She really owed Morgan an apology.

In her office, holding on to the phone receiver, Belle listened to the voices chatting in the hallway. She might be shaking inside and this most recent bombshell wasn't helping, but she needed to be strong for her girls. She glanced up.

Callie, wearing a green vinyl apron over her jeans and sweater, stood in the doorway. "Any news yet?"

Not the news Belle had been expecting to hear. "No, darlin'. Don't forget with the three-hour time difference, it's still morning out there. You can't ask a hen to lay an egg before she's ready."

"But we're ready here." Regina sat on the edge of the desk. She didn't have her camera in hand, which told Belle how worried the photographer must be. "I've already eaten three slices of Natalie's banana cake trying to calm my nerves."

"Are you calm?"

"Nope. Just full."

Belle placed the receiver in its cradle. "Charlie sounded hopeful after talking to officials in Idaho."

"Is that who you were talking to?" Callie sat on a chair. "Charlie?"

"No, I haven't heard from him." Well, not in the last half hour. He'd gone home to pack for the trip west. Belle drew in a breath for strength. "I was on the phone with Rupert."

"The poor guy." Regina sighed. "He must be out of his mind with worry."

Callie nodded. "When do Rupert and Charlie fly out there?"

Belle wished she didn't have to answer that question. "Rupert isn't going."

Disappointment flared in Callie's green eyes, something Belle had witnessed a million times before until Jared had entered the florist's life and love had blossomed this past spring. "But he's her boyfriend."

"He has to go." Regina tensed. Belle knew the photographer had learned how important sticking together as a couple was. "Serena's going to need him."

Belle took a calming breath. It didn't help. "Rupert broke up with Serena in April."

"What?" the two women said at the same time. Their mouths remained opened. Their eyes wide.

"But it's November." Callie sounded dumbfounded.

"I knew something was up." Regina's brown eyes

darkened. "But Serena said things were okay and they seemed to be the perfect couple."

"Serena hinted things weren't so great, but she didn't seem that concerned," Callie admitted. "Everything always works out for her."

"That's so true." Belle shivered, feeling as if she'd failed the young designer. Serena looked as if she had it all, and Belle never had to worry about her like some of the other girls. "But appearances aren't always what they seem."

Regina nodded.

Callie pressed her lips together. "I still don't understand why she didn't tell us."

"She must have her reasons," Regina said.

Both the girls sounded hurt and worried. Belle wished she had answers for them. "Remember, this is something Serena needs to tell us on her own, when she's ready, even if we want answers now."

But that didn't stop the pain all three of them felt with Serena gone. It seemed like a piece of Belle's heart was missing along with the designer. She wanted Serena found ASAP.

Regina hopped off the desk. "So if Rupert isn't going to Idaho, who is going to be there for Serena?"

Belle straightened. "I am."

CHAPTER SEVEN

HE NEEDED to have his head examined.

Stomping around in the snow with flurries falling from the sky didn't make a lot of sense to Kane. Neither had kissing Serena. He'd only wanted to kiss her once, not a full-on make-out session, but when she'd pressed against him and kissed him back...

At least gathering firewood gave them time and much-needed space away from each other. He glanced her way. But she was getting a little too far away.

"What are you doing?" he asked.

Serena waved her hot-pink cell phone in the air with a bare hand. "Seeing if I can get a signal on my cell phone."

City girl. He tried for patience. Failed.

"Forget about that and put your gloves back on before you get frostbite." He watched her pull his gloves onto her hands. "Look for fallen trees, branches, anything that looks like it might burn."

"Okay."

Nothing was okay.

Kissing Serena was about the dumbest thing he'd done lately. Sure, he'd enjoyed it. One taste and he wanted to kiss her again. But he couldn't let himself get caught up in the moment again. Putting the moves on a woman who couldn't call a cab and was forced for survival's sake to share his bed violated his personal code of conduct.

Kane brushed the snowflakes from his hair with his sock-covered hands. Maybe the rough landing had shaken up more than the plane.

He shot a sideward glance at Serena, whose feet sunk into the deep snow as she made her way back toward him. "Be careful."

"I'm being careful," she said. "I know how to take care of myself."

Distance, he reminded himself. "And your damn dresses."

"You helped with the dresses." She smiled at him. "In fact, you've helped with everything."

Even distance wasn't proof against her smile. "You don't make it easy."

"I know, but I'm trying to be less…"

"Of a pain in the ass?"

"Hey." She placed her gloved hands on her coat-covered hips. "You said I had a cute ass."

"I did. You do. But you can still be a pain."

"I'm trying to be—"

"Not so self-reliant, independent, stubborn?"

Her mouth quirked. "I was actually going to say more receptive."

To his help? To his kisses? To him? Only the first mattered. He focused on a large branch lying in the snow. "That would make things easier."

He looked at her bright blue eyes and flushed cheeks.

Then again, maybe not.

Kane dragged the branch to the end of the trail leading

back to the cabin. Serena added a smaller branch of her own.

"I'm not used to admitting I can't handle everything out here myself," she said quietly.

"You don't have to." She'd shown glimpses of vulnerability before, but now she didn't seem so afraid to let him know what she was feeling. "Just don't pretend you can."

"I won't."

Kane might find her emotional honesty attractive on one level, but it was also damn inconvenient. Her being vulnerable to him did not mean he would be vulnerable to her. He was not going there. He didn't open himself up to anybody.

And that was the way he was keeping it.

On board a plane bound for Idaho, Belle stared out of the window. The sight of the landscape below, the acres of green fields giving way to tree-covered mountainsides, reminded her of Serena and Kane lost somewhere in the wilderness. Belle closed her eyes for a moment. She needed time to regroup, put her game face on as Callie, resident poker player expert, called it.

Callie, Regina, Natalie, Audra and Julie.

Belle hated leaving them alone, but they had each other. Serena needed someone to be there for her. Still, a few hours ago the tears had fallen like raindrops during a Georgia thunderstorm. The hugs and goodbyes had mingled with their hopes and fears. Belle knew she'd left the shop in strong, capable hands. The five women would keep The Wedding Belles running smoothly until she returned with Serena.

If she returned with Serena...

Belle blew out a puff of air.

"Hang in there." Charlie sat in the aisle seat next to her. "We can't give up hope."

"I'm trying." The compassion in his voice tugged on Belle's heartstrings. "But not knowing anything is hard. Part of me is afraid of what we might find when we get there."

"Sometimes not knowing is better," Charlie admitted. "I remember…"

"What?" She leaned toward him. "Tell me, please."

"Three years ago I got a phone call from Kane telling me his mother, my wife, had suffered a heart attack. He asked me to meet him at the hospital. What he didn't tell me was that the massive coronary had killed her."

"Oh, Charlie." Memories of losing Matthew, tucked deep in her heart, floated to the surface. She remembered the emotions as if they were brand-new and raw, not nine years old. Disbelief, shock and loneliness had rooted themselves in her heart only to be pruned, somewhat, with the passage of time. Belle covered Charlie's hand with her own. "That must have been horrible."

"Not at first. I didn't know," he said. "As I drove to the hospital I worried she might need surgery. That scared me, but the idea of her dying? My mind wouldn't let me go there or I would have fallen apart."

Belle gave his hand a gentle squeeze. "When my husband, Matthew, got sick I knew it was serious. He was older than me, but I believed with all my heart he would recover. I don't know how I could have given him the support, the care he'd needed if I'd thought he was leaving me."

"I had worked everything out in my head by the time I arrived at the hospital. How she would recover, what needed to be done and then Kane told me and…"

"Your world fell apart."

Charlie nodded.

"Mine, too," she said. "At first you have so much to take care of, all the paperwork, the people around you. I felt as if I was living in a fog."

"But the work ends, the people go away and the cloud of shock lifts. And you're left…"

"With nothing." Belle felt a connection, a new bond growing between her and Charlie. "And if you're like me, you're utterly lost, don't know what to do and end up making some really bad decisions."

Surprise filled his eyes. "I thought I was the only one who did that."

"Oh, darlin', I wish that was the case because I made some doozies. A stuffed Thanksgiving turkey had more sense than I did those first two years."

He laughed. So did Belle.

"I'm happy you're with me." His brown eyes darkened to the color of espresso. "No matter what we find out, we'll make it through."

She nodded.

"We'll keep each other from making any doozy mistakes, too," he added. "That's what friends are for."

Friends.

Belle thought she only wanted friendship from Charlie. But sitting here with her hand on top of his, talking with him this way, the word didn't seem nearly enough for her.

Must be the situation, she rationalized. The heightened emotions. The terrifying unknowns. Nothing else made sense.

"Do we have a deal, Belle?"

She pulled her hand from the top of his to shake on his words. "Deal, darlin'."

* * *

That evening, Kane sat across from Serena. She stared at the remnants of their dinner—canned stew, crackers and dried fruit—littering the table. Not exactly gourmet fare.

"Thanks for cooking dinner tonight," he said. "The meal hit the spot after all that wood-gathering."

She placed the wrappers from the crackers on her plate. "That wasn't cooking. I wish the biscuits had turned out."

"Hey, I'm impressed you even attempted biscuits." He leaned back in his chair. "How are your ribs? Sore?"

"A little."

But the rest of Serena's muscles ached, especially her back. Pilates and running, her normal workouts, couldn't compare to gathering firewood in the falling snow.

What she wouldn't give for a massage.

She stretched, happy she'd changed out of her skirt and sweater into her flannel pajama bottoms and a turtleneck. As long as she didn't have to make a late-night run to the outhouse, she'd stay comfy and warm.

Serena glanced around the small cabin, surprisingly content. The crackling wood in the stove kept the temperature comfortable. The propane lighting provided a soft glow. And her companion...

"Dessert?" Kane asked

She would rather have that massage. But dessert was a safer bet than Kane's hands soothing, massaging and making her feel all better. "Let me clean up first."

"No, dessert comes first. Always."

As he rummaged through the food, she studied him. Kane was a contradiction. One minute gruff, the other giving. Serena appreciated his softer, gentler side. To be honest, she kind of liked being taken care of. Not that she would ever tell him that. Or anybody for that matter.

For so long, she'd had to be reliable, successful and independent. She'd dressed to glossy perfection and portrayed the image of a successful wedding dress designer with practiced flair and finesse. But out here in the mountains, in this cozy little cabin with Kane, she could just be herself. She could forget about everyone else's expectations and relax. She could finally be…free.

He extended his arm and offered her a handful of truffles. "Here you go."

She took a heart-shaped chocolate wrapped in cellophane and tied with a lavender ribbon from his hand. "Thanks."

"Just one?"

"This will hit the spot."

"Chocolate always does."

"A man after my own heart." Serena felt his gaze on her. "What?"

"I thought you were a no-chocolate girl."

She unwrapped the piece. "Why?"

"At the bridal show, you didn't eat a chocolate. I figured you were a perpetual dieter who scorned sweets."

"Are you kidding?" She raised the truffle to her nose and sniffed. Heavenly. "All of us Belles, except Natalie, eat wedding cake samples all the time. Chocolate is my favorite."

Serena bit into the crisp dark chocolate shell. The taste exploded in her mouth. Sweet and rich with a hint of bitterness. The creamy inside melted in her mouth. "Mmm."

"That good?"

Nodding, she savored the texture as she took another bite. Oh-so-yummy, but addictive. A little like a kiss from Kane. You wanted more than one taste. But like the handful of truffles he offered her, one was more than enough. Any more wouldn't be smart.

When she was finished, a faint sugary scent remained on her fingertips. At least Kane's kiss hadn't left that on her lips. Serena looked across the table at him. "Aren't you having one?"

"I had two." A devilish grin appeared. "You were too busy enjoying yours to notice."

"Sorry."

"Don't be. I like a woman who can appreciate what's good for her."

"I consider myself a chocolate connoisseur," she said.

"And how do you become a chocolate connoisseur?"

She smiled. "By eating lots and lots of chocolate."

"Then I must be a connoisseur, too." He picked up the carafe he'd brought from the plane and filled their glasses with water he'd melted from snow. "Make sure you drink all of it. You don't want to get dehydrated."

As Serena sipped the warm water, a comforting silence settled between them. They were more like a couple on a vacation in a mountain cabin than two strangers stranded together in the wilderness.

He drank from a mug. She watched him, mesmerized, wishing his lips were touching hers instead. Her cup slipped from her right hand, but she caught it with her left, only spilling a few drops.

Uh-oh. If she weren't careful, she could be the one crashing to the floor. Serena rose and cleared the table.

"You like playing house, don't you?" Kane asked.

As she carried the plates, she glanced his way, suddenly cautious. "I don't play house."

"Never?"

"Never," she admitted, thinking about her sister, Morgan. "I've seen what can go wrong when you play."

"You surprise me, Blondie."

"What do you mean?" Serena asked.

"Underneath all that shine and glamour, you're kind of an old-fashioned girl. Cleaning the cabin. Cooking dinner. Now the dishes."

Old-fashioned? Serena tried to decide whether she was offended by his comment. "It's not old-fashioned to want a clean living space. I grew up doing chores."

"I never did chores." Kane stood. "My mom or the housekeeper did everything."

Serena had been the one to do everything. She'd done her own chores and her sister's, too. Anything she could to make things...perfect.

He took the dishes from her hands. "I've got these."

"I don't mind," she said automatically.

She reached for the dishes, but he wouldn't let go. "I do."

The two held on to the plates as if they were made of fine porcelain, not plastic.

"What are you doing, Blondie?" Kane asked finally. "Trying to earn a gold star on your chore chart?"

Serena blushed. How could he know her so well? "Well, I always did get a lot of gold stars."

"Such a good girl." His lips curved in a teasing, charming, coaxing smile. "Let me do the dishes tonight."

Reluctantly she let go. "Then what will I do?"

"To earn those gold stars?" His eyes gleamed. "I'm sure we can think of something."

The dishes were clean, the fire stoked. All Kane needed to do was crawl into bed. Strike that. Bed brought up the image of rolling around with one sexy blonde who kissed like a dream. Scowling, he rubbed the back of his neck.

"Are you all right?" Serena asked. "You look tense."

He fought the urge to laugh. "I'm fine."

Her pretty blue eyes widened in sympathy. "It's the bed. It's not really big enough for two."

Unless they slept stacked like firewood. And then Kane would guarantee they'd get no sleep at all.

"The bed's fine," he said. "I just need—"

You.

"—a pillow," he finished lamely.

Serena, sitting at the table, perked up. She pulled one of her boxes toward her and searched through it until she pulled out a plump, purple velvet square. "A-ha. One pillow."

Kane raised his eyebrows. "That wasn't in the booth at the show."

"I know. I didn't use it because I couldn't find the slipper."

Kane had no idea what she was talking about. "What slipper?"

"The glass slipper. Cinderella's slipper?"

He continued to stare at her.

She sighed. "You know. Fairy Godmother, Prince Charming, stroke of midnight, happily ever after."

He shook his head. "I don't believe in that stuff."

"Stuff?" she asked.

"Fairy tales and happy endings."

"Why not?"

Thinking about his father and his ex-stepmother left a bitter taste in Kane's mouth. "Happy endings aren't possible because love is transitory. It doesn't last. It can't. As soon as a so-called love is gone the other person is on to the next one."

A beat passed. And another.

The only sounds were the fire in the stove and their breathing.

"It isn't always like that," she said.

This conversation was making him...tired. He headed toward the bed. Maybe she would get the clue he didn't want to talk about this.

"I believe fairy-tale endings exist. That there are people out there who will stand by the one they love through it all, good or bad," she continued, her words full of longing. "Disappointment or failure won't matter because even when things are at their darkest or someone has fallen or whatever horrible thing might happen, the love will remain strong, solid, forever."

He was more moved—and more shaken—than he wanted to admit. "You believe that if you want to."

"What do you believe?" she asked softly.

Looking into her blue eyes, Kane thought he'd like to believe in her.

And that scared him even more than her talk about forever.

He deflected her question with a smile. "I believe in the benefits of a good night's sleep. Toss that pillow over here and let's get some shut-eye."

The next day passed slowly. Snow continued to fall, keeping them trapped inside the cabin. Serena sketched new dress design ideas. Kane worked on an electric box from the plane. By the time evening came and dinner was over, she was ready to do something to work off some energy and take her mind off their plight. Anything.

She glanced at Kane sitting at the table. Okay, not anything.

Serena paced the small confines of the cabin. The smell

from the woodstove seemed to intensify and she longed to feel a cool breeze on her face. What she wouldn't give to smell the ocean or cocoa butter, something tropical.

She'd counted the mice scurrying across the floor—three—and wondered if naming them would be a good idea. She had to do something to keep herself occupied. Boredom might lead her and Kane to do something they shouldn't in order to, well, keep themselves busy.

Serena couldn't think about him that way. Walking away from his father the way he had, told her that he didn't believe in unconditional love. Not that what he believed mattered to her. Still a flicker of disappointment shot through her.

"Bored?" he asked.

"A little."

"Cabin fever is no fun," Kane said.

That was better than another kind of fever. She gulped. "I'm sure we can think of something to do."

She was sure they could. That's what worried her. Outside, a wolf howled somewhere in the distance.

"I have a game for couples to know each other better somewhere," she suggested. "But we're not a couple."

"No, but we are sleeping together."

Serena glared at him.

He laughed. "Don't worry, you're still the kind of girl a guy would want to take home to meet the parents. My father thinks you're great."

She smiled. "Your dad is so sweet."

"He has his moments." Kane got this faraway look in his eyes when he talked about Charlie that suggested he wasn't as indifferent to his dad as he pretended.

The wolf howled again, the lonely cry cutting through the cold night air.

"What about your mom?" she asked, intrigued enough to want to know more about Kane.

"If my mom were still here, she would like you," Kane said, his voice full of warmth.

Serena sat across from him. "What was she like?"

"She was the best and had so much love to give." A soft smile formed on his lips. "The two of you...you have a lot in common. She was into clothes, loved to sew and subscribed to a stack of fashion magazines. My mom would have talked your ear off about what you do and she would have invited you shopping."

Kane's tone spoke of a deep love for his mother. His words wrapped around Serena like an old quilt, comfy and warm and stitched with affection. "She sounds wonderful."

"She was."

The two simple words spoke volumes when coupled with the emotion—the love—in his eyes. And that was when Serena realized Kane Wiley wasn't totally the loner, the free spirit he claimed to be. She had seen his passion with his flying and experienced it with his kiss. She'd also realized that he felt loss deeply. Buried inside had to be a man with a streak of romance, longing for commitment. If only she could get to see that side of him...

"Tell me what your parents would think if you brought me home to meet them."

"They would not like you at all."

He laughed.

Oh, no. Had she said that out loud? Her cheeks burned. "It's just my parents have a pretty well-defined view of who would make an acceptable...partner for their daughters. My parents are overachievers. That's what they raised my sister, Morgan, and me to be."

"Looks like they succeeded."

With me at least. "They want us to be happy."

"Happiness to them is having you marry some guy in a suit with a solid background, a stable job and a good income with the potential for more so you will have whatever you want or need."

"Pretty much."

"You want the same thing?"

His words hung in the air, as if they floated in front of her like a movie special effect. *You want the same thing?* She thought about what she wanted most of all. She wanted her plans to be realized. She wanted to make people happy. She wanted…

An answer formed deep inside of her and burst to the surface. "I want true love."

"Ah, the fairy tale again." He studied her. "You've got everything figured out."

She raised her chin. "I've got a plan."

"Let's hear it."

"Well, once I find Mr. Right, we date for a year, are engaged for a year, get married, buy a house, wait another year before we get pregnant and then we have a baby."

Kane laughed. "I don't know whether to be impressed at your knowing what you want or worried for the poor guy you choose."

Her cheeks felt warm. "Well, I'm a planner."

"Nothing wrong with that except sometimes plans don't work out the way you think they will."

"Tell me about it." Serena sighed. Kane was so easy to talk to. She'd been more up-front and honest with him, whom she'd known—and fought with—for only a couple of days, than with the women she'd known and worked with for years. "I'm missing the most important thing in my plan. Mr. Right."

"Hey—" he reached across the table and touched the corner of her mouth with his fingertip "—smile, Blondie. He's out there."

"You think?" She cringed at the insecurity in those two words.

"I know," Kane reassured. "Think positively."

She felt anything but positive. "He's out there. Somewhere."

"Absolutely. You'll find him."

Serena nodded once and stared down at the table.

"Look." He lifted her chin with his finger. "I'm about as far away from Mr. Right as you would want, but if you'd like, I could be your Mr. Right Now."

CHAPTER EIGHT

MR. RIGHT NOW.

Kane shook his head in self-disgust. What was he thinking?

Like Miss-Seeking-Happily-Ever-After-Tied-Up-In-A-Neat-Little-Bow would settle for a torrid three-day or less affair with a no-strings flyboy.

Not that he didn't like the idea. He liked it a lot. He liked her a lot.

Which was part of the problem.

She'd be a lot easier to resist if she were the spoiled ice princess he'd pegged her as at their first meeting.

The wolf howled again. Louder this time. Closer.

Serena's forehead wrinkled. Her mouth tightened.

Uh-oh. He rose from the table and snuck a peek out of the window. The darkness prevented him from seeing anything. "The howl is likely a neighbor's dog barking. The wolf won't bother us."

Or shouldn't under normal circumstances. But with their luck...

The howl turned into howls.

Right on cue. Kane shook his head, but he shouldn't have been surprised.

Turning slightly, Serena craned her neck to peer at the door. "That sounds like more than one wolf."

"Probably just a family," he said nonchalantly, wanting to take the wariness in her voice away. "A dad, mom, pups."

"You mean a pack."

The howling continued. Intensified. He heard shuffling outside. Something scratched at the door.

A layer of tension filled the cabin. The lighting seemed to dim. Serena's lower lip quivered. Not a lot, but enough so he noticed. She looked stiff, tight, scared. Maybe he'd mistaken tension for fear.

Kane didn't feel like smiling at the moment, but forced one anyway. "We're inside. They're outside. No worries."

"No worries," Serena repeated, but kept her head turned and her eyes focused on the door. If she kept that position for any length of time, she would add twisted neck to her injuries.

Not on his watch.

Kane carried his chair over and wedged the top under the door handle. "Wolves usually stay away from humans. I've never known a wolf to open a door, but just in case these Idaho ones know any special tricks, the chair will add a little insurance."

As she turned to face him, her tense shoulders relaxed. "Thanks."

He blew out a puff of air. Now what? "So…"

"So what does a 'Mr. Right Now' do?"

Damn. Kane thought he'd gotten away with that one scot-free. He was trying to resist temptation, but if temptation—or Serena—threw itself in his lap… "Whatever you want him to do."

The howling continued, but Serena didn't glance back.

She stood instead. Her gaze, a mix of anticipation and alarm in her eyes, met his. "Would you hold me?"

In a New York minute. The vulnerable look on her face and the sexy way she looked in her pajamas smacked him right in the gut. He sat on her chair and pulled Serena onto his lap. "How's this?"

"Nice."

Nice didn't begin to describe how good holding her on his lap felt. More like perfect.

Wolves howled outside. Wind blew through the trees and rattled the windows. Wood burned in the stove, crackling and popping, the now familiar scent of smoke lofting in the air.

Kane still felt as if nothing else existed. Nothing else mattered. He wrapped his arms around her. Soft and warm and all his. Well, for as long as she allowed.

"Thank you," she murmured.

He should be thanking her. And the wolves. "No problem."

It wasn't.

Not now.

Ask him again in a few minutes.

"It's probably silly to be frightened of a few overgrown dogs," she said. "I think the wolves were the final straw after everything that's happened. I'm not very good at this adventure stuff."

He ran his finger along her jaw to her chin. Soft with a determined edge. Like the woman herself. "Being out here alone is nothing like being back in Boston."

She smiled. "But I'm not alone. I have you."

Kane swallowed. "For now."

He was not in this for the long haul. One of them had to remember that.

She leaned back, giving him the chance to nuzzle his nose against her hair. The scent of strawberries, sweet and fresh and juicy, filled his nostrils. The smell reminded him of spring, flowers blooming and sunny days, not a day in early November with drifting snow outside as far as the eye could see. He took another sniff. Her lotion? Or just Serena?

The answer didn't matter.

Not with her on his lap in his arms cuddling against him as if she belonged there. His blood boiled, pounding through his veins with purpose and direction. That could be embarrassing. He needed to think cool thoughts. Arctic thoughts might work best.

"You want to know something?" Serena asked.

Anything to stop thinking about her and the way she smelled. "What?"

"Even though I feel out of sorts tonight, I'd rather be here than in Boston."

Her words headed straight to his heart, crashing through his defense system with their sincerity. "Me, too."

And if Kane were smart, he would end this right now. The situation had *bad news* written all over it. She wasn't looking for something temporary. He wasn't looking for something permanent. Someone was going to get hurt.

Not hurt.

He…respected Serena too much to hurt her, to take advantage of her trust and the situation.

All Kane wanted to do was hold her. Well, not all. But it would do. It had to.

He pulled her closer, careful of her ribs, mindful of where he placed his hands. Her heartbeat drummed against him, the increasing tempo matching his own.

Another noise sounded outside the door. Wind, wolf? Hard to tell.

Serena turned, her face right next to his. Her warm breath fanned his cheek. Big blue eyes stared deep into his, probing and searching. Attraction buzzed between them.

Kane's self-control slipped a notch. Okay, two.

She'd asked him to hold her. She'd wanted comfort, but the flash of desire in her eyes and her parted lips told him she also wanted…

"Kiss me," she whispered. "Please."

She wasn't going to have to ask twice.

Brushing his lips over hers, Kane wanted to soothe her. Calm and reassure her, too. He wanted his kiss to make her feel special, cherished and adored. The way a woman should always feel.

This kiss was different, sweeter and softer than their ones yesterday, but just as good. With each passing moment, he struggled to keep the kiss gentle and not allow his growing desire to take over. Hard to do when she was in his arms and kissing him. Talk about heaven on earth.

It couldn't get much better than this.

She leaned into him, into the kiss, pressing her lips against his. Her tongue sought, found, danced with his.

So much for tenderness.

His blood pressure spiraled. Logical thought disappeared. Common sense fled.

There was only here and now.

Only Serena.

The realization should have bothered him more than it did, but Kane didn't care. Right now this…she…was all that mattered. He ran his hands through her hair, the short strands sifting through his fingers.

Pulling her closer, he deepened the kiss. She tasted like chocolate. Expensive and rich and filling. He wanted another taste. And another.

As his tongue explored her mouth, she moaned. The husky sound excited him, bringing a twinge to his groin.

Her fingertips ran along the muscles on his back. Rubbing, kneading, exploring. Her eagerness pleased him. Turned him on. Made him want more.

Want her.

Want all of her.

Damn. This was getting out of control. Who was he kidding? The situation was reaching breaking point.

Kane had to stop kissing her. Now.

Before the kisses turned into something more. He couldn't do that to Serena even if she were the one who asked for the kiss. She needed more than he was willing to give her. She wanted a man who would commit. Just like Amber and every other woman he'd known. He wasn't that man.

He kissed Serena, soaking up the taste of her for one last time and pulled away. Her breathing ragged, she looked at him with those big eyes, eyes clouded with desire for him, and full lips, lips bruised and swollen from kissing him. He'd never seen a woman look more beautiful or sexier.

Kane struggled to breathe.

"Wow." She scooted off his lap and stood next to the table. "I'm not sure what to say."

"Thank you would suffice."

She smiled shyly. "Thank you."

"Anytime. I mean, if you want something or need…"

"I know what you mean, Kane."

That made one of them because he hadn't a clue.

"What now?" Serena asked.

Oh, he had lots of ideas, but none of them would be good for her. Or, come to think of it, him. "Sleep."

"Sleep?" She sounded a little confused.

That made two of them.

Why did she have to be so sweet, so pretty, so damn sexy? Why did she want to find true love instead of hot sex? Why couldn't they…?

"Maybe I should sleep on the floor," he said. "On blankets."

"You want to sleep on the floor?" she asked, her voice as soft as a snowflake. "Is that really what you want to do?"

Forget about what he wanted to do. That would only make things worse. "It's probably a good idea tonight. Taking this physical stuff any further—"

"Wouldn't be smart," she finished for him. "But I hate for you to sleep on the floor. What if we were to agree to be on our best behavior, a gentleman and a gentlewoman, and made sure nothing else happened?"

"Would you feel comfortable enough with that?" he asked.

She nodded. "I trust you, Kane."

Her words pierced his heart like an arrow shot at the bull's-eye. Direct hit.

He nearly staggered back a step.

But his heart didn't hurt. It wanted…more.

That meant one thing. Serena was getting too close. Kane knew exactly what he had to do or rather what he couldn't do. No more cuddling, no more kisses and no more Mr. Right Now.

Tempted or not, his heart was off-limits. And he wasn't about to change that.

"We have pinpointed a possible location," on-scene Incident Commander Logan Michaels explained to Charlie and Belle at a mobile command post in the Clearwater

National Forest. He pointed to a large topographical map with red marks and circles drawn on it. "The weather has the air search grounded again, but a search and rescue team is riding to Gold Meadows on horseback. In a situation like this, we put calls out for assistance. County and state lines don't matter much. We've got a unit from Missoula, Montana, waiting to assist with the evacuation and another group on standby."

Excitement surged through Belle. "Wonderful news to start the day."

She hugged Charlie, who spun her around as if she were sixteen not sixty-five. Heat rushed up her cheeks.

He placed her on her feet. "Sorry about that."

"No need to apologize." The tingles in Belle's stomach actually felt good. "I didn't mind."

And that was the truth. She liked having someone to lean on after so long.

Charlie's eye-reaching grin filled Belle with surprising joy.

"How did you pinpoint them?" he asked.

"Cell phone technology," Logan said. "A local cellular company found pings from one of the phones."

One. At least one of them was alive. Belle muttered a silent prayer. She hated being greedy, but one of them surviving wasn't enough.

Charlie looked at her. His mouth tight. His jaw set.

Belle didn't know him well, but she knew enough about him to know the question he wanted answered. A question he wasn't capable of asking himself. "Do you know whose cell phone had been turned on? Kane's or Serena's?"

"Serena's," Logan answered.

A shadow crossed Charlie's face. Belle reached for him, linking her hand with his. "That doesn't mean—"

"I know."

"Kane could be using the phone," she said. "We don't know enough to make any assumptions."

"Belle is correct, Charlie," Logan said. "Your concern is understandable given the circumstances, but there are so many unknowns we just don't know. What you can count on is the experience and expertise of the SAR unit out there searching for Kane and Serena."

"SAR?" Belle asked, thinking of the Asian disease from a few years ago.

"Search and Rescue," Logan explained. "You won't find a better group of men and women. One of the best SAR experts in the country is out there, too. Jake Porter. He's from Oregon Mountain Search and Rescue and was training our unit this past weekend. When the call came in on Sunday, he decided to stay on and join the team in the field."

Belle forced a smile. "Well, you can't ask for more than that, can you, darlin'?"

The strain on Charlie's face eased. "I guess you can't. We appreciate your efforts, Logan. And everyone out there in the cold snowy weather looking for Kane and Serena."

"You're welcome." Logan pointed to a map. "Just so you know, Gold Meadows has been used in the past as a helicopter landing site while fighting forest fires. There's also a small cabin there with provisions, light and heat."

"More good news," Belle said.

"It could be. I will let you know when I hear more news," Logan said. "I also want to let you know the media has picked up the story. You may be asked for a statement. It's your choice if you do or don't. The sheriff's office has a public relations liaison who will work with you."

"Thank you." Belle and Charlie spoke at the same time.

His gaze caught hers. His brown eyes seemed to see right inside her, straight to her heart. Warmth flooded through her like a sip of hot cocoa with a dash of Peppermint Schnapps mixed in. The reaction was unexpected, but surprisingly not unwelcome.

The realization set off about a zillion warning bells in her head. She'd had her chance at the love of a lifetime with her beloved Matthew. She didn't want a boyfriend let alone something serious.

But still Belle found herself sneaking a peek at the handsome and charming Charlie.

The next morning, Serena woke feeling rested and warm as if she were waking in her own bed at home, not a rustic little cabin in the woods. Kane lay with his chest against her back, his arm draped over her hip and his legs entwined with hers.

She felt his breath on her neck. The warm puffs of air comforted her. The same way his snores had during the night.

She'd held up her end of the bargain and so had he. Kane had been the perfect gentleman, as promised. Just as she knew he would be. But that hadn't made things any easier.

She touched her lips. Slightly swollen as if she'd used a plumping lipstick. But these lips were strictly the result of Kane, not some cosmetic recipe.

Kiss me, please.

Serena couldn't believe she'd said those words. She wished she could blame her lapse on fear over the wolves and a sudden realization that they were truly lost, but she knew better. Being held had eased her worry, but ignited a spark. One that didn't want to be doused.

She'd wanted to be kissed. She'd needed to be kissed. By him.

Only him.

Kane had delivered. His kisses made her feel safe, secure and accepted. Without her usual gloss of manners and accomplishments, without the armor of designer clothing, without styling gel and concealer, he made her feel beautiful. Sexy. Herself.

She could be herself and that was enough. Freeing.

Serena glanced at him, her heart filling with satisfaction. She couldn't forget this wasn't real. They were playing house—make that cabin—with no one else around except a pack of wolves, birds and an occasional mouse scampering across the floor. What happened here would never have happened back home. It couldn't.

Still the experience only reaffirmed what she wanted in life. Serena was tired of living up to other people's expectations and demands. She wanted a man who would love her for herself. Without strings. Without conditions. She wanted to find what she'd found temporarily in Kane's arms.

If only it could be him…

No. She couldn't allow herself to even daydream about that. Kane Wiley could never be her Mr. Right. He'd admitted that himself.

But still her heart wanted him.

Not going to happen.

All Serena had to do was push emotion aside and look at the situation logically. Look at Kane that way, too. Mentally she composed a list of everything wrong with him:

1. Does not love unconditionally
2. Cannot forgive

3. No longer believes in happily ever after
4. Values freedom more than anything including relationships
5. Kisses so well that reasons 1-4 don't matter

Darn him.

Not a problem. In spite of number five, she had learned from Morgan's mistakes and would not repeat them herself.

Serena pulled her leg away from his and crawled off the bed quietly. The wood floor was cold beneath her socked feet. She padded to the window. No sight of any wolves, but snow fell. Disappointment settled in the bottom of her tummy. Snow meant another day and night in the cabin. At least another twenty-four tempting hours with Kane.

Don't think about that.

Instead Serena got busy. She added wood to the stove to keep the cabin warm, dressed in her heaviest skirt and reminded herself to always pack warm clothes when traveling. She needed to use the outhouse, but hesitated at the door. What if the wolves were still out there? She opened the door slowly. Pawprints were everywhere.

"Going somewhere, Blondie?"

The rich sound of his voice sent the butterflies in her tummy flapping their wings. Those were going to have to stop right now. "I was seeing if the wolves were still out there."

"Are they?" he asked.

Feeling tongue-tied, she shrugged.

What was going on? She was Serena James, the hottest new name in wedding dress design. She had a great job, her own flat. She always knew the right thing to say whether talking with a friend or giving a sound bite. She was capable, successful and reliable. But Kane made her feel like she was back in junior high school, thin and awkward-looking, standing against the wall by herself, waiting to be asked to dance at the ball.

"Want to wear a pair of my pants?" he asked.

"I don't think they'd fit but if they did I'd have to stop eating."

A corner of his mouth turned up. "I'm sure with your vast fashion expertise you could figure out how to keep my pants on you."

"Thanks, but this skirt is wool." She remembered how intimate wearing his shirt the first night had felt. His pants might be worse. No more intimacy allowed!

"Suit yourself." He grabbed a pair of jeans from his bag. "I'm going to change clothes then I can make sure there aren't any more four-footed visitors hanging around outside."

Serena looked out of the window at the falling snow. She felt as if she were falling, too, and didn't like the feeling one bit. The only way to get what she wanted was to be in control. She'd figured that out years ago.

As the teeth of a zipper being undone filled the quiet cabin, a flare of heat burst through her. She grimaced at her reaction. So much for self-control.

She didn't understand why Kane had such an effect on her, but somehow she had to learn how to control her reactions. No way was she going to do anything with Mr. Wrong she might regret.

Even if she might like it.

During breakfast, Kane kept the topics of conversation light—weather, food and sports teams. Anything to distance himself from her because the first thing he'd wanted to do when he woke up and saw Serena was kiss her. So much for off-limits.

Time to get serious.

"I'm going to hike out to the plane," he said.

"I'll come with you."

"No." The word came out harsher than he intended. "Stay here and doodle in your book."

"Do you mean this book?" She pulled a notebook out of her bag. "This is a sketch pad. I use it to come up with design ideas."

"Then stay here and work." He ignored the hurt in her eyes. He couldn't afford to care. "It's better than you getting cold."

"I don't melt in the cold."

A knock sounded on the door.

Serena looked at him.

Another knock.

"I don't think it's the wolves." He sprang out of his chair and opened the door. Five people stood outside. The first four wore matching green jackets. The fifth, hanging back a ways, wore a red and black jacket. Kane smiled. "We are so glad to see you."

"I'm Ray Massey," the first in green, a man in his early forties, said. "With the Idaho County Sheriff's Posse."

"Kane Wiley." He motioned behind him. "This is Serena James. Come in."

The team entered the cabin, making the space even more crowded.

"Are either of you injured?" Ray asked.

"Serena has a cut on her head and bruised ribs."

"We all are Wilderness First Responders and a couple of us are EMTs, too," Ray said to her. "Can we examine you?"

"That's fine," she said.

"Freeman and Porter," Ray ordered.

Freeman wore a heavy green jacket with the words *Sheriff's Posse* written in black on the back. Porter wore a black and red jacket with the initials *OMSAR* written in white on the front and *rescue* on the sleeves.

"Nice setup. Warm. Dry." Ray looked around. "Good job."

"Good job getting to us," Kane said. "How'd you find us?"

"Cell phone pings."

Serena's little pink phone. He'd told her to put the damn thing away. Good thing she hadn't listened to him. He admired her resourcefulness and stubbornness, but felt like an idiot for not pulling out his own cell phone.

Kane looked over at her, feeling a burst of protectiveness when he saw the two men examining her bare stomach. The one in green knelt in front of her while the one in red and black stood.

"Don't worry," Freeman said to Serena. "I've done this before."

"On a dummy," one of his team members teased.

"Nah, don't you remember?" another team member said. "He got his junior certification last week."

Serena laughed, the tension evaporating from her shoulders.

"You're in good hands, miss," Ray said. "Freeman's new at this, but Porter is from Oregon Mountain Search and Rescue. He knows exactly what he's doing."

She looked up at Porter. "I've seen those mountain rescues in Oregon on the news. I'm sure I'm in good hands."

"Hey," Freeman said. "We have mountains in Idaho, too."

Porter winked. "You've got foothills here, kid."

All three laughed.

Serena caught Kane staring at her. "What?"

He took a deep breath. It didn't stop the strange feeling in his stomach. "Good job, Blondie. You and that hot-pink phone of yours got us rescued."

"Really?"

Ray nodded. "The cell phone company used your pings to determine your location."

"That's great." Her eyes twinkled. "Guess I contributed something to this adventure after all."

"You contributed a lot more than that, Serena." As a thousand-watt smile lit up her face, Kane's mouth went dry. And that was when he knew. Oh, maybe he'd already figured it out but hadn't admitted to himself. Now he had no doubt. She'd gotten under his skin somehow and wormed her way into his heart.

Good thing they were getting out of here.

"Her head is healing nicely with the two butterfly bandages. No sign of infection. No evidence of a concussion," Freeman said to Ray. "Her ribs are sore. Bruised, but she should have an X-ray to rule out any kind of fracture. She can get out on her own."

"Porter?" Ray asked. "How'd the newbie do?"

"The newbie did fine," Porter said. "Good assessment, kid."

"Let's get going, before the snow really starts falling." Ray clapped his hands. "We've got clothes for you to change into. We may have to do something about those boots though, miss. Those heels might cause some problems."

"You'd be surprised what she can do in them," Kane mumbled.

Serena shot him a warning look. "That's fine, Ray."

"We'll try to save them if we can. We'll line your feet in plastic bags to keep them dry," Ray continued, smiling at her. All of the rescue team seemed to be smiling at her. Not that Kane blamed them. She was beautiful. "We're on horseback so we can pack out as much as we can. The rest will have to wait until spring."

"I don't need anything but my purse and the dress bags," she said, the competent, strong-willed dress designer re-emerging.

"Dress bags?" Ray asked.

"Those bulky white things hanging on the bunk," Kane answered. "And trust me, she won't leave the cabin without them."

CHAPTER NINE

"WE'RE almost there, Serena." Jake Porter encouraged her along the snow-covered trail as they traveled on horseback. The way he had for hours. "Warm enough?"

"Toasty and dry in these clothes you guys loaned me." She appreciated his humor and upbeat attitude, not to mention his killer smile and blue eyes, but she was ready to get there. Wherever "there" might be. "Thanks."

Kane rode thirty yards behind her with one of the wedding dress bags. The others were spread among the rescuers. She smiled at him.

He smiled back and gave her the thumbs-up sign. He was happy. They were on their way back to civilization. She was safe. So why did it feel as if she were riding to her doom?

Serena concentrated on what was in front of her. The rows of trees stood like sentry guards on the side of the trail. As they came to a swinging bridge over the Lochsa River, the hair on the back of her neck stood up. She gripped the reins tightly. But the horse knew what to do and crossed without incident. They continued up the trail another two hundred yards until they reached...a trail-head. Her breath caught in her throat.

"Welcome to Eagle Mountain Trailhead." Ray, who led the group, glanced back and grinned.

"We're here?" she asked.

"I told you we were close," Jake said.

"I thought you were trying to keep me motivated."

He grinned. "That, too."

"You guys did a good job." A bittersweet relief washed over her. Now she could go home. She'd also have to say goodbye to Kane. Her chest tightened. "Thank you."

Serena emerged from the path and saw trucks, SUVs, police cars and four media vans with satellite dishes crammed into the gravel pullout. A uniformed official helped her off the horse.

"Your boyfriend will be out soon," Ray said, standing by her side.

"My boyfriend? No, he's my—" what was he? "—my pilot."

Ray looked from Serena to Kane, glowering as he rode from the trail, and gave a masculine-sounding grunt. "Right."

A few people, reporters, barked questions at her. Cameras flashed. She crossed her arms over her chest.

"Ignore them," Ray advised, a protective arm around her back. "You can decide later if you want to talk to the media."

She inhaled deeply, the cold, icy air stinging her lungs. "Why are they here?"

"The two of you made headlines," he explained.

Kane stood next to them. She fought the urge to scoot closer to him. "Slow news day, huh?" he asked.

"You know it." Ray laughed. "Come on, let's get you guys inside the trailer."

Serena hesitated. Life hadn't stopped with their disappearance. Only their lives. Now everything would probably change back once she stepped inside the trailer. She looked at Kane, hoping for some sort of sign things would stay the same, the way they had been at the cabin. The odds were low. The chances were slim, but still she hoped.

"Ready, Serena?" he said.

Serena, not Blondie.

Too late. She felt like a cement block had taken the place of her heart. Things had already changed.

Four microphones, each with a different channel—eight, thirteen, seventeen and twenty-three—and four digital voice recorders sat on the table in front of Kane. Four cameras were pointed in their direction. Talk about overkill. One would have been too many.

Kane leaned back in his chair at the community medical center in Missoula where they'd been taken for checkups after being debriefed and returning their borrowed winter gear. All he wanted was for this press conference about their non-newsworthy experience to end.

"Well, I couldn't exactly wear one of the wedding dresses," Serena answered yet another stupid question.

The audience, consisting of a handful of journalists, four television reporters and two high school students, laughed. But the entire White House Press Corps could have been present and the result would have been the same. In her borrowed surgical scrubs and hair that hadn't been washed in days, she had captivated the media. Kane, too. He forced himself not to stare. It wasn't easy. She shone, tossing out witty sound bites like Halloween candy.

Pride welled in him. She'd been through so much yet she'd demonstrated such grace and grit in dealing with everything today. Everything since Sunday. Saying good-bye wasn't going to be fun, even though it had to be done.

"Though Kane suggested I should," Serena added.

Her confidence bloomed under the spotlight. He'd seen the same thing at the bridal show. Super Serena. But Kane missed the woman he'd gotten to know at the cabin. He hadn't seen a glimpse of her since they'd stepped in the trailer earlier. Actually since they'd left the cabin with the rescue team. Where had she gone?

"Were you scared when you had to land on a snow-covered meadow, Kane?" a reporter in the second row asked.

A "yes" or a "no" answer wasn't going to satisfy the perched vultures. They would keep asking questions until they got the quote they wanted. Kane didn't want to waste time. He decided to take a page out of Serena's playbook and give the reporters what they wanted.

"There can be an element of fear whenever something goes wrong in the cockpit. But you're so busy reacting that emotions take a back seat. At least until you realize the plane is barreling toward a dense forest of trees and there's nothing you can do to stop it. Then, yeah, you're scared."

"Were you scared, Serena?" the same reporter asked.

"I was terrified. I kept praying Kane was as good a pilot as he said he was." She glanced sideways at him and smiled. "Turns out he was."

Her compliment made him feel so good. He sat straighter, as if showing people she was right, realized what he'd done and leaned back again.

"How would you describe your relationship with each other after your ordeal together?" a woman in the back yelled.

He thought about sleeping with his chest pressed

against her back. The next day when he'd kissed her for the first time and she'd surprised him by kissing back. Then last night when she'd sat on his lap and asked him to kiss her. His temperature jumped ten degrees.

"Want to take this one?" Serena asked, apprehension clear in her eyes.

He remembered her pseudo-boyfriend, her insecurity and her need to project a positive image. She might be Super Serena, but she wanted help with the question. He wasn't about to turn her down. Kane nodded.

"First, I'd like to clarify something," he said. "Ordeal doesn't exactly describe what we went through. There were no hysterics. We had little choice where we landed, but we kept our cool. We had what we needed to be comfortable—a warm place to stay, water to drink and food to eat. Serena might look like a city girl, but she knew how to survive in the wilderness. She kept trying to get a signal on her cell phone and that led to our rescue. The swift action of the search and rescue team got us out of the wilderness area in hours. Wouldn't you agree, Serena?"

"It was actually kind of fun. Well, except the night a pack of wolves paid us a visit."

"You're lucky they only dropped by one night." The on-site incident commander, Logan Michaels, sat to Kane's left and drank coffee as if his life depended on caffeine to stay awake. No doubt he hadn't slept in a while. "Those wolves and their incessant howling drove out a team of field researchers a couple of years ago."

"Then it's a good thing we were found before the wolves came back." As Kane spoke, reporters scribbled notes. "As for your question, Serena James started out as a passenger, a wedding dress designer from Boston. But she's so much more than what she does for a living. Serena never gave up or gave in, even when she was a little worried. She deserves full credit for making our location known to authorities so we could be found. I'm proud to call her my—" *girlfriend* "—my friend."

"Thanks, Kane." Her gaze, full of gratitude and warmth, met his. "I consider you my friend, too."

He didn't want to be her friend, damn it. But anything else—

"What do you plan on doing now?" another reporter asked.

Serena turned her attention back to the crowd. "I'm flying to Boston and getting right back to work with The Wedding Belles."

"What about you, Kane?" the same reporter asked.

He thought about all he'd lost in Gold Meadows—his home, his livelihood, his heart. No, he'd almost lost that, but not quite. The other things, however...

"I need to talk to the insurance company and the Forest Service about my plane and to someone in Seattle about the contaminated fuel. That will probably occupy my time for a while."

And a good thing.

He needed something to think about so he could put Serena James out of his mind. Because that's exactly where she belonged, even if his heart didn't agree.

"We can do this tomorrow, darlin'." Belle's eyes clouded with concern. "You look tired."

Tired didn't begin to describe how Serena felt. She wasn't sure whether the ride out or the press conference or pretending she and Kane were just friends had been more taxing, but she couldn't crawl between the sheets of the motel bed yet. "I need to take care of this."

She opened the closet door to where six no-longer-white dress bags hung. The small space smelled like the cabin. Serena fought the rush of memories of her and Kane. She'd just said goodbye to him an hour ago, but it seemed like days. "The smoke from the woodstove seeped into the bags. I hope it's the bags, not the dresses. Otherwise…"

"Don't borrow worry." Belle held on to six new dress bags a local bridal store had sold her to transport the dresses back to Boston tomorrow. "Trust me on this one."

"I will." Serena fought the tears stinging her eyes. She'd been battling an internal struggle and felt guilty. So many people had been worried. So many people endured the cold, snowy weather to look for them. But Serena wished she were still at the cabin with Kane, where she could just be herself. "Having you here means so much. I don't know what I would have done if I'd walked into that trailer and only seen strangers."

"You had Kane with you."

Not really. "It's not the same as having someone you love there. Thank you for coming all this way to be with me."

Belle set the bags on the bed. She enveloped Serena in one of her trademark hugs. "I'm glad to be here, darlin'."

The scent of Belle's perfume comforted Serena like the smell of her favorite chocolate cake. Her friends who worked at The Wedding Belles were what really mattered. What happened at the cabin had been simply…a dream.

And yet, she'd felt more real, more alive, more herself there. Kane's praise about her courage and uncomplaining attitude had been real, too. Not like a dream at all.

"I kept your parents updated."

"Thanks." And then it hit Serena. If Belle had called her

parents, she had probably called… "Did you talk to anyone else?"

"Yes."

Rupert. The air evaporated from Serena's lungs. She struggled to breathe.

"Let's not worry about that now," Belle said. "We'll have plenty of time to talk about things later. Once you're rested and back home. Okay?"

Serena swallowed around the snowball-size lump in her throat as she felt herself drifting back to the way she'd been before the time in the cabin. Kane would never have let her get away with an evasion like that. "Thank you again."

"Anytime, darlin'."

Serena unzipped the first bag with a hesitant hand. All the dress bags looked alike. She had no idea which gown was inside which bag. Each catch of the zipper felt like a countdown to the moment of truth. Afraid to look, she closed her eyes and pushed the bag off and away.

Belle released a rebel yell.

Serena's eyelids sprang open. She stared at a perfectly white wedding dress made of chiffon with crystals sprayed across the gown. "Thank goodness."

"It looks perfect."

She studied the gown as if inspecting a perfect jewel for a flaw. She left no thread unexamined, but found no problems. Oh, the dress was a little crushed and a lot wrinkled, but nothing steaming or a careful pressing wouldn't fix.

"It is perfect." Serena sniffed the fabric. "And no smoke smell, either. I don't believe it."

Belle grinned. "Believe it."

Serena put the gown into a new bag and zipped it up.

"On to the next one."

She unzipped the bag. Not even halfway down, she stopped.

Belle grimaced. "That's not just smoke I smell."

"Mildew maybe."

"Let's see how bad it is." Belle gasped when the dress came out of the bag. "It's…"

"Ruined." Tears prickled Serena's eyes seeing the water and dirt spots on the diamond-white satin with a champagne tulle lace overlay. Small holes had destroyed the Alencon lace around the neckline. Had a mouse gotten inside somehow? "At least it's a sample dress from the new collection, not a custom gown."

Like Callie's dress.

Don't borrow worry.

Easier said than done.

With a heavy heart, she continued on. To her surprise, the next two dresses came out fine. One, a sleeveless silk with a cutaway skirt, and the other, a satin with embellished lace on the bodice and sleeves. Wrinkled, but fresh smelling. Neither, however, was Callie's dress.

When Serena came to the next dress bag, her heart pounded in her ears. She was almost afraid to go on. Unzipping the next bag, she recognized the beading on the bodice.

Her hand froze. "This is Callie's dress."

Belle sucked in a breath.

The zipper went down three more inches and Serena's heart plummeted. The air whooshed from her lungs. She sagged against the door frame.

"What is it?" Belle asked.

"Callie's dress—" Serena's voice cracked "—it's ruined."

As she pulled the dress bag away, a mouse fell out. Belle screeched and jumped away. Serena was too dejected to care.

She stared at what had once been her most exquisite creation. A strapless A-line corset-back gown with delustered satin alternating with rows of scalloped lace giving the dress a fairy-tale feel yet a strong, contemporary silhouette. Swarovski crystals, bugle beads and seed beads embellished the bodice. The dress had been designed with Callie in mind, but now…

Forget calling what remained a wedding gown. The wet, dirty, smelly and holey dress looked like a farce, a bad joke gone too far. It wasn't fair.

Serena fought back the tears. She had to be strong and hold herself together. She needed to show Belle she could handle this. But inside, she trembled, a potent combination of failure and disappointment grabbing hold of her. She longed to have Kane here, for him to tell her everything would be okay, for him to help her fix this the way he had everything else since landing in the meadow.

"You're going to have to use one of the gowns you have back at the studio for her," Belle said calmly.

"No." Serena raised her chin. "I promised Callie I would take care of her dress. I owe her a one-of-a-kind creation and that's what she'll have."

"Callie's wedding is less than two weeks away," Belle said. "You've already lost this week and still have other obligations to meet, darlin'."

"Don't worry about a thing. I can do this."

And Serena would.

As fingers of sunrise broke over the mountains to the east, Serena sat in a corner booth at the coffee shop attached to the motel in Missoula, Montana. She warmed her cold hands on a steaming cup of coffee.

"Mind if I join you?"

The familiar male voice brought a sensation of pleasure rippling through her. Kane. She'd missed him so much already, which made no sense. She'd only spent a night away from him, but what a night.

Sleep hadn't come easy. Not at all really, and she'd tried to take advantage of the insomnia to think about Callie's dress. That had only made Serena anxious and lonely.

She fought the urge to throw herself against his chest and bawl about the ruined wedding dress for her friend's upcoming fairy-tale wedding. He would hold her and make her feel better. The way no one else could. And then she remembered. Kane wasn't into dresses, and he didn't believe in fairy tales.

She raised her coffee and took a sip. "Sure."

Kane placed his coffee cup on the table and sat across from her. He wore jeans, a green shirt and a brown leather jacket that made his eyes look hazel. His hair was damp as if straight from the shower. His razor stubble was gone, replaced by smooth skin she longed to feel rubbing against her cheek.

"Sleep well?" he asked.

"Not as well as I thought I would."

"Me, neither."

Clean and casual, he looked entirely too delectable. She wanted a taste. Instead she dug into another bite of her buttermilk pancakes with maple syrup.

Kane whistled. "That's some breakfast."

She eyed her plate of scrambled eggs, pancakes, bacon and fruit. "I was hungry."

"A couple of days of granola bars, honey-roasted peanuts, pretzels and crackers will make you crave a real breakfast."

"I wasn't tired of the food we had at the cabin." She remembered the many wrappers that had piled up during their meals. "I liked the cabin. Well, except for the wolves, the mice and the outhouse. There's something to be said for flush toilets."

His smile reached his eyes, and her heart beat faster. "You didn't go away."

"Excuse me?"

"The Serena I got to know at the cabin. I thought she'd disappeared, especially after Super Serena wowed the media with her sparkling brilliance."

"Brilliance?"

"I needed sunglasses, Blondie."

She smiled at his use of the nickname. "I was trying to get through the press conference the best way I knew how."

The only way she knew how, by reverting to what she did best—putting on a perfect facade. Maybe Super Serena did exist.

"You did great," he said. "You're back in your element."

"I don't feel like it," she admitted. "I feel like the only scarlet and gold cap-sleeved on a rack of strapless diamond whites."

Kane raised his cup and took a sip. "That bad."

"You have no idea what I just said."

"Nope, but I could tell from your tone that you feel out of place and that matters to me."

"Why does it matter?"

"I like you."

"You like me?" Not good enough. "Like me how?"

A beat passed. "As I said at the press conference, you're my friend, Serena."

Her heart deflated a little even though being just friends made sense. As Audra would say, anything else wouldn't be logical. "You're mine, too, but…"

The word hung out there. She was afraid to say more. Still she might not get another chance. "What happened at the cabin…?"

"It was…"

"Nice?" she offered.

"Great."

"Yes, great," she admitted. "I didn't know how you felt."

"You know I like you, Blondie. I'm attracted to you, but we want different things."

"We do." And taking what happened at the cabin any further made no sense. Kane understood that. So did Serena. But the thought of never seeing him again…hurt.

"I just came in for a quick cup of coffee." He pushed back his chair. "So maybe I'll see you around."

A brush-off. "You planning a trip to Boston?" she asked lightly. Stupid question. He didn't plan.

His gaze met hers. "I could be."

Oh, heavens.

Friends, she reminded herself. They wanted different things. "Then I'll see you in Boston sometime."

He nodded once.

Her heart thudded. She couldn't wait.

"I've got an appointment with the Forest Service this morning about my plane." He stood. "Have a safe flight home."

She hated to see him go. "Good luck with your plane and, well, everything else."

He leaned over and kissed her on the forehead. Nothing more than a friendly brush of his lips. "Goodbye, Blondie."

"Bye, Kane."

He left the coffee shop and got into a nondescript blue sedan. As he backed out, he waved at her. She waved back.

Mr. Right, Mr. Right Now or Mr. Wrong, Serena didn't care. A sigh escaped from her lips. She hoped sometime came soon because she really wanted to see him again.

"Thank you." As Belle took her suitcase from Charlie at Logan International Airport in Boston, her hand brushed his. Tingles shot up her arm. She ignored them, the same way she paid no attention to the warmth settling over the center of her chest. "I don't know how I would have made it through without you…your friendship."

"I feel the same way." His gaze held hers, and her heart melted a little. "I'll give you and Serena a ride home."

His continued generosity touched Belle. She glanced at the restroom to see if Serena was out yet. "That's sweet of you, but Regina's husband, Dell, arranged for a limo to take us home."

Charlie's smile didn't reach his eyes. "Riding home in style."

"Serena deserves it."

He raised Belle's hand to his lips and kissed it. "So do you."

The heat in her cheeks matched the temperature of the blood racing through her veins. Blushing at her age? But she wasn't used to a man switching attention from one of the girls to her. Belle pulled her hand away from his and adjusted the purse strap on her shoulder.

"When can I see you again?" he asked.

She hesitated. Sure, he was an attractive and wealthy man. She'd enjoyed his company, they'd relied on each other during the stress-filled days and become closer. But now that the crisis was over, seeing him again might not be such a good idea. He was a nice man, but Belle didn't want to lead him on.

"That hard to answer, huh?" he added, humor lacing his words.

Maybe she shouldn't put too much thought into the decision. Belle smiled. "Give me a call, darlin'."

That was the best she could come up with right now.

Anticipation filled his brown eyes. "I will."

His lighthearted grin took ten years off his face. Her heart sank. She was already nine years older than Charlie. Add ten to nine and… She didn't want to think about the total.

He wrapped his arms around her and squeezed. His hug shouldn't have surprised her. They'd held and comforted each other in Idaho. Support was no longer necessary, yet a part of Belle didn't want it to end.

Uh-oh. She was acting like one of her girls when they met a new beau. Maybe this wasn't such a good idea.

She stepped out of Charlie's embrace. "I need to get Serena home. She looks as if she hasn't slept a wink and she's been so quiet. Do you know if anything happened between her and Kane that we don't know about?"

"Kane said they were friends."

"Friends like us?" Belle asked, wondering if Serena was keeping more secrets to herself.

"He didn't elaborate, but I think you know I want to be more than your friend, Belle."

She nodded. The way Kane looked at Serena reminded Belle of the way Charlie looked at her. The elder Wiley was a true gentleman, but the younger seemed to be more of a ladies' man. That could spell only one thing for Belle's already heartbroken young designer—T-R-O-U-B-L-E.

CHAPTER TEN

THE Monday after she'd returned to Boston on a thankfully uneventful flight, Serena sat in her studio trying to reconstruct Callie's dress, but nothing seemed to be working. Serena didn't have enough of the diamond white delustered satin left so she was using a regular white satin instead. The fabric, however, had bluer overtones and didn't drape as well as the original. The seed and bugle beads seemed to disappear against the satin's higher sheen. Should she use more crystals or a tinted lace? Both would change the look of the dress. Who was she kidding? The fabric already did. Maybe she should come up with a new design.

Tossing a piece of embellished tulle onto her worktable, Serena glanced at the giant calendar hanging on the wall. Twelve days until Callie and Jared's wedding. Two fittings would need to be scheduled in. Time for alterations in between. Serena had the Brodeur bridesmaids flying into town this weekend for measurements. She couldn't forget about the Craggin fitting scheduled for Tuesday and the Cross fitting scheduled for next Thursday. And then there was Callie's surprise shower on Wednesday night. Serena rubbed her pounding head.

Closing her eyes, she imagined Callie's finished wedding gown but saw the cabin instead. Serena could smell smoke and pine and hear the rattle of wind against the windows. If only she could be there with Kane, instead of here alone.

Not good. Serena opened her eyes and glanced around her studio. How come what she'd always wanted no longer seemed…enough?

A knock sounded on the door separating the studio from the rest of the shop. She checked her watch. Her next appointment was over an hour away. "Come in."

"I brought in a new cake to taste." Pink and purple chopsticks, most likely painted by Natalie's twin daughters, secured the pile of blond hair on the top of her head. In her well-worn jeans and blue sweater that matched the color of her eyes, she looked more like a college student than a mom and talented cake maker. "It's chocolate."

"My favorite."

"I know." Natalie never brought cake into the studio due to all the white fabric. The petite baker hopped up and sat on a nearby stool. "How's it going?"

Serena ignored the calendar and forced a smile. "Good."

"You've been working so hard since you got back."

"Lots of winter weddings. And Callie's gown." Serena picked up one of the bodice panels. "I wish…"

"What do wish?"

"Nothing really. Do-overs aren't possible."

"A lot of us wish they were." Natalie sighed. "What would you change if you could?"

"Nothing."

"Come on," Natalie challenged. "You're the one who brought it up. There has to be something."

If Serena could be herself with Kane, maybe she should try to be more honest with her closest friends.

"I would have told you all about Rupert as soon as it happened." She looked down at her worktable. "I should have told you all."

"You did finally tell us the truth and answered our questions," Natalie said. "That couldn't have been easy for you."

"Or any of you." Serena looked up at her. "I really am sorry. I just didn't want to disappoint any of you."

Natalie smiled softly. "Just remember, next time we're here for you. We love you."

"I will."

"You'd better." Natalie sounded every bit a mom. "Now go get a slice of cake."

"I'd love one." Serena knew the baker, a diabetic, couldn't taste her own creations and relied on the Belles for their opinions. "And thanks, Nat."

"For what?"

"For being my friend."

"Anytime. That's what the Belles are for." Natalie beamed. "I'm going to see if Audra wants a slice."

Serena made her way into the reception area. The front desk was empty. She picked up a slice of chocolate cake with a raspberry fruit filling.

As she raised a forkful of cake, the scents of chocolate and icing filled her nostrils. Okay, things could be a lot worse right now. She took a bite. The chocolate flavor exploded in her mouth. The not-too-sweet raspberry filling complemented the cake and icing perfectly.

As she ate, the doorbell rang. With a mouthful of cake, she opened the door. Kane stood on the porch in a pair of black pants, a black turtleneck and his brown leather jacket. She choked on the bite.

His dark eyes narrowed. "You okay, Blondie?"

She nodded, struggling to swallow. "Cake."

"Can I have a taste?"

Serena scooped a bite with her fork and fed it to him.

"That's the best cake I've ever tasted." He smiled at her.

Her heart thudded. And that's when she knew. She wasn't Kane's friend. She was in love with him. Even though she'd only known him for a few days, they had been the most intense days of her life. He was totally wrong for her and didn't fit any of her plans or her life, but she didn't care. All she wanted was to be with him.

That realization scared her to death.

"You look good," he said.

"Thanks." The appreciation in his eyes made her forget she'd been up half the night, hadn't showered this morning and wasn't wearing lip gloss. "How did things go with your plane?"

"I can't get it out of Gold Meadows until spring, but the insurance company declared it a total loss based on the pictures and the report write-up."

"Kane." She reached for him, but pulled back her arm. "I'm so sorry."

"No worries," he said. "I'll buy another."

"And fly away again."

He nodded.

"When do you plan to do that?" she asked lightly, trying to sound like it didn't matter to her.

"As soon as I can."

Serena felt as if her clothing had been stitched too tightly and she couldn't breathe. Not that she should be surprised. He'd never pretended to be anything but what he was.

He handed her a medium-size white shopping bag. "For you."

She peeked inside and saw white tissue paper.

"Go on," he urged.

Serena pushed aside the paper. Something gray and white was there. She pulled the stuffed animal out and smiled. "A wolf."

"A little something to remember your adventure in Gold Meadows."

She would never forget it. Or him. She cuddled the wolf. "That was so thoughtful of you. Thank you, Kane."

He hooked his thumb through a belt loop. "Do you have time for a cup of coffee?"

Yes. She wanted to see him even if things weren't perfect. *No.* He would just leave again, so why bother? "I, um, have an appointment in an hour and I should be working."

"My dad told me what happened to a few of your dresses."

"You've been talking to your dad?" she asked.

"I'm staying with him."

"Good." Maybe they could start working out some of their differences. That would be good for Kane and Charlie, too. She smiled. "He must be happy to have you around."

Kane shrugged. "If you've been working so much you probably need caffeine or something besides cake to eat."

"There's nothing wrong with cake."

"Nope, but you can't live on cake alone. You need coffee, too." He grinned. "Come on, I promise I won't keep you."

The problem was she wanted him to keep her. Forever. She swallowed hard.

"What do you say, Blondie?"

Serena wanted to say yes.

Maybe she could convince him that they would be good
for each other. That he could find what he needed right here
in Boston. Or maybe not. And he would fly off chasing his
notion of freedom again. She stared at the wolf in her
arms. "One cup, then I have to get back to work."

Walking on the sidewalk with Serena felt weird to Kane.
The sounds of traffic on the street, the squeal of breaks and
the blare of horns were a far cry from the snow-swallowed
silence of the wilderness. The smells of exhaust and
garbage made him miss the fresh pine and smoke scents.
But he was happy to be with Serena. He'd missed her so
much that when he'd seen the wolf in a store window in
Missoula, he'd bought it for her without a moment's hesitation.

"We weren't gone that long," he said. "But I'm not used
to being back in the real world yet."

"Me, neither." Serena looked up at him with big round
sunglasses covering her eyes. She wore a trendy wool coat,
black boots and a knee-length skirt. A multicolored cap
covered her blond hair. "I never really paid attention to all
the different noises in the city before, but now I really
miss the quiet of the woods. I keep thinking about the
cabin."

And he'd been thinking about her. Too much.

Like me how?

Serena's words and the look in her eyes at the restaurant that morning had haunted Kane for the past four days.
He had thought being away from her would keep her out
of his thoughts and off his mind.

Wrong.

Which was why he needed to see her. To prove to

himself these strong feelings for her meant nothing, that he was hooked on a silly fantasy, nothing more.

"So…" she said.

He stopped on the curb waiting for the light to change. "So you've been busy."

"Yes, the work keeps piling up." She shoved her gloved hands in her pockets, reminding Kane of when she had worn his gloves, and smiled. "It's been hard getting back into the swing of things, but I'm checking things off the To Do list."

Kane had wondered how she was managing since returning home. He'd pictured her in full coping, press-conference mode. Super Serena to the max. But he could see now, he'd been wrong about that.

Despite the usual perfection of her appearance and even a smile on her face, she looked tired and stressed and a little sad. Instead of those things making her less beautiful, they only made him care for her more.

Real, not fantasy.

Self-preservation told him to run away as fast as he could. He could find a new plane anywhere. But Kane knew how vulnerable Serena James was. He didn't want to hurt her.

They entered a corner coffeehouse where they ordered drinks to go. Serena picked up a sandwich, too.

"What's really wrong, Blondie?" he asked on the walk back to the shop. "You've got a smile on your face, but you don't look happy."

"What do you mean?" Her brows drew together. "I've got almost everything a girl could want. Of course I'm happy."

"I'm not buying it." He removed her glasses. "I see a woman who's tired and stressed."

"I worked late last night and forgot to eat dinner and breakfast." She flashed him a brilliant smile. "I'm a little hungry, but okay."

"Good thing you bought a sandwich." He placed the sunglasses back on her face. "But a person doesn't have to feel good to smile as long as they know how to flex their facial muscles. That's what my mom used to say when she was trying to get me to admit I'd had a bad day."

Serena sipped her latte. "Did it work?"

"Usually." Kane wished his mom was here so he could talk to her about Serena. "Why don't you just tell me what's going on? Unless you want me to start guessing."

"Please don't."

She sounded horrified at the thought. Chalk another one up to Mom. A smile pulled at his lips. "So…"

"The biggest thing right now is Callie's dress," Serena explained. "She's my friend and the florist at The Wedding Belles. Her dress was one that got ruined. Destroyed, actually. Her wedding is a week from Saturday and I'm not even close to having something ready so I can fit her for alterations."

"You need help."

"I can do it myself."

"Can you?" he asked. "Or is that Super Serena talking?"

"There is no Super Serena. Just me. And I can do it."

She sounded capable and sure of herself. He wasn't buying it. "You can do it if you don't sleep or eat or waste a single moment of time."

Her mouth formed a perfect *O*. "We hardly know each other, yet you seem to know me the best of all. How is that possible?"

"It's a gift." He studied her, trying to see beneath that perfect facade. "Let me help you."

She drew back. "You?"

The offer had been an impulse, but Kane liked hearing the sound of her laughter and knowing he'd been the reason for it. If worst came to worst, he'd get to spend some time with her. No regrets there. "Yeah, me."

"What do you know about wedding dresses?"

"Less than you know about planes," he admitted. "But I can be an extra pair of hands, a sounding board, someone to bring you food, whatever you need."

"Mr. Right Now?"

Oh, man. Kane rocked back on his heels. "If that's what you want."

She looked down at her coffee and he felt like a heel. She wanted so much more than he could give her.

"In any case—" she pressed her lips together and met his eyes "—you're leaving."

"I'm not leaving until I find a plane. The right plane. I have a few to look at, but what's a few extra days in Boston if I get to help you?"

Those baby blues of hers widened. "A few days."

The hope in her voice and the anticipation in her eyes slammed into him. Suddenly following through on his offer didn't seem such a good idea. Kane nodded anyway.

"Okay, then," she said. "You're hired."

When Kane had agreed to help Serena, he hadn't really known what he was getting himself into. He hadn't really cared. What had he promised her? A few days. No big deal.

But helping her out felt good. Things had remained platonic, too. He wasn't about to take advantage of her.

"Can you please move that one about three inches to the left," Serena asked.

But he'd never thought he'd be standing in one of

Boston's finest mansions hanging wedding dresses on the walls of the impressive dining room. "No problem."

And it wasn't.

He enjoyed seeing Super Serena in action. The way she took charge of the decorating for Callie's surprise wedding shower tonight reminded him of a military leader in action. Serena executed her orders with quick decisive steps. So far he'd strung wide satin ribbons around the dining room and now was hanging wedding dresses on fancy hangers with big bows.

He moved the dress he was holding the requested three inches. "How's this?"

"Perfect."

Her favorite word.

He had to admit Serena James was pretty damned perfect herself. Not that he planned to do anything about that.

Okay, Kane had feelings for her, but he wasn't about to hurt her, especially when she was going through such a hard time remaking that damned wedding dress. He would help her and then he would leave.

"There's one more gown," she said.

"Where do you want it?" he asked.

She pointed to the spot. He moved the stepladder and hung the dress.

Sure, he'd thought about taking things further. But there was no sense starting something he couldn't finish.

"How's that?" he asked.

"A little to the left."

He'd learned with the seven other dresses not to guess-timate. She'd only make him redo it. "How little?"

"An inch and a half."

Good thing he'd asked. Kane moved the dress, pleased with the work they'd done.

Serena impressed him. She'd transformed the dining room into the perfect setting for a bridal shower. No wonder people spoke about her creativity with awe. She really was something.

He climbed down from the stepladder. "What do you think?"

She spun around slowly, taking in each dress, all the ribbons, every bow. "It works."

"It's fantastic," he said. "And I'm a guy. I'm not supposed to notice stuff like this. Good job."

She smiled. "You, too."

"You deserve all the credit. You're the one who came up with the idea and told me what to do."

Something in her eyes changed. "You know, there's been something else I've been wanting to tell you to do ever since you came back."

"What?" he asked, intrigued.

"This." She leaned over and kissed him.

The feel of her mouth against his, her lips pressing and probing, sent his temperature skyrocketing. He'd been pretending that he hadn't wanted to kiss her. That she hadn't meant much to him.

But he had and she did.

She tasted sweet and warm as she moved her lips over his. He wanted more. Hell, he wanted all she was willing to give.

Kane brought his arm around her, running his fingers through her hair. He explored every inch of her mouth, and she his. He soaked up the feel and taste of her, kissing her as if there were no tomorrow. He felt as if he'd found the place where he belonged and he never wanted to leave again. He was finally home.

The kisses continued until she slowly and gently pulled away. Serena stared at him with wide eyes and swollen, thoroughly kissed lips.

"That's what you've been wanting to tell me to do since I came back?" he asked.

She lifted her chin. "Yes."

He smiled, as he brushed strands of her bangs that had fallen over her right eye. "You are so beautiful, so brave, so perfect."

"You think?"

"I know." He kissed her lightly on the lips. "I might have to stick around Boston a little while longer."

Her smile lit up her face. "There's nothing I'd like more."

At the monthly poker and margarita night, Serena glanced at the clock on the wall of Regina's kitchen. The guests should have arrived for Callie's surprise wedding shower.

Now all they had to do was get the bride-to-be into the dining room. Good thing Part B of Operation Poker Plan was already under way.

Audra flipped her long blond hair behind her shoulder. "I'm all-in, too."

Callie gasped as the pile of chips in the center grew taller. "The entire table is all-in? That's impossible."

Serena looked at her partners in crime—Audra and Regina. The other Belles—Natalie, Julie and Belle herself—were busy in the dining room.

"This doesn't make any sense. There aren't that many good hands." Callie's face scrunched. She studied the cards on the table. "Serena never goes all-in. Could it be a certain pilot is leading you to take more risks these days?"

"Maybe."

"You and hottie flyboy seem pretty chummy," Regina said.

"We're getting chummier." Serena took a sip of her margarita thinking about what had happened earlier. "I kissed him this afternoon."

"And?" Callie asked.

Serena got all tingly inside. "It was absolutely, positively toe-curling wonderful."

"I'd like to experience a kiss like that," Audra said. "That is, if I ever planned to date again."

"You will," Serena encouraged. "And I hope you find someone who makes your toes curl."

Callie's eyes softened. "It's nice to see you opening up and talking about Kane like this."

"It feels good," Serena admitted. "Hey, don't we need to see who wins this huge pot of chips?"

Regina nodded. "Let's see your cards, ladies."

Serena laid her pair of threes on the table. The other two had nothing but a couple of face cards.

"I can't believe you guys went all-in on those hands. It's as if you wanted to lose." Callie flipped over a full house. "I win."

"Great hand," Audra said.

Callie moved the stack of chips in front of her and took a sip from her frozen margarita. "Not a bad haul, but I can't believe how fast the game ended."

Serena nursed her own drink. She still had work to do and a part of her hoped Kane might stop by. She bit back a sigh. "Luck of the cards."

Callie shuffled the deck. "We have time for another game."

"How does the new buffet look in the dining room, Regina?" Audra asked.

"I'd like to see it," Serena added, not wanting to delay Part C of the evening's plan.

"Let's all go and see it." Regina stood.

"But then we're going to play some more." Callie picked up her drink and followed Audra. "This time next month things will be different. I'll be a married woman."

Regina led the way, surreptitiously picked up her camera from the kitchen counter on her way toward the dining room. She crossed the threshold first. Next came Audra. Then Callie.

"Surprise!" a group of twenty women yelled.

Flashes from Regina's camera blinded Serena, but she kept a smile on her face. The photos would go into a wedding shower album the photographer wanted to put together for their friend.

"How did you guys do all this?" Callie asked Serena.

"While we played poker, Belle, Natalie and Julie set up and snuck guests into the dining room."

Callie stared wide-eyed. "I can't believe how quiet everyone was."

Julie smiled. "Belle threatened some nasty Southern torture to anyone who so much as sneezed."

"We Southerners know how to control a crowd, darlin'," Belle said.

"I had no idea," Callie admitted. "Though everyone going all-in at once was a little strange. But it's all so wonderful. Look at those wedding dresses hanging on the walls. Amazing."

Regina handed Callie a fresh margarita. "Using the dresses as decorations was Serena's brilliant idea."

Serena appreciated the compliment. "Well, I couldn't exactly ask our florist and decorating idea generator for help, now could I? I had to come up with something on my own."

"The gown I wore when I married Matthew is next to the window," Belle said.

Callie turned and sighed. "Lovely."

"Dated, but still pretty and so little," Belle said. "There wasn't quite so much of me back then."

"We wouldn't want you any other way," Audra said, and the rest of the Belles agreed.

Belle sniffled. "What would I do without you girls?"

"I don't know what I'd do without any of you. Thank you." Callie blinked. "This is so much more than I ever imagined having."

Everyone knew Callie hadn't had the easiest of times, but things had changed for the better since she'd joined The Wedding Belles and fallen in love with Jared Townsend.

As Serena thought about Kane, she wiggled her toes. He didn't seem to be in any hurry to leave Boston. He wanted to help her. He'd kissed her back. That had to mean he had feelings for her, but she had to be patient. She couldn't force Kane to love her. She didn't want to force him to run, either. She just wanted him to tell her how he felt about her. She imagined her and Kane as a couple. Like Callie and Jared. The image filled her with warmth.

"A toast." Serena raised her glass. "To Callie and Jared. May their love for one another never stop growing. Even after the wedding, the honeymoon and the kids."

Everyone laughed.

"Kids?" Callie teased. "I may need another drink."

Serena continued. "Best wishes on your journey toward your happily ever after."

"Hear, hear!" The guests raised their margarita glasses. "To Callie and Jared."

"Thank you," Callie mouthed.

Nodding, Serena smiled, though celebrating was the last thing she should be doing right now. Callie trusted her to get the dress done, but Serena wouldn't have missed tonight for the world. Even if being here meant working another late night.

Her friend was worth it.

Callie deserved the perfect wedding gown for the perfect wedding. Serena wasn't about to let her down.

CHAPTER ELEVEN

BY SATURDAY night, Serena was overwhelmed and exhausted. She glanced at the clock. Nine o'clock. All she wanted to do was go to sleep. All she could do was work on Callie's wedding dress. If Serena finished the gown tonight, she could work on the embellishments tomorrow and be ready for a fitting on Monday. That would allow plenty of time for alterations.

Kane stood behind her and massaged her tense shoulders. "You're all bunched up, Blondie."

She almost moaned with relief. "It's been a long week, but you being here to help has made it better."

"I'm happy to help." He kissed her neck. "I was thinking I could spend the night here."

Her insides fluttered, then tensed. "Tonight?"

"I could take better care of you if I was on-site so to speak."

"No." The word rushed from her mouth. "I'm too busy, too distracted. I want your first night here to be perfect."

His mouth tightened. "Why does everything always have to be so perfect with you?"

Because that's how things should be when I tell you I love you. She couldn't tell him that. "It just does."

Great, she sounded like a little kid.

"I'm not trying to get you into bed, Blondie." His gaze held hers. "I'm only trying to take care of you the best way I know how."

She looked at the mannequin wearing Callie's almost finished dress. "Not tonight."

"Why not?"

"I don't have time."

"I'm not asking for your time. Just a space on your couch."

She shook her head. "I... That's not good enough."

He stepped away from her. "You mean I'm not good enough."

"I never said that."

"You didn't have to." The hurt in his voice clawed at her heart. "You're too busy chasing your vision of perfection to see something right and real in front of you. Can't you cut me some slack?"

"Slack?" Her voice rose. Serena had thought Kane understood her, but he didn't. He couldn't. "I have to finish the dress."

"Or kill yourself trying." He picked up a piece of lace and waved it in the air. Though the lace was white, she didn't think he was surrendering. "Is a dress worth all this? The sun will still rise tomorrow if you don't get it done."

"I have to have it done."

"Then ask for some help." He dropped the fabric. Tenderness filled his eyes. "Your friends would be here in a heartbeat."

"Callie trusts me. She's counting on me," Serena explained, feeling as if everything she held dear was about to unravel. "I have it under control."

"I'm sorry, Blondie, but you don't."

She stiffened.

"You've got to stop pretending. Look at the toll this is taking on you. Your health. Your life. It's destroying you. I won't let you keep this up."

"You won't let me?" No one told her what to do. Her temper flared. "I can do this. I will do this. I don't need anybody's help. Not even yours."

His expression shuttered. "Well, thanks a lot."

She stared at the wedding dress, her heart aching as if she'd lost her best friend. "What do you want me to say?"

"I'm sorry would be a good start."

She'd thought he accepted her for who she was, not who he wanted her to be.

"Why?" Pain, raw and jagged, sliced through her. "So you can get in your plane and fly away with no hard feelings? That's what you do best, isn't it? Take off when you don't get what you want?"

"You're way off base. This has nothing to do with me." His gaze hardened, accused. "Nothing will ever be perfect enough for you, Serena. I don't know why I've stuck around and even tried."

Emotion clogged her throat. Her stomach clenched. She couldn't breath.

Everything she'd thought about, dreamed about and planned for was coming to an end. And she felt helpless to stop it.

She'd known what Kane Wiley was like from the very beginning. He'd even told her himself. The quintessential Mr. Wrong, but she'd pretended that he could be her Mr. Right.

Well, he was right about something. It was time to stop pretending.

"Then I guess," she said, her voice trembling, "you'd better go."

* * *

Kane sat in his rented car, his hands on the steering wheel to keep them from shaking. He needed to calm down before driving away.

He took a deep breath, unsure what had just happened.

Why? So you can get in your plane and fly away with no hard feelings. That's what you do best, isn't it? Take off when you don't get what you want?

Serena had it all wrong. This wasn't about him. He hadn't wanted a relationship. He avoided them like bad fuel, but both had found him in Seattle.

Now he was sitting in his car staring at a brightly lit flat. Outside looking in. That's how Kane usually liked things. Distant, removed, safe. But at this moment he felt none of those things. Kane felt as if someone had yanked his entire life from him. His home, everything he'd wanted, was gone yet again.

That hurt.

And made him feel…stupid.

When was he ever going to learn? Love equaled pain. No two ways about it.

Maybe he shouldn't have pushed her when she was already tired and stressed out, but her mood didn't affect the basic situation.

Little Miss Perfection wasn't going to change. Super Serena was back and not going away. She wanted her perfect life and he didn't fit in. He'd been a fool to think that he could or that she would let him.

Kane should have known better.

Next time… There wasn't going to be a next time.

Heartbroken over what had just happened, Serena sat on the middle of her living room floor staring at the dress she'd been working on for days. Over a week actually.

Tears filled her eyes, but she blinked them away. She wanted to cry over Kane. She wanted to cry hard, but still had too much to do.

She focused on the gown. Even with the new fabric, Callie's dress, almost complete, wasn't coming out right. Serena had been ignoring the truth, but couldn't any longer. Her broken heart splintered more. She was going to have to start over. Which meant she would never be able to make Callie the kind of dress she deserved to wear on the most special day of her life.

Serena cradled her head in her hands.

Her fault. She'd failed. She'd let her friend down in the worst possible way.

Tears stung Serena's eyes, but surrounded by yards of delicate fabrics and lace, she kept them at bay. Not that she had time to use the fabric to make a new dress from scratch now.

What was she going to do? How was she going to tell Callie?

Serena hugged her knees.

All her plans had disintegrated, leaving her nothing to fall back on, nothing to hold on to or reach for. How could everything go from perfect to disaster so quickly?

You're too busy chasing your vision of perfection to see something right and real in front of you.

Kane's words rushed back to Serena. Her shoulders slumped. She had just been trying to do the best she could. What was wrong with wanting a perfect life or a perfect man or a perfect wedding dress?

Perfect wedding dress. Serena repeated the word. She straightened and stood. Maybe…

She padded her way to the hall closet and opened the door. Hanging there, wrapped in plain muslin, was her almost-completed dream wedding gown. A perfect wedding dress. For her perfect marriage to the absolutely wrong for her Rupert.

She uncovered the gown.

Serena felt no excitement, no joy, no longing the way she had before. Her needing the dress had simply been a dream, a wish that hadn't come true. Chasing a vision— make that a clouded vision—of perfection, most definitely. She sighed.

But Callie's dream was very much alive. Her and Jared's happily ever after still existed. She deserved this gown to start her new life with her husband.

Not perfect. Not for Serena any longer.

But just right for Callie. And right here.

This gown would be the one.

Serena placed the dress on the mannequin. She grabbed her sketch pad, sat on the floor once again and drew how she wanted the completed dress to look. Not for her, but for Callie.

Thirty minutes later, Serena was ready to begin the transformation, but she'd learned her lesson. She couldn't do this on her own. She needed help to make sure she got this dress finished on time.

Just remember, next time we're here for you. We love you.

Serena knew exactly who to call—The Wedding Belles. Her friends would understand. They would help her. Nothing, not time or tiredness, would stop them from creating a spectacular wedding gown for Callie.

The oohs and aahs filled the dress design studio on Monday night after Julie had put out the calligraphy-script Closed sign and locked the front door. The only question remaining was whether the bride liked the gown or not. Serena held her breath.

"It's absolutely perfect." Tears glistened in Callie's eyes as she stared at her reflection in the three-panel mirror. She spun around on the carpeted platform. "I love it even more than the first dress."

So did Serena. She hadn't let her friend down.

The dress, the one she'd spent weeks designing and stitching with an "I do" in mind, was no longer hers. Each stitch, each bead, each crystal may have been sewn with love in mind, but not the forever kind. The friend kind. She'd turned the dress into Callie's dream gown. Sleek and neat. Not at all what Serena had planned for herself, but perfect for Callie.

Belle clasped her hands to her chest. "You are the most beautiful bride."

Callie's smile lit up her face. "You say that to all the brides."

"Because it's true."

She stared at her reflection in the mirror. "Thank you, Serena."

"Don't thank me." Serena had learned her lesson in time to save Callie's wedding gown, but not in time to salvage her relationship with Kane. "For the past two days, we all worked on the dress."

"Thank you, everyone." Callie's voice bubbled with excitement.

Everyone spoke at the same time. Laughed. Hugged.

Callie looked at Serena. "Is it horrible if I say I'm glad you got stuck in the wilderness and the other dress got ruined?"

"Not at all," Serena said.

"I know Kane has been a big help to you. I want to thank

him." Callie glowed the way only a bride could. "Is he around?"

"I haven't heard from him." The honest answer tore Serena's heart in two. "I think he might have left Boston."

The studio went dead quiet. All six pairs of sympathetic eyes focused on Serena.

"I've seen how he looks at you, darlin'." Belle touched her shoulder. "He'll be back."

Serena knew he wasn't coming back. She'd wanted to apologize after all he'd done for her. For the past two days, she'd tried calling him both on his cell phone and at Charlie's. He hadn't returned any of her messages.

"It's okay," she said to her friends.

And it was. Or would be. Someday.

Kane had made his choice, and so had Serena. He didn't want her if she didn't behave the way he wanted, but she was tired of trying to please everyone all the time. She wasn't going to do it any longer. Especially for someone who ran away from commitment, the very thing she wanted most of all.

She couldn't be what he wanted, and he couldn't give her what she wanted. That, unfortunately, was the bottom line.

"She's a beauty, son," Charlie said about the business jet Kane wanted to buy two days later. "But have you thought this through?"

"I'm a pilot. Flying is how I make my living. I need a plane."

"Do you want to go back to that lifestyle, flying here and there, never staying in one place, with one person, for long?"

"I never left that life, Dad." Kane stared at the inch-thick sales contract. His grandfather had guaranteed what the insurance payout wouldn't cover. The only thing missing—Kane's signature on the paperwork. "I like my freedom."

"You can change how you live and still experience freedom."

Kane thought about Serena with her wide blue eyes and big, warm smile. He'd been willing to try, but she hadn't been willing to accept the man he'd tried so desperately to be for her. "I don't need to change anything."

"I used to think that way," Charlie said quietly. "After your mother…"

Kane looked up from the contract. "After Mom what?"

His father stared down at his shoes. "I loved your mother so much. She was my life. After she died, I missed her so much and I wasn't ready to face what had happened. I wasn't ready to change. I liked being married. I liked having someone there."

"So you married Evangeline."

Charlie nodded. "I was looking for a replacement more than anything. I know it hurt you, Kane."

"It did." A ball of emotion clogged his throat. "I guess I'd been in denial or something, but when you got married it made Mom's death seem more real. I finally had to accept she wasn't coming back. I wasn't ready to do that. I couldn't understand how you were ready to do that so quickly."

"Losing your mother was the hardest thing I've ever had to go through. But worse, I lost you, too," Charlie admitted. "I hope you can forgive me someday."

Kane didn't want to forgive. Holding on to the grudge—his anger—was easier than opening himself up to more hurt. But he knew his mother would have wanted him to at least hear his father out. "I'm listening."

"Marrying Evangeline was a mistake. I thought I loved her, but I didn't. I should have listened to you. I should have listened to a lot of people. I'm so very sorry, son." The sincerity in his father's voice struck a chord deep inside Kane. "I don't know if I'll ever love another woman the way I loved your mother. That doesn't mean I can't love a different way. There is someone I would like to pursue a relationship with if she'd have me, but I want your blessing this time."

"Are you talking about Belle?"

"Yes."

Kane took a deep breath and exhaled slowly. A part of him understood what his father was talking about. The other part still hurt. But holding on to his anger made little sense. He couldn't change what had happened. Not with his dad. Not with his mother. "If that's who you care for, go for it, Dad."

"Thank you, son," Charlie said, his voice grateful. "What about you and Serena?"

"It's complicated."

"Love always is."

Love?

"I tried to ignore your mother's death and live my life the way I always had. But I learned you have to face things head-on even if it's not easy. There's no avoiding the bad stuff. If you don't do it now, you'll only have to do it later."

His father's words sunk in. Had Kane been avoiding whatever went wrong in his life or getting upset when he didn't get his way?

So you can get in your plane and fly away with no hard feelings. That's what you like to do best, isn't it? Take off when the going gets tough?

Serena's words played in his mind. He thought about

his mother's death, his dad's second marriage, so many other things including Serena herself. She was right. He had run away. And he was doing it again.

"No matter what you decide, I love you." Charlie patted Kane's shoulder. "I'll always be here for you, son."

And that's what it was all about, he realized. Being there for those you cared about. Kane didn't want to spend his entire life leaving on a plane, flying from place to place. He remembered the home his parents had created for him, the love inside the walls.

Something so good wasn't easy to make happen. There were no guarantees, and the hard stuff required work. He'd avoided that all these years, but he was finally ready. He hoped he wasn't too late.

"Thanks, Dad," Kane said. "I'm sorry it took us so long to talk about this."

Charlie smiled. "We have plenty of time ahead of us."

"Just not right now." Kane moistened his dry lips. "Could you give me a lift?"

"Where to?"

"Wherever Serena might be, but we may need to make a stop or two on the way."

"Come on." Charlie headed down the stairs of the plane. "You navigate, and I'll drive."

Kane preferred being behind the wheel, but this time he'd happily sit in the passenger seat. "Let's go, Dad."

Serena cleaned up the mess in her living room, piling the fabric, lace, tulle and beading into a box. Once this stuff was back at the studio, she could put the entire wedding dress fiasco behind her. Too bad she couldn't do the same with Kane.

Kane.

Tears welled in her eyes. Serena hadn't known him that long, but she'd never experienced such emptiness, such loneliness since he'd been gone. Her heart felt as if all the blood had been squeezed out. Every beat hurt. She picked up the stuffed wolf from the couch.

How had she come to this? All her plans in ashes. Her plans…

Serena nearly laughed. Her plans hadn't been worth much. They hadn't kept her from falling in love with Mr. Wrong. She hugged the wolf.

Her heart wanted Kane still. No one else would do, even though he could never give her the kind of love and commitment she wanted. The truth cut deep, the raw wound threatening to swallow her whole. She wiped tears from the corners of her eyes.

Pathetic.

She'd wanted to be loved so badly, to have a family of her own, that she had been willing to engineer her future, plan everything, including the man she wanted to marry. She set the wolf down. At least she'd recognized the trap and wouldn't be caught in it again.

If only…

No. Serena wasn't looking back. She didn't want to look forward, either. She needed to stop planning and start living.

A knock sounded at her front door.

Serena wasn't expecting anyone. She picked up a tissue and blew her nose.

Another knock.

Go away.

And another.

The doorbell rang.

Fed up, Serena tossed the tissue in the garbage can and stormed to the door. "This had better be important."

She threw open the door and saw…

"Kane."

Tears exploded from her eyes.

"Serena?" he asked, his voice filled with concern.

She must look a fright. No makeup, unwashed hair, grungy clothes and red, puffy eyes. "Yes?"

"Seeing you like this…" He wiped the tears from her face with his thumb and led her inside, closing the door behind him. "I'm sorry. I shouldn't have left like that. I should have returned your calls, but you were right. Anytime something doesn't go right, I run away. I may think I'm chasing freedom, but all I'm doing is holding on to grudges and not looking back because it hurts too much."

She stared at him, shocked yet hopeful. She wanted to believe him.

His gaze lingered, practically caressed. "You and I aren't so different, Blondie."

"I'm sorry, too," Serena said, her eyes locked on his. "You were right about me. I get so focused on a goal I ignore everything else, every other possibility, including what's right in front of my face. Whether it's a wedding dress or…"

Choked up, she couldn't continue.

"We like having control of a situation, but when we don't, it's damn difficult." Kane inhaled sharply. "When my mother died, I had no control over anything. One minute I was trying to help my father, then the next thing I knew he was dating, engaged and remarried. I did the only thing I could. I left. I'm tired of leaving, Serena."

Her eyes met his. "But you said that's what you wanted to do. You want freedom—"

"I did, but freedom is no longer enough."

Serena was almost afraid to ask, but she had to know. "What do you want now?"

"You."

The air whooshed from her lungs. She struggled to breathe, to think.

"But flying is your life," she managed.

He smiled. "My hobby is flying. Loving you is my life."

Her heart melted. Her knees nearly gave way.

"I don't care if we're in Boston or stranded in the wilderness, whether you're designing wedding gowns or gathering firewood, I want to be with you. And I mean you, whoever you want to be. Serena, Super Serena or Blondie."

Serena touched her hand to her heart that seemed to be dancing to a tune of its own. "I don't know what to say."

"You don't have to say anything." The sincerity of his voice brought a lump to her throat. "I love you, Serena James."

The words she'd wanted to hear. She'd waited to hear them. But she'd had it all wrong. No special plans were necessary to say those words. The words themselves were perfect no matter when or where they were spoken. She swallowed. Hard. "I love you, too."

Kane pulled her toward him and kissed her. He kissed her lips, her cheeks, her neck. She felt as if he were kissing her heart and her soul. She couldn't be happier, feel more complete.

"I always had to be the good girl, never disappoint, so I put on this facade, always doing the right thing, saying the right words, never deviating from my plan. And that worked. Until I met you."

She pulled back and gazed into his eyes.

"I needed to give Callie the chance for the kind of wedding I always wanted, with a dress she'd always remember, but pushing myself to my limit took its toll on my time, my temper…and us. I learned my lesson though. When I finally realized I couldn't finish the dress myself, I called my friends, but by then you were…"

Gone.

The unspoken word echoed between them.

"I'm here now."

"Yes, you are." A peace filled her. "I finally realized I don't always have to be Super Serena all the time. I don't always have to do the right thing. In fact, I've learned I can be incorrect about what's right for me, especially about something very important."

"What's that?" he asked.

"Who was Mr. Wrong and who is Mr. Right."

His smile crinkled the corners of his eyes. "Who might that be?"

She stood on her tiptoes and kissed him hard on the lips.

"You are creative, smart, generous and beautiful, Blondie." His rich laughter wrapped itself around her heart. "I love you."

Joy filled her heart and overflowed. "I love you, too."

"Just to prove I mean what I said—" he dropped down on one knee and pulled something from his pocket "—will you marry me?"

She stared at the small glass slipper he held with his fingers. Inside was a simple, elegant diamond ring. She knew in her heart this was right. Not only was this the beginning of their fairy tale, but the start of a much better life, a life full of love.

"This ring belonged to my mother," he said. "It probably has to be resized. Or if you don't like it, I can buy you another. I want it to be perfect."

Serena put her fingers over his mouth. She didn't need to look at the ring. All she had to see was the love in Kane's eyes, real and right in front of her. "It's perfect. I love it."

"Does that mean—?"

"Yes." Her insides tingled. She had never felt so content or fulfilled in her life. "I love you. I would be honored to marry you, Kane Wiley. Or should I call you Mr. Right?"

"Call me whatever you want." He picked her up and twirled her around. "I don't care as long as we're together."

She laughed. "You know this means I have to design another wedding dress."

He set her down. "I can't wait to see what you come up with for yourself."

Thinking about standing at the altar with Kane at her side, Serena smiled. "Neither can I."

EPILOGUE

November 22nd

THE Castle at Boston University, a Tudor Revival Mansion, looked stately with its ivy-covered exterior. The interior matched expectations from the outside with its regal columns, inviting fireplace, crystal chandelier and wall of arched windows. The perfect space for a wedding reception, especially with the Belles in charge.

Callie and Jared's wedding was going off without a hitch. No detail had been overlooked. Guests enjoyed champagne cocktails and passed appetizers while the wedding party had photographs taken. An elegant catered sit-down dinner was served followed by the cake, a four-tiered white chocolate cake with raspberry filling decorated with Callie's favorite flower, the stargazer lily. Taking her cue from the monthly poker nights and not one to be totally traditional, Callie had made memorable center-pieces for each of the round linen-covered tables by filling extra-large margarita glasses with stargazer lilies and adding a piece of snake grass for the stirrer.

Now that the food and cake had been served, Belle and Julie, the only two Belles not members of the wedding party, removed their headsets and joined the others to watch Callie sing a romantic ballad to her husband on the DJ's karaoke machine. She swayed with the music, the yards of shantung silk of her gown swishing back and forth as she sang her heart out. Callie might have once believed Mr. Right didn't exist, but no one could mistake the love in her eyes and in her voice now.

Listening to her talented friend sing about believing in fairy tales brought a sigh to Serena's lips. A happy ending was in store for her friend. Serena couldn't be more pleased. She knew exactly how Callie felt about Jared because Serena felt the same way about Kane.

She leaned back against him, resting against his strong chest as if she'd been doing it her entire life. He wrapped his arms around her, and his warm breath caressed her neck. "Is this the kind of wedding you want to have?"

Once upon a time, Serena would have answered yes without hesitation, but now...now that she'd experienced a love so wonderful, so right, she no longer knew what kind of wedding she wanted. Or, to be honest, cared.

"As long as we say 'I do' and sign on the dotted line, it doesn't matter how we get married. The details aren't important." Serena stared at her hand, at the four-pronged set diamond solitaire engagement ring that had belonged to Kane's late mother. "What matters is how much I love you and what happens after the wedding."

"Have I told you how much I love you?" Kane whispered.

"About ten minutes ago."

"I won't wait so long the next time."

Serena smiled as Kane kissed her neck.

After Callie finished her song, Jared picked up his bride and kissed her, to the delight of the clapping audience.

"You really can't sing?" Kane asked Serena.

"Nope, but I still sing in the shower."

He grinned. "That's a performance I can't wait to see."

"Don't you mean hear?"

Kane whistled a little ditty.

Natalie's twins, Rose and Lily, ran across the dance floor in their matching flower girl dresses. They looked sweet and innocent in their white dresses with pink and cranberry ribbons, but the two were always up to some sort of mischief.

"I hope our children look exactly like you," Kane said, his voice full of warmth and love.

The DJ made an announcement asking all single women to come onto the dance floor. Serena laced her fingers with Kane's and turned to Audra and Natalie. "You two had better get out there."

"Looks like we're the only single Belles left, Natalie," Audra said.

The baker smiled. "Don't forget Belle."

"The six of us couldn't drag her out here." Natalie stepped forward two feet. "Let's not disappoint Callie. There are enough single women we won't have to worry about catching the bouquet way back here."

"Good," Audra said. "Because I'd rather catch the flu than the bouquet."

Natalie stared lovingly at her twin daughters, standing front and center, eager to catch the bouquet. "Me, too."

Callie stood with her back to the crowd and held the bouquet up in the air for all to see. Long stems of pink and white stargazers were tied with three neatly tailored bands of cranberry ribbon trimmed with clear crystals that looked like buttons, coordinating with the ones on her gown. Crystal accents stood up a half inch between each bloom throughout the bouquet. Callie wound up her arm as if she were pitching a fastball for the Red Sox and let her bouquet fly. Over the heads of the reaching women and right into the arms of...

Natalie.

The *Wedding* PLANNERS

MILLIONAIRE GROOMS

Don't miss the last three heartwarming stories
in the Wedding Planners series!

Wedding Planners: Millionaire Grooms

Chef: Who will Natalie cut her own wedding cake with?

Cooper Sullivan is at the top of his career. But
seeing Natalie again makes Cooper realise that the
only thing he never won – and the only thing that
really matters – is her heart.

Accountant: Will Audra's big-day budget include a millionaire groom?

Tycoon Dominic needs help with his newly orphaned
nephew, and he knows exactly who to ask. But every
smile from his new nanny starts making him want to
swap his playboy nights out on the town for nights
in with Audra and the baby.

Planner: Julie's always been the wedding planner – will she ever be the bride?

Julie Montgomery is the happiest girl in town until
she discovers the gossip about her fiancé. Matt must
learn that marriage is about sharing everything –
even his deepest secrets!

Coming next month from M&B™

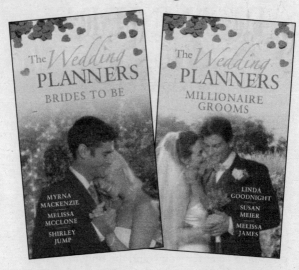
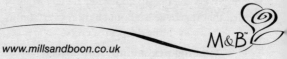

Secrets always find a place to hide…

When DEA agent Rodrigo Ramirez finds undercover work at Gloryanne Barnes's nearby farm, Gloryanne's sweet innocence is too much temptation for him. Confused and bitter about love, Rodrigo's not sure if his reckless offer of marriage is just a means to completing his mission – or something more.

But as Gloryanne's bittersweet miracle and Rodrigo's double life collide, two people must decide if there's a chance for the future they both secretly desire.

Available 6th February 2009

Passion. Power. Suspense.
It's time to fall under the spell
of Nora Roberts.

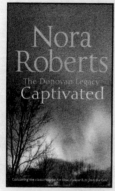

2nd January 2009

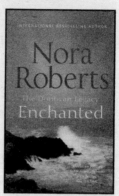

6th February 2009

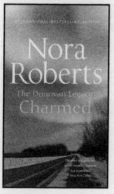

6th March 2009

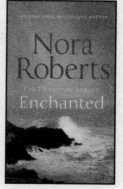

3rd April 2009

The Donovan Legacy
Four cousins. Four stories. One terrifying secret.

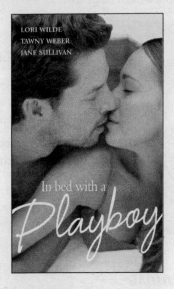

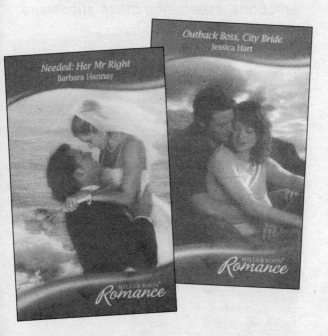

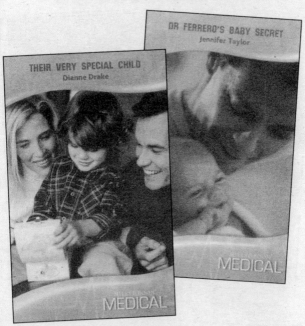

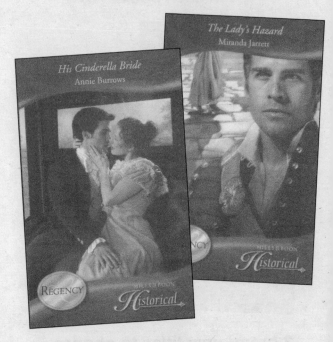